" . . . Don't Take My Sunshine Away."

The phone rang. Her chest tightened.

She lifted the wall extension and listened to the music coming through the receiver. *You are my sun-shine, my only sun-shine* . . . That particular song had been a favorite of hers when she was a kid. Now it was raising goosebumps along her arms.

She moved to hang up when a muffled voice whispered, "Suzanne . . . ?"

She was about to say no, wrong number, when the voice said, "Alexandra Suzanne . . . ?" If speaking her name was meant to shake her up—it did. She squeezed the receiver. . . . *never knew de-ar how* . . . click . . . *much I love you* . . . "Alexandra." A whisper. "I hear you breathing. So pretty. Always so pretty. Not for long."

She slammed down the receiver. Jerked her hand away.

The phone shrilled a second time. She jumped, rapping her knuckles painfully on the edge of the counter. It rang five . . . six . . . seven times before curiosity overrode her growing apprehension. Lifting the receiver slowly, cupping a hand over the mouthpiece and holding her breath, she listened

"Alex, let me hear your voice. Talk to me, Alex." . . . *happy when skies are gray* . . . "Such a tiny bikini. Was that the way you were brought up, Alex? To flaunt your body . . . beautiful body . . ." . . . *please don't take my sun-shine away* . . .

DORIS MILES DISNEY IS
THE QUEEN OF SUSPENSE

DO NOT FOLD, SPINDLE OR MUTILATE (2154, $2.95)
Even at 58, Sophie Tate Curtis was always clowning — sending her bridge club into stitches by filling out a computer dating service card with a phony name. But her clowning days were about to come to an abrupt end. For one of her computer-suitors was very, very serious — and he would make sure that this was Sophie's last laugh . . .

MRS. MEEKER'S MONEY (2212, $2.95)
It took old Mrs. Meeker $30,000 to realize that she was being swindled by a private detective. Bent on justice, she turned to Postal Inspector Madden. But — unfortunately for Mrs. Meeker — this case was about to provide Madden with a change of pace by turning from mail fraud into murder, C.O.D.

HERE LIES (2362, $2.95)
Someone was already occupying the final resting place of the late Mrs. Phoebe Upton Clarke. A stranger had taken up underground residence there more than 45 years earlier — an illegal squatter with no name — and a bullet in his skull!

THE LAST STRAW (2286, $2.95)
Alone with a safe containing over $30,000 worth of bonds, Dean Lipscomb couldn't help remembering that he needed a little extra money. The bonds were easily exchanged for cash, but Leonard Riggott discovered them missing sooner than Dean expected. One crime quickly led to another . . . but this time Dean discovered that it was easier to redeem the bonds than himself!

Available wherever paperbacks are sold, or order direct from the Publisher. Send cover price plus 50¢ per copy for mailing and handling to Zebra Books, Dept. 2921, 475 Park Avenue South, New York, N.Y. 10016. Residents of New York, New Jersey and Pennsylvania must include sales tax. DO NOT SEND CASH.

NIGHT STALKER

CAROL DAVIS LUCE

ZEBRA BOOKS
KENSINGTON PUBLISHING CORP.

This book is dedicated with love to my grandmother.
  Ethel Katona
and my mother . . .
  Helen Christian

ZEBRA BOOKS

are published by

Kensington Publishing Corp.
475 Park Avenue South
New York, NY 10016

Second printing: March, 1990
Printed in the United States of America

Prologue

The paperboard box was covered with a muted blue paper in a tiny primrose pattern. The lid, a grayish white Currier and Ives winter scene, came into focus. Then the papers and documents sticking out from within.

The fit had passed.

His head hurt. The pain, boring into his eye socket, leveled off.

He lay in a fetal position on the floor and clutched the letter.

Sweat drenched his clothes, stung his eyes. He heard the scratching, and almost screamed before he realized it was only the needle aimlessly tracking the final grooves of the records. His knee jerked.

He straightened, grabbed the mattress, and rose part way to the bed before falling back. He pulled himself along the floor to the table that held the cheap record player, rolled over and scooted upward to sit with his back wedged into the corner. Finally, his arm heavy and numb, he reached the stylus and scraped the needle across the record. The song began to play. *You are my sun-shine* — click — *my only sunshine* — click. . . .

He dropped the letter, looked down at his hands and arms, touched his face. No fresh bites or scratches. He ran his fingers through his wet hair. No areas of tenderness. His breathing eased.

He trembled when he picked up the letter. It was addressed to her. "Not yet," he whispered aloud. He let it fall and reached for the box. He caressed the soft padded lid with an angry hand.

The box had been hers. Many years ago it had sat on her bedroom dresser, a solitary vanity. She had owned no cosmetics, no perfume or jewelry.

The box was his now. He saw her, smelled her, heard her voice. He shuddered.

He pulled out the document and traced the embossed letterhead with his fingertips. The stiff parchment, veined in green, rustled crisply. Her name was there. And *his*. The drill bore into his eye. . . . *Please don't* — click — *take my sun-shine a-waaay.* . . .

He snatched up the letter and reread it. He felt his muscles begin to knot. His knee twitched and jerked. He drew his legs up to his chest, dug his heels into the threadbare carpet, and pushed, forcing his body back into the corner. He grabbed his legs and arms, struggled for control. He breathed spasmodically. *Don't go,* he told himself. *Don't go!* He wadded the front of his shirt into a ball and bit down on it. The scream stayed in his throat.

Pop! Pop! The pain was gone. He had teetered, but had not gone over the edge. The scratching sounds had not come to turn his bowels into a roiling inferno. The acrid odor of burning hair and flesh had not come to fill his nostrils. The monsters had been cheated.

He smiled. In place of the fear and pain, he felt a glorious rage. He had stayed in control, mastered it, beaten it. That delicious rage grew, throbbing, intensifying with each beat of his heart. With a fierce

6

sanity, he began to formulate his revenge.

"They'll pay," he whispered. "They'll both pay." . . . *and I hung my head . . . and cried.*

Chapter 1

Over the persistent scratch, scratch, Alexandra Carlson heard the sizzling sound of disaster. She smelled the acrid odor of something burning.

She crossed the kitchen, flung open the door of the broiler, and watched the last of the toasted garlic loaf blacken. Sitting on her haunches, she pounded a fist against her thigh and sighed.

The scratching went on.

She cursed softly as she fumbled the bread out from under the broiler and dumped it into the garbage.

She brushed her hands against the tails of her oversized shirt, tossed her shoulder-length hair away from her face, and glanced up at the clock. Past noon already? Where had the time gone? With a feeling of urgency and exasperation, she hurried around the breakfast bar to the dining-room slider. Blackie stood at the door, his claws working at the glass, scratching.

"So c'mon, get in here," she said to the tom as he sauntered in, tail twitching peevishly.

No sooner had she closed the door than the cat turned to it and scratched to go back out.

"Ohhh, no you don't, buster. I've no time for that today." She opened the door wide and left it open. Smoke escaped outside.

Alex went back to the kitchen. As she dumped the ingredients for the devil's food cake into a bowl, she could hear Blackie meowing on the redwood deck—a guttural cry that Alex called his bitchy tone. What's with that damn cat now? And where, she wondered uneasily as she switched on the electric mixer, was the other one—Blackie's contrasting sibling, the chalky she-cat?

The whirr of the beaters brought her mind back to the birthday party she was giving Greg that night.

Gregory Ott had turned forty. To show her appreciation for all the times he had been there for her, the times he had escorted her to art function after dull art function, and the times he had just been a good friend and companion, she wanted to reciprocate. She rarely entertained, especially with big affairs like tonight where there'd be a lot of stuffed shirts, but for the past three weeks Greg had been hinting outrageously for a party. It was the least she could do.

Fifty minutes later the cake came out of the oven, slightly burned and definitely lopsided. No problem, she thought, that's what frosting is for. This cake—all chocolate—was for Greg only. The sheet cake waiting to be picked up at the bakery would serve the party guests.

Blackie rubbed against her legs. He made strange throaty sounds.

"Where's Winnie, huh, boy? Is she getting better chow at another establishment?" Alex bent down and scratched Blackie's head. His meow was low and forlorn.

Alex checked the time again. She had a few minutes before she had to leave for the bakery.

"Okay, let's go have a look."

Just as she passed the wall phone, it rang. She snatched up the receiver impatiently.

"Hello?"

"Hi. Is this the Carlson residence?" a man asked.

"That's right," she said, looking beyond the deck to scan the hillside for a small white form.

"Alex?"

"Yes?"

"Hello, Alex," the speaker sounded hesitant, unsure. "It's David Sloane. Maybe you don't remember me. I used to work with your husband at Norday Investments before I got transferred to Dallas. Joe and I played racquetball together on Saturday mornings."

"Oh, yes . . . Dave." A vague image wove in and out of her mind. "Yeah, sure. How are you?"

"Couldn't be better. Is Joe around?"

Alex laughed uneasily. "It's been a while, hasn't it? Joe and I were divorced three years ago. He lives in California now."

"Oh."

"I could give you his number if you like?"

There was a pause, then, "No, that's all right. It's just that . . . well, I'm in Reno for a couple days and I don't seem to know anyone here anymore." He cleared his throat and continued in a light tone. "So you and Joe are divorced? Alex, if I'm not being too forward— last minute and all that—perhaps we could get together tonight. Dinner? A movie? Your choice."

"Uh . . . well . . ."

"You're married again?"

"No."

"Really? Well then, if you don't have plans . . ."

"I do have plans. I'm sorry."

There was a long pause. Then, "Don't be sorry. Hey, you don't know me, so why should you go out with me? Look, I'll survive. Thanks anyway."

It was true, she didn't know him. But hell, she was having a party. A large party. So what difference would one more person make? And what better way was there to meet someone than at a social event with lots of people.

She invited him. He accepted.

As she hung up, she felt a tingle of excitement. He sounded pleasant enough. And, God knows, the only

11

male companionship she'd had in a long while was Greg—but he didn't count, at least not in that way.

Gregory Delaney Ott, Esq., had stepped into Alex's life twelve months after her divorce. They'd dated several times. She liked him. He certainly seemed to like her. Just as she had been about to succumb to Greg's overt advances, she'd discovered he had a roving eye and a weakness for any attractive female with an IQ above fifty. His secretary of three years worked overtime with her boss two nights a week—the bulk of the work being conducted on the office couch. And ex-wife number four cleaned his house, washed his clothes, and shared his bed one night a week. Although Greg worked diligently to seduce Alex, she managed to keep their relationship platonic. Greg, thrilled by the challenge and not likely to give up short of victory or death, was enjoying the chase immensely. He could be crude and obnoxious at times—that was Greg's way—but Alex knew him for what he was; a warm, loyal, caring person.

Blackie meowed.

A noise overhead made Alex look up. Winnie on the roof? Had to be. Often the cats climbed the apple tree, leaped onto the low-hanging wood shakes of the roof and stalked the birds nesting in the eaves.

She glanced at the clock. Damn! There was so much to do yet.

In a hurry to finish in the kitchen, she frosted the still-warm cake. The chocolate frosting peaked proudly for several minutes before collapsing, running down the sides, and pooling on the plate. I'll fix it later, she told herself. She grabbed her purse and hurried down the stairs to the foyer, anxious to get to the bakery before it closed.

Alone in the house now, Blackie paced fitfully, his tail twitching in spasmodic bursts. He jumped onto the counter, jumped down. He scratched at the glass of the slider, meowing. Suddenly he stopped, his body stiff. With ears pointed and alert, he looked upward, listening. His tail bristled. Then, even more agitated, he resumed his scratching at the glass door.

Alex spritzed mineral water on her face to set her makeup, then dabbed Opium at her temples. She stood back and, looking in the full-length mirror on the closet slider, adjusted the belt on her new silver-gray satin Cossack outfit.

Her long, dark brown hair, lightly teased, lifted up and away from her ears showing off silver and emerald earrings. The brilliant green stones intensified the green of her eyes.

Not bad for an old broad with a grown kid, she thought, turning one last time. Satisfied, she turned off the light and left the room.

Bob and Margie Meacham were the first to arrive. The Meachams along with their two sons, Junior and Stevie, and Gypsy, the big sheepdog with one blue eye and one brown eye, were like family to her. At thirty-six, two years younger than Alex, Margie glowed with the youthfulness of someone who was pampered by an older, doting husband and loved every minute of it. Her bright blue eyes were set in a face of eggshell skin that had somehow escaped the freckling characteristic of her Irish lineage. Her short curly hair was the color of an old penny.

Margie steered Bob to the wing-chair rocker in the living room, pushed him down, handed him the TV remote unit and a bowl of mixed nuts, and said, "Stay out of our hair." She joined Alex in the kitchen.

"Almost bought that outfit myself," Margie said.

"Really? You approve then?"

Margie stared at Alex reflectively.

"What?" Alex frowned, looking down at herself.

13

"Lord, when I think back to the Alex Carlson I met fifteen years ago, I can't believe that this woman standing before me now could actually be the same person. Remember her?"

Alex smiled, nodding.

"Not a lick of makeup. That gorgeous dark hair hacked off in a shag. I'd bet you didn't own one piece of jewelry. And those things you called clothes—good God, they dressed snazzier at the state Woman's Correctional Center."

"I owe it all to you." Alex curtsied.

"It was all there, begging to come out. I felt like the fairy godmother in Cinderella."

"So where's my prince charming?" When Margie turned and shot her a disapproving glance, Alex added. "Never mind. Don't answer that."

Margie lifted the sheet cake from the box. "How many are you expecting for this shindig?"

"About twenty. Mostly friends of Greg's. Lawyers, judges, politicians. I don't know half of them."

"Ahhh." Margie's brows worked up and down. "Perhaps he invited someone you might take a fancy to."

"Perhaps."

"If you weren't so persnickety, that is."

"Me? Persnickety? Well, it just so happens I invited someone tonight. A man. A very nice man."

"Who?"

"You don't know him."

As Alex reached for the cocktail toothpicks, she knocked over a box of dry cat food. Suddenly her stomach knotted tightly. She had forgotten about Winnie. Winnie was out there somewhere. Something was wrong. The cat had never stayed away this long.

The doorbell rang.

"That's probably the birthday boy," Margie said. "I won't be a bit surprised if he's wearing his birthday suit."

"Hey, c'mon. Greg's raunchy, but he's not *that*

14

raunchy."

"Hah!"

Alex went downstairs to the foyer. Instead of Greg, she opened the door to a tall, trim, blond-haired man with a mustache. David Sloane. In one hand he held a bottle of wine, in the other a half-dozen red roses.

"Hello," he said quietly. "Am I early?"

Alex swallowed and said, "No, not at all. Come in."

He handed her the roses and stepped inside.

"Thank you. They're beautiful."

"I didn't know you lived on a mountain. Do you have it all to yourself?"

"It's not quite a mountain. And no, I share it with a few others."

He looked around the foyer, down to the lower level, then up into the living room, and finally straight down the hall to her bedroom.

"Unusual layout," David said. "Trilevel?"

"Uh-huh. My father was the architect. As you can see he shied away from the norm."

"I remember now. Joe called it the 'upside-down' house. It's fantastic. You must be crazy about it?"

Alex tried to smile. It came off weak, nebulous. "Come on up. I want you to meet some good friends of mine."

As she led the way upstairs, she wondered how she could have forgotten what he looked like. He was gorgeous.

The party was in full swing when Greg Ott, leaning over Alex's shoulder as she refilled the ice bucket, whispered in her ear, "Who is he?"

"Who's who?"

He lit a cigarette, inhaled deeply as he looked into the dining room where Margie and Bob were talking to the tall, fair-haired man in the blue suit.

"You mean David Sloane? I could've sworn I introduced you two."

"Correct. But who is he?"

"A friend of my ex-husband."

"That's some endorsement. So how come he's at my party?"

Alex turned and stared at him somberly. "I'm sorry, Greg. I didn't think you'd mind. He's in town, alone, and I thought—"

Greg held up a hand. "Honey, don't dignify that moronic remark with an answer. I'm jealous and I hate him, but that's my problem, not yours." As he stared at Sloane, he ran a hand through his full, yet prematurely gray, hair. "Now that I'm forty, maybe I'll color my hair."

"I like it just the way it is."

"Yeah?"

"Yeah."

Greg smiled. "Go on over and talk to them. Margie's trying to get your attention."

"I baked a cake for you to take home. Promise me you won't laugh," Alex said as she moved away.

Bob, a real-estate broker and a native Nevadan who harbored a fierce love for every rock and piñon tree in the state, was talking with Sloane when Alex joined them.

"Ah, our illustrious hostess. Lovely party, Alex," Margie said. She turned to her husband and straightened his string tie. "Daddy, will you get me another drink?"

"I could use another one myself. I'm not used to being around all these courthouse folks." Bob took Margie's glass and wandered off toward the bar.

"So, David, you and your wife used to play tennis with Alex and Joe?" Margie said, avoiding Alex's eyes.

"It was racquetball . . . with Joe." Sloane's eyes met Alex's. He gave her a knowing look. "There's no wife."

Margie smiled and forged on. "Alex, David was telling us he has friends in the building trade."

16

David turned to Alex. "You're thinking of building something?"

She nodded. "Adding on. An art studio above the garage. It's something I've always wanted. Y'know, elbow room, high ceiling, north light. Then, instead of driving to the art center three days a week, I can give my painting classes right here."

"Anything I can do," David said, smiling. "I'll be more than happy to be of help."

"How long will you be staying?" Alex asked.

"Oh, didn't I mention I've been transferred back to the Reno office?"

"I thought you said you were in town for just a couple of days?"

"No. You must've misunderstood. I said I've been in town for two days."

"Oh?"

"I do have friends in the building trade. I might be able to get you a deal on labor and materials."

"These friends, they live in Reno?" Something worried at her subconscious.

"Yeah."

Before she could absorb that bit of information, Judge Bennett and his wife were announcing their departure. Alex excused herself to see them to the door.

Just before midnight, Greg listing slightly from too much to drink, came up behind Alex and, locking his arms around her, kissed her on the neck. Her heel caught his shin.

He groaned and released her. "Be nice, now. It's my birthday."

"That's doesn't give you an excuse to manhandle me." She flicked ashes from his tie. "Are you having a good time?"

"I'd have a good time anywhere you are." He leaned down to kiss her lips but found her chin instead.

"You're drunk."

"Absolutely. I better spend the night."

Margie strolled up. "We'll take you home."

"Why do you hate me so?" Greg said to Margie.

"How can I hate someone who just turned forty? Happy birthday, darling."

"You're a heartless hussy."

Margie made kissing sounds at Greg. For Alex's benefit, as she moved away she tipped her head toward the windows, where David Sloane stood looking out, and mouthed the words, "Go for it."

"What'd she say?" Greg asked, frowning.

"C'mon, let's get something in your stomach besides Beefeater."

The telephone rang.

Alex gently pushed Greg in the direction of the buffet table. She worked her way around a knot of people at the breakfast bar to answer the phone.

"Hello?"

There was a pause on the line before she heard mumbling and what she thought was the word *cat*.

"Sorry. What?"

More mumbling. This time, though, she distinctly heard the caller say "cat."

Guests talked and laughed all around her. Someone was running water in the sink. A chorus of "For He's a Jolly Good Fellow" broke out. Alex frowned. She put a hand over her ear to hear better. "I'm sorry, I can't hear you. Could you speak up, please?"

No response.

"Hello? Hello?" She heard a series of clicks. Then the dial tone came on.

The doorbell rang.

What was that all about? she wondered. She hung up and hurried down to the foyer. The call was forgotten when she opened the door to a uniformed policeman.

"Do you live here, ma'am?" the officer asked.

"Yes."

"There's been a complaint. Disturbing the peace."

"You're kidding?" Alex said.

Greg leaned over the rail from above. "What's going on, babe?"

Alex shrugged. "Police."

Greg took the stairs two at a time. His arm went around Alex, pulling her to him. "What's the problem, officer? Jesus—Gunther, I should've known it'd be you."

"Evening, Mr. Ott. I'm sorry to interrupt the party, but I'm just following up on a disturbing the peace complaint," Gunther said.

"Who's complaining? Which one of her two neighbors was it?"

"Anonymous call, sir."

"Although it is my birthday party, Gunther . . ." Greg said slowly and carefully, "given to me by this beautiful lady . . ."—he kissed Alex's cheek—"and all the most important people . . . in the state . . . are at this very moment—as we speak—upstairs . . . it is far, and I repeat far, from being a boisterous affair."

Guests began coming down the stairs. After thanking Alex and extending best wishes to Greg, they uttered goodbyes and filed out in pairs. Within minutes, it was obvious the party was over.

"Look what you did, Gunther," Greg said. "You broke up my party."

"He didn't break up anything," Margie cut in. "Tomorrow's Monday. Some people work. C'mon, Greg. We're driving you home."

"I'm not leaving till my birthday's over."

Margie looked down at her watch. She counted backward from ten. "Okay, it's over. I have your cake. Say goodbye."

"I'm not leaving till this goddamn spoiler does," Greg whined, nodding at the policeman.

A short burst of laughter erupted from Alex before she could control it. Greg, though being childish, was funny when he was juiced. The corners of her mouth quivered.

Gunther shot Alex a penetrating look before melding in with the departing guests.

"Oh-oh." Alex said. "Officer Gunther is ticked at me."

"The guy's a bootlicker, an ass kisser, a brown-nose, a sycophant of the most toady kind," Greg said.

Alex kissed his cheek. "Happy Birthday."

"Alex, don't touch a thing," Margie called over her shoulder. "I'll be over in the morning to help."

Alex watched as Margie and Bob escorted Greg out between them. Then there was no one.

Before going back inside, she called out softly, "Winnie? Kitty?" An owl responded. Alex shivered. Wasn't there some folklore about the hoot of an owl and death? No, that was a wild bird loose in the house. Maybe it was both. *Who cares?*

She went in, closed the door, and flipped the deadbolt. She pulled off her shoes, dropped them at the base of the staircase, then, taking deep breaths and massaging the back of her neck, she climbed the stairs to the living room.

"Nice party."

Alex started and spun around. David Sloane leaned against the wall in the dining room.

"I thought they'd never leave," he said.

Alex smiled uneasily. She began to gather glasses. "I'm sorry if I wasn't a very good hostess. But . . . well, it was Greg's party."

"Your boyfriend?"

"A friend."

Pushing away from the wall, he crossed the room to the unbroken line of windows that faced south. "Quite a sight. Ever take it for granted?"

She put the glasses on the dining-room table, turned, looked out the window, then shook her head. "Uh-uh." It was true, she never tired of looking at the panoramic view of Reno, Sparks, Washoe Valley, and the High Sierra mountain range.

"May I have one for the road?" he asked, holding out his glass.

Alex hesitated a moment. She felt less relaxed in his presence now that she was alone with him. He smiled. She took the glass.

"What are you drinking?"

"Whiskey, rocks."

From the kitchen Alex called out. "So tell me, Dave, are you glad to be back in Nevada?" With a drink in each hand she turned and was startled to find him standing directly in front of her. She held his glass out to him. He ignored the drink, took hold of her upper arms, and began to run his hands slowly down, then up the satiny fabric of her blouse.

"Nice. Very soft. Very sexy." His hand moved to a lock of hair on her shoulder. "May I confess something?"

She tilted her head.

"When Joe and I played racquetball at the gym, I couldn't wait to see you each week when you dropped him off and picked him up again. I thought you were really something. And that hasn't changed." He gently twisted the hair around his fingers. "Joe made like you were a personal possession of his. Did you know he talked about your sex life—yours and his?" He moved his face in close to hers.

Alex pulled back, pushed his drink into his hand, and maneuvered around him. As she headed for the living room, she heard a low chuckle behind her. She felt a chill.

"Dave, I hope you won't be offended if I ask you to drink up and leave. I'm really tired. It's been a long day. The roses were—"

Without warning he grabbed her from behind and spun her around in the circle of his arms. His mouth came down hard on hers. His lips were rigid and

21

crushing as he tried to force his tongue into her mouth.

With a twist, she pulled her head free. Pushed at him.

He tightened his grip. "Your friend's a real fondler, isn't he? And you seemed to like it. How about getting friendly with me?" His hand cupped her buttocks. Then it was tugging on the zipper of her slacks.

Breathing hard, struggling silently, Alex pushed at him. His breath was raspy in her ear. His arms pinned hers to her sides. She tipped her head forward and bit into his shoulder. He grabbed her hair, yanking her head back until she thought her neck would snap. She looked at his face. He was smiling. But the hard, icy glint in his eyes told her he was far from amiable. Her mind was racing. She felt dizzy. Sick to her stomach. His hand had found a breast and was kneading and pinching.

Date rape. No, this couldn't be happening, she thought as panic rose.

He loosened his grip to reach for the top button of her blouse. Alex brought both hands up and pushed hard against his chest. He grabbed at her, getting a handful of the blouse. Buttons popped, flying in all directions. The blouse lay wide open. The bra and the tops of her breasts were fully exposed.

"Get out! Get out right now!" she said, backing away.

He lunged at her like a lumbering, enraged drunk, snatching a piece of the blouse as she turned to run. She slapped at him. Her fingernails scraped over skin. There was a tearing sound as the fabric ripped up one side. He lost his grip on the material and staggered backward. She prayed he would fall. He regained his footing, but Alex took that moment — those crucial few seconds — to run to the far wall in the dining room. Her hand flew to the red button mounted on the wall.

Holding a finger within an inch of the button, she

said in a hoarse whisper, "Emergency alarm. Come any closer and I'll press it—so help me God, I'll press it."

Stopping in his tracks, he looked from her face to the button and back again. He's debating, she thought, weighing his chances of reaching me before I can push the button. Don't let him think.

"C'mon." She beckoned with her fingers. "C'mon, I'd love to have you thrown in jail for assault and attempted rape."

He put his hand to his ear and then brought it around to look at it. Blood stained his fingers.

"Bitch. Rotten bitch." He took a step forward. Rage made his face terra-cotta; his eyes bulged. "You'll be sorry."

"Get out!" she said tightly, lightly placing a trembling finger on the red button. "I'll give you to the count of five. One . . . two . . ."

"You won't call. Rape is tough to prove these days. Real tough," he said quietly.

"Three . . ."

"I can make you out a liar—"

"Two . . ."

He stormed from the room, his heavy footsteps shaking the house as he tromped down the stairs. She heard the front door open and slam shut with a resounding bang.

Her breath exploded from her lungs in a rush. Her hand dropped to her side. She took a step away from the wall, about to leave her post to lock the door after him, when she froze. If he were faking her out, only pretending to leave, she was in a world of trouble. She held her breath, listening. She heard no sounds of soles on concrete, no car door opening and closing, no engine turning over.

"You sly bastard," she said over a lump in her throat. She picked up the phone and dialed 911. At the exact moment the dispatcher said "Reno Emergency,"

23

she heard a car engine rev up. She quickly hung up the phone. The last thing she wanted was the police out at the house again.

The phone rang.

"Reno emergency calling. Is this 555-2300?"

"Yes." Alex's heart pounded.

"Did you just dial 911?"

"I'm sorry . . . it was a mistake."

"Is there a problem, ma'am?"

"Not anymore." She watched the red taillights rapidly descend the tenth of a mile driveway. The car turned the corner onto the main road. "Someone I know tried to get a little physical with me. He's gone now."

"An assault, ma'am?"

"Sort of."

"Do you need assistance?"

"No, really. It's okay. He's gone now."

"Are you unable to talk freely at this moment?"

"No. I can talk. Everything's fine."

"If you have further problems, call —"

"Yes, I will. Thank you. Sorry again."

Alex hung up. If she had known a tracer detected and recorded the phone numbers of all callers, she wouldn't have been so hasty. She went to the window, feeling foolish, shaken.

"Goodbye, asshole. Thanks for the roses."

She peered down at herself and quickly stepped back from the window. Slowly undoing her belt, she surveyed the damage to her new blouse. Trashed.

Her father's words came back to her: "Don't trust men, Allie. They only want one thing." Yeah, tell me about it, she thought grimly.

The clock struck the half-hour, twelve-thirty. After locking up, Alex filled the sink with soapy water and left the dirty dishes to soak overnight. All she wanted to do was go to bed and pray that sleep would come.

She turned off the kitchen and dining-room lights.

Her hand moved over the "panic button" on the wall. The button looked commanding enough. Red—the color of panic. She pressed the button firmly. A loud metallic *clank-clanking* came from the overhead area of the patio. The automatic aluminum awning noisily clanked into place over the redwood deck. Thank God the creep hadn't called her bluff.

Blackie scratched at the glass of the sliding door. She let him in and stepped out on the deck.

"Winnie," she called. "Winnie, kitty, kitty?"

The air was crisp and filled with the spicy aroma of sage. Alex shivered. *Winnie, Winnie, where are you?*

There was nothing she could do that night, but first thing in the morning she would look for her cat.

Alex set out on foot in a futile attempt to find her cat. As she was returning to the house she heard shouting, then caught a glimpse of a man as he stormed around the side of the house waving his arms frantically and yelling: "Here you—scat! Scat, scat! Get outta there you goddamned, filth-spreading varmint!"

It was Otis Hawkins, her yard man.

Alex's property, located on the side of a hill, consisted of five acres of craggy ridges, sagebrush, and rocks. *Better Homes and Gardens* would have described it as "natural landscaping." The area actually landscaped was no greater than the yard of the average tract home. Spread out below, to the west, was the Wild Woods Golf Course. The proximity of the lush course considerably increased the value of Alex's property.

She rounded the corner of the house, heading into the rear yard. "Mr. Hawkins?!"

He stepped out of the storage shed, wiping his mouth on the back of his hand. "Over here," he said. He hiked up his faded jeans, eliminating some of the bag in the seat. He was forever hiking up his pants, only to have them glide back down and come to rest beneath his massive gut.

"I'm looking for my cat. Have you seen her? The white one?"

Alex waited, looking into his perpetually bloodshot eyes, and wondered again what it was he had fermenting in the shed?

"Ain't seen that one. Saw the black one though. He's been using that fill earth I brought in for the garden, y'know, using it for a potty place." He jerked his bullet head in the direction of an ordinary mound of dirt. "Lord knows its got plenty land around here to do its nasty business without using my clean earth. I seen him just minutes ago, going and then covering it over like cats do. Course it gets uncovered when I shovel." As he spoke, puddles of saliva formed in the corners of his mouth. Wet. Shiny. A glistening, beaded thread of spittle stretched and retracted from his upper lip to his lower lip, stretched and retracted hypnotically.

Alex pulled her gaze away, turned. "I'll see what I can do."

"Coyotes, maybe."

"What?" She turned back.

"Coyotes maybe got your cat. Happens all the time in these hills."

"I thank you, Mr. Hawkins, for that enlightening bit of information."

He grunted again. "Y'asked."

"My mistake." She found her eyes drawn to the craggy hillside, wondering if a carcass with white fur lay up there in the sun drawing magpies and other scavengers. Her throat tightened.

"I put that window screen back on for you."

She gladly brought her attention back to Hawkins. "Screen? What screen?"

"The one on your bedroom window. It was laying there on the ground."

"How do you suppose it got off?"

"Musta been them boys what belong to that friend of yours. I been meanin' to talk to you about 'em. Been climbin' the apple tree again, they have. One of them branches was near broke off."

He was referring to the Meachams' two preteen sons.

"Mr. Hawkins, trees are for boys to climb," Alex said, smiling complacently.

"Boys? Humph. No better'n monkeys."

Would he feel better if she were to rip their offensive little fingers off one by one? she wanted to ask. Or perhaps having the boys locked away in reform school until their heinous tree-climbing days were over would be more to his liking?

Instead Alex said, "If you see the white cat, let me know, okay?"

He mumbled something under his breath, then turned and walked back to the shed.

Maybe she should have a talk with Junior and Stevie. They were typical boys, but sometimes they did get a little overzealous in their tactical maneuvers.

Alex was about to return to the house when she heard a shout.

"Hey, you there! Wait!"

She spotted Thelma Klump, a purple and green apparition, pedaling laboriously up the driveway on her ancient bicycle. Her legs pumped up and down, up and down like two well-oiled pistons.

Although Thelma Klump was her nearest neighbor to the west, Alex was certain the spinster was not making a neighborly call. The feud had begun eighteen years ago when Alex's father had built on the land below Klump's. Exhausting every avenue open to her the woman had fought, unsuccessfully, to prohibit construction of Carlson's trilevel house. Her view, she claimed, was being severely obstructed.

The last time Alex had been subjected to the woman's wrath was three years ago, when Klump had arrived at her house in the same alarming manner to inform Alex that her son Todd—now eighteen and in college five hundred miles away—was a trespasser and a thief. Todd had invaded Klump's property, she claimed, and ripped off a peach from a tree.

Now here the woman was again. Her face, Alex noted as she reluctantly went to meet her, no less red, her clothes no less eye-catching, than the last time.

Klump didn't waste time on social amenities.

"Are you the owner of a cat?"

Alex's pulse quickened. "Winnie?"

"Winnie, schminnie, I don't know names," Klump said caustically. "The black one."

"Oh." Blackie, Alex thought, feeling a heavy disappointment.

"Your damn cat's been prowling around my bird feeder, stalking the birds. He appears, thank heavens, to be a stupid, clumsy bastard. But he could get lucky."

Poor Blackie, Alex mused. Four years ago someone had taken two kittens for the "Big Ride." She had found them, scrawny, half-starved, wandering along the ridge, mewing pathetically, and had taken them in. In all that time neither Blackie nor Winnie had stirred the community's ire. But now, two complaints in one morning—uncanny.

Concerned about Winnie and still upset over the incident with Sloane the night before, Alex was in no mood for this pettiness. Seeing Klump pedaling up the driveway hadn't sweetened her disposition any either.

"Your complaint is duly acknowledged. I'll file it along with the 'disturbing the peace' complaint of last night." She began to walk away.

"I don't like your kind, Mrs. Carlson."

Alex stopped, turned back around. "Oh? And what kind am I, Miss Klump?"

"I don't like cats either. I have a pellet gun and, by God I'll use it. I give you fair warning." Klump coasted down the driveway. Over her hunched shoulder, she

28

shouted, "I give you fair warning, Mrs. Carlson! Bell that damn cat!"

Several hours later, wearing white shorts and a tube top, Alex was stretched out on a lounge chair at Margie's. Indian summer had come to Nevada in October. The sun's rays warmed and relaxed her. The poolsweep was making soft, rhythmic sounds that lulled her. Margie, reclining in the shade of the patio, was not as considerate.

"Okay, out with it." She used her Nurse Ratchet tone, sweet yet commanding.

"Whatever do you mean?" Alex said, sitting up to adjust the tube top. She avoided Margie's eyes.

"I walk into your house to find you shredding rose petals with the subtlety and refinement of a lunatic. I doubt very much that the roses did something to piss you off, so that leaves the bearer of the roses. What happened?"

"Nothing."

"Alex?"

"I already told you. Winnie's missing, and old lady Klump's on the rampage again. The yard guy was bitching about Blackie. Oh, yes, by the way, 'them monkeys of yours been climbing the apple tree again . . .' "—she mimicked Hawkins—" 'One of them branches was near broke off.' Also the screen was off my window and—"

"Did he lie to you? Was he married after all?"

"I have no idea."

"Did he uh . . . get a little too friendly?"

Alex turned to Margie, their eyes met and held; then Alex, articulating each word carefully, said, "He tried to rape me."

Margie sat up slowly. "Oh my God, Alex—no!"

"Yes."

"Are you sure?"

29

Alex buried her fingers in her hair and squeezed her palms against her temples. "Jesus, Margie."

"I'm sorry, honey." Margie came over to sit beside Alex. "Of course you're sure. It's just that—God, he seemed like such a nice guy. Handsome, suave . . . uh . . . uh . . . well, shit, a megamarvelous man."

"Yeah. I know what you mean."

"Did you call the police?"

Alex shook her head. "It was so . . . so . . . First it was scary. Then it was . . . degrading."

"That sonofabitch. You should've called the cops on him. What if he comes back and tries again?"

Alex hesitated before saying, "I'll shoot him." She felt Margie staring at her. She turned her head to look her friend in the eye. "I'll shoot him."

They studied each other briefly; then Margie pressed a finger to the red skin of Alex's thigh. "C'mon, let's get you out of the sun. You're burning."

After dinner Alex played a game of Scrabble with Junior and Stevie, and then, refusing the Meachams' offer to spend the night, she said her goodbyes and drove home.

The sun had set. The magenta sky above the mountains graduated in hue to a deep Prussian blue. Clouds, looking like strips of gauze, glowed pink. Alex parked in front of the house. She called out Winnie's name several times before unlocking and opening the front door.

"Blackie!" she called, switching on the foyer light. "Hey, guy, if you've got to go, better get your scrawny tail out here."

Blackie let out a mournful mew and dashed out of the bedroom. His short fur bristling up along his back, his tail fat and stiff like a black bottlebrush, he disappeared out the door into the night.

It wasn't like Blackie to go out without greeting her. The hair rose on the nape of her neck. Her sunburned skin suddenly felt icy. She looked first through the open front door, then down the hallway to her room. Every nerve in her body tensed. Her muscles began to twitch like a handful of Mexican jumping beans. I shouldn't go in there, she reasoned, as she put one foot in front of the other, heading toward that room. She thought of the old horror movies she was hopelessly addicted to, and how she hated the part where the nosy heroine creeps silently down the dark passageway or cellar steps to certain doom—Todd used to say that anyone that stupid deserved to die. Then she was standing in the bedroom doorway.

Alex fumbled for the wall switch and flipped it up. With the sound of her pulse beating in her ears, she gripped the doorframe and stared into a room of total chaos.

Sweaters, underwear, shorts, and tops—torn or sprayed with black paint—hung over the edge of the drawers and littered the floor. On the queen-sized bed, which sat on a raised platform, lay the drawer from the night stand, its contents scattered across the quilted spread. The spread had been slashed repeatedly. Perfume bottles lay smashed on the floor at the base of the wall they had been hurled against. The room reeked of a hodgepodge of cloying scents.

Alex's feet, independent of her brain, continued to move forward. Illustrations from her worktable in the studio alcove were cast haphazardly on the floor. Pencils, pens, and an assortment of art paraphernalia lay in a pool of black India ink. A rivulet of the indelible liquid had flowed to the edge of the table and then puddled on the ceramic tiles below.

She began to back up. Out of the corner of her eyes, she detected a movement to her left. Fear gripped her like a cold, scaly hand on the back of her neck. She whipped her head in the direction of the movement and stared into wide, frightened eyes. A sharp cry leaped out of her mouth. It took her a moment to realize that the image—hair fastened in a twisted knot

31

atop the head, skin glowing — was a reflection of herself in the closet mirror. Alex's body sagged limply, then tensed again. Scrawled across the full length of the mirror, in what looked like blood, were the words: "the monsters are waiting."

Something so intense, so terrifying, flashed across her mind that she gasped. Oh God, no! No, it's not *possible!*

Chapter 2

She felt numb, drugged. She should call someone. Get help. Now, of course, she told herself, was the time to call the police.

Alex crossed the room to the telephone. The base of the Trimline lay on the bed; its coiled cord hung over the edge and out of sight. For the first time since entering the room she became aware of a muffled, consistent beeping coming from under the bed. She wondered how long that beeping tone would continue on a phone left off the hook? Several minutes? An hour? Indefinitely? She knelt cautiously and peered under the bed. The green glow of the receiver's night light met her eyes like a rescue beacon.

Taking hold of the cord, she dragged it out from under the bed, pressed the button to silence the *beepbeepbeep* that seemed to be keeping perfect time with her heart, and dialed the police.

"My house—broken into," she croaked out.

"Give me your name and address, and don't hang up until I terminate this call," a deadpan voice responded.

After sputtering over the familiar information, Alex asked, "How long will it take someone to get here?"

"Hold the line." Alex heard static, the dispatcher's voice talking to someone else, after what seemed like an eternity, "Two cars are responding now. They're in the neighborhood. Ma'am, is there anyone in the house with you?"

"No, I live alone."

"Can you go to a neighbor and wait for the patrol cars?"

"No, there are none close by."

She heard the sirens in the distance.

"I think they're coming now. I can hear them." The sirens wailed, getting closer, coming up to the house. Through the open front door she could see red and blue lights swirling around and around, throwing an eerie glow over the outdoor landscape. Blue, then red passed alternately across Alex's body, making the veins in the back of her hand appear prominent and the pallor of her skin a sickly hue. Car doors slammed. She watched a uniformed policeman bound up the brick steps and halt in the doorway with a hand on his holstered revolver.

"They're right out front," Alex said to the dispatcher. "This call is now terminated."

She hung up, rose from the bed, and hurried to meet the police. Halfway down the hallway, she slowed. The same policeman who had been out to the house the night before stood in the doorway. The one Greg had insulted. He stared at her silently.

Another policeman came up behind him and leaned in toward her. "We got two officers checking out the grounds, ma'am. Are you all right?"

"Yes."

"What happened?"

"Somebody . . . or maybe several of them . . ." She waved a hand in the direction of the bedroom. "Come in, see for yourself."

"Did you see anyone leaving the premises?"

She shook her head.

"Okay, we'll have a look," he said, removing the gun from his holster.

The two officers checked through the house, one room at a time, starting with the master bedroom and then proceeding to the lower level. She followed behind them, not knowing what else to do, too nervous to just sit.

"Hey, Adams—Gunther," someone shouted from upstairs. "Come check this out."

The owner of the voice, standing on the deck that ran the length of the kitchen and dining room, waved an arm through the broken pane in the window over the double sink.

"Watch out for the glass, it's everywhere," he said as Alex and the officers entered. There were shards of broken glass strewn about on the countertops, in the sink, on the tiled floor. "I don't know what to make of this. He'd have to be Tom Thumb, or a contortionist, to get through this hole."

Alex bent to pick up a large piece of glass from the floor.

"Please, ma'am, don't touch anything till the crime investigators have come and gone."

Crime investigators? Lately Alex had been so busy preparing for her one-woman art show, she hadn't paid much attention to what crimes might be occurring right under her nose. Wasn't someone murdering women and dumping their bodies in the river? No, that was in another state, not Nevada. Nevada, she remembered grimly, had the two prison escapees. One of them had been serving time for murder, the other for rape and assault.

With her heart pounding, Alex heard Officer Adams ask her to take a seat. She sat in the rocker, kicked off her sandals, pulled her feet up under her, and crossed her arms. Her skin felt hot and dry.

"I'll just get a statement from you before Detective Holmes arrives," Adams said, taking a chair opposite her. "He'll ask you to repeat everything, I'm afraid."

She nodded.

Gunther stood in the middle of the room. As Alex spoke he looked on casually, smiling whenever her eyes met his. He acts amiable enough, she told herself, but it is obvious he doesn't like me. She was sure his animosity toward her had something to do with Greg and his gin-loosened tongue.

The doorbell rang.

"That's probably the sergeant. Gunther, you want to get the door?" Adams asked, but Gunther was already going down the stairs.

Alex heard voices then footsteps on the parquet floor. These last became muffled on the carpeted stairway. Adams stood. She had a compelling urge to stand as well, but decided against it. Instead, she lowered her feet to the floor and turned her head to acknowledge the man whose face was just coming into view. Her eyes locked onto a pair of penetrating ice blue eyes.

"Evening, Jus," Adams said.

"Hello, Billy." The sergeant took several steps into the living room. He looked over at Alex.

Alex realized she was staring at him. She lowered her eyes.

"This is Mrs. Carlson's home," Adams explained. "Mrs. Carlson, Detective Holmes."

"Hello," she said quietly.

Holmes nodded, then turned to Adams again. "What have we got, Billy?"

Alex studied the sergeant's face with an artist's eye. Interesting, she thought, but not heart stopping. So what was it about him that had given her that initial jolt? She got her answer when he glanced over at her. Of course—the eyes, cool and piercing and totally out of character with the rest of his face.

"We're not sure yet," Adams was saying. "The only room disturbed was the master bedroom that is aside from the kitchen where the perp broke out a window pane."

"Let's start there," Holmes said.

Alex stared at the backs of the two policemen—one in uniform and one not—as they walked into the kitchen.

Glass crunched under their feet on the kitchen floor.

"I find it hard to believe that he entered through that small space," Adams said. "The glass at the bottom would've cut him up good. And everything else seems in order according to Mrs. Carlson's statement. She has a couple of TVs, an expensive stereo system, a video recorder/camera setup, silver flatware, even a coin collection . . . not touched."

Feeling Gunther's eyes on her, Alex glanced over at him. He was standing stiffly in the middle of the room, arms folded at his chest. This time he failed to smile. She looked away.

Adams and Holmes walked out of the kitchen. Holmes looked first to Alex, then to Gunther and again back to Alex.

"Mrs. Carlson, do you have an idea what, if anything, is missing?"

She shook her head, answered, "No."

"Would you care to show me the room that was disturbed?" he said, adding, "Please."

The doorbell rang again as they stepped down into the foyer. Holmes stopped, turned to Adams, and said, "CSI. Let him in, and have him start on the deck and the area around the broken window." Turning to Alex, he asked, "Do you live alone?"

"Yes."

"We'll need her prints," Holmes said to Adams.

Alex walked down the hall with Holmes behind her. She suddenly felt self-conscious in the tube top and shorts. Turning to stand sideways in the doorway, she said. "This is it."

"Don't touch anything for the moment," he said. "Just look around and tell me if you notice anything missing."

Alex stepped into the room. She felt his eyes on her. With a feeling of uneasiness, she surveyed the ruins of her bedroom.

Her gaze fell on the deep gash along the top of the oak dresser and she quickly looked away, her stomach knotting painfully. Look at everything objectively, she told herself, as though it belongs to someone else.

"The jewelry box is open." They both reached the dresser at the same time. Chains and beaded necklaces were hopelessly tangled and entwined around one another.

"It looks like it's all here." She lifted up the whole mass of jewelry by one clasp. "There's nothing of value here, just costume jewelry. I keep my good stuff in this drawer." Alex reached for the handle of the small drawer. He stopped her by putting his hand on her arm.

Lifting a gold pen from the inside pocket of his jacket, he inserted it through the handle loop and pulled. Nothing happened. "Do you have a key?"

"It's under there." She pointed at the small lamp on the dresser. "Is it okay?"

He nodded.

She lifted the lamp, took the key, and opened the drawer. He allowed her to look through the contents of the two velvet boxes. Nothing, as far as she could tell, had been taken or even touched.

"Go ahead and look in the other drawers—don't touch the wood."

All of the drawers were pulled out to some extent. Not relishing the idea of sorting through her panties and bras with a strange man at her elbow, she said, "There's just clothes—no valuables."

He shrugged and looked around. Spotting the studio, he started to move in that direction, only to stop and look down at the floor. Across the top of his shoe was the lacy strap of the beige demibra he was standing on. He bent over, lifted his foot, picked up the bra, then dropped it into the open drawer. Without a word, he continued on to the alcove. Going down on one knee, he looked at the half-dozen drawings scattered over the floor without touching them. "Yours?"

"Yes."

"You're very talented."

"Thanks."

"There's no need for you to check in here. I'll have CSI go over this area."

"CSI?"

"Crime Scene Investigators. Sorry about that. We cops like to make everything mysterious and secretive."

He walked to the sliding door, pulled back the drapes, put the pen to a corner of the handle, and pushed. The door remained closed. "You were away when the break-in occurred?"

Alex nodded.

"And the house was locked?"

"Yes."

"Let's hope there's a print or two for Hank to get excited about."

"Hank?"

"CSI. I was trying to give you a break from the technical jargon."

"Stick with one or the other, you're confusing me."

"You're beginning to get the picture." A corner of his mouth turned up slightly.

"Aren't you going to ask about this?" Alex pointed to the mirror with the printed words he had walked by without so much as a glance.

"Did you think I hadn't noticed?"

"I was beginning to wonder."

"What can you tell me about it? Do those words have a significant meaning to you?"

She turned away. "No, none." Her voice cracked strangely.

Gunther appeared in the doorway. "Sergeant," his voice rattled Alex, making her jump. "Mayer and

Cooly have gone. Adams is taping cardboard over the broken window. You want us to hang around when he's through?"

"No," Holmes said. "You two can head out. I'll take it from here."

Gunther turned to leave.

"Tell Hank we'll need him down here when he's finished upstairs."

"Yes, sir. I'll do that, Sarge." His eyes lingered overly long on the bed and its contents before he finally turned and walked from the room.

"Anything missing from there?" Holmes gestured toward the bed as he watched Gunther retreating down the hall.

She stared at the items from the night-stand drawer that were strewn over the spread. *Oh, my God.* Alex closed her eyes tightly for several seconds. That night-stand drawer had been her most private of private niches, and because it was so private, she'd kept it locked. On the face of the night stand was a deep gouge. The wood above the lock was splintered and chipped. Her face burning, she stared at the personal articles displayed unsystematically like junk merchandise at a flea market. Her small, travel douche kit lay next to the open powder blue case of her diaphragm — though she'd switched to the pill ages ago, for some reason she'd kept the obsolete contraceptive. On the open pages of her five-year diary lay a sex manual, the words *100 Positions with Graphic Color Photographs* splashed boldly across the cover — it had been given to her and Joe as a gag on their tenth wedding anniversary.

She stood frozen, not making a move to touch anything; instead, she shut her eyes again and expelled her breath.

"Go ahead and put those things away," Holmes said as he stared out the window into the darkness. "If possible try not to touch the outside of the drawer."

She quickly tossed everything back in the drawer. As she slid it back into the night stand, she paused and sucked in her breath, "The gun . . ." she whispered. Holmes was beside her in two strides. "The gun my husband bought for me. It's gone!"

"What kind of gun?"

"A .22, I think. A revolver. Oh, my God!" Alex hurried across the room to the dresser. She knelt down. After tossing all the sweaters and knitted caps out of the bottom drawer, she sat there, hugging a cardigan to her chest and staring numbly into the empty drawer.

"They're gone too," she said. "My father's dueling pistols."

Alex and Holmes sat upstairs in the dining room. The uniformed policemen had gone.

"Would you like coffee?" she asked. "Instant?"

"I'd love some, thanks."

After slipping on sandals to walk on the glass-crusted floor, Alex turned the burner on under the kettle, swept the glass to one side, then returned to the dining room. She joined Holmes at the windows.

The sky was brilliant with stars. The moon, glowing a warm orange, was in a three-quarter phase. A light breeze, stirring from the west, the same direction as the broken window, tapped at the heavy paperboard. Wind chimes on the deck tinkled randomly. Shuddering from a sudden chill, Alex hugged herself.

"You're cold," he said, looking over at her. "Why don't you go down and put on something warmer?"

"It's the combination of sunburn and overwrought nerves hitting me all at once."

He nodded. "Do you have the serial number of the .22? A description—any information on it?"

"Yes, downstairs."

She went down to the study, she found what she was

looking for after sorting through a dozen receipts and warranties for merchandise she hadn't owned in years. She made a mental note to clean out the files.

On her way back upstairs, Alex stopped at the closet and took out a long navy cardigan sweater and put it on. She pushed the sleeves up to her elbows.

The teakettle was just beginning to whistle when she returned. "Joe is one of those organized creatures. It's all there." She handed Holmes the papers, then stepped around the breakfast bar to the kitchen. She took down two cups.

"Mind if I take this along with me?" He looked over at her. "I'll return it to you."

"Take it," she said, pouring water over the coffee crystals.

He leaned back, ran a hand through his hair. "So, as far as you can tell, all that's missing is the guns?"

"As far as I know, yes."

"You're sure the guns were in the house prior to the break-in tonight?"

"I'm sure." Just the night before, after the incident with Sloane, Alex had slept with the night-stand drawer open and the .22 within reach.

She carried the cups of coffee into the dining room. The man from CSI came up the stairs. He stopped at the top.

"Excuse me, folks. Jus, can I have a word with you?"

Holmes and the fingerprint man went back down to the foyer. Alex heard whispering. Minutes later she heard the front door open and close.

Holmes came back to the table and sat down. The CSI man had been the last to leave.

"Seems he didn't leave any prints. Hank got a lot of smudges, some clear ones of yours. But that's it."

"I see. So what happens now?"

"Now I investigate. I'll start with your neighbors. They might have seen someone prowling around."

"That should be easy. I only have two. Both live

42

above me. The O'Briens to the east and Thelma Klump, the wicked witch, to the west."

"O'Brien," Holmes said, writing in his notebook, "and Klump, was it?"

She nodded. "Don't expect much cooperation from Miss Klump. She's sort of the neighborhood dragon lady."

"May I make a suggestion?"

Alex nodded.

"Since you live alone, I think it'd be wise to spend the night somewhere else." He gestured toward the kitchen window where the flimsy illustration board covered the opening. "He may come back, and he can punch that out with a pinkie."

"Why would he come back?" She was trying to keep the rising alarm from her voice.

"Mrs. Carlson," he began in a patient tone, "you're missing three guns . . . and that's all. You might have interrupted him—scared him off. A sharp burglar would've had all your valuables in a matter of minutes. I've been in this business long enough to know your house is a burglar's paradise. Now either he was a gross amateur or he was interrupted by you or someone before you."

"What if he just wanted a gun?"

"That's another possibility. A man on the run, let's say a dangerous fugitive from a prison, would want to be armed. If that's the case, he now is."

"And you think he'd come back?"

His answer was a penetrating stare.

"You know, you're scaring me," she said barely above a whisper.

"If it's the only way I can make you understand the seriousness of the situation, well then, get scared."

"I am. But I don't believe he'd come back." Alex said it more to convince herself than Holmes. She waved a hand in the air. "With the police and everything . . . my stuff can't be that appealing to a burglar."

"We haven't determined yet if he is a burglar. He left you a calling card on your bedroom mirror."

Alex had pushed the written message back into the recesses of her brain. Holmes had plucked it out. Spread it out before her.

"Do you have somewhere you can go? Friends? Relatives?"

"Yes," Alex said absently. "Friends."

"Why don't you give them a call? Then when you're ready to leave I'll walk out with you."

She went to the phone.

"Mind if I take off my jacket?" he asked.

"Please," she said, glancing down at her bare legs. "I guess I'm a little underdressed tonight. Afraid I didn't have a chance to change clothes when I got home."

His eyes flickered over her legs as he removed his jacket. He turned to hang it on the back of the chair. Alex noticed he was wearing a holstered gun. She also noticed he was tall, his body was well proportioned and muscular—not with the bulging overdeveloped muscularity of a body builder, but with enough sinew to deter the average bully.

She lifted the receiver and checked her watch simultaneously. Ten-fifteen. She hoped the Meachams weren't already asleep.

Margie answered the phone on the fifth ring. They spoke for several minutes. Alex hung up, turned to Holmes. "It's all set. You don't have to wait."

"I don't have to, but I will." He tore a piece of paper from the pad. "I wrote down the names of two security control firms here in town. You might want to look into having an alarm system installed. It's pretty isolated up here. A couple of flood lights might help too."

Alex nodded, taking the paper.

"Your homeowner's insurance should cover the cost of the window, the vandalism, and the guns. I assume the pistols were insured?"

"Well insured. They're French dueling pistols, early

44

nineteenth century. Very valuable. They were given to my great-grandfather by the Marquis Achille-Claude."

"Was there an inscription?"

"Yes, inside the case. 'To my good friend Captain William Bently — Louis Benigne Achille-Claude.' "

Holmes wrote it down. "There's a good chance we'll recover your heirlooms from one of the downtown pawnshops. If not, at least they're insured."

"I hope you find the pistols. You know, sentimental attachment and all that."

Holmes nodded.

Alex drew in a deep breath. "Well, I'll get my stuff. I won't be long." She hurried downstairs.

She avoided looking at the words on the closet mirror as she took a tote bag and hastily stuffed in a cotton jumpsuit, the demibra and a pair of panties that had miraculously escaped the spray paint. She moved into the bathroom. What cosmetics had not been smashed or dumped into the toilet and basin, she tossed into the bag. A feeling of reckless desperation was closing over her. This was her home. Despite her ambivalence toward it, she had felt safe here. Oh, God, would she ever feel safe here again?

At the bedroom door she paused, her eyes drawn irresistibly to the message. *Monsters. Waiting.* The walls began to close in. The house itself folded in on her, black, oppressive, suffocating. It was his house. He could make it do anything he wanted. If he wanted it to hurt her, there was nothing she could do to stop it. She squeezed her eyes shut and hurried through the doorway. At the end of the long hallway she stopped and leaned against the wall until the panic left her and she felt in control again. She had wanted to run.

Within moments, she and the detective were outside. He was writing something as she climbed into her car. He handed her a business card.

"If you find anything else missing, or if something comes up pertaining to the case, no matter how trivial it may seem to you, call me at one of those numbers. The top number is headquarters; just ask for the detective division."

As she drove away she wondered if Blackie would be all right? She had no thoughts of Winnie. Winnie was not a part of the nightmare.

Chapter 3

The following morning, expecting to be received coolly, if not disdainfully, by Thelma Klump, Holmes was momentarily taken aback when the large woman, wearing a canary yellow jumpsuit and matching shoes, greeted him with a warm smile and a steady stream of chitchat. She ceremoniously placed him in a fat leather recliner — obviously the seat of honor in the garish, ornate living rooom — and hurried off to make herbal tea. The "dragon lady" appeared pleasant and cooperative.

Several minutes later she returned, a brilliant spot of rouge now on each cheek, effortlessly carrying a tray bearing a silver tea service, cups, and sweets. She sat across from the detective.

"A brownie, Detective Holmes?" Klump held out a plate of chocolate-frosted brownies. "They're home-made. I don't use that package stuff."

"No, thank you."

"Mine are moist. The secret's in adding a bit of oil to the batter."

"I'm sure they're great, but I have to watch my blood sugar."

"Pity." She poured the tea, handed him a cup.

"Ms. Klump, the —"

"Oh, call me Thelma. I'm not into the *Ms.* business."

"The home of your neighbor, Mrs. Carlson, was

broken into last night and I wondered—"

"You don't say. How dreadful. Is she all right?"

"She's fine. Mrs. Carlson wasn't at home when the intruder entered. Now, did you—"

"We're so isolated up here. I'm not complaining, mind you; I'm a country girl, born and raised. But sometimes . . ."

"Who lives in the house east of you and Mrs. Carlson?"

"That'd be the O'Briens. But there's no point in you going there. They winter in Arizona, Labor Day to Memorial Day. Place is all closed up."

"Did you notice anything out of the ordinary yesterday? Someone in the area that didn't belong? A vehicle cruising back and forth?"

"Nooo." She toyed with a silvery curl on her forehead. Justin noticed dingy gray-brown strands at the nape of her neck, sticking out from under the wig. "And you can bet I'd notice. I live alone and I keep my guard up. A woman living alone must always keep her guard up. With the O'Briens gone, there's only Mrs. Carlson and myself for a good quarter-mile. I'm forgetting her son. Nice young boy."

"Do you know Mrs. Carlson socially?"

"No, no I don't." She sipped her tea. Looked rueful. "But it's not for lack of trying, mind you. The few times that I've tried to be neighborly, Mrs. Carlson has . . . well, shunted me. And none too gently."

"Does she appear to be a loner?"

"Hel— Heavens, no!" she said with force. "That one dotes on attention. Quite popular with the gentlemen, y'know. Now mind you, I'm no snoop, but I do take pleasure in fiddling in the yard and I can't help but notice, living above her as I do, the cars coming up the driveway and . . . and going down the following day."

"More than one car at a time?"

"No. Different cars. Different times."

48

"Were you in the yard yesterday afternoon?"

"I was."

"Yet you saw no one at her house?"

"No one except her. She sunbathes on her deck nearly every morning—in the altogether. If you ask me I'd say that's perverted behavior. Wouldn't you, Sergeant?" Justin made no comment. "I was planting ground cover all afternoon at the edge of the bluff. If someone had been down there prowling around, it's not likely I would've missed them. Of course, I did come inside to take my meals, and . . . well, who knows . . . ?"

"Did you see Mrs. Carlson come home?"

"She left the house at eleven and returned at dusk."

"You're very observant."

"We're two women alone. Neighborhood Watch applies to even remote areas like ours. I'm sure Mrs. Carlson would report a prowler up my way."

"Aside from the men coming and going, would you say thing are generally quiet down there?"

Klump cleared her throat. "No, I would not."

"Oh?"

"You have only to check within your own police department to get that answer."

"I'll do that, but perhaps you'd care to enlighten me while I'm here."

"Two nights ago she was having one of her rowdy parties. At midnight the police arrived."

"You called them?"

"Not me. I'm not that sort of neighbor. Granted, I'm no saint, Sergeant, but I'm tolerant. And I've seen plenty."

Holmes waited.

Klump picked up the cue. "More than once, coming home from an evening out, she's had trouble maneuvering her car around the rocks lining the driveway. People like her have no business being on the road."

After quickly drinking his tea, Holmes thanked her and left.

He headed for his car, then circled back and walked to the edge of the bluff. As he stood under a peach tree, looking down at the Carlson house, he mentally sorted and filed Klump's account. She could be an excellent witness, he thought. Intelligent, cooperative, keen-eyed. But perhaps she was too cooperative? Perhaps she tended to embellish certain points, understate others? According to her statement, she'd witnessed nothing pertaining to the crime. And his main objective was to obtain factual and useful information necessary to advance the investigation. Mrs. Carlson's personal activities were none of his business. She was a victim, not a suspect.

He watched as two cars drove up the long driveway and pulled to a stop at the front entrance. He recognized one as Alex Carlson's. A redheaded woman exited from the tan station wagon. She and Alex Carlson disappeared into the house.

At the Meachams' earlier that morning, Alex had lolled in the shower, leaning against the tiles with eyes closed, forceful spray stinging her sunburn, until the water cooled. She had avoided looking at herself until after her shower. The steamy mirror, a nebulous veil, masked the dark circles and the puffiness around her eyes.

An hour later she and Margie were trying to put some order back into her bedroom. Margie, taking a box of broken cosmetic jars and perfume bottles out to the trash, had left the bedroom slider open to air out the room.

With Windex and paper towels, Alex approached the closet mirror. Trepidation slowed her pace. The words *the monsters are waiting* seemed to breathe on their own. It's an optical illusion, she told herself, light playing on the mirror. But knowing that, she still could not control that erratic voltage that skittered to each nerve ending.

She squirted Windex over the words, then bent over, picked up the roll of paper towels, unrolled several sheets and ripped them off. Wadding the towels into a ball, she brought her hand up to wipe the mirror. She froze.

The glass cleaner had loosened the dried substance the words had been written in. Red tracks, splaying out, ran down the mirror and joined in places. No longer did it spell words. The words, somehow, someway, had become living things. Monsters. Hideous red monsters with needle-sharp teeth and claws. *Monsters eat little children . . . eat little children . . . eat . . .*

"It's blood."

Alex gasped and spun around.

"I'm sorry, did I scare you?" Holmes stood at the open slider.

She turned back to the mirror. It held thin pinkish streaks. Nothing frightening. Nothing ominous. Her body went limp. With the back of her hand, she brushed the hair from her eyes.

"The way you were staring at the mirror, I thought you might be wondering what it had been written in. It was blood. Animal blood."

"Thank you, Detective Holmes. I shall sleep better knowing that," Alex said finally.

"May I come in?"

"Come in." She pressed the towels to the mirror and scrubbed.

"I've just come from interviewing your neighbor, Thelma Klump. She makes brownies from scratch."

"If you ate one, you may need a stomach pump." She glanced over at him. "Did she see anything."

"Unfortunately, no." Holmes walked around the

51

room. He stopped before some sort of crude design spray-painted on the wall above the bed. With his hands clasped behind his back, he studied it. "Do you know anything about devil worship?"

"I sat halfway through the *Exorcist*. That's about the extent of it."

"Then you wouldn't know if this was a satanic symbol?"

"No," she said guardedly. "Would you?"

"I've been involved in a few occult cases. In this town most of them are the result of mixed-up kids trying to make a statement. They have initiation rites, and sometimes they carve or tattoo satanic symbols into their flesh." With his hands in his pockets, he swung around to face her. "And then there's the real thing."

"Would they do something like this?"

"Yes. They feed on fear. Evoke power from the shock and terror of their victim."

"Do you think this case involves satanism?"

Holmes turned back to the painted wall. He paused for an undetermined amount of time before saying, "No. Two reasons. There aren't enough symbols — these people want recognition. The second is the absence of a ritualistic killing. Cats and dogs make convenient sacrificial offerings."

At the mention of cats, Alex thought of Winnie. Blackie had been acting strange since the day of the party. Did he know something?

Margie walked in. She looked from Alex to Holmes. Without mincing words, she said to him, "Who are you?"

"Margie Meacham, meet Detective Holmes," Alex said by way of an introduction. "He's come by to fill me in on all kinds of goodies. Blood writing. Satanical deeds. It seems the only thing we're missing is the slaughtered lamb."

"Don't mind her," Margie said to Holmes. "She always gets sarcastic when she's scared."

Holmes smiled.

"Is it okay to paint the walls?" Alex asked.

"Sure. We have the pictures." He scanned the room, gave the design a final look, then said, "I have to get back to the station." He stepped to the door, but turned around to face Alex. "If you haven't called the alarm system company, I suggest you do it today. With those two prison escapees still at large, their business is booming. You also might want to lock up after me." He went out the door.

Margie closed the slider, lowered the latch. Staring off in the direction in which Holmes had gone, she said evenly. "I don't suppose you noticed that your detective has one crackerjack bod?"

Alex smiled as she rubbed at the mirror.

Two hours later, after the kitchen window had been replaced, the locks changed on all the doors, the house put somewhat back in order, and Margie was on her way home, Alex flopped on the couch, rested her head on a throw pillow, and closed her eyes.

So he had actually followed through on his threat, she thought. David Sloane had said she would be sorry. *God, was she sorry*. Sorry she'd ever laid eyes on the slimy bastard.

She picked up the phone, dialed the number for Norday Investments, and, before she could lose her nerve, asked for David Sloane.

"Mr. Sloane is out of town," the receptionist said.

I don't doubt it, Alex thought bitterly. "When did he leave, do you know?"

"He left yesterday morning."

Alex sat up straight. "Are you sure? Yesterday was Monday. You're sure he left in the morning?"

"Who's calling, please?"

"Uh . . . Mrs. Chambers. I had an appointment

with him yesterday. We were to meet for lunch. He didn't show."

"I'm sorry, Mrs. Chambers. I'm sure he tried to get in touch with you to cancel. It was imperative that he and Mr. Norday be in Fort Worth for a conference."

"Are you certain he left in the morning?"

"Positive. I drove Mr. Sloane and Mr. Norday to the airport."

"But you didn't see them get on the plane?" Alex asked tightly.

"Actually, I did. David—Mr. Sloane, that is—had left the Landon folder on the backseat of my car. I hand-delivered it as he was boarding the plane."

"I see."

"He'll be back in the office tomorrow morning. May I take your number and have him return your call?"

"No, that's all right. I'll call again." Alex hung up slowly. Damn, that certainly shot down her theory. The break-in had occurred sometime in the late afternoon, Monday. If David had left in the morning, there was no way he could have done it.

The phone rang. Groaning, she lifted the receiver.

"Hi, Mom, guess who?"

Todd's voice sounded so close. Her stomach fluttered. Just hearing from him cheered her up. "How are you, honey? Where're you calling from?"

"I'm fine. I'm at Dad's place."

"How is your father?"

"I thought you could tell me."

"What?"

"Dad's not at home, so I figured he was there with you. He said something about flying in for some tax papers. Did he call you?"

"No."

"Then he's probably out sailing. So how've you been, Mom?"

"Great, hon, just great," she lied. She had been

tempted to tell him about the break-in, decided there was no point in upsetting him. He'd only worry. "What tax papers did your father want? Is he being audited again?"

"Yep. There's no slipping by those crafty computers."

"What year."

" 'Eighty-five."

"I'll dig them out. Tell him to call me."

"Mom, I know you just got rid of me, but is it okay if I come home for the weekend?"

"This weekend?"

"Yeah."

"Honey, I'd love it. But why?"

"A couple things. Homesick for one."

"Tracey for the other," Alex answered for him. Tracey, a senior in high school, was Todd's girlfriend.

"I promised to take her to some school dance. It'll only be for one night. Dad's paying for the flight."

"You don't have to convince me. Come on home. I doubt I'll see much of you, what with your friends and all, but it'll be great having you here—even for a short time." They talked about Todd's school, the fraternity he had joined, the California weather, and Joe's obsession with *Lexy*, his sailboat. She ended the conversation without mentioning the break-in.

The lower level of the house, where Todd's room, the guest room, and the study were located, was cool and dim. Alex found the tax papers and put them on the desk. She was about to leave the room when something about the desk top made her pause. She'd waxed the furniture in this room five days ago. In the left corner a narrow ribbon of polished wood gleamed through the fine layer of dust that had settled on the surface. What had been on the desk that wasn't there now? she wondered. Of course. The photograph. The framed eight-by-ten photograph that Todd had given to her as a birthday present four years ago was gone.

She pulled open the desk drawers slowly. Pencils, pens, paper clips, all the usual paraphernalia of a desk lay inside . . . undisturbed.

She collapsed into the swivel chair to think. The last time she'd been in this room was the night before — with the police. They were finishing up in the study when they were called upstairs. They had not returned. But no — she had come back into the room to get the papers on the gun for Holmes.

She stood, walked to the file cabinet, and pulled out first one drawer, then another, until all five drawers were open. All was in order.

Todd couldn't have taken it. It was here, on this desk, after he'd left home. It had to be somewhere in this room.

She checked the bookshelves, the small closet and all the drawers large enough to hold the thick oak frame.

It didn't make sense. She stood at the desk and, rubbing the tight muscles at the back of her neck, wondered if — and more mystifying — *why* someone would take it.

A loud bang, like a sonic boom, shook the house. Alex jumped, spun around, knocking a dried-flower arrangement off the desk. Her heart held off a beat, then promptly made up the lost beat by thumping a rapid tattoo in her chest.

When the lawn mower sputtered into action, she exhaled slowly and silently cursed Hawkins. After taking the power mower out of the garage, the fool had just let the heavy door drop, shaking the house on its foundation.

She picked up the vase and dried flowers, laid them on the desk, and moved around to the telephone. She dialed the police, asked for the detective division and then Sergeant Holmes.

"Holmes speaking."

"Sergeant, it's Alex Carlson."

"Yes, Mrs. Carlson."

"I really feel foolish calling you about this, but you said if I found anything else missing . . ."

"What's missing?"

"A photograph." She cleared her throat nervously. "A framed eight-by-ten photograph from the study."

"A photograph of what—or whom?"

"Me. That is to say, the photograph was of me." Alex closed her eyes and, with her fingers, pinched the bridge of her nose.

A long silence. What was he thinking?

"Are you sure you didn't move it? Maybe you gave it to someone?"

"I tore the room apart looking for it, every nook and cranny. Whoever broke in has also been in the study."

"I wasn't aware of that."

"Well, that makes two of us. I didn't notice anything missing last night."

"You mentioned you had a son in college. Could he have taken the picture without your knowledge?"

"No."

"Anything else missing from that room?"

"I don't think so."

"Okay," he said. "I'll be out to take a report as soon as I can square away some priorities here—say a couple of hours?"

She looked at her watch. It was eleven o'clock.

"In the meantime," he went on, "I want you to go through the entire house, everyplace you think the perpetrator had access to. That includes all the drawers in your bedroom." When she did not respond, he continued. "*Specifically* the drawers that contain underthings. Do you understand?"

She understood. With that understanding came a sharp prickly sensation on her scalp. "Yes," she said slowly. "I understand."

57

She replaced the receiver without saying goodbye and, not at all thrilled with her mission, walked into her room and began the task of searching through her underwear drawer.

She had thrown out all the slashed and spray-painted clothes. Very little underwear had escaped. Sorting through the dresser drawers, the trash, and even the laundry hamper, she could not find one pair of her lace bikini panties.

Detective Sergeant Justin Holmes hung up slowly. There was something about the break-in that gnawed at him. And there was something about this Carlson woman that seemed out of kilter.

He picked up the receiver and called downstairs. From the duty officer he determined which officer had been dispatched to the Carlson resident the night of October fourth.

He dialed the squad room and asked for Gunther.

"Yes, sir," Gunther said. The two words sounded crisp, heavy with respect. Respect, Holmes thought, and wondered why the word when used in conjunction with Gunther came out cynical?

"You responded to a complaint at the Carlson home on the fourth, is that right?" Holmes asked.

"Yes, sir. Anonymous call. Disturbing the peace."

Holmes waited, finally said, "Tell me about it."

"She was having a party . . . Mrs. Carlson, that is. I went out just before midnight, sir."

"A rowdy party?"

"Hard to say, sir. By the time I got there it was breaking up."

"You've had two encounters with Mrs. Carlson in one week. What's you opinion of her?"

"Well, sir, I'd rather not say. After all, she is supposed to be the victim. What I think is irrelevant."

The words "supposed to" didn't go unheeded by Holmes.

"Unofficially, Gunther, what's your opinion of her?"

"She keeps bad company."

"Care to explain?"

"She and that attorney, Ott. It's common knowledge that Ott is a pervert. I'd question the scruples of any woman who's involved with him. Then there's the other guy."

"Other guy?"

The voice lowered, became muffled. Holmes could visualize Gunther's lips pressed to the mouthpiece.

"At the door while she's talking to me, Ott's all over her and she's letting him do what he wants. Then, after everyone leaves, she's alone with this other guy. They stood at those big windows acting mighty friendly. He had her blouse open."

"I don't understand. Where were you?"

Gunther cleared his throat. "I stopped at the bottom of her drive, there on Rockridge."

"Oh? Why?"

"My report, sir," he said, clearing his throat again.

"Anything else?"

"No, sir. The rest, sir, is speculative."

Justin could almost see Gunther smile. "You wouldn't happen to know who the other guy was? The one she was friendly with at the window?"

"Not by name. But he was driving a snazzy sports car. Corvette, I think. Typical cock's-mobile." Justin had to smile—he owned a Corvette. "Texas plates."

"Pardon?"

"The plates on the Corvette, sir, Texas issue. Dallas to be exact."

"I'm impressed, Gunther."

"And it was personalized."

"Oh yeah? What'd it say?"

"LUV2WIN."

59

Holmes jotted it down. "Thanks, Gunther." He hung up, dialed again.

With a little checking, Holmes discovered that at twelve-thirty on the night of the party someone from the residence of one Alexandra Carlson had dialed the emergency number 911 and then had hung up on the dispatcher. Holmes had the dispatcher play back the ensuing conversation.

". . . it was a mistake . . . Someone I know tried to get a little physical with me. He's gone now."

Definitely Alex Carlson's voice.

Peculiar that she hadn't said a thing to him about a possible assault.

He picked up the phone, dialed information, and asked for the number of the State Department of Motor Vehicles in Austin, Texas.

The discovery of the missing underwear gnawed at Alex like acid eating into metal. When one o'clock had come and gone with no sign of the detective, she felt a growing irritation. When nearly three more hours had rolled around and still no Detective Holmes, her nerves felt raw, exposed. She could have been doing something constructive, such as painting for her show. Instead she was pacing, playing the waiting game.

At four o'clock, just a little more than an hour before she had to leave for the art center to teach a painting class, Holmes showed up.

She opened the door to see him standing on the bottom step of the brick porch, gazing up the hill.

"Your cat?" he asked without looking her way.

She spotted Blackie lying on a large flat rock.

"Yes. Is he doing something illegal?" she said, not bothering to hide the irritation in her voice.

"He's being a cat."

With one forepaw crossed over the other, Blackie

looked around in a bored, lazy way. Gingerly, he lifted his paws and Alex, with a sinking feeling in her stomach, saw a small furry animal run out. Blackie had caught a field mouse. This wasn't the first time she had seen him in action. Fear, torture, and finally death. The cat versus mouse game had always sickened her.

Alex looked away, but out of the corner of her eye she saw Blackie leap off the rock. He was allowing the prey a little more freedom . . . spicing up the game.

"Could we go in? If you don't mind I'd rather not watch him make the kill."

Holmes followed her inside. "Did you make an appointment for the estimate?"

"Estimate?"

"The alarm system."

"Oh, that. No, not yet."

"What are you waiting for?"

"I've been a little preoccupied."

"In light of the new circumstances, I'd have thought securing your home would be your first concern."

"It's right up there at the top, Sergeant, but—"

"What if he comes again while you're here alone in the house. What will you do? Scream? Run to a neighbor? Sic your cat on him?" He was staring at her intently.

"Now wait a minute . . ."

"No, you wait a minute. There are at least a dozen ways for someone to forcibly enter this house. He didn't have a problem getting in before, and he won't have one now."

She stared at him. Then, slowly nodding her head, she said, "You're enjoying this. You enjoy scaring me, don't you?"

"Is that what you think?"

"Yes."

"You should be scared. You should be terrified.

61

Unless, of course, you know something I don't know."

"You seem to know everything, Sergeant!" Alex shot back at him. Then, breathing deeply, making an effort to calm herself, she went on. "Look, I don't want to fight with you. I'll call them, all right? I wouldn't want to complicate your job."

"It's just a matter of precaution, Mrs. Carlson."

Alex nodded wearily. She led the way downstairs. In the study, Holmes circled the room slowly. "Find anything else missing?" he asked, taking the notebook and pen from his pocket.

"Yes."

He stared at her.

Alex felt herself tensing. She hesitated before saying, "A couple pairs of panties."

"Were the missing items in a drawer or in the laundry?"

"Is that question relevant?"

"It's relevant. I'm trying to establish the sort of character we're dealing with here."

"I see." Whose character? she wondered. She busied herself with putting the dried flowers back in the vase. "I don't know where they were taken from. I just know they're gone."

"Anything else?"

"No. I don't think so. Could he be dangerous?"

"What sort of frame was the photograph in?"

Why is he being so evasive? she wondered. He treats me as though *I* were suspect. He believes me, doesn't he? Why wouldn't he? Who would want to make up such things?

"Mrs. Carlson, the frame."

"A thick oak one with ornate brass corners. Very heavy."

He leaned on the edge of the desk and flipped the page of the notebook. "Describe the picture to me."

"It's a color photograph of me, in a bikini, standing

62

on the deck of a sailboat."

Holmes stared at the notebook, pen poised to write. After pausing a full ten seconds, he jotted on the paper. "Anyone else in the picture?"

"No, just me."

He exhaled. "Okay, I guess that's all I need." He bent down and picked something off the carpet. A dried flower. The flower was crushed.

"Throw it away, please," she said, pointing to the wastebasket in the kneehole of the desk. "It's broken."

He nodded, dropped the flower in the wastebasket. He stared after it, then he bent down and lifted the wastebasket, his eyes riveted inside.

"I thought you said you looked everywhere in this room?" Without waiting for an answer, Holmes tilted the wicker basket so Alex could see the frame at the bottom. He reached in and pulled it out by the felt stand. The frame was empty.

Alex's stomach tightened painfully.

"I'll just take this along . . ." He paused, his back tensed.

Before she knew what was happening, Holmes was out of the room, climbing the stairs two at a time and unfastening the catch on his holster. He opened the front door and stepped out onto the porch.

She ran after him and nearly careened into his back as he stood just outside the door. He took several cautious steps forward, looking right and left.

Hawkins appeared unexpectedly from the side of the house. He stopped when he saw Alex and the man with her.

"Oh, Miss Carlson, sorry if I scared you. I . . . uh . . . I thought I left some prunin' shears in the yard," he said, hiking up his pants.

"Hawkins, I didn't hear you drive up," she said.

"Yeah, well I figured I left them shears down there by the mailbox. When they wasn't there, I just walked on up to the house. Didn't mean to be botherin' nobody."

"You didn't find them?"

"Naw. But that's okay; they'll turn up." He scurried by without so much as a glance at Holmes.

"Who was that?"

"The yard man."

"Hawkins," he said speculatively. "Does he have a first name?"

"Otis. Why?"

He reached inside his jacket and fastened the catch on his holster. Gazing out over the landscape, he said, "Mrs. Carlson, would you please bring me the frame. Don't touch anything but the felt backing."

Oh! He could be so damned infuriating, she thought. One minute he was saying too much — scaring the hell out of her — and the next he was close-mouthed and secretive — also scaring the hell out of her.

When she returned he was standing at the car with the door open. He carefully slid the frame into an envelope marked Evidence.

"I'll be in touch," he said, climbing behind the wheel and starting the engine.

Alex headed for the house before he could pull away.

From the living room, she watched him turn his car around, accelerate down the hill, then turn the corner. She didn't see his car pass between the trees on Rockview Drive. Strange. He must have pulled over just beyond her drive.

She located the two security-alarm phone numbers Holmes had given her. As her fingers touched the receiver, the phone rang. She picked it up. There was a long pause then a click, followed by the dial tone. She replaced the receiver slowly, puzzled.

The grandfather clock chimed the half hour.

"Oh shit!"

She was going to be late for her class. She hurried downstairs to get her art supplies.

Holmes pulled to the side of the road alongside a willow tree, shut off the engine, and sat staring straight ahead.

Last night there'd been no doubt in his mind she was telling the truth. Now he wasn't so sure. What is her game? he wondered. She didn't look like the kind of woman who played games. Serious games. Illegal games. But it took all kinds.

Was she lonely like Mrs. Quinz in Hidden Valley, who repeatedly fabricated intruders and disturbances for a few minutes of companionship? Not likely. No, he doubted that Alex Carlson would have much trouble finding companionship, at least not among the male gender. She was too damn pretty. Christ, she was better than pretty, she was a knockout. Dark, silky hair. Large gray-green eyes. A sensuous mouth — made even more sensuous by the nervous habit she had of biting down on her lower lip, sucking on it until it was full and glossy. And her body — yeah, she had a body. Those shorts she'd been wearing revealed long shapely legs. And that stretchy top certainly concealed very little — when she had gotten cold, standing at the window, he hadn't been able to keep his eyes off those two buds rising . . .

"Shit," he said, snapping the sun visor down. He leaned over to look out the passenger window. Through the drooping limbs of the willow tree he could see the house quite clearly. Someone was standing at the windows in the center of the living room. This was probably where Gunther had pulled over to watch a man and a woman embracing. From this distance, there was no doubt that what Holmes was looking at was a human form. But the sex was questionable. Open blouse? No way. For Gunther to see what he claimed to have seen, he would have had to scope them in with binoculars. Or perhaps he had left the patrol car and closed the distance on foot.

That brought up another matter. At about the time Gunther was spying on two lovers, an emergency call had been made indicating a possible assault.

Who was lying?

As Holmes watched, the form moved away from the window.

This morning, on the phone, when she called to report a missing photograph of herself—in what? a bikini, for Christ's sake—he had planted a seed. Given her a suggestion. Dangled the bait. And she had taken it hook, line, and sinker. So Mrs. Carlson had discovered her panties were missing? Very interesting.

And something else was interesting. All these odd occurrences began to take place shortly after her son left home.

Holmes thought back to the night of the break-in. When she had discovered the .22 missing from the night stand, she had been quick to assume the pistols would be gone as well. A little too quick, perhaps?

She lived in an expensive house. The mortgage and upkeep on such a place would be costly. Financial support from her ex may have ceased when their son turned eighteen. How lucrative could art classes be? A hefty insurance payoff could alleviate her financial worries for a while.

When he got back to the station, he would again try the number that the DMV in Austin had given him for one David Leroy Sloane, registered owner of a late model Corvette. Somebody had some answers.

Holmes sighed, shook his head slowly. First he'd find out what her game was. Then he'd decide what to do about her.

He started the car and pulled away.

Scratching and shuffling. That's okay, he thought, nothing to worry about. Hear it all the time. They can't get in. No way can they get in.

The shuffling became louder. Very loud. Suddenly his arm was grabbed in a vise-like grip. Needle-sharp teeth sank into his wrist. He screamed.

Tearing himself out of the dream, flailing his arms and legs and gasping for air—air that was not heavy from smoke and that horrible stench within the smoke—he felt, in his arm, that familiar aching pain.

He sat up in bed, rolled the sleeve of his shirt back and examined the oval of angry dashes on his wrist. He knew if he put his mouth just so over the oval, his teeth and the marks would fit neatly, like pieces in a jigsaw puzzle.

Would the nightmare ever let go? Most of the time he was able to wake up before the thing actually sank its teeth into him. But not always. He rubbed at the scars. Not always.

"Do you have nightmares, Allie," he whispered.

Reaching into the back of the radio, he pulled out the photograph. He studied it carefully, his fingertips lightly tracing over her image.

"So pretty."

He lifted a pair of flesh-colored bikini panties to the side of his face. With thumb and forefinger, he rubbed the silky material, chanting, "Pretty . . . pretty . . . pretty."

His other hand reached out and gently stroked the thick white fur of the cat. She began to purr.

"Wanna go home, kitty? Wanna go home to Allie?"

Winnie purred louder.

In the spacious north room of the art center, Alex moved from one easel to another, critiquing and at times picking up a brush, dabbing it with paint from the palette, and demonstrating on the student's canvas in front of her. The class was full, fifteen students. All were female except for one elderly man.

Harry Bodkin called out to her from the next easel.

"Be right with you," Alex said to him. "While you're waiting, change your turpentine. I see you've got it all muddy again."

She pointed to his metal cup of turpentine. Bodkin bobbed his head.

"Lovely, Mrs. Couch," Alex said. "I suggest, however, that you play down the flowers in the background. Soften the edges. That's it; smudge them up a bit. Better, much better."

Alex carefully stepped over the two canes lying beside the stool on which Bodkin was perched. She touched his arm. "What's the problem, Harry?"

"You don't get down this way often enough," he said, pouting. "From the time you leave till you get back here, I always manage to make a mess of things."

Alex studied his canvas. He was working on a still-life setup on a table standing against the wall. She noticed he'd hardly put any paint to canvas since her last round.

"Oh, Harry, it's coming along just fine."

He nodded, grinning in such a way that Alex knew he hadn't heard a word she'd said. "Fix it up for me, will you, missy?"

Smiling, Alex took the offered brush and began to paint. Within minutes her world transpired into a one of shadow and light, hard and soft edges, rich and muted colors. She crawled into the painting, wandering blissfully in a place that she knew well, a place where nothing could hurt her—where no monsters existed. With a chilling shudder, she wondered what had made her think of that.

She stopped painting when she realized her students were packing away their art supplies. It was time to close up shop.

"There you go," Alex said to Bodkin, handing back the brush.

"I could watch you paint all day," he said.

"I'm sure you could." Alex knew that Harry Bodkin would apply a few more inconspicuous strokes, sign his name, and then hang the painting in the dining room of the Golden Era Complex where he lived, priced, thank goodness, too steeply to sell.

As she picked up paint-soiled paper towels and Styrofoam coffee cups, she called out goodbyes. The last of the students filed out, so she walked down the row of still-life setups and switched off the spotlights. The room was quiet and smelled strongly of oil paint, linseed oil, fixative, and turpentine. Alex washed and dried her hands at the ancient, rust-stained sink.

She took her supplies to the storage room, propped the door open, and, guided by the light from the studio, backed in. Easel in one hand and standing tray in the other, she worked her way down the narrow row of folding chairs to the back, leaned the easel and tray against the wall, and turned around just as the door slowly closed, shutting out the light. Alex froze. Acutely aware of the blackness, the musty smell, the suffocating heaviness, she felt the room closing in on her. Her pulse pounding in her ears, she took several faltering steps forward. Panic rose. She wanted to scream out, but forced herself to stop.

"Cool it," she whispered. "Keep cool."

She breathed deeply, once, twice. Then, with as much aplomb as she could muster, she leaned to the left, reaching out, until she felt the cold metal of a folding chair. Okay, she told herself, you're in the storage room. There's a way out. The door is just a few steps away.

She took a step, moved her hand along the top of the chair to the adjacent chair. It's only a room. With lots of air. It's not like before. There's a light switch here

69

somewhere . . . somewhere. Her hand moved along the wall until she felt the switch. She flipped it on. Light from the bare bulb flooded the tiny room. Alex collapsed with a sigh against the wall. Instantly she felt her composure returning. She told herself there'd been no reason to panic. There was no danger. Not like before. And thinking that, she let memory take her back in time. Back to the day when her father had saved her life.

On that hot August day when Alex was five and her sister, Lora, was seven, the two girls, disobeying their father's rule about not leaving their own yard, climbed the fence into the back lot. They wanted to play hide-and-seek in the brick ruins of the Acme Laundry. Lora had counted down while Alex ran frantically around the yard rejecting one hiding place after another in her search for the perfect one. On the west side of the building, at the bottom of the cellar steps, she found what she was looking for. The old refrigerator was small and square and surely, Alex thought, cool. She climbed inside and quickly pulled the door shut by the shelves lining it. Within an instant she was transported into a world of heavy blackness. It dawned on her almost immediately that she didn't like this hiding place. It smelled rank and moldy, and she had to hold her breath to keep from drawing in the stink. And instead of being cool, as she had hoped, it was hot, unbearably hot. She decided to wait until she couldn't hold her breath any longer, and if Lora hadn't found her by then, she'd have to show herself. Her lungs began to hurt. Her head felt light. Her legs were starting to cramp. She fumbled in the black box for a handle . . . for something with which to open the door. There was nothing, just the slimy shelves. With lungs about to burst, she braced her feet on the door and pushed with all her might. She might as well have tried to push the building off its foundation. Air . . . had to have air. Opening her mouth, she sucked in the heavy foulness, filling air-starved lungs with it. A fit of coughing seized her. She coughed and gasped. She beat fists and bare feet against the door. Pain stabbed through her feet as the metal shelves twisted and bent inward from her weight. Tears and mucous smeared her face as she frantically fought for her life. She cried, kicking and clawing and sucking in that rancid air until there was no more, good or bad, to suck in. Dazzling white lights danced before her eyes. She stopped struggling. The light made her unafraid, calm, tranquil—happy even.

Suddenly the light was unpleasant. Slivers of brightness pierced through her eyelids and sent pinpricks of pain into her head. Cool air chilled her wet face and body. She shook violently as a voice said over and over, "Allie, breathe! Damn it, Allie, breathe!" She pulled air into her lungs—in and out with her sobs. "Breathe, Allie, breathe," her father had whispered, gently rocking her.

And so began the daily warnings.

Alex pushed herself away from the wall of the storage room. She untied her smock and pulled it off. With the hem, she wiped the wetness from her face before hanging the smock on the hook behind the door. She left the room, turned out the light, and gently closed the door. Picking up her paint box and canvas totebag, and taking one more deep breath, she stepped out into the front hall where Velda Lancaster sat at her desk.

Velda was the founder and curator of the Silver State Art Center. The building had once been the home of the Lancasters. When Velda's parents had died in an automobile accident in 1949, leaving her the large estate overlooking the Truckee River, she had founded the Center that now consisted of a dance studio, two workshops, a recital room, and an art gallery.

Velda glanced up from a stack of papers, a startled look on her face. "Alex, for heaven's sake, what's wrong?"

Alex swallowed, then smiled wanly. Her heart was beating more normally now. "I thought I saw a mouse in the storage room."

"Oh, dear. I'll have Stan set some traps in the morning."

Alex checked her watch. Nine-fifteen. "Working late, Velda?"

"Mailers. Oktoberfest is nearly upon us." Velda peered over the top of her bifocals. "Can I count on you as an 'artist in action' again this year, dear?"

"I'm yours."

"Your portrait sketches are one of the highlights."

"Flattery will get you everywhere. See you next week."

"Oh, Alex, I almost forgot. I sold one of your paintings this evening."

"Which one?"

"The nude."

You're kidding!" Alex felt a rush of excitement. "I put an outrageous price on that. Did the buyer take it with him—or her?"

"Him. And yes. Paid cash and insisted on having it now. In fact he left with it just minutes ago. I have a feeling he was willing to pay more. He was quite taken with it." Velda tipped her head and added in a whisper. "He wanted to know if you were the model."

"Really? Well"—Alex smiled, raising an eyebrow— "he'll never know, will he?" She waved goodbye and pushed through the main door. At the top of the steps she paused, inhaled deeply, smelling a tinge of wood smoke in the night air, then hurried down the steps. She strode across the parking lot to her silver two-door Nissan feeling exuberant about the sale of her painting. With that money she could have her bedroom repapered and new carpet installed. Or perhaps it would even pay for the alarm system.

After stowing her art paraphernalia in the trunk, Alex unlocked the car door and opened it a crack. Suddenly an alarming feeling of anxiety rushed at her like a blast of frigid air. She sensed she was being watched, not just looked at, but observed—intently. Instinctively she bent, looking through the window into the backseat. Nothing.

Anxious to get safely into her car, she yanked on the handle. A hand appeared from nowhere and held the door closed.

Alex spun around with a gasp, her heart thumping madly in her chest. The man blocking her way was an ex-student, Scott Withers. The fact that she knew him failed to ease her anxiety.

"What do you want, Scott?"

"Just thought I'd say hello. You don't come over anymore." He tipped his head in the direction of the pizza parlor across the street.

"And you know why I don't," Alex said evenly.

Scott, a handsome, twenty-eight-year-old university student, waited tables at Gina's Pizza. After painting classes Alex had gotten into the habit of crossing the street to Gina's for a salad, pizza, and a glass of wine. Scott had loitered at her table, asking about her classes. He'd signed up for lessons. With an overinflated ego, accustomed to getting what he wanted, he had made his move, instantly and without finesse, at the close of the first class.

"Okay, so I might've come on a little too strong the first time. How 'bout giving a guy a second chance?"

"I never offered you a first chance."

"Shit, just 'cause you're older than me doesn't mean we can't have something special between us."

Alex sensed a strong innuendo in his last words.

"Forget it, Scott."

"Hey, lady, you should be flattered."

"I'm not."

"Look damn it, I signed up for those fucking classes. I thought that's what I had to do to get you to go out with me."

"I refunded your money. What do you want, compensation for the time wasted in my class?" she said sarcastically.

He bobbed his head, grinning. "Yeah," he drawled. "My place . . . tonight."

"Drop dead." She tried to push his hand away.

"Alex!" Velda called from the side door of the center. "Everything all right out there?"

Alex pulled open the door and climbed into the car, slamming and locking the door.

Scott swaggered backward several steps, his hands locked behind him. He bent at the waist. "I'll call you."

Alex started the engine and drove away without looking back.

Chapter 4

Midnight.
He stared down through the tinted bubble into her bedroom.
A soft light coming from somewhere to the left of the room
illuminated the bed directly below the skylight. He could make
out her shape in the center of the bed. She was lying on her back
with her legs to one side, her hands by her head. He watched as
she rolled onto her right side, then tossed over to her left. "Can't
sleep, huh, Allie?" he said quietly under his breath. "Good.
That's good."

He could sit up here on the roof watching her for hours. And
he had, many times. But right now he had things to do.
Important things. He pushed himself up, crouching on the balls
of his feet; then, taking one last look at her, he began to creep
silently down the wood shakes toward the apple tree.

Alex opened her eyes. She looked over at the clock.
Twelve-six. The room was softly lit by the glow from
the bathroom—the night light she had refused to give
up from her childhood. Lying awake, she listened to
the creaking and groaning of the house as it settled. It
was back again, that irrational feeling of being
watched. The oval skylight above her bed looked down
like a dark and sinister eye.

God, how she hated that skylight. When her father built the house, he had insisted on it. She had decided that when the construction on her new studio began, she would get rid of the damn thing.

An all too familiar sense of oppression crept over her, making her shudder. It seemed like ages since she'd felt that heavy, suffocating sensation. God knows, she thought, in the past three days my emotions have run the gamut — anger, fear, desperation, shock, and even revulsion. But they all took a backseat to the wretched dirge that was trying to worm its way up from the past.

She pulled her legs up, curling into a fetal position, and thought of Joe and the dissolution of their sixteen-year marriage. Then she thought of her mother and sister. And finally, the inevitable thoughts of her father pressed forth, overpowering all else. *Why, Daddy, why won't you let me go?* Her mind drifted back to the beginning, back when it had all turned bad.

Her father, William Bently, had hired the carpenter, at a dollar an hour over union scale, to build the addition onto the back of their suburban California house. Happy to put out a little more to have the job done right, he had hired Fritz Lambert, the best carpenter in the trade. The Bentlys' new family room would be the pride of the neighborhood.

Her mother wrote the letter, propped it on the mantel against the photograph of her two young daughters, then ran off with the hired man. Mrs. Bently and Fritz made only one stop before heading out of town, the Downey Federal Bank, where she cleaned out the joint savings account of fifteen thousand dollars.

Four hours later William arrived home from the office. He smiled when he looked into the family room to see his daughters and their friends sitting on a braided rug watching some inane kiddie show. Television in the early fifties was in its infancy. The neighborhood children flocked to the Bently house.

William found the letter on the mantel.

He sent the neighbor kids home. He put the toe of his shoe through the small screen of the Motorola. Then he took a claw-toothed hammer to the new paneling of the family room.

Five-year-old Alex and her seven-year-old sister, Lora, stared wide-eyed, in terror of the madman who only moments before had asked for kisses and hugs. They watched him lift a bar stool and hurl it through the picture window. The three matching stools followed. The girls clung to each other as their father, wildly swinging the fireplace poker, smashed all the glasses and bottles behind the bar. When he finally became too exhausted to swing the poker, when there was nothing left to break or slash, he collapsed on the gutted loveseat, in tears. The girls cried with him, though neither of them knew why they were crying.

The following day William pulled his daughters out of Wirtz Elementary School. Why, they wondered, had he taken them out just two weeks before the end of the term? And why did he carry on so, crying every day? Their mother would come back. She never meant to leave them *forever*.

Four months later Fritz was back in town—alone.

William, stony calm on the outside, raging out of control inside, looked up the man who had seduced his wife—lured her away from her family. He learned that Joy had left the carpenter in Florida for a two-bit race-car driver. Although William attacked his wife's spoiler with his bare hands, fracturing his skull in two places, his rage remained constant.

From the day Joy Bently climbed into that Ford pickup with her white Samsonite suitcase and headed out on the highway, never to return, life for the three people she had left behind changed drastically.

Alex forced the past back into the recesses of her mind—where it belonged, she thought. The present

77

was already more than she could handle.

She thought of Todd, and immediately the oppressiveness began to ease. She missed him terribly. Her son, the baby who had arrived within a year of her marriage to Joe, the child who had always been her main source of love and pride, was now a grown man living away from home. He was coming home from school this weekend. His unguarded optimism and playfulness were what she needed. She would make his favorite dishes. Tomorrow she would make fruitcakes, she thought dreamily, Todd loved fruitcake chock full of dried dates and nuts.

The insensate veil of sleep had begun to envelop her when, suddenly, alarmingly, she felt as if she were plummeting down a black well. She jerked awake.

The phone was ringing.

Apprehension gripped her.

She reached out, her hand hovering hesitantly above it. Calls in the middle of the night could only be bad news. She drew in a deep breath, lifted the receiver to her ear and said softly, "Yes?"

There was no response.

"Hello?" More impatiently, "Hello?"

She pressed the lever down then released it. Nothing. Whoever had called was still on the line. "Hello." Several seconds later she slammed down the receiver.

Flopping back onto the pillow, Alex squeezed her eyes shut. So it's going to be one of those nights, she thought grimly. Whenever thoughts of her father trespassed into her waking state of mind, sleep became nearly impossible. The smell of fresh interior paint was strong. A patchwork of shadows dissected the room, cutting across the walls and furniture. An owl screeched.

Alex pushed herself up into a sitting position. From the night-stand, she picked up the TV remote unit and switched on the set. Flipping through the channels rapidly, she paused, then backtracked until she found the dark, Gypsy-looking man whose leg muscles bulged as he ran in-place on a sandy patch of lush Hawaiian soil, counting down to high-impact aerobics: "*Ichi, ni, san, shi.*"

Over the beat of the music she heard something else. A scratchy sound, like the rasp of an old phonograph record. She turned the volume off on the set and listened. Definitely scratching. Blackie? He had gone out earlier in the evening and hadn't returned by bedtime. Since the nights were still warm, she had decided to leave him outside. He could sleep on the deck chaise lounge.

The scratching went on, becoming more insistent and impossible to ignore. With an exaggerated sigh, Alex threw back the blankets and slipped out of bed. The blue light from the television flickered behind her, lighting her way as she padded barefoot along the cold tiles of the hallway. For the umpteenth time since Todd had left, she sensed how utterly cold and disquieting this damned house could feel. Most evenings when Todd had lived at home, she had been alone, but for some reason it was different now.

As she approached the foyer, the scratching became louder. It was coming from upstairs, at the dining room slider. Turning right, she climbed to the upper level. The scratching stopped. Cocking her head to the side, she listened. Wind chimes and crickets, nothing more. The upstairs was dark, but enough moonlight washed across the deck and spilled in through the slider for Alex to see there was no cat at the door.

"It's the chaise lounge for you, cat," she mumbled. She turned and headed down the stairs, back to bed. Something began to scratch at the front door. Alex stiffened. Fear gave her heart a boost, making it beat faster.

Although the front door was on the ground level, Blackie rarely scratched there. He preferred to climb the wooden steps to the deck. At the slider he could see into the living room. That was also where he would find his water, kitchen scraps if there were any, and an occasional unsuspecting sparrow.

Breathing deeply, Alex moved to the door, put her eye to the peephole, and flipped the switch for the porch light. Blackness. The bulb must be burned out again, she thought; then she remembered that there was moonlight. Enough to see faint light at least.

Pressing her ear to the solid wood door, she heard a shuffling sound. Too heavy for a cat. Her heart banged in her chest.

She backed up from the door, turned, then ran down the hall to the telephone in her bedroom. She snatched at the receiver, then, holding it to her chest, not dialing, she paused, listening again. The minutes ticked away with only the sound of her pounding heart and the steady hum of the dial tone in odd duet.

Hold it a minute, she told herself, calm down. Before you do something rash, think this out.

Would she have been so jumpy tonight if she had not let her thoughts go back into the past? The awful bad dreams that had haunted her childhood were just that—bad dreams. Remember that, she told herself— bad dreams, nothing more.

She forced herself to think about what she had actually heard, seen.

A scratching. Blackie.

A shuffling. Not Blackie.

The absence of any light from the peephole.

She punched 911.

A scream shattered the stillness. Was it human or animal? Was it a cat?

Answer the phone, Goddamn you!

Another scream. There was no doubt this time—it was a cat in pain. And following the scream came a thud at the door.

"Reno emergency," the dispatcher said.

"Carlson! Rockridge Drive!" she shouted. "Get out here!" She dropped the phone, ran down the hall to the front door, and threw it open. Then she screamed.

Chapter 5

Alex reeled back from the door, the scream echoing in her head. She looked away and then, as if compelled, looked back again at the thing sprawled in a white heap at the threshold. It wasn't entirely white, though. Red splotches stained the beautiful long white hairs of Winnie's belly.

"Winnie?" Alex whispered, bending down. "Don't be dead, Winnie."

But she knew Winnie was. The cat's eyes were already glazing over. Her tongue, covered with clinging bits of gravel and dried grass, poked out of a mouth that was open and frozen into a cavern guarded by needle-sharp teeth. The cat looked strangely deflated.

Alex reached out to touch Winnie, but found she couldn't do it. Her hand, instead, pressed against the door for support. She felt something slick on her palm. Nearly a third of the way up on the outer facing of the front door she saw a wide streak of blood. She wiped her hand roughly on her robe, shivered, drawing in a ragged breath.

Tears filled Alex's eyes and coursed down her face. Poor kitty. Sweet kitty. Of the two siblings, Winnie had been the more affectionate, nuzzling, purring, and even sleeping at the foot of Alex's bed. When she had failed to come home three nights ago—three, was that all?—Alex had feared the worst, though not knowing for sure had made it easier somehow. Cats were known to be fickle, moving to suit their moods and tastes. And because Winnie hadn't been involved in the latest horrors, Alex had really not given her much thought. Now Winnie seemed to be a part of the nightmare—a fatal part.

The patrol car arrived several minutes later. Two male officers and a police dog. Alex told them all she knew, up to opening the door and finding her cat dead on the mat.

The officer bending over the cat said, "Coyotes, I'd say."

"I don't think so," Alex answered. And then she told them about the vandalism the night before.

"We know about that, Mrs. Carlson. But I don't think this has anything to do with that. Look here," he said, the end of his black shoe wedged under the cat and he rolled it over. "Gutted. Coyotes do that."

Alex looked away, revulsion and grief washing over her. "Are you saying that a coyote killed my cat and then dropped it off on my porch?"

"It could've just come home to die. Cats are tough."

"They're also very private and prefer to die alone."

"Then tell me what you think happened."

"I think someone called me first to wake me up and then murdered my cat and threw her against the front door."

"Threw her?"

"Yes, threw her." She pointed to the streak of blood on the door.

"What reason would someone have to do that?"

"I don't know. To scare me. To hurt me." Fresh tears ran down Alex's face. "I don't know. Oh, God, I don't know."

"Elliot!" the officer called out to the other policeman

who was walking with the leashed dog, shining his flashlight around some shrubs at the base of the hill. "Hey, Elliot, bring Caesar up here."

Caesar trotted up the steps with Elliot close behind. The German shepherd approached the cat warily. He sniffed at it, starting from the head and ending at the tail. Then he sat down and looked from one officer to the other.

Alex's teeth began to chatter. She hugged herself, shivering.

"Mrs. Carlson, go on inside. We'll take care of your cat for you."

"What will you do with her?"

"Well, uh . . . dispose of her properly."

"Aren't you going to do an autopsy to determine what killed her?"

"If you make a request, then yes, ma'am, we will."

"Although you think it's a waste of time. Right?"

His silence confirmed it.

"Leave her," Alex said quietly. "I'll bury her myself."

"Yes, ma'am. I . . . uh . . . I'll wrap her in something for you." He turned to Elliot. "Get a plastic bag from the trunk, huh?" He turned back and paused before saying quietly, "I'm really sorry, Mrs. Carlson."

She nodded.

He leaned against the porch lamp. The light flickered.

"Looks like you got a loose bulb here." He jiggled the lamp. "Don't think I don't know how you feel," he said, reaching underneath and twisting the bulb; light washed over his hand. "I had a manx. A tougher house cat you won't find. I lost him to a coyote."

"Mr. Sloane will see you now, Sergeant," the receptionist at Norday Investments said the next morning. "Second office on the left."

Justin thanked her, walked down the hall, and entered the large corner office. The Norday suites were on the tenth floor of the Richmond Building. The view was to the east, toward the airport and the mountains of Virginia City.

"David Sloane? Sergeant Holmes," Justin said, extending his hand.

The man behind the desk rose quickly to his feet, shook Justin's hand. "Afternoon. What can I do for you, Sergeant?"

Sloane's hand felt wet, clammy.

"Just a few questions, if you don't mind?"

"Always willing to cooperate with the RPD. Have a seat."

"You're acquainted with an Alexandra Carlson, Mr. Sloane?" Justin asked, sitting.

"Alex? Of course. Her husband once worked at this office."

"When was the last time you saw her?"

"Well, I uh . . . I saw her Sunday night, as a matter of fact."

"Social visit?"

"Well, yes, I guess you'd say it was social."

"Did she happen to say if she was having any problems?"

"Problems? I don't think— What sort of problems?"

"Problems of any kind? Financial problems?" Justin noticed the tension in the man's face easing. Sloane leaned back in his chair, put both hands behind his head, exposing damp perspiration stains under the arms of the cotton shirt. The room was cool, almost chilly.

"She's an artist. She teaches painting classes. That's how she supports herself."

"That's a big house she lives in. Lots of land. Art classes must be very lucrative."

"Must be. She has plans to build a studio onto the

85

house. She asked if I could get her a deal on material and labor."

"Would you mind telling me a little about her? Disposition? Personality? Her general makeup?" Sloane dropped his arms, let them swing along the sides of the chair. "How did you learn we . . . uh, know each other?"

"I didn't get your name from her. She has no idea I'm speaking to you or that I even know the two of you are acquainted."

"Then how—?"

"Your car was seen at her home on the fourth. Texas DMV supplied your name."

"What's she done?" Sloane sat forward eagerly.

"I didn't mean to imply she had done anything. If you'd rather not discuss her, I can appreciate that, Mr. Sloane."

Sloane was silent for several moments. "If you intend to interview all the men who know her, you have your job cut out for you, my friend."

"Why do you say that?"

"Look, don't get me wrong. Alex is a lovely lady. And she's bound to attract men . . . lots of men. The plain truth is she goes through them like someone with a head cold goes through Kleenex."

"You're speaking from personal experience?"

"Sergeant, I have a great little woman back in Dallas. She'll be joining me as soon as the sale of the house is final. I wouldn't want what I'm about to tell you to get back to her, you understand what I'm saying?"

Justin nodded.

"Alex has been coming on to me for as long as I've known her."

"How long is that?"

"About eight years." He looked up at Justin. "She's been divorced three." When Justin made no comment,

86

Sloane continued. "Her husband didn't trust her one iota, and he was damn jealous of her. Christ, if he had thought anything was going on between his wife and me, I wouldn't be here talking to you now."

"Her husband is out of the picture now."

"True. Very true. And she's a great-looking woman, Alex is, but I don't fool around on Sara."

"Yet you went to see her Sunday night. Why was that?"

"Dumb. Just plain dumb. She invited me to a party. I'm alone in town—till Sara gets here, that is—and it was something to do." Sloane straightened the papers on his desk. "Alex can be very persistent. She's used to getting her way. And if things don't go her way, she can be extremely spiteful. 'Hell hath no fury like a woman scorned,' huh, Sergeant? When I wouldn't play her game, she threatened to call my wife. Y'know, tell her we had a thing going between us. Spite, plain and simple." Sloane sighed. "If I were you, I wouldn't take everything she says as gospel." He paused, then added, "Has she tried to come on to you, Sergeant?"

Justin shook his head slowly.

"Well, at the risk of sounding egotistic, it's my opinion that that little woman is shopping for an influential meal ticket."

"Mrs. Carlson's house was broken into late Monday afternoon. A few things were taken. Among the stolen property was a pair of dueling pistols—"

"Dueling pistols?"

"Yes. She was pretty shook up about the loss. Sentimental attachment."

Sloane laughed. "Sentimental, my ass. Look, I'm not big on antiques, and I don't know a dueling pistol from a popgun, but that didn't stop her from trying to sell those guns to me."

"When was that?"

"Last time I saw her. Sunday night. She asked me to

stick around after the party and have a look at them. My friend, she wanted to show me more than a pair of pistols."

Lightning flashed across the entire southeast skyline. The clap of thunder followed approximately seven seconds later.

In the dimly lit living room, Alex stood at the window looking out in fascination at the clouds being propelled northward by the wind. Through gaps in them the sky was a striking shade of Windsor blue. For one instant the eyes of Detective Holmes flashed into her mind. Why, she wondered, had *he* come to mind?

She had buried Winnie that morning at the back of the house in a wild strawberry patch. The hole she'd dug had been deep. After filling it in, she'd rolled a large rock across it so other animals would not dig up the carcass. Blackie had rubbed against Alex, mewing pitifully, as she had said words that comforted no one.

Another flash of lightning—so bright, she automatically stepped back—lit up the sky. Her father would turn over in his grave if he knew she was tempting fate by standing within inches of electrocution—paternal warning number three hundred sixty-four. Five seconds later the boom of thunder acknowledged the lightning. "Getting closer," she said aloud.

After gathering an armful of wood from the deck, Alex dropped the logs into the canvas hammock beside the round fireplace. Brushing wood chips from her hands and clothes, she went to the kitchen.

She turned on the radio and was filling the teakettle when the phone rang. Another bright flash filled the room, and the thunder rumbled immediately, before the sky could turn dark again. "Right on top of us now," she said as she reached for the phone.

Heavy static crackled through the line, making her

"Hello" sound hollow in her ear. The static went crazy, like a Geiger counter poised over a mound of scrap metal; then the wild clicking eased into a low hiss.

"Who is this?" Still no one spoke. Alex pulled the receiver away from her ear and stared at it. When she put it back to her ear there was no sound. She hung up slowly.

The wind screamed. The high wailing wound down to an agonizing moan, only to rise and fall again and again.

The phone rang again. Cautiously lifting the receiver and pressing it to her ear, she listened without speaking. Not all the hissing on the line was interference. Someone was breathing. She was certain she heard raspy, uneven breathing.

"All right, what the hell do you want? Thelma Klump, is that you?" She was rewarded with a loud click.

The phone shrilled again as soon as she hung up. Alex grabbed the receiver. "What?!"

"Well, a thousand pardons."

"Margie? Oh, I'm so glad it's you. I thought you were that telephone creep."

"Honey, if I were you I'd call that detective and tell him about it."

Alex sighed. "I don't know. Maybe."

"I'd make up calls if it would bring hormone man out to my house."

"I know you would."

"Seriously, Alex, tell him."

The entire room lit up. Thunder rocked the house, shaking windows and doors. The wind howled and battered against the windows. Alex loved electrical storms, but she was getting more than she'd bargained for tonight.

The doorbell rang, startling her.

"Margie, there's someone at the door."

89

"Who?"

"I don't know. I didn't see a car drive up."

"Don't answer it, you don't know who's out there."

"It's probably Greg."

"It could be the guy who broke into your house. It could be the prison escapees."

"Margie, you're letting the storm rule your imagination," Alex said, but she suddenly felt cold.

"Don't hang up. If you must answer the door, then just put the phone down. I'll stay on the line and if you're not back in . . . say . . . four minutes, I'll call the cops."

The Westminster chimed through the house again. "Okay, here goes."

"Alex, be sure to use the peephole and—"

"If I don't answer the door soon, whoever's out there will have given up and left, or frozen to death on my porch, so hold on."

"Remember—four minutes . . . I'm timing . . . *now.*"

Alex reached the door as the bell chimed again. She flipped on the porch light, peered through the viewer. Although there was light, she saw no one. *Oh no,* she thought, tensing, *not again.* "Who is it?" she called out.

"Mrs. Carlson, it's Justin—" The last name was carried off by the wind.

Justin? Did she know a Justin? "Who?"

"Detective Holmes, RPD." His face came into view.

Alex let out her breath. She glanced in the mirror by the door and quickly tucked her baggy sweater into the waistband of her jeans. She unlocked the deadbolt, leaving the safety chain in its track, and opened the door a crack.

"Sergeant?"

"It's not a fit night out for man or beast." Justin Holmes nodded at his feet where Blackie sat hunched, head nuzzling his pantleg. Alex closed the door and unhooked the chain.

"Hurry, get in here . . . both of you." Blackie bounded over the threshold. Justin quickly followed. Alex closed the door.

He was wearing snug blue jeans and a pastel blue, Ralph Lauren polo shirt. A golden locust leaf nestled in his hair above one ear. Alex reflexively reached up to remove it. His eyebrow arched upward as her hand touched his hair.

"A leaf." She quickly withdrew her hand, showed it to him, then crumpled it.

He nodded and ran a hand through his tousled hair.

They stood facing each other awkwardly. "Are you here on official business?"

"That depends." His windbreaker was slung over his shoulder, held by two crooked fingers. She took it, hung it over the bannister knob and turned back to him.

"Have you found out anything?"

"I've found out quite a few things, Mrs. Carlson. The more I learn, the more confused I become."

"Do you plan to share your findings with me?"

"Why don't we both share what we know."

"I've already told you everything I know." Alex felt as though he was setting her up to be interrogated.

"Have you?" He stared at her intently. "What do you know about an assault?"

Her hand flew to her mouth. She turned abruptly and ran up the stairs to the living room.

Holmes charged up the steps after her. He stopped her by grabbing her around the waist and pulling her roughly around to face him. "What the hell's going on?" he said tightly. "What are you playing at?"

He smelled fresh, woodsy and masculine. "The phone," she said, short of breath from her dash up the stairs and across the room. "Margie's on the phone. She'll call the police if I don't let her know there was no

91

big brute lurking on the other side of the door."

He released her so unexpectedly she had to put her hands up against his chest to steady herself.

"Better talk to her then. One brute from the RPD should be enough for any defenseless woman."

She snatched up the phone. "Margie? Margie, are you there?"

After several moments Margie said, "You were gone four minutes and thirty-two seconds. I was just looking up the number for the police."

"It's 911."

"Is that a signal? Do you want me to call them?" Margie whispered.

"No, it's not a signal. And why are you whispering? Everything's all right." Margie was going to love this. "It was — it is — Detective Holmes. You remember Detective Holmes? From the break-in?"

"You're kidding? One of Reno's finest just happens to come out on a dark stormy night. How apropos."

Reno's finest was standing at the windows, hands in the back pockets of his jeans, looking out at the storm.

"Sooo, what's he doing there?" Margie asked.

"I don't know."

"Can't talk, huh? Is he standing beside you, gazing longingly down at you with those electric blue eyes?"

"You can be very exasperating, my friend," Alex turned her head slightly to steal a glance at Holmes. Their eyes met briefly before he tuned his head away. "I have to go. I'll talk to you tomorrow?"

"Tomorrow, my ass. Call me after he leaves. Unless of course, he doesn't leave before my bedtime . . . which is very, very late."

Alex could hear Margie's laughter as she slowly put the phone down.

"This is fantastic. Stupendous." He turned to look at her. "You're not having a problem with your lights, are you?"

"No. I was doing just what you're doing now . . . watching the lightning in the dark."

They stared at each other silently for several moments. Justin broke eye contact first. "Just happened to be in the neighborhood. Didn't see lights up here. Thought I'd just run up and make sure everything was okay."

"I see." No one just happened to be in her neighborhood. Whatever was on his mind, she was certain he'd get to it in his own good time.

She walked to the lamp on the end table and reached down to switch it on.

"Don't," he said softly. "Don't spoil the effect. Unless being alone in the dark with me makes you uneasy?"

She laughed lightly. Why was he here? "Can I offer you something. Coffee. A drink?"

"Scotch, if you have it."

"Scotch I have." She walked into the kitchen, turned on the twenty-watt bulb above the stove. "Ice, water, soda?"

"Ice and a little water, please."

The room brightened, dimmed, and brightened again. Thunder rumbled on the second flash.

She poured J&B over ice, added water. After turning the burner on under the teakettle, she returned to the living room and handed him his drink.

"You're not joining me?" he asked, taking the glass.

"I have the kettle on. Hot buttered rum and storms go hand in hand."

Alex bent down to stack logs in the fireplace. He took one from her hand.

"Here, let me do that." She watched as he stacked the logs into what looked like a miniature log cabin, then stuffed a wadded sheet of newspaper inside the little house. "You're not afraid of electrical storms?"

"I'm crazy about them. The element of danger, maybe." The kettle sputtered. She went to the kitchen, made the buttered rum, then joined him at the window.

"Dangerous situations intrigue you?"

"No, not really. Not if the danger pertains to me personally."

"Did I upset you by popping in unannounced?"

"You might have if I hadn't been on the phone with Margie. She was my lifeline, so to speak."

"Was it your idea to have her stay on the line?"

"No, hers."

"She's a bright lady."

"Meaning . . . *I'm not?*"

"That depends on what you'd have done about an unexpected visitor had she not been on the phone."

"I would have done just what I did."

"And if a man had identified himself as Detective So-and-so from the RPD, would you have opened the door to him?"

I probably would have, she thought. But damn it, what does he expect from me? "I let *you* in. Did I make a mistake?"

"Perhaps. You don't really know me. My being a cop doesn't automatically make me trustworthy."

"What if I asked you to leave?"

"You can ask, but I'm in now. If I choose not to leave, what could you do about it?" He stared at her with an unreadable expression.

"Is this a test?" She was beginning to feel extremely uneasy about his visit. "Did you come all the way up here tonight to see how I'd handle myself in such a situation?" His eyes were fixed on hers. Her question went unanswered. She swallowed hard and continued, "Look, I live alone . . . and I don't much like it. I'm having a few problems in my life right now, which I also don't like. But I'm learning, day by day . . . I'm learning."

"I don't want you to learn the hard way." His tone

was smooth and cool. "I'm a cop. It's my job to protect people and to help them protect themselves. On the average, women are too damn trusting. Every day some woman, somewhere, opens her door to a stranger or climbs into a car with a man she doesn't know well enough to trust. The serial murderer has relatively no problem luring a victim. He can be attractive, sociable, and very charming. Mrs. Carlson, there are more Ted Bundys and Ed Kempers hiding in the woodwork than even the crime experts would care to admit."

She studied him a moment before saying, "You don't think much of women, do you?"

"I think a great deal of women or I wouldn't bother trying to save their necks. At this moment there are two very dangerous criminals loose somewhere out there. They may be in Brazil by now, and then again they may be right here in your neighborhood."

"I'm acutely aware of that. I read the newspaper. I called the numbers you gave me, plus practically every security company in town. I told them I wanted an alarm system installed as soon as possible." She dropped onto the swivel rocker, draping her legs over the arm of the chair. "When they finished laughing, they said maybe, just maybe, they could get out here by the end of the month—for an estimate. You were right; the escapees are good for their business."

"Shit." He lowered himself to the floor with his back against the brick firepit, his knees drawn up. A blinding flash of light caused him to blink instinctively.

"So now what do I do?"

"Are you afraid?"

"I'm scared out of my wits. I've been getting these phone calls. Tonight I got two before you came."

"Phone calls? Obscene calls?" He looked at her as though carefully watching for a reaction. Almost as if he was trying to judge her credibility.

"No one talks. But I heard breathing." She looked out the window to see a bolt of lightning zigzag to the ground on Rattlesnake Mountain. There'll be brush fires tonight, she told herself.

He was silent—deep in thought for several moments. "Phone calls now, is it? Any more wild parties, midnight visits, 'sort of' assaults?"

Alex stiffened. She hadn't told him about those things. Who had he been investigating? *Her?*

Disbelief, frustration, anger, one after the other washed over her. "How do you know—how did you find out?"

"It's my job to know."

After a long pause, with both of them staring at each other, Alex said slowly, "Sergeant, since your investigation seems to be directed toward me personally, then you must know that last night one of my cats—missing since the night of the break-in—was found at my front door, dead, its stomach ripped open."

He sat quietly gazing into the glass in his hand. The orange and scarlet light from the fire glowed on his face, reflecting the flickering flames in his eyes.

"I don't believe this," she said. "You haven't been doing a damn thing about the break-in. Has all your time on this case been spent digging into my personal life?"

His eyes came up slowly to meet her. "The break-in. Now that's a very perplexing matter. Someone breaks out a window too small to come through—why? You say the house was locked up, yet there was no other sign of forced entry. And of the property you claim was stolen, the only item of any great monetary value—the pistols—would, in my opinion, be very difficult to fence."

"What are you saying?"

"Are we dealing with some sort of mysterious entity

here, Mrs. Carlson? A phantom perhaps? I doubt it. I think you should know that filing a false police report is a criminal offense. Insurance fraud is also frowned upon."

Alex was so outraged by his accusation she was at a loss for words with which to defend herself. But why should she defend herself? She hadn't done anything wrong. She was a victim. But no. To this man, sitting across from her, drinking her liquor, warming his back at her fire, she was something else. She was either a kook or a criminal. Or both.

She stared at him, nodding her head slowly. When she spoke, her voice was calm, quiet. "You're too clever for me, Sergeant. Yes, I'm the witch who lives on the hill, practicing deadly satanic rituals and . . . and evil mumbo jumbo. You saved me a call by dropping in tonight. I was just about to report a homicide. Quite a few homicides, actually. It might interest you to know that not only did I murder my own cat, but for years I've been luring men up here, seducing them, then cutting their throats. Their bodies are hanging like sides of beef in my basement. Care to see?"

"I want some straight answers."

"You can go straight to hell!" Alex slammed her mug on the floor, it tipped over, spilling the buttered rum over the carpet. She rose with such vigor that the chair rocked precariously on its pedestal as she headed for the stairs. "After you get out of my house!"

He bounded to his feet and grabbed her arm, wrenching her around to face him. "You started this, Mrs. Carlson, and I'm going to see it through. The average citizen can go years, possibly his entire life, without police intervention. You've had four independent incidents in a very short time. I just want to know what the hell's going on? Is it too much to ask that I get some straight answers?"

She tried to twist her arm free. He grabbed her other arm, holding both firmly.

"Who tried to assault you on the fourth of October? Take your time. I'm sure you'll think of something intriguing." Alex glared at him. "Talk to me, damn it, I've wasted enough time on you as it is."

"What do you plan to do. Twist my arm? Handcuff me to the bannister?"

"I could take you in for questioning. I could request that you be evaluated by a qualified psychiatrist."

"And I could have you up before the police commission on charges of duress and police brutality. You're hurting my arms."

Holmes released her. One hand pawed through his hair. He sighed deeply. "I'm sorry. You're absolutely right. That was uncalled for."

Alex instinctively massaged her arms. Although the sunburn stung slightly, he hadn't hurt her. But if he stayed any longer, implied that she was lying again, she didn't know if she'd be able to refrain from hurting *him*. She had felt a strong urge to smash her fists into his face.

"I'd like you to go now."

"Mrs. Carlson, please. Who assaulted you that night?"

"You find out. That's your job. I'm now the suspect, remember?"

They stood facing each other, tense, wary. Finally he nodded. He got as far as the stairway when the phone rang. He turned slowly. They looked at each other.

"You take the kitchen phone, I'll get the one in here," he said. "When I signal, pick it up and answer just as you normally would."

"Why? You've already made up your mind. Why trouble yourself?"

"Just do it . . . please."

She moved to the wall extension. They picked up

their respective receivers on the fourth ring.

"Hello?"

No one spoke. She heard the breathing. She glanced over at Holmes. Her pulse throbbed. Then:

"Suzanne?"

Alex gripped the receiver tightly.

"Suzanne, is that you?" The voice was deep, raspy. A mere whisper.

"No." Alex felt the blood rush to her head. It was him. Something told her it was the man who had been calling her. Her middle name was Suzanne. Could that be coincidental?

Looking at Holmes, she jabbed her finger at the receiver, mouthing the words, "It's him."

The connection was broken.

Her hands were shaking. Instead of feeling confident and safe with a policeman by her side, Alex felt grave apprehension. There was something about the voice that made her skin feel as if it were too tight for her body.

"It was *him*." Alex slammed down the phone.

"How can you be sure? You said no one spoke to you before."

"The breathing, the . . . the . . ."

"And why would he talk this time?"

"How the hell should I know!"

Her entire body shaking now, Alex moved to the window, hugging herself. Someone out there knew a lot about her. And she was at a disadvantage—she knew nothing about him. No, that wasn't entirely true; she knew he had a thing for skimpy underwear and he had her picture, revolver, and heirloom guns. She knew that much about him because she felt certain the person on the phone was the same person who had tossed her stuff around, had made off with what he wanted, and then, last night, had brutally murdered her cat. What does he want? she wondered. Why me?

Jesus, why me?

With her hands clenched tightly into fists, she stared across the valley at Rattlesnake Mountain. The glow of a campfire flickered — no, not a campfire, the beginning of a brushfire.

The storm was waning with only an occasional flash of lightning in the eastern hills. The thunder rumbled far off in the distance. A spattering of raindrops began to pepper the window, making sharp pinging sounds as the wind propelled the drops against the glass.

Her gaze dropped to the weather vane attached to the white fencepost. The wooden duck was swirling back and forth in semicircles, its wings churning like pinwheels. Not committed to any particular direction, the duck jerked left and right crazily, wings pulling through the air like an Olympic swimmer going for the gold.

Absorbed in her own troubled thoughts, Alex had momentarily forgotten about Holmes until she felt his hands on her arms. Her body stiffened. She jerked her head up to glare at his reflection in the glass. He immediately dropped his hands and stepped back.

"Come lock up after me."

On weak legs she followed him down to the door. "I'll have a patrol car cruise the area tonight." He took out a notepad. "May I have your husband's phone number?" When she stared at him questioningly, he added. "It's about the handgun. I need more information."

She gave him the phone number.

Alex watched as he took his jacket from the bannister knob, walked to the door, and opened it. Before he went out, she said, "David Sloane."

He turned to her his eyes staring into hers. Understanding flashed in his eyes. He nodded. Then he was out, pulling the door shut behind him. She locked the deadbolt and fastened the safety chain.

He was an arrogant, smug bastard. But for some reason unknown to her, Alex wanted very much for him to believe her.

He had to believe her.

Chapter 6

The following morning, Justin called David Sloane. He told Sloane that Mrs. Carlson had implicated him in an act of aggression on the night of the party.

"Christ!" Sloane had spit out. "That's just what I was telling you about, Sergeant. She was all over me after everyone had left that night. I'm ashamed to admit this, but I wanted her . . . wanted her bad, though I came to my senses before it went too far. That's when it turned ugly. She snatches up the phone and says she's calling the cops and she's gonna tell them I tried to rape her. Now, really, Sergeant, do I look like your typical rapist?"

Justin was about to tell him there was no such thing as a typical rapist, then decided against it. "Why didn't you mention this when I talked to you yesterday?"

"I didn't see any point. To be truthful, I thought she'd been faking the call. Y'know, pretending to dial 911. I just said, 'Screw it,' and headed out, disgusted with the whole affair."

"I see. Well, thank you, Mr. Sloane."

"Glad to be of help."

Justin then made a call to California. He got through to the Newport Beach branch of Norday Investments, and after a long delay the secretary connected him to the office of Joseph Carlson. The man sounded gruff, out of sorts.

"Mr. Carlson, Sergeant Holmes, Reno Police Department here."

"I don't know what this is about, Sergeant, but I've got an important meeting across town in less than ten minutes. If you could get back to me in—"

"I'm calling in regard to your ex-wife, Alexandra Carlson."

A pause. "Is she in some sort of trouble with the law?"

"I was hoping you could help me straighten out a few things. Would you mind answering a question or two?"

"This pertains to?"

"The break-in and burglary at her Rockridge address. I understand the stolen handgun had been purchased by you, is that correct?"

Another pause. This one longer. "I don't know what the hell you're talking about."

"Your ex didn't tell you that on the fifth, her house was broken into? That several guns, among other items, were taken?"

"No."

"Do the two of you . . . uh . . . communicate with each other?"

"Of course. Our son lives near me, goes to college at USC. We're civilized. We do speak—about important things, at least."

"Well then, can you think of a reason why she would keep something like that to herself?"

"Not the foggiest."

"Mr. Carlson, can you tell me something about your wife's—ex-wife's—background?"

"I really do have a meeting to get to, Sergeant."

"I realize that, but this is important. Perhaps we can arrange to meet—"

"I'm planning to come into Reno in a week or so. I could call you when I arrive."

"I was thinking within the next couple of days, Mr. Carlson. At your office, if that's convenient?"

"Yeah. Sure. I'll put my secretary back on. She can set up an appointment. I must go."

A moment later Holmes was making an appointment for the coming Monday. This will work out fine, he thought. His daughter and her mother lived in the neighboring city of Huntington Beach. He'd combine business with pleasure.

As far as the workup on Mrs. Carlson was concerned, he knew no more now than before. The case began as a routine B and E—breaking and entering—burgary and vandalism. Then the delayed discovery of a stolen photograph and panties. And now this thing about a dead cat—a murdered pet, according to Alex Carlson. Why was it that everything he'd casually suggested somehow came to be? He remembered telling her that the act of satanism was remote because of the absence of a ritualistic killing. "Cats and dogs," he had said, "make convenient sacrificial offerings." Voilà—dead cat!

She had stuck to her story even after he'd practically accused her of illegally filing false police reports and insurance fraud. If she was telling the truth about the cat, the calls, the vandalism, all of it, then someone truly had it in for her. And that someone could be dangerous.

But it seemed the more he dug up, the weaker her case became.

Alex had finished her Thursday night class, stowed her totebag and paint box in the trunk of the car, and was about to get into her car when she felt a hand lightly touch her shoulder. She gasped, jerking around.

Velda Lancaster pulled back, eyes widening.

"God, Velda, you scared the hell out of me!"

With her hand splayed over her chest, Velda said, "I scared *you*? Lordy, my heart's thumping to beat the band. I thought sure you were going to deck me."

"Sorry. I thought you were . . . well, someone else."

"Who? That young man I saw talking to you the other night?"

She had almost said no, not that young punk. Someone else. Someone whose idea of fun was to kill a defenseless cat. Instead she nodded and said, "Thanks for calling out. Scott's harmless, but he can by pushy."

"Is there something wrong, dear? You haven't been yourself the past week."

Alex was tempted to tell the elderly curator everything, but didn't know how or where to begin. Instead she said, "Everything's fine, Velda."

"Then you're working too hard. You should take some time for yourself." Velda handed her a slip of paper. "New student. I sent him a supply list and told him I'd call when there was an opening."

"Thanks, Velda."

Velda waved and walked back into the building. Alex climbed into her car and quickly locked the door. She wiped her sweaty palms on the front of her jeans. Although the night was warm and windless, she felt cold. Again she sensed she was being watched. Instinctively she glanced across the street, fully expecting to see Scott staring at her from the parking lot of Gina's. She saw no one. God, am I becoming paranoid as well? she wondered. She started the engine and pulled away.

Within a block of the center, in her rearview mirror, she picked up the bright lights of a car.

Looking in the side mirror, she could see by the colored plastic appendage on the roof that it was a police car. Although blinded by the lights, Alex could barely make out a lone policeman behind the wheel. She checked her speedometer—under the speed limit. She signaled, then swung a right onto the freeway ramp heading north. The lights stayed fixed in her mirror. Jockeying for a lane, her speed increasing, she soon forgot about the police car. When she exited the freeway a mile from her house, she noticed the lights again. They stayed close behind until she made the turn onto the street that crossed her drive. The lights were still there, but dropping back.

She turned left onto the road that was posted Private Drive and stopped. Turning in her seat to look out the back window, Alex caught a glimpse of a motorcycle passing and then she watched as Gunther slowly drove by. He was staring straight ahead, seemingly unaware of her car stopped at the entrance of her drive. He turned at the first intersection and disappeared.

Alex sat there, hands gripping the steering wheel tightly, her heart thumping hard beneath her breastbone. Had he been following her?

From his bed Justin reached out, pushed aside the alarm clock and a package of throat lozenges on the night stand, and not finding what he was looking for, pulled his hand away. The luminous hands of the clock pointed to half-past two. What was I looking for? he wondered. *Cigarettes*. The night companion. The friend that kept him company when he was waiting, or nervous, or just couldn't sleep. Although he'd quit over a year ago, the urge—not an urge exactly, more like a pang—zapped him now and then like an electrical shock.

106

Before reaching out, he'd been lying in the dark, arms crossed behind his head, thinking. Alex Carlson's face materialized before him again. His mind went back to the last time he'd seen her. The night of the storm. He remembered the disappointment he'd felt when her hand, reaching up to his hair, had come away with a leaf. He remembered the feel of her against him when, pulling her into his arms, he had stopped her mad dash to the phone. She'd been on his mind a lot. At first he'd told himself it was the strangeness of her case that had her weaving in and out of his head throughout the day. But when she began to invade his private thoughts, his sleep, it was time to unfold it, give it a brisk shake, spread it out, and have a good look. Okay, what was it about this woman that played on his mind?

She was no dawn nymph. He assumed she was close to his age. She was pretty, but he'd known others who were prettier. However, there was something about her, something more than the general construction of her face and body. She was different. Hell, he was intrigued, like a kid marveling over an unusual breed of butterfly. After a while, when the uniqueness wore off, boredom would set in. She was different, that's all. Certainly not special. No, damn it, not special.

Since divorcing Yvonne seven years ago, Justin had fiercely guarded his bachelorhood. Not that he didn't respect the institution of matrimony. It worked fine for some couples. His parents had been happily married for almost twenty-five years until death took them both, huddled together, one cold January night. It might even have worked for him if he had married someone other than Yvonne. Or he might still be married to her—he shuddered at the thought—if he hadn't interrupted her and the detective-lieutenant as

107

they were conducting their own undercover work.

Years ago he had gotten over the pain and anger of coming home unexpectedly one day to find his wife bare-ass naked with another man in their bed. Justin had calmly turned and left the room. Over his shoulder, he had said softly, "Lieutenant, when you're through, may I have a word with you out back?" Before Justin could clear the hallway, the lieutenant had shouted the names of the other two cops—uniform and plainclothes—Yvonne had also gone to bed with. Justin had sat at the redwood patio table, a can of beer gripped tightly in his hand, and waited. He waited, thinking about the men the lieutenant had named. He could go after them, break their faces, maybe get his own face broken, but was she worth it? He decided she probably wasn't. He could go to the day care center and pick up their three-year-old daughter and just take off, for Canada, maybe. But he wouldn't do that. Casey loved and needed her mother. And, he knew, Yvonne—no matter how she felt about him—adored their daughter. He waited over an hour. No one came out the back door. The next time he saw Yvonne was four weeks later at the courthouse. She begged Justin to take her back, swearing to be faithful. He knew he would never trust her. She had lied too many times in the past. The first few years of their marriage he'd suspected she had lovers. He'd even confronted her. She had accused him of being irrationally jealous. She will never lie to me again, he told himself. At least not in affairs of the heart.

Thinking of Yvonne never failed to put his emotions in the proper perspective. Let the other guy get all sloppy and sentimental. Let him feel the pain. Justin had had his. He wasn't having any more, thank you.

Justin climbed out of bed and, naked, headed

toward the kitchen. In the refrigerator was a cold Heineken and the makings for a thirty-two ounce Dagwood sandwich.

Alex had been dreaming. She was walking down an endless stone passageway toward an eerie light. As she walked, she brushed cobwebs from her face. They clung to her hair, softly stirred against her cheek. The light she was moving toward dimmed, then went out, leaving her in total darkness. In the blackness she heard scratching. Something caressed her face. She felt a paralyzing numbness.

Her eyes flew open. She moaned.

It's only a dream, she told herself, staring wide-eyed at the skylight above the bed. She was beginning to relax and feel drowsy again when she felt a fluttering on the side of her face — so like the cobwebs in the dream. Frantically swiping at her face and pillow, she cried out, sat up, switching on the bedside lamp. The thing that had awakened her was now batting itself furiously between the bulb and the lamp shade — a moth. A moth had been on her pillow, fluttering its wings against her face.

"*Christ Almighty,*" she muttered, a hand going to her pounding chest. "Blackie!" The cat was regarding her curiously. "Sic it. That's your job."

Blackie looked at the end of her pointed finger, yawned, then lay back down and began to clean his paws.

"Thanks, I'll remember this when you whine for that dried cuttlefish I can only find in the oriental market." As Alex reached for the light, deciding to leave the moth where it was, she heard a muffled thud above and to the right of her room. Kitchen — something had fallen to the floor in the kitchen. Blackie was blameless, Alex reasoned as she watched the cat draw a paw over his face. With her heart cranking up again, she slid out of bed, put on her robe, and looked around for something with which to protect herself, something heavy. She spotted the cast-iron soldier on her work table. With both hands she picked up the statuette, then cautiously headed upstairs, turning on lights as she went.

Nothing was out of place. Everything appeared normal. No one was in the house.

Back in bed a few minutes later, frightened and perplexed, she clutched the iron statuette in icy hands. She stared at it, thumbs stroking the smooth contours of the steely face. She had bought the eighteen-inch union officer from a sculptor in Carmel because it had reminded her of her father. Handsome, commanding, and as rigid as the metal from which the piece was cast.

Again she found herself wondering if her childhood would have been different if her mother had not run away. She thought so.

Almost immediately after that day, William had become a martinet, relentless in his quest to protect, or perhaps, hold on to, his two little girls. The invisible seine he had cast over them seemed to grow smaller as time went on. Supervising his daughters cut disruptively into William's career as a budding architect. He was fired from his job. He borrowed money to open his own architectural business. The family room was converted into an office. He dropped his friends and ignored the attentions of available women attracted to a handsome man nobly trying to raise two motherless daughters. Long before either girl reached puberty, Lora and Alex felt stifled by his constant presence. His daily lectures. His warnings.

Cosmetics were forbidden. Upon finding a tube of lipstick under Lora's mattress, William scribbled Passion Pink words across her vanity mirror, "Cheap hussies wear painted faces." He selected their clothes. His range of colors narrowed with each passing year. Quaker drab, Pilgrim brown, and cadet gray hung like burial shrouds in their closets. For school, he chose plain cotton dresses with high necklines, always a size too large. For play, he bought long pants and baggy tops. Undergarments were plain white cotton. Shoes were sensible, ugly, and wore like iron. Fad apparel, shorts, and swimsuits were strictly taboo.

By the time Alex was thirteen and Lora fifteen, Lora rebelled. During lunch period, at the beginning in her sophomore year, Lora left the school grounds, went to the shopping center, and stole jewelry, cosmetics, and clothing. Clothing that, to her way of thinking, showed off her ripening figure to its fullest. These clothes she stashed in her locker. Every morning before the first bell, Lora changed from her dowdy dresses into sweaters and skirts so tight they fit like celluloid. After the last bell she washed away the makeup, removed the jewelry, and changed back.

That same year, Lora began to sneak out of the house late at night. Alex heard the giggles of other kids as they ran with her across the backyard and let themselves out the side gate. On the nights Lora stole out the window it was impossible for Alex to sleep until her sister was safely back in bed.

Before long something unforeseen happened to take up what little slack in the reins William left in tethering both girls. Surprisingly, Lora was not to blame. Although Lora would suffer along with her sister, and would run away from home less than a year later, it was Alex who brought the roof down around their heads shortly after her fourteenth birthday.

One evening, on a rare occasion when Alex was alone in the house, a boy she knew only slightly

111

conned his way inside. Within minutes he maneuvered her to the couch, pushed her down, and fell on top of her. She struggled as his hands grabbed eagerly and his wet mouth sought hers.

"Filthy pig!" a deep voice boomed from across the room.

Alex looked up to see her father, a colossal figure, standing in the dining room, the evening newspaper twisted in his hands, his face purple and distorted with rage. He lurched forward. But before he could cross the room, the boy rolled off the couch, scrambled to his feet, and, without stopping or looking back, charged out the front door.

William towered over Alex. "Nothing but a filthy pig," he said through clenched teeth. "Barely fourteen and already whoring around."

"Daddy . . . !"

"Sluts. All women. No-good sluts."

"Daddy . . . honest to God, I—"

"How long has this been going on? I leave you alone for a few minutes and look what happens."

"It wasn't—"

"Do you open your window for them at night? Let them crawl into your bed? You're just like your mother. Was she satisfied with a loving husband? Was she content to raise you and your sister? Was a new home in a nice neighborhood good enough for her? No! And when that scum she whored with ran off and left her, did she come home? Ask our forgiveness? No, no. She took up with more scum. Who knows how many bums have lived off her and the money she stole from me—stole from all of us. Who knows how many men have used her in these nine years."

"Daddy, I'm not like her."

"Liar!" he shouted. "Like mother, like daughter. Look at your sister. She thinks I don't know she

112

sneaks out her window at night and runs with those delinquents. No better than her mother. She's a two-bit floozy. But you—I prayed you'd be different. Christ, why was I burdened with daughters? I'd trade the both of you in a minute for just one son."

Tears filled Alex's eyes, rolled down her cheeks. She whispered, "Oh, Daddy."

"Allie, my God, Allie." He dropped to his knees, crushed her to him. "Baby, I'm so sorry. I didn't mean that. Not one word of it. I love you with all my heart. I love Lora. I wouldn't trade you sweet girls for anything in this world." He kissed her face, his tears mingling with hers. "Tell me you love me. Tell me you'll never leave me like your mother did."

Sobbing, she whispered, "I love you, Daddy."

"Whose baby are you?"

"Yours, Daddy."

William had then listened to Alex's explanation. To her surprise, he had absolved her of all blame. A pretty girl such as she was fair game, he had declared. Men would try to use her, then toss her aside. Her mother, he'd said ruefully, had probably been used up years ago. If she was still alive, only God knew what had become of her—or what she had become.

The lectures multiplied. The warnings grew more vivid and frightening.

Suddenly Lora changed. She no longer sneaked out at night. Her moods became variable. She had screaming tantrums one day, was solemn and weepy the next. Six months later she took off without a word to anyone.

Alex hadn't thought about Lora in a long time. She wondered what had become of her? Was she happy? Married with a nice family? Or had she chosen the wayward route of their mother?

The house creaked. She shivered. God, how she

113

hated this house. With Todd gone, she should sell it and move into something smaller. Yes, that was exactly what she should do. But she knew she never would. Whatever it was that held her here controlled her life as well.

With a burst of angry frustration, she shook the statuette, shoved it under the pillow, and pounded it with balled fists, crying, "Let me go! Let me go!"

He paused in his search through her purse when he heard her call out. The words had sounded like, "Let me go!" Was she having a nightmare? No, not her, he thought bitterly. Her sleep was peaceful, filled with good dreams and happy times. Not like his. Had there ever been a night when he had not awakened in terror, his screams echoing in his head? Yes, of course, many years ago — when she had been with him — his dreams had not all been bad.

Earlier that evening, after deliberately dropping a book to the floor, he had quietly stepped into the pantry. Minutes later, through the wooden slats, he had watched her enter the kitchen clutching a metal statuette in her white-knuckled hands. She had crossed the room to peer out the window above the sink. Then, standing stiffly at the breakfast bar, her fingers drumming nervously on the very book that had been responsible for bringing her upstairs, she had looked around the room. Finally, leaving the lights burning, she'd gone back downstairs.

He thought she had looked so beautiful in that white wrapper, her long hair loose and full, her eyes exquisitely frightened.

He shook his head hard to clear his thoughts, then went back to the task at hand. He put away her appointment book, then lifted out her address book. He opened it and sorted through it page by page, his mind cataloguing certain names and numbers. Sometime later, he returned the book to the exact compartment in her purse.

He scanned the room. Everything was in place. He went down the stairs to the foyer. But instead of turning toward the front door, he turned the other way and, his jogging shoes soundless on the tiles, approached her room. The bathroom light was on. Just before reaching the doorway, he went down on all fours and, like a panther, crept the rest of the way. At the far end of her room, in the dark grotto of her painting alcove, he stood. He looked on as she slept, a mixture of love and hate painfully gripping at his gut like a deadly toxin.

Chapter 7

From his desk at the station, Justin called his daughter in California. Her stepfather answered the phone.

"Dan, its Justin. Casey around?"

"Yeah, sure, Jus. She's out in the garage, getting the camping gear together. I'll get her."

A few moments later. "Hullo, Justin." It was Yvonne. Her voice low and sexy. Always working at it, he thought.

"Hello."

"Casey's so excited about this camping thing. She wanted to practice sleeping in the tent. I had to disappoint her. It looks like rain."

"Tell her it doesn't take practice, it takes tolerance."

"When will you be picking her up?"

"In the morning between eight and nine."

"You're not driving down, are you?"

"No, flying. Tell Casey no hotrollers, hair blower, or any electrical appliances. Make sure she takes warm clothes. I'm leasing a car at the airport, so there won't be much room. Did she find sleeping bags?"

"We got everything on your list. You have change coming."

"Put it in her bank account."

"I don't know why you won't let Dan lend you his

pickup. He wants to, y'know?"

Good ol' Dan. The lieutenant had taken his wife and daughter. Now he wanted to lend him his pickup truck. Sounded like a fair exchange. Don't be an ass, Justin thought. The only one he missed was his daughter. And though Dan had been a royal prick— sleeping with his wife, then badmouthing her, only to turn around and marry her in the end—he seemed an okay stepdad to Casey. Justin had hated it, though, when they took Casey over four hundred miles from him.

Yvonne was insisting. "It'd be a lot easier with a truck."

Justin said nothing. After a long pause she cleared her throat. "Well, here's your daughter. We'll see you when you get here."

"Hi, Pop."

"Hey, pumpkin."

"If it rains are we still going?"

"If it rains we'll camp out in a Howard Johnson's. We'll pitch the tent on the floor, unplug the TV, and tell ghost stories around a Bic lighter."

"Oh, Daddy." She giggled. "No, really?"

"We're going."

"Aww ri-ight!"

"See you in the morning, sweety. Get a good night's sleep. It may be your last until you're back in your own bed."

"Okay, Dad. Love you."

"Love ya too." He hung up. He checked his watch. It was after eight P.M.

Detective Frank de Solo stopped at his desk. "Jus, Roberts and I are heading to the Pit Stop when we check out. Wanna join us?"

"Not tonight, Frank. I'm leaving now. Gotta catch a plane early in the morning. Taking my kid camping."

"No shit? How old is Casey now?"

"Ten going on making me an old man."

117

Five minutes later, pulling out of the parking garage, he surprised himself by turning right instead of left. He took the freeway and exited at the off ramp closest to Alex Carlson's. A minute later he was driving slowly past her house. The lights were on in the living room. He looked up the driveway and saw only her car. He pulled to the side of the road. His attention was drawn to the dining room where, from his worm's-eye view, he caught a glimpse of the top of someone's head, moving toward the kitchen.

Watching for several minutes without seeing anything more, he shoved the gearshift of his Corvette into first. "What the hell am I doing here?" he said aloud. He punched the gas pedal, spraying gravel behind him as he whipped into a U-turn and accelerated back the way he had come.

Alex reclined in the tub, her head resting on an inflated pillow, her thoughts as hollow and vapid as the soap bubbles crowding around her in the scented water. She scooped up a large bubble and brought it to her face. When she lightly blew on the bubble it burst with a wet plop in the palm of her hand. She sighed. "Yeah, my sentiments exactly."

She stepped out of the tub, dried herself slowly, and slipped on a silk kimono she had bought in San Francisco's Chinatown. Then she headed upstairs.

Alex smelled the smoke before she saw it. The battery-operated smoke alarm shrilled into action just as she caught sight of the gray cloud hugging the ceiling. She froze on the stairway.

Fire.

On TV, she'd seen Dick Van Dyke enact the simulated house-fire scene a dozen times. If she did what she was supposed to do — head for the exit — the whole place could burn down before she could reach an outside phone.

118

Alex ran up the last few steps, turned the corner, and looked into the kitchen. A dish towel lying on the counter beside one glowing electric burner was almost completely in flames. She ran across to it, knocking over Blackie's food dish. Her bare feet crunched painfully on dry cat food. Grabbing the edge of the towel, she dragged it along the counter into the sink. Ashes and red embers scattered wildly throughout the room. She felt and smelled the hair on her arm singeing as she turned on the tap. The water hit the towel with a hissing, sizzling sound. Choking smoke invaded her nose, was sucked into her lungs. She coughed. Her eyes stung and watered. With her bare hands, she slapped at the live embers that had settled on the kimono. The tops of her feet felt as though fire ants were making a meal of them. She patted her head, making sure her hair was not about to burst out in flames.

When she was certain the fire was out, both on the towel and herself, Alex turned off the burner and silenced the fire alarm. Inhaling deeply, she rubbed at her eyes with the backs of her hands, then slowly looked around the room. Dark smoke stained one oak cabinet and the ceiling above. Hundreds of tiny charred holes dotted the silk of her kimono. Her hands were black, but not burned. Cat food stuck to the bottoms of her feet. She brushed it off and rolled up her sleeves.

All the while, as she cleaned up the grimy soot from the kitchen and herself, swept the floor, discarded the burnt towel, and applied antiseptic to the burns on her feet, she wondered how she could have been so dumb as to have left the burner on and the dish towel so close to the electric coil.

The phone rang. Her chest tightened.

She lifted the wall extension and listened to the music coming through the receiver. *You are my sunshine, my only sun-shine* . . . That particular song had been a favorite of hers when she was a kid. Now it was raising goosebumps along her arms.

She was about to hang up when a muffled voice whispered, "Suzanne . . . ?"

She was about to say no, wrong number, when the voice said, "Alexandra Suzanne . . . ?" If speaking her name was meant to shake her up—it did. She squeezed the receiver. . . . *never know de-ar how* . . . *click* . . . *much I love you* . . . "Alexandra." A whisper. "I hear you breathing. So pretty. Always so pretty. Not for long."

She slammed down the receiver. Jerked her hand away.

The phone shrilled a second time. She jumped, rapping her knuckles painfully on the edge of the counter. It rang five . . . six . . . seven times before curiosity overrode her growing apprehension. Lifting the receiver slowly, cupping a hand over the mouthpiece and holding her breath, she listened.

"Alex, let me hear your voice. Talk to me, Alex." . . . *happy when skies are gray* . . . "Such a tiny bikini. Was that the way you were brought up, Alex? To flaunt your body . . . beautiful body . . ." . . . *please don't take my sun-shine away* . . .

She pressed the disconnection lever and hurled the receiver, as hard as she could, across the dining room. It clunked off the wall, denting the plaster, and bounced back over the carpet to where she stood. The coiled cord swung back and forth as the receiver spun lazily inches from the floor. She rummaged through her purse, dug out the card Holmes had given her. Then, rapidly punching the number of police headquarters, she asked for the detective division.

"Detective de Solo," a deep voice said.

"Detective Holmes, please."

"Sorry, ma'am, he left about twenty minutes ago. Something I can do for you?"

"No, I mean yes. I'd like to leave a message for

him."

"What's the message?"

She gave him her name and number. "Please have him call as soon as he gets the message. It's important."

Had she locked the front door?

She dashed to it, turned the deadbolt and fastened the safety chain. The sergeant would have made a federal case out of the unlocked door and justifiably so. She worked her way through the house, checking all the doors and windows. As she double-checked the lock on the dining-room slider the phone rang again.

She hoped it was Holmes.

"Alex," the whisper. "Alex . . ." Her heart was racing as she slammed down the phone and called the police again.

"Detective de Solo."

"This is Alex Carlson again. Has Detective Holmes returned or . . . or called in for his messages?"

"No, ma'am. Look, if you have a problem, maybe I can help."

"Someone is calling me."

"Are these calls obscene? Threatening?"

"I'm not sure."

"Don't encourage him. Hang up immediately without saying anything further. I suggest you look into getting an unlisted number?"

"Yes, yes, I will."

"Call the phone company first thing in the morning. That should do it, ma'am."

Alex wondered if it would be that simple? Nothing was simple anymore. She hung up and dialed the second number on the card. No answer.

Calm down, she told herself. You're getting shook up over a couple of lousy phone calls. He just wants to scare you; don't give the bastard the satisfaction of knowing he's succeeding.

She turned on the television, curled up in the

rocker, and attempted to lose herself in a sitcom. But when the phone rang for the fourth time, her muscles tensed anew.

"No way, pal," she said aloud. Reaching over to the phone on the end table, she lowered the volume.

Each ring seemed to get closer together and last longer. "Stop!" she screamed at the linear desk phone. "Give up, you stupid sonofabitch!"

She snatched up the phone.

The muffled voice started right in, "Oh, Alex, you shouldn't hang up on me. It's taken me a long time to get up the nerve to talk to you. Alex . . . ?" When she didn't speak or hang up, the voice continued, "You can be such a cold bitch. It hurts to be shut out. And you've shut me out. It hurts, and when I hurt I wanna hurt back."

Alex bit down on her lip, chewed at it.

"So where's the cop tonight? The one that was there last night? The one that's got the hots for you?"

Everything inside her turned to stone. He was watching the house. Had been watching the house last night when Holmes was here. Her eyes instinctively went to the tinted panoramic windows.

"Do you know where your cat is? Would you like me to bring this one home too?"

She let the receiver drop to the floor and, reaching over slowly, depressed the lever on the phone, held it down for a long time. Her finger ached from the pressure. Her hand and arm trembled.

She was close to falling apart. She had to get herself under control.

She left the receiver on the floor and ran downstairs to the bathroom. As she shook out half the pills from a bottle of Valium, she wondered how many she should take. Had they lost their potency? The pills were three years old, prescribed to her after her divorce from Joe. It had been such an ugly divorce, with Joe making threats and accusing her of sleeping

122

with practically every man in town. Her hand trembled as she popped one pill into her mouth, then another, washing them both down with water cupped in her palm. .

She headed back upstairs, turning off the lights as she moved through the house. In the dark she had a better chance of seeing someone outside. No one could see in. She wanted to call Margie, then remembered that she and Bob had gone to the Red Rose Tavern to practice the two-step.

In the kitchen, she took the flashlight from under the sink and turned off the overhead light. She pulled out the drawer with the kitchen knives. They glinted malevolently in the beam of the flashlight. She wondered if she could use a knife on someone, even in self-defense? The thought of plunging a blade into a living, breathing body sickened her. Unless she made direct contact with a vital organ, she'd have to repeatedly stab and stab and stab. The blood. There would be so much blood.

Momentarily abandoning the knives, she poured a hefty shot of brandy. Like a gunslinger in an old Western, she put the glass to her lips and tossed the liquor down her throat. After the coughing eased, she went back to the knife drawer. Deciding against the long, black steel-bladed knife, she took hold of a keen boning knife. She left the flashlight burning on the kitchen floor. Total darkness on top of everything else would drive her mad. As she crossed the kitchen tiles she stepped on a hard nugget of cat food. Is Blackie dead now? she wondered, a sick feeling in her stomach.

She began her vigil in the swivel rocker.

Her head felt light. Her body tingled. Her tense muscles softened like warm marshmallows. When her eyelids became heavy, she willed them to stay open — to stare unflinchingly into the blackness of the deck beyond. The blackness became complete.

Her eyes flew open. *Don't fall asleep. Please God, don't let me fall asleep.* In an attempt to keep her eyes open, Alex let her gaze dart around the room. It flitted from one place to another, until, spotting the telephone receiver lying on the carpet four feet from her, it paused. Was he still on the line? Could he hear the creaking of the chair springs as she methodically rocked back and forth, back and forth?

The sudden jerking reflex of her body brought her back to a state of semiconsciousness.

She had dozed off. For how long? And what had caused her to wake up so abruptly?

Someone was out there.

She tried to focus her eyes, blurred from sleep and the Valium, on the grandfather clock. The face of the clock was shadowy, indistinct. It began to chime. She counted eleven.

There!

She distinctly heard something that time—out on the deck—the creaking of wood. Then the sound of metal clicking against metal. That sound could only be the handle on the sliding door, Alex told herself. Someone was out there, trying to get in!

With a racing heart, eyes straining to look through the glass door, she pressed her palms firmly to her temples in an effort to think. It was important that she concentrate . . . to rationally plan her moves.

The knife! Where was it? Sliding from the chair onto her knees, Alex groped about frantically in the dark for the knife. In desperation she thrust her hand down and along the side of the cushion and felt a shocking, sickening sensation as the sharp blade sliced across one finger.

Ignoring the throbbing pain, she grabbed the knife, scrambled across the room and, with her breath coming in ragged gasps, rose to her feet at the portion of wall between the glass door and the kitchen telephone. She lifted the receiver to her ear. Dead.

The phone was dead.

"Oh, you stupid fool!" She cursed herself as she stared at the living-room phone, its receiver lying useless on the floor. She had disconnected it earlier. Did she want to cross ten feet of open space, in full view from the deck, to get to it? With a despairing moan she replaced the receiver, wincing at the sucking sound her sticky hand made as it reluctantly came away.

Then, her body pressed flat to the wall, she held the knife in both hands at chin level and felt the warm blood run down her hands and arms. In the darkness the blood was the color of black ink.

For what seemed like an eternity, Alex stood there, straining to hear the intruder. She wondered how long she would be able to keep this up. Soon her legs would collapse if she didn't do something. She steadied herself as best she could. Then, leaning slightly to her right, she looked through the glass door. The south portion of the deck was visible. Covered redwood table and chairs sat serenely in testimony of summer past; of normal uncomplicated days unhampered by panic and fear. Nothing, with the exception of her beating heart, moved or made a sound.

She leaned out farther. Then, like an explosion, a loud clank shattered the silence. Abruptly she pulled back, slamming her head against the wall, biting her lower lip. Her legs gave out, and she slid to the floor. Blood flowed into her mouth. She swallowed over and over, shuddering.

The metallic clanking went on for what seemed an eternity. The automatic deck awning moved into place, activated, she realized, by her shoulder pressing against the button when she leaned forward to look outside. A final clank and the motor wound down.

Holding her breath, she listened. She heard the sound of something sharp being scratched against the glass. Then, as she exhaled with a rush, the scratching was followed by two welcome and wonderful meows.

Blackie? Good Lord, it was Blackie. He was alive!

Relief flooded through her weak muscles. She found the strength to rise and place herself in front of the door. "Oh, you stupid, beautiful cat," she breathed, leaning forward. "You scared the living hell out of me. I'd skin you alive if I wasn't so glad to see you. Was that you making all the noise?"

Blackie stood on his hind legs, front paws scratching persistently on the glass. Alex hastily unlocked the door. At the same moment the latch went up, a pair of shoes suddenly appeared beside Blackie. Alex gasped as her eyes shot up from the shoes to see a tall dark figure—with only the glass of the unlocked door separating him from her.

She opened her mouth to scream, but no sound came out as fear imprisoned every muscle in her body.

The door slid open. The man took hold of her wrist, pried the boning knife from her hand, then stepped inside, closing the door behind him.

"Mrs. Carlson, it's all right. It's Justin Holmes."

The sight of Holmes released the paralysis. As Alex brushed the hair from her face with the back of her bloody hand, an arm circled her waist. With a meek cry she leaned against Justin. His hand gently pressed her head to his shoulder. They stood together, silent, swaying, like two lovers dancing, oblivious to the rhythm of the music.

After a time he pulled away from her to turn on the dining-room light. When the brightness made her moan and cover her eyes, he quickly dimmed it. "Jesus," he said huskily, his eyes moving from her face to her feet and back up again.

126

He took in the blood on her face and hands. Scarlet rivulets, now drying, traveled from her hands down her arms and into the sleeves of the kimono. The kimono was twisted, gaping open.

He untied the sash of the robe and pulled the two pieces together. "Here . . . help me," he said softly. He lifted her limp hand and placed it between her breasts to hold the bodice while he tied the sash. "Was anyone here?"

She tried to shake her head, but the motion was more like a roll than a shake.

"Is that a yes or a no?"

She moved her head from side to side, shrugging her shoulders.

"Where are you bleeding from? You've got blood on your face and in your hair." Lightly parting her hair, he looked for a wound.

She lifted her trembling hand. The blood still oozed from the cut, thickly coagulating.

He inspected the cut. "Come." With one hand around Alex's waist and the other hand holding her bleeding hand, he led her into the kitchen. She stood rigid as he dampened paper towels under warm water and carefully washed the blood from her face and beneath her chin. After closely inspecting her lip where she had bitten it, he switched the warm water to cool. "Put your hands under the faucet. Do you have Band-Aids?" She pointed to a drawer beside him and then lowered her hands under the icy water and kept them there until he shut off the faucet a minute later.

When he finished drying her arms and hands, he applied the Band-Aid to her finger. Then he led her into the living room where he gently deposited her in the rocker.

She lifted her feet, tucked them under her as she stared at the stain on the arm of the chair . . . blood, so much blood—on her, on the phone, on the knife,

127

on his shirt, all that blood from a little cut on the finger. Had she actually contemplated stabbing someone to death?

Holmes went into the kitchen again. He returned with a small glass filled with amber liquid. "Drink this," he said, putting the glass in her hand. He removed his jacket and started to take off the gun and holster.

"Don't take that off!"

"It's all right. Drink the brandy."

She drank half of it down in two swallows. It burned her throat, coursed warmly into her stomach. She took another deep swallow.

He bent and placed a hand on each arm of the chair. "Look at me. I said, look at me." She obeyed. "Did you take anything this evening?" He stared first into one eye and then the other. "An upper? A downer?"

Her head nodded twice.

"How many did you take?"

She held up two fingers and stared blankly at the Band-Aid.

"Oh, shit." He took the glass from her hand. "Then you don't need this. Are you in the habit of taking drugs?"

She shook her head.

"Terrific."

In a foggy state, Alex watched him straighten, turn, and step to the phone. After replacing the receiver, he returned and sat on the edge of the end table, swiveling the rocker around to face him. He pressed a knee to each armrest. He leaned in. "Talk to me . . . please."

She opened her mouth to speak, but no sound came out. Panic rose in her. People had been known to become mute from trauma, their larynxes paralyzed by fear. Except for the one outburst regarding Holmes's gun, she hadn't said a word. But she could

128

talk, she thought with relief, if she said those words, she could still talk.

"Talk to me."

She licked her dry swollen lip. "He . . . he said the same thing."

"*Who* said *what?*"

"The man on the phone said, 'Talk to me, Alex.' " Each word was an effort. "He called again, and . . . and he talked to me. It was better when he didn't."

"What else did he say?"

She thought hard. "He had my picture. He said I liked to flaunt my body." Alex looked down at her legs. The kimono had pulled apart, exposing bare skin to the hip. Holmes reached over and covered the leg with the silky material.

"What happened to your robe?" With a thumbnail he picked at one of the burnt holes.

"Fire . . . in the kitchen. I left the burner on. A dish towel . . ."

"Okay, back to the call. What else did he say? Think. Think hard."

There was something, something very important she had to tell Holmes, but what was it?

"Did he make any sexual overtures?"

She thought about that, then shook her head. "He said I was pretty." She laughed dryly. "I didn't say thank you. I've always had this thing about not being able to accept compliments gracefully."

"Mrs. Carlson, look at me. Try to pull yourself together. Did he threaten you in any way?"

"I don't know . . . I mean, I'm not sure it was a threat. He said I had hurt him and he wanted to hurt back. He said something about you." Her eyes bore into his. "He knows so much about me."

"What do you mean?" He gripped the arm on the chair. "What are you talking about?"

"He knows about you. That you've been out to the house. He watched you come and go last night. *He's watching me."*

Holmes ran his hand roughly across his face and sighed sharply. He took one of her hands in both of his. It lay limp between his fingers. He began to twist the ring on her little finger around and around, seemingly fascinated by the row of small diamonds. Lifting his head, he looked into her face, meticulously scanning her features as he squeezed her hand gently — squeezed and relaxed, over and over. He looked into her eyes, his gaze holding hers so long and with such grave intensity that she had an overwhelming urge to comfort *him.*

She began to cry. "Oh my God, my God," she moaned, staring back at him. "He killed my cat, and he wants to hurt me. Stop him. Please stop him before I go crazy. *Please.*"

"Alex . . ." he whispered so tenderly that had she not been watching his face she would have believed him incapable of such sensitivity.

He stood, lifting her with him. She buried her face in his chest as his arms closed around her, holding her tight. "Don't be afraid. Have a good cry. Go on, Alex, let it all out."

Deep gasping sobs, wrenched from somewhere far down inside her, rushed outward in a great torrent. He held her as she cried. She cried until her chest hurt from the violent heaving and gasping. She cried, hiccuping, until she thought her throat would close up. She cried until she had no more tears. His shirt was damp from her tears. Dark smudges of mascara mingled with the dried blood on the white knit fabric.

Alex was immensely tired. The Valium and brandy encased her mind and body in a sheath of soothing dullness. After finally allowing herself to release the tension through her tears, she was totally depleted.

He carried her across the room and, with her limp body in his arms, half-sat, half-reclined in the vee of the couch. Lying across his lap, her head against his shoulder, her face pressed to his neck, Alex drew her legs forward to lie in a fetal position. One of his arms rested across her back, hand on her hip; the other hand stroked the hair from her face.

Fresh tears filled her eyes and rolled down her cheek. Alex sobbed again, so quietly this time that the sobs were barely audible over the rhythmic beating of Justin Holmes's heart.

The clock chimed twice. Someone was in the house. Someone evil and sinister, looking for her. Wanting to hurt her. Quietly, carefully, Alex lifted the telephone to call Holmes. What was that number? God, why couldn't she remember the number. Where was the card he had given her? As she looked around, the plastic receiver suddenly came alive in her hand. It took the form of a snake, writhing, coiling. The dial tone, sounding like someone breathing in a raspy hiss, sent chills up her spine. The cord was winding around her hand and throat. She struggled with it. Flung it from her. Turned and ran. The inky night, as she opened the door to escape, offered only terror with its warning sounds of hissing and rattling. Thousands of red eyes, like bits of burning coal, glowed in the dark, paralyzing her legs, freezing the blood in her veins. And then Holmes was holding her tight. "Don't be afraid," he said.

Suddenly she was no longer frightened. She felt safe. At peace. He was holding her. Caressing her throat, her shoulder, her breast. Her body began to feel warm, tingly. She didn't want to wake up from the dream . . . she wanted to sink down and let it carry her along, release her from the horror of the nightmare. She moaned softly. The sound was cut off by warm lips covering hers. Startled, she pulled her head back, opened her eyes, and stared into those clear blue eyes. Then she remembered. And she realized that what he was doing, what she was feeling, was not a dream.

His hand was inside her kimono. "No," she said weakly, pushing at his hand. "Please . . . no."

"Why not?" he whispered against her mouth.

She tried to sit up. He gently held her down.

"Go back to sleep, then." His hand pulled away from her breast and out of the kimono. "I won't bother you."

She immediately fell back to sleep.

Chapter 8

"Leave me alone."

Blackie was licking Alex's eyelid. The rough raspy tongue sent shivers of pain through her tender, heavy head. She opened her eyes a little at a time and took in the light room. Why did the mornings always have to be so bright in Nevada? And the sun so persistently available? She was on the couch with her head resting on a small throw pillow. She sat up sluggishly, lifting the afghan that covered her.

Except for Blackie, she was alone. Traces of a dream teased at her brain. No, not a dream, she thought—recall, a mental impression. As much as she wanted it to be a dream, fragments of reality tore into her like bits of shrapnel. The calls . . . the fear. She rubbed her eyes and something scratched her face. Holding out her hand, she examined the Band-Aid on her index finger—she remembered that part too.

Where was Holmes?

She rose slowly, holding onto the back of the couch for support, then went into the kitchen. After washing down an aspirin with two glasses of icy tap water, she fed Blackie and let him out. It was seven-thirty. All she wanted to do was crawl into bed and sleep away the misery in her head and body. Todd was due in around eleven A.M. His girlfriend, Tracey, would pick him up at the airport. Alex didn't expect to see him until late afternoon, and then only for a short time before he had to dress and leave for Tracey's school dance. Today he belonged to Tracey. Tomorrow he was Alex's. Then it was back to California for him.

The note was on the breakfast counter. As she poured a glass of orange juice, she leaned down and read the message through squinted lids. Each word stabbed at her brain.

Will call you approx 10 A.M.

Jus

She took her juice and headed down to her bedroom.

.

At the same moment that Alex was reading Justin's note, he was knocking at the door of his daughter's house in Huntington Beach.

Yvonne answered. Justin noticed she was dressed, hair done, face freshly made up. He remembered her as being a late riser. She invited him in and led the way into the living room.

"Is Casey all set?" Justin asked.

"Has been for days now. Last night she slept with her backpack. Perhaps I should say she took it to bed with her. I doubt she slept a wink all night."

"Could you get her, please?"

"She's not back yet."

"Not back from where?"

"Her paper route. Dan took her in the car this morning so she could be done before you arrived. You're early."

"What paper route?" Justin felt a slight irritation.

134

This was the first he'd heard about a paper route.

Yvonne smiled complacently. "She's had a route since the beginning of summer."

"Christ, Yvonne, she's only ten."

"At least you didn't say 'Christ, Yvonne, she's a *girl.*'"

"That was coming."

"She wanted to make some money, and you know what a tomboy she is. She loves it. It's good for her."

He wanted to bluster, condemn, but he knew Yvonne was right. He suspected his nose was slightly out of joint because he hadn't been informed — consulted actually. "Yeah, well . . . paper routes are hard work. I know, I had one. Is she walking or biking?"

"Walking. That is when Dan's not taking her. He's overprotective, like you."

That did nothing to assuage Justin's crimped ego.

"How about a cup of coffee?" Yvonne asked, moving into the kitchen.

"No thanks. I'll pack the car while I'm waiting. Where is everything?"

"In the garage. I'll show you."

Justin followed Yvonne as she crossed the kitchen and went through a door into the garage. A small pile of camping paraphernalia sat on the floor just inside the door. He bent down and began sorting through the stuff. Tent, two sleeping bags, a lantern and flashlight, fishing poles and tackle box, ice chest, an assortment of cooking utensils and dry goods — he had told Casey they would shop for groceries on the way out of town. As he took inventory he sensed Yvonne staring at him. She was leaning against the wall of the garage, her hands slowly moving up and down along the tight denim of her thighs. Without looking up, Justin asked, "Does

135

Casey have hiking boots or good walking shoes?"

She moved away from the wall and came around behind him as he knelt. He felt her fingers lightly touch the hair at the back of his neck. Pretending not to notice, he brushed his hands together and stood.

"Any decent tennis shoes will do," he said lamely.

Her arms went around his waist. Coming up on her toes, she whispered in his ear, "You're lookin' good, Jus."

"Yvonne," he said quietly, "knock it off."

"I was such a fool," she said, as if he hadn't spoken. "Dan's a nice guy, but it's you I think about when we make love."

"I was a nice guy, too. Who did you think about when we made love?"

She kissed his mouth. Her arms went around his neck, her body pressed against his. "I've never cheated on Dan. But I would, in a minute, for you."

The lies never stop, Justin thought. They come so easy to her. Is it possible she believes her own lies?

"Oh, Jus, you always knew what I liked. What made me crazy. Touch me, Jus. Touch me like you used to."

Justin sensed that he could have her now, right here in the garage of the house where her husband and daughter lived. Wouldn't that be a kick, to have Dan walk in and find his wife and her ex screwing on a pile of camping gear. There were a few snags, he thought: he wasn't into revenge; Casey was too precious to him to ever hurt; and he simply didn't want Yvonne anymore.

"Yvonne, let's cool it, shall we?"

"Jesus, I love the way you smell." She nibbled his earlobe. "I know you feel uncomfortable here. But I've been thinking. I'll come to Reno next week. Stay

136

at your place."

Looking soberly into her eyes, he said. "Not here, not Reno, not anywhere." He reached out and poked at the button for the automatic garage-door opener. The door began to lift. Yvonne pulled away from Justin just seconds before Dan's pickup swung into the driveway.

Justin saw Casey bouncing up and down in the cab, grinning and waving.

Ten minutes later he was on the road with her, heading for the mountains and the Coldsprings campgrounds.

At ten-twenty A.M. the phone rang. Alex reached over and lifted the receiver on the night-stand.

" 'Lo." It was all she could manage at the moment.

"Alex?" Justin's voice.

"I think so."

"How are you feeling?" His voice sounded cheerful and far away.

"You don't want to know." She massaged the back of her neck. "It may put a damper on your good mood, Sergeant."

"Try me. And my name is Justin."

"Okay, Justin. First though, a question?"

"Shoot."

"Last night . . . when I was asleep . . . did you beat me about the head and body with a blunt instrument?"

He laughed. "That bad, huh?"

"Owww," she groaned. "Please."

"*That* bad?"

"Worse."

"Take a couple of aspirin and crawl into bed."

"I took an aspirin. I'm in bed."

"How's the finger?"

"It's the only part of me that doesn't hurt. I haven't looked at it yet. It's all I can do to breathe and talk, I'm not prepared, mentally, to cast my eyes on torn and mutilated flesh."

They were silent for several moments. "Thanks for tending my cut last night . . . and for staying with me," she said. "Did you get any sleep?"

"A little." A pause. "Listen, I've arranged to have your number changed to an unlisted one. The phone company will be out to your place Monday morning. I want you to call the station sometime after four that day and give me your new number. I should be back in town by then. If I'm not, just leave a message that you called, don't give out your number, okay?"

"You don't trust the police department?"

"The fewer people who know that unlisted number, the better."

"Where are you?"

"A gas station in the San Bernadino Mountains. More commonly known in these parts as Big Bear."

Alex heard a child's voice in the background say, "C'mon, Daddy. It's starting to get cloudy."

"Coming, baby — Alex, when I get back we're going to have to have a long talk. I can't do my job if you continue to withhold information from me. I'll want a list of your male acquaintances."

"What do you mean by male acquaintances?"

"Men you've dated; are presently dating. Men you've seen on a regular basis for one thing or another for, say, the past twelve months. For instance, your doctor, Hawkins, anyone that does a service for you. Got that?"

"Yes. I think so."

"Oh, by the way. I had to use your front-door key

138

to lock up after myself this morning. I didn't want to leave the door unlocked. Will you need it before Monday?"

"No, I have others."

"Take the phone off the hook at night. And, please, for God's sake, use some caution." He hung up without saying goodbye.

Before going back to sleep, Alex called Margie and related the events of the previous night. Margie offered to bring one of Bob's twelve-gauge shotguns by later in the day. Alex gratefully accepted.

"Daddy, are you sure you know how to do that?" Casey asked. "If it starts to rain now . . . *bum-mer.*"

Justin was inside the tent holding it up with his shoulders and head as he tried to erect it. One side went up and the other came down. "Where the heck'd you get this piece of sssh—?"

"I borrowed it from the Connell brothers next door. They go camping all the time."

"Couldn't you have bought us a new one? One with instructions?"

"Eddy Connell said this one was all broke in. Besides, I thought you said putting up a tent was second nature to you."

"This isn't a tent, it's a Chinese puzzle." Justin grunted. "I could use some help. Come in here and hold it up in the middle."

Casey giggled. "Oh-oh," she said, stepping through the nylon opening. "I just felt a big, fat rain drop."

"You really know how to apply the pressure."

An hour later the tent was up—listing slightly westward—and equipped with the bedrolls. They had gathered wood and set up camp. A circle of rocks and an old oven rack constituted the combina-

139

tion cooking facility and campfire. They'd each gone in search of ideal roasting sticks for weiners and marshmallows, and Justin, taking his pocket knife, had whittled his to a point, then had done the same for Casey's forked twig—which she claimed was perfect for doubles. The prepared sticks they set aside until dinner.

Justin hung the lantern on the branch of a fir tree. He then turned, surveyed the site that would be their home for the night, and nodded approvingly. "Looks great, huh, kid? Fit for a king. We'd better put the food up so as not to encourage the bears."

"Bears?" Casey let fall an armful of firewood and looked up, alarmed. "You didn't say anything about bears."

"Little guys," her father said quickly. "Won't hurt you. We'll keep the food in the trunk of the car; then they won't get at it."

"Let 'em have it, Dad. I don't want them coming in our tent while we're sleeping, scrounging for it."

"Don't worry, your ol' man will protect you." He tugged playfully at the gob of hair on top of her head; it reminded him of Pebbles Flintstone's hairdo—without the bone. "Get your pole. It's time we went after our dinner."

"Let's make a bet," Casey said casually. "A buck to the one who catches the first fish."

"And a buck for the biggest fish."

"And a buck for the most fish."

"You're on."

Justin had ended up forking over three bucks to Casey. Her two pan-sized brook trout had been their dinner, along with a can of Chef Boyardee beef ravioli, fried potatoes, and roasted weiners. He had let Casey make up the dinner menu. Over the open

140

fire—a blazing inferno hot enough to warp the soles of their walking shoes—they'd toasted marshmallows for "s'mores" and sipped instant hot chocolate as they listened to "Mystery Theater" on the car radio.

In the middle of the night, when they were snug in their sleeping bags, the storm clouds that had been building ominously all day finally let loose. Rain came down in a torrent.

Lying on his back, the smell of wet nylon sharp in the chilling air, the steady patter of rain lulling him, Justin, though exhausted from his sleepless night with Alex Carlson, could not sleep. He thought about Yvonne and her play for him in the garage. The first few years after they'd been divorced, he'd stayed away from her as much as possible. Not because he'd feared she would come on to him, but because it hurt too much to be near her. The past couple of years he had finally come to accept her with indifference. She was a beautiful woman, sexy as all hell, but she did nothing for him now. Absolutely nothing. Women like her had no substance. Women like her . . . like the one with the haunting eyes—like Alex Carlson—women like that had looks, sex appeal, but . . .

"Daddy?" Casey whispered when the rain began to pound on the top of the tent.

Just turned his head toward her voice, "Yeah, baby?"

"Is this thing waterproof?"

"Sure."

"Ohhh, I don't think so, Daddy." Justin could hear Casey moving around, struggling to get out of her bag. Halfway out, she tumbled over, said "Shit," and knocked against one of the poles. The tent caved in on her side. Justin groped for the flashlight, finding a shoe, a hairbrush, and the lamb's wool-stuffed

141

animal Casey slept with still, but no flashlight. Suddenly light exploded in his eyes, blinding him. Casey had found it. She was standing in a crouched position, the sleeping bag up to her waist and twisted about her ankles, the tent a damp shroud around her head and shoulders. Rainwater, leaking from a faulty seam, was dripping from her nose and chin onto her Minnie Mouse sweatshirt. Her face was beginning to scrunch up.

"Casey?" Justin tossed off his bag and reached for her. She was about to cry, and it was all his fault. It had been his idea to go camping. She had never been out all night in the wilderness like this, sleeping in a tent, cooking over a campfire, relieving herself in the bushes. What an idiot he was to take her in October instead of the summer. He had scared her with his mention of bears. And he had forgotten to warn her about poison ivy—which he was certain she had tromped through on her way down to the creek. Even something as innocuous as roasting marshmallows had had dire consequences for her when she had attempted to blow out one that had caught fire only to have it stick to her lip, burning her. And now this. She was wet and scared and having a miserable time.

Sputtering sounds came from her and her shoulders shook. "Daddy!" she said, and burst out laughing. She pounced on him, laughing, squealing as she rolled over him to a dry spot on his other side.

"Casey . . . ?" Justin began, before also breaking up in laughter.

"I'm . . . having the best time . . . ever. But next time . . . let me . . . put up the tent," she squeaked between bouts of laughter. "I put it up . . . by myself . . . in the back yard in no time. And . . . and . . . and it stayed up!"

"Why, you little rascal. You stood there and let me make a fool of myself and you didn't even offer to help."

"Momma said to let you do it. She said men had to show women how nacho they could be."

Justin laughed. "*Macho*, monkeyface, not nacho. And your mother was right. There was no way on this earth I would've let you pitch the tent."

By morning the storm had passed, leaving behind crisp, radiant verdure, bright with reflecting sunshine.

At eight o'clock Sunday morning, Alex looked in on Todd. He was sleeping soundly, one leg and one arm hanging out of the bed. She crept in quietly and began to pick up the formal clothes he had tossed around the room only hours before. As she hung up pants and jacket, she thought back to the night before and how great he'd looked in a white tux. Todd was tall and thin, with Alex's dark brown hair and gray-green eyes. He had his father's clear olive complexion. Her son, she reasoned with the objectivity of a mother, was more than just handsome and charming, he was wonderful. The best.

"Mom, I'll do that," Todd said, his eyes still closed.

"Go back to sleep. It's early."

His eyes opened. "Naw. I don't wanna blow my whole day in the sack. I can sleep on the plane going home." He sat up and roughly rubbed the palm of his hand along his jaw as a man with a morning beard would do. His cheeks were smooth, nearly hairless.

"Breakfast?" Alex asked. "We have bacon, ham, or sausage. I'll make eggs, hashbrowns, and English muffins."

143

"You know what I've been craving since I left home, Mom? Some of your famous crepes. Real crispy around the edges like only you can do. Rolled with strawberry jam and covered with powdered sugar. Is that too much trouble?"

"I've missed them too. It's not something I'd make for just me." She tousled his hair. "Half an hour."

After breakfast Todd insisted on doing household repairs. He fixed a toilet in the downstairs bath; it had been running for months. Now it no longer ran, but to flush it, Alex had to hold down the handle. A clicking noise in the kitchen ceiling fan compelled him to tear it apart. When he couldn't get it back together again, Alex assured him that, without doubt, it had been on its last leg.

She kept him out of her bedroom. The carpet still bore the insult of black spray paint and the long gash on the dresser top was still visible after repeated efforts to rub it out. Todd would want to know how those things had happened. It was better that he never did.

Todd took his mother out to dinner. She chose Roma's, an Italian restaurant near the airport.

Sitting at a window table, they watched the traffic on Plumb Street. "I'm going to miss you—again," Alex said.

"Yeah, me too."

"I'd forgotten how handy you were around the house," she teased.

He chuckled. "That's a ploy we men use. Act helpful, screw up a few jobs, and we're home free. Dad taught me that."

"Yes. I remember now," Alex said reflectively. She pushed thoughts of the past away. "Will Tracey be at the airport to see you off?"

Todd shook his head and snapped a breadstick in

half. "We've come to an agreement. We're both smart enough to know that long-distance relationships are the pits. I've been away a little over a month. Last night was sort of a test. It turned out to be a goodbye."

"How do you feel about that?"

He stared off into the distance, his expression somber, pensive. Alex wanted to put her hand over his, but resisted. He slowly brought his gaze back to hers. With a widening grin, he said, "Mom, the women at USC are so radical. I'd be a fool not to avail myself of their charms." Laughing now, he added. "They love me. I'm not sure there's enough of little ol' Todd to go around."

She squeezed his hand. "I think I've lost a son."

"Have no fear. I'll be back for the holidays. Maybe as early as Thanksgiving. By then I should feel the need to recuperate. Y'know, charge my battery."

Justin and Casey had spent the day fishing and hiking. On the way home they stopped for dinner at an Italian restaurant that Casey loved. Between slurping yards of spaghetti, she had beamed and said, "Daddy, I love you. Camping with you is so cool. I wish I could be with you every day." He had replied, "So do I." And meant it.

When they'd pulled into the drive, Dan came out to help them with the camping gear. Casey ran to him, planting a kiss on his cheek, and Justin felt a painful surge of jealousy. He realized he had transferred his jealousy from Yvonne to Casey. Dan was a good man, Justin admitted reluctantly, and a good stepfather. Would he feel better if his daughter had to live with some creep who resented the fact that she was another man's kid? She was lucky to have someone like Dan. It was Dan who wasn't so lucky, Justin told himself as he thought of Yvonne.

He drove the rented car to a motel in Newport Beach. In the morning, after a much-needed good night's sleep, he would have his interview with Joseph Carlson; then it was back to Reno and his full caseload.

Chapter 9

The man was nothing like what Justin had pictured. For some reason he had assumed Alex's ex-husband would resemble physically someone . . . well, someone like David Sloane. There was no comparison. Joseph Carlson, squatting amidst the iron contraptions of the nautilus equipment, was short and balding, with puffy, oversize features. He seemed charged with such an abundance of nervous energy that Justin expected to hear the crackle of static electricity when the man's fingers touched the metal equipment.

"Hope you don't mind meeting me here," Carlson said, nodding his head to indicate the workout room in the executive offices of Norday Investments. He stepped aboard the treadmill, flipped the switch, and got his feet moving on the conveyor belt. "This is where I conduct any business not related to the firm."

"You do this every day?" Justin asked.

"Without fail." He rubbed his sweaty face with a velour hand towel. "You'll find juice and mineral water in the fridge there. Help yourself."

"I'm fine, thanks." What Justin needed was coffee. Strong, caffeine-laden coffee. He'd spent a sleepless

147

night—his third in a row—at the Beachcomber Motel where the occupants of the adjacent room had kept him awake, first with the cacophony of a party, then a lover's spat, and finally at dawn, the rhythmic thumping against the wall as the lovers made up.

"What's Alex got herself into?"

"I'm not sure. For starters her house was broken into and vandalized. Her cat was killed and she seems to think it was murdered by the same person or persons who broke in."

"On the phone you mentioned something about a stolen gun."

"Guns. A .22 revolver and a pair of antique dueling pistols."

Carlson had slowed his pace as Justin talked; now he picked it up again. "What was it you wanted from me?"

"Some information, Mr. Carlson."

"You've got my undivided attention for—" he consulted his watch, a gold Rolex—"thirty-one minutes. Ask away."

"Can you think of anyone who would want to undertake a vendetta where your wife is concerned?"

Keeping up the same pace, Carlson stared at the far wall as though he hadn't heard. Finally he shook his head.

"How about yourself?"

"I bear Alex no grudge. The divorce was about as ugly as they can get. And I must confess, it was I who made it so, but that was three years ago. I can save you the trouble of checking on my whereabouts the night of the fifth. I have no alibi. I took a couple of days off and went sailing on my boat. Alone. No one saw me take her out." Without missing a step, Carlson leaned over the rail and lifted a plastic bottle. He tipped his head back and shot a stream of water into his mouth. He wiped his face again with the towel. "What makes you think it might be a vendetta?"

"She claims to be getting anonymous phone calls. She's under the impression this person has been, in some way, hurt by something she did."

"That puts me right at the top of the list, doesn't it?" When Justin failed to comment, he went on. "Second on the list would be her father."

"Her father? I thought he was dead."

"He is. But he still seems to control her life. That house she lives in, he built it for her, you know. We were married sixteen years and I couldn't get her to leave it. I would have built anything she wanted . . . anything." He slowed his pace, took a swipe at his face with the towel. "I met Alex at the University of Nevada in her freshman year. We dated and decided to marry. We went to her father, more as a courtesy than anything, for his blessing. He said, and I quote: 'Over my dead body.' And it seems that's the way it turned out. He died a week later."

"He felt you weren't good enough for his daughter?" Justin thought of Casey and wondered how he would react when the time came.

"Not just me. No one was good enough for her. I never saw a man so determined to hold on to someone. And it wasn't because he couldn't take care of himself. It was . . ." Carlson cleared his throat. "Sometimes I think his death wasn't an accident."

"Suicide?"

"Yes."

"How'd he die?"

"A boating mishap. On Lake Pyramid. The body was never found. As you know, Sergeant, that's not unusual in those waters. Lake Pyramid appears, at times, quite reluctant to relinquish its victims. He

149

may have died, but all those years I felt as though he were reaching out from his watery grave and grasping onto her. Our marriage was doomed from the start." He laughed. The sound was dry and without humor. "And just like her father, I found it difficult to let go."

"Why was he so possessive? Do you know?"

"Alex's mother ran off with another man when she and her sister were little. It seemed to devastate him. He came down pretty hard on both girls. Hardly let them out of his sight. I guess the sister couldn't take it. She ran away in her teens. This man was a kook. I mean, a real kook." Carlson's breathing was heavier now. He squirted more water into his mouth. "When Alex and I began to date, she was eighteen. A grown woman. I caught the guy following us more than once."

They were both silent. Carlson glanced at his watch.

"I won't keep you, Mr. Carlson. One more question. Do you know David Sloane?"

"Sloane? Sloane? Oh, yes, Dave. Sure. Used to play racquetball with him years ago." He stared hard at Justin. "What about him?"

"He was at Mrs. Carlson's the night before the break-in. From what she said he—"

Carlson cut in, his voice nearly a growl. "Sonofabitch. She denied it! Denied it like she denied everything. Yet I knew . . . I knew there was something going on between those two back then." He hopped backward off the moving belt. A vein throbbed in his temple. "That bastard. He was making it with my wife and buddying up to me at the same time. Christ, I knew—" Carlson looked up at Justin. "Forgive me. Didn't mean to go off like that. Those old battle wounds tend to flare up now and

150

again." He twisted at the towel, lowered his head. "When I married her, she was something of a plain Jane. I mean, I knew she was beautiful, but she didn't. Then she meets this woman, her best friend now, and this meddling bitch makes her over into the woman Alex is today. She gets gorgeous and suddenly I'm not good enough anymore." He wadded the towel and threw it into the corner. "If there is nothing more, Sergeant Holmes, I'd like to get on with my day."

"No, there's nothing more." Justin rose.

"Sorry I couldn't be more helpful."

To the man's drenched back as he hurried through a door into a shower/locker room, Justin said quietly, "On the contrary, Mr. Carlson, you've been most helpful."

At seven Monday morning Alex awakened to the sound of Hawkins cranking up the power mower just outside her bedroom window. After mowing the lawn, he and the weed-eater in short order took care of the tall grass around the trees and shrubs while a Nevada Bell lineman set Alex up with a new unlisted phone number. While Hawkins was blowing the leaves from the driveway with the noisy contraption strapped to his back, a man from Vanguard Security gave Alex an estimate on an alarm system.

Hawkins's love affair with the ear-splitting equipment continued on into the afternoon. Then, suddenly, it became blessedly quiet.

Moments later the doorbell chimed.

Alex opened the door to Hawkins. He stood on the mat, wet leaves sticking to his boots, a large, stiff red leaf sitting upright on his flannel shirt. The leaf, looking like a bird perched on his shoulder, curled toward his ear as though about to share a secret with him. Alex noticed his eyes were more bloodshot than usual.

"Sorry to bother you, ma'am, but I'm runnin' late—what with the leaves and all. I got another job to go to from yer place, and I was s'pose to be there now. I was wondering if I could use your phone? Y'know, tell 'em I'm gonna be late."

She hesitated.

"Won't be but a minute, and you can get on back to what you were doing."

Reluctantly she opened the door. "There's a phone in the study. Right down those stairs and through that first door."

He nodded, then tramped down the stairs, leaving a mushy trail of sodden leaves on the carpeted steps.

Minutes later he was tramping back up, grinding the wet dirty leaves deeper onto the carpet. Alex's hand rested on the knob, ready to close the door as soon as he passed through. He stopped at the top of the stairway.

"Mighty nice of you to let me use the phone." He leaned against the wall. "You sure got a great place here. I bet the rest of it's somethin', huh?"

He was rummier than she thought if he expected her to give him a tour through the house. "You'd better get going, you're late as it is."

"Ain't in no hurry now. 'Sides, it was just ol' lady Clifford. She's a widda. I got lots of widdas and divorced gals I do work for. Lots of em are alone . . . and lonely, too."

Alex opened the door wider.

He ambled slowly to it, placed a grubby hand on the frame. "You had a real busy morning here, what with all the vans coming and going." When she made no comment he grunted, removed the hand from the door frame, and stepped out on the porch.

She had the door nearly closed when he turned and, putting out a hand to halt the door, stared silently at her.

She stared back. "What?"

"That ol' gal that lives up the hill," he said finally. "The one with the bike. She popped over last week when you wasn't home."

"Klump?"

"She wanted to know about some building plans." Alex shook her head, confused.

"Y'know, that art studio you're gonna do. She said she got this notice from the planning committee."

"What did you tell her?"

"That you was gonna build it on top the garage. She got real hot about that. Hope I didn't go an' cause no trouble for ya?"

Alex sighed. "No, it's okay," she said absently as she closed the door. She turned and leaned against it. Damn it. That was all she needed right now. To be involved in a heated building dispute with a fanatic like Thelma Klump.

She heard Hawkins's footsteps going down the porch steps. A moment later she heard footsteps across the porch again, then a light tapping. What the hell did he want now, she wondered? Impatiently she pulled open the door.

Instead of Hawkins it was Justin Holmes.

"Hello," Alex said, feeling a strange tugging in her stomach at the sight of him.

He stared at her in a peculiar unnerving way. "Was that Otis Hawkins I saw just leaving your house?"

"Yes."

"Do you usually invite your hired help in?" he asked, moving slowly through the door.

153

"He asked to use the phone to make a business call. I couldn't very well say no."

"You have a hard time with the word *no?*"

She stared at him curiously.

"Well, do you? Have a hard time saying no?"

She struggled to control her voice. "No. No, I don't. What's your problem, Sergeant?"

"Problem? No problem. Let's just say it would've spoiled my day if I had arrived here to discover that you'd been raped, beaten—maybe murdered—by a man who only wanted to use your phone to make a business call." He shrugged his shoulders nonchalantly. "No problem."

"Hawkins has been working here for months."

"Has he? What do you know about him?"

She opened her mouth to speak, then closed it. "Yes?"

"Nothing. I don't know anything about him. What do you know about him?"

He turned and closed the door.

"Well, damn it, tell me," she said.

"He's not involved in the break-in—at least I don't think he is."

"Stop playing games with me. Tell me," she said, her voice rising.

He took her arm and guided her to the stairs. "Do you think we could go upstairs and sit down, before I curl up in your entry hall?" He walked behind her up the stairs. "You're looking at a man who hasn't slept ten hours total in the past three nights."

In the living room, she said. "Sit down. I'll get you some coffee."

"Thank you." With a sigh, he sank down on the couch.

She poured what was left in the pot into a mug, prepared a fresh pot, then carried the mug into the

154

living room.

"You'll have to start with this," she said, handing him the mug. She crossed to the rocker. "It's strong enough to drive you to your knees or, at the very least, grow hair on your chest."

"Can never have too much, I suppose." He ran a hand over his chest. "Would you mind sitting over here? I'm too tired to shout across the room."

She moved to the couch.

"Everything go okay the last couple nights?" he asked, massaging the back of his neck.

"Yes."

He looked down into the steamy mug. "Good."

"The security people were out today. The alarm will be installed at the end of the month. The phone people were out as well."

He nodded.

"Sergeant . . . Justin, what were you doing on the deck that night?"

"De Solo called me. Said you sounded pretty uptight about some caller. Your line was busy, so I drove over. All the lights were out, but your car was in the driveway. I was coming up the front steps when I heard this ungodly clanking noise coming from the back. So I came around. The rest you know."

"How long were you there . . . on the deck?"

"A minute or two before you unlocked the door for the cat."

"Someone else was on the deck."

"I didn't see anyone."

"Long before you arrived, I heard footsteps and someone trying to open the slider."

"Alex, you were pretty much out of it that night. The mind, under stress, can imagine the weirdest things."

155

She expelled her breath, rose to her feet and began to pace the room. "Justin . . . what's happening? What does he want from me?"

"I don't know." Their eyes met. "I just don't know."

She walked to the windows and stood looking out. "He keeps a vigil on my house. I think he's been watching me for a long time."

"Oh?"

"I've had this feeling—I can't explain it. He knows about you, and yet he doesn't seem concerned. In fact, I sensed he was intrigued by the challenge. I think he knew you were here the night he called and asked for 'Suzanne.' Suzanne is my middle name, and he knows it."

"Can you think of anyone who would want to make your life miserable?"

"No, not anyone who would do the things he's doing."

"Did the voice sound familiar?"

Alex was about to say yes. Decided against it. She was sure the detective had some doubts about her mental state. If she told him that the voice, though muffled and possibly disguised, sounded like a voice from the past—nineteen years in the past to be exact—he was certain to think she was crazy. Dead fathers don't talk to their daughters on the phone.

"No. But then the voice was merely a whisper." She came back to the couch and sat. "Hawkins. You were going to tell me about Hawkins."

"Right. Hawkins. Well, here it is. He was convicted and served time for murder. Sixteen years ago, in a drunken stupor, he strangled to death a prostitute."

Alex was silent. Somehow the news was no surprise to her. Not that Hawkins fit a conventional image of a murderer; there was no such stereotype

156

as far as she knew. It was something else, something that had made her reluctant to let him in her house, or even to talk to him in the yard—a gut feeling, so to speak.

"He was convicted on a charge of second-degree murder because—before he had killed her—she had bashed in his head in order to roll him.

"The man served his time. And as far as anyone knows, he's been clean the two years since his release. I'm only telling you because I feel you have a vested interest."

Alex nodded. She was a woman living alone in a remote area. With all her other problems she didn't need an ex-con, with booze in the shed and keys to her garage, hanging around, looking for reasons to come inside. He was coming back on Friday; she'd tell him then that she had no more work.

For the first time since he had come in the door, Alex noticed how exhausted Justin looked. A fine dark stubble covered his face. His eyes were as bloodshot as Hawkins's had been.

"Why haven't you slept in three days?"

"What do you intend to do about Hawkins now that you know?"

"I asked you a question."

"I ask the questions, not you. Will you let him go?"

"I'll tell you what I intend to do about Hawkins *if* you tell me what I want to know."

"Madam, don't force me to handcuff you to the bannister and twist your arm."

"Sergeant, don't force me to report you to the commissioner for police brutality."

They both smiled.

His face became serious. "Let's talk. About important things. But first, did you make out that list I

157

asked for?"

"Yes. It's downstairs. I'll get it."

Alex rose, went down to her bedroom, found the list, then returned upstairs.

"Some are students. The art center will have their addresses and phone numbers. Will you be contacting these men?"

Justin's head rested against the back of the couch. There was no response.

"Justin?"

She quietly moved around before him. Justin's eyes, under the lids, darted from side to side. He was dreaming, the vividly colorful, revealing dreams of the first stage of sleep.

Alex backed up to the rocker and sat. She studied his face as he slept. He has a good face, she thought. Handsome in its simplicity. The stunning blue eyes, now hidden, gave his face its intensity, making it exceptional. In repose, he looked peaceful, angelic, younger than his thirty-eight or thirty-nine years.

She was attracted to him; there was no doubt about it. Although the events of the night he had spent with her on the couch had been fuzzy at the time, she'd obviously been moved by his show of compassion. Compassion? What does that prove? she asked herself. Greg Ott is compassionate and, forever, just a good friend.

The telephone rang. She picked it up quickly, cutting off the first ring. A woman, identifying herself as the assistant operator, asked if she had reached the residence of A. S. Carlson. Warily Alex answered, "Yes." Lieutenant Kreps of the Reno Police Department was on the line, would she accept the call. Again she said, "Yes."

"Mrs. Carlson, Lieutenant Kreps. If Detective

Holmes is still there, I'd like to speak with him, please?"

"Yes, of course."

She went to Justin's side and shook his shoulder gently. "Justin?"

"Ummm?" With his eyes still closed, he snaked an arm around her waist, pulled her down across his lap. His stubbled jaw rubbed coarsely against her face. His lips moved across her cheek to her mouth. He kissed her. She pulled her head back.

"Justin, there's a phone call for you. A Lieutenant Kreps."

His eyes flew open. The pressure of his arms slackened. She stood up awkwardly.

"Kreps? Where?" He looked around, confused.

"On the phone."

Fingers buried in his hair, he rubbed his eyes with the palms of his hands. "I fell asleep."

She handed him the phone from the end table. She felt his gaze on her as she picked up his coffee cup and crossed the room to the breakfast counter.

"Holmes speaking. Yes, Lieutenant." After a long pause, "On my way."

He stood up, stretched, and looked at his watch. "I have to leave. Sorry to have fallen asleep on you." Tearing a sheet of paper from his notebook, he handed it to her along with a pen. "Phone number."

She wrote down the number and handed it back with the list. He stuffed the papers in his coat pocket as they walked to the front door.

"You'd better get some rest," she said. "You look terrible."

"I'm flattered that you noticed." He lifted her hand, placed her house key on her palm, then went out the door.

As Alex locked up, she stared reflectively at the

159

grimy fingerprints on the door frame—a residue of Hawkins's presence. But it wasn't Hawkins she was thinking about. It was Justin. Justin asleep, pulling her down on his lap and kissing her. Justin obviously aroused—she'd felt his erection against her hip—by a dream figure. The look of confusion in his eyes when he had awakened to find her in his arms made her wonder just *who* it was he'd thought he'd been holding?

Chapter 10

Otis Hawkins lived within sniffing distance of the Lockwood dump. When Justin pulled the moss green Ford Fairlane onto the vacant lot and up the rutted drive, Hawkins gave him a cursory glance before turning back to what he was doing—taping a sheet of clear plastic over the window of his ancient aluminum travel trailer. Justin pulled up alongside Hawkins's pickup truck.

As he got out of the car, he saw the cloud of dust his tires had stirred up envelop the stocky old man. Hawkins ignored it as he ripped off a piece of electrical tape from the roll with his teeth, and slapped it over one corner of the plastic.

"You here 'bout the Carlson woman?" Hawkins asked without turning around.

"That's right."

"Yer wastin' yer time then. I got nothing to say."

"Well, since I've come all the way out, how about I ask a few questions for the hell of it?"

Hawkins shrugged his shoulders.

"You know about the break-in, correct?"

"Yeah. Miss Carlson told me 'bout it. She wanted to know had I seen anyone snooping around."

"Had you?"

"Just that old biddy up the hill from her."

"Klump?"

"That's the one." He cleared his throat and then spat on the ground. "Like I tol' Miss Carlson yesterday, she was asking about the new building."

"What new building?"

"Miss Carlson's new paint room. The one she's gonna build on top the garage. The old lady was foaming at the mouth about it."

"Why should she care?"

"Says its gonna *ob*-struct her view." Hawkins walked to the pickup, hiking up his pants as he went. He pulled out a smaller piece of plastic, brought it back to the trailer, and held it up to the next window, checking its size. "Maybe it will an' maybe it won't. But one thing's for sure, the ol' buzzard's a real pisser and moaner. One day last week the two of 'em were beefin' out by the driveway. I heard the old lady say somethin' 'bout a gun."

"What sort of gun?"

"Didn't hear what sort. Just heard *gun*."

Justin made a note on his pad.

"What's your opinion of Mrs. Carlson?" Justin asked. He had stepped forward, taken hold of the plastic, and held it while Hawkins ripped off a piece of tape and stuck it on.

"She pays good, and she lets me do my work without buttin' in."

"What's your personal opinion of her?"

"Hot stuff. Real hot stuff. But shit, I don't hafta tell you that."

"Does she have a boyfriend? Someone steady?"

Hawkins shrugged. "Woman like that mostly plays the field. Say, ya got a cigarette?"

With a reflexive motion, Justin reached up. He patted his empty shirt pocket. "Sorry, I quit."

Justin decided there was nothing more to gain by questioning Hawkins.

As he drove back to town he pondered the information about Alex and her neighbor. They had squared off lately. The hassle over the construction was of little or no concern to him. But the gun was another matter.

His next stop was the Rivercliff Complex—duplex office suites that were priced to sell at a mere half million. He pulled into a parking slot with a sign that read: Reserved for clients of Gregory D. Ott, attorney. Parked in the adjacent slot was a late model, white Mercedes, the big one, the one that cost as much as a middle-class townhouse. The personalized plate read *GOTT ESQ.*

Inside the spacious, contemporary reception room a pretty secretary in her late twenties was saying goodbye to an elderly couple. She looked from them to Justin, the wide smile intact.

"Hi. May I help you?"

Justin identified himself and showed his shield. "I don't have an appointment, but I'd appreciate it if Mr. Ott could squeeze me in for a few minutes."

The secretary lifted the receiver, buzzed, then spoke. "Greg, there's a Detective Holmes out here. He doesn't have an appointment. Can you talk to him?" She looked up at Justin and asked, "What does it pertain to?"

"Alexandra Carlson," Justin said.

"He said Alexan—Okay." She hung up. "Go right in." She pointed to a pair of sliding oak doors with stained glass inlays.

Justin crossed the room. The carpet, thick and cushy under his feet, was bone white. He pulled open the door and stepped in.

This room was twice the size of the reception area. Aside from the standard ceiling-to-floor bookshelves with their impressive leather and gilt law tomes, the entire north side of the room was windowed in French panes. A transom, with more stained-glass inlays, ran the length of the window. The desk, though massive as desks go, seemed dwarfed by the surroundings. The desk was unoccupied.

"Well, I'm glad to see you've decided to take this thing with Alex seriously and do some investigating," Greg said. He was standing to Justin's right, sprinkling food into the oceanic-sized aquarium. "You *are* conducting an investigation, are you not, Detective Holmes?"

"I am."

"I mean, you *are* here to investigate a crime and not to conduct a character check of . . ."—he turned to Justin, the canister of fish food still poised over the tank—"the *victim.*"

"A little of both, perhaps," Justin said, undaunted by Ott's cynicism.

"A little of both," Ott repeated sarcastically, nodding his head. He pulled a cigarette from a pack in his shirt pocket and lit it. "Well, ask your questions. I'll decide whether they have relevance and if they're leading in the proper direction."

"How long have you known Mrs. Carlson?"

"Objection. Not relevant."

"Would Mrs. Carlson have reason to fabricate a crime?"

"Contempt! You're in contempt—"

"Come on, damn it," Justin said, feeling his composure crumbling. "Knock off the theatrics, Ott. You know as well as I do that everyone is suspect. I have a job to do. My caseload is straining at the seams. If I'm chasing a phantom, I want to know about it."

"I feel for you, Holmes."

"Yeah, I know." Justin walked to the window and looked down. He watched the Truckee River, low at

164

this time of year, coursing its way through town on its final leg to Lake Pyramid. "It's common knowledge you have no use for cops. The feeling is mutual. I'm not wholly convinced Alex Carlson is telling the truth. But I'll tell you this, Ott, if she is, then she could be in danger. Grave danger."

There was a long pause. Justin felt the attorney was weighing his words, deciding if he should cooperate, and if so, how much.

"Like you said, Holmes, you have a job to do. Do it. I'm not telling you shit about Alex. Her credibility, her character, is none of your fucking business. If anything happens to her because you were dicking around, looking behind the wrong bushes, you'll have me down on you so hard you'll wish you had gone into another line of work."

Justin crossed the room to the door. He stopped, turned around to Ott and said, "Thanks for the help."

"Anytime." Ott went back to feeding the fish.

Justin sat in the car until his breathing evened and his hands were no longer tight fists. It's a good bet the lawyer is in love with Alex Carlson, he thought. Ott had had that pathetic, tormented look when he'd spoken of her.

He scanned the list of men she had given him. Alongside the name Ott, Alex had written "friend." Justin ran a line through it. The next name on the list was David Sloane. She had written nothing alongside his name. Justin ran a line through that as well, but added a question mark.

Other names had been lined out earlier. The housekeeper of Edward Scoggin had informed Justin her employer was presently on his honeymoon in Australia.

That morning Justin had called Sergei Borodin, the owner of and mechanic at the service station Alex used on a regular basis. Despite the man's thirty-odd years in the U.S., he had managed to hang onto his charming, yet unintelligible Russian accent. Alex had said nothing about the person on the phone having an accent.

Two other names had been scratched off the list. Robert Meacham, the husband of her best friend Margie, had told him Alex was a saint. Justin hadn't bothered to call Dr. Fields, Alex's gynecologist.

Four names remained. They were bracketed: students.

Justin drove to the Silver State Art Center.

After introducing himself to Velda Lancaster, he inquired about Alex's classes. He was told she instructed three workshops a week. Fifteen students at ten dollars a head per class. She also held a space in the gallery.

"Many men take her classes?"

"No. Mostly women," the curator said. "Men sign up, take a few classes, then drop out. I think they feel uncomfortable around so many females. But Mr. Bodkin, that sweet old dear, loves being the rooster among all the hens. The widow ladies fuss over him something awful."

"This Bodkin, he's an elderly man?"

"Eighty-one and still going strong."

Justin made a mental note to scratch Bodkin off the list. "Do you keep a list of her students — past and present?"

"Why, yes. The names go on the Center's mailing list. We send out flyers of upcoming workshops."

"May I see the list?"

"The entire list?"

"Just Mrs. Carlson's students, please."

She pulled a folder from the filing cabinet, handed it to him.

Justin opened the file and began flipping through the paper. "There must be two hundred names here," he said.

"She's been teaching for three years. Summer workshops in addition to her regular classes. Would you like a photocopy of the list?"

"Please."

As the copier spat out sheets of paper, Velda pursed her lips, lowered her head to peer over the rim of her bifocals. "Sergeant Holmes, your interest in Alex, is it . . . I mean, has something happened to her?"

"You'll have to ask her that."

"Oh. Yes, of course." She handed the copies to Justin.

"Did you happen to notice anyone hanging around the center? Maybe asking about Mrs. Carlson?"

"Can't say that I have."

"Thank you. You've been very helpful." Justin crossed the room.

"Oh, Sergeant? I don't know if this is important or not. There was a young man—took one class of hers, dropped out like the others—but I recall one evening as Alex was going home, I saw her and this young man together in the parking lot. He seemed to be blocking her way. You know, trying to keep her from getting into her car."

"When did this happen?"

"Not more than a week ago."

"What was his name?"

Velda Lancaster pressed her lips together, shook her head slowly. "He signed up for the class sometime in September. His name would be on that list. Handsome fellow. Although much too young for

167

Alex Carlson."

Instead of going straight out the front exit, Justin found himself detouring into the gallery. The huge room was divided by partitions. He moved slowly from one group of paintings to another until he found her work. He stood back and stared, clearly impressed.

What he had seen on the floor in her work area the night of the break-in had been only sketches. Displayed before him now were true works of art. Bursts of light exploding against shadows, luminosity, lacy shapes with various contrasts strongly defined. Each canvas or paper conveyed a personal statement of the artist. The paintings, though unmistakable in subject matter, appeared to have been established by mood — an array of moods.

A small watercolor commanded his attention. It was a night landscape. Midnight blue and black. The heavens, so vast that all distance was lost, glimmered with stars. Justin stepped closer, read *Depth,* by A. S. Carlson. It was not for sale.

He checked the prices of the other paintings and realized that if she sold only one or two a month, she'd have no trouble keeping the creditors from her doorstep. He took another long look at *Depth,* then left the gallery.

As he drove back to the station, Justin mulled over the information he had gathered so far.

Of the five men on the list who had been willing to talk to him, including last week's interview with David Sloane, each had offered a different profile of her. From a gifted saint to a vindictive bitch. There was nothing cut and dried about Alexandra S. Carlson.

Damn it! He was letting this woman get under his skin. Against his better judgment he had already made moves on her twice. The night she had gone

168

to pieces, he had not intended to kiss her. It had just happened. With a beautiful, sexy woman curled up in his arms, her breast partially exposed through the opening of her kimono, he'd found himself thinking with his little head instead of his big head. And last night was an enigma to him. Exhausted, he had fallen asleep on her couch, and damned if he hadn't dreamed about her. She was in his arms, in his bed, naked. With rising passion, about to enter her, he had suddenly woken up. She was in his arms. Not naked. Not in his bed. But on her couch. He wished he knew under what circumstances she had come to be there.

He wanted no part of her. He was footloose and fancy free. The last thing he needed was a teasing, spiteful woman complicating his life. She could be trouble—in more ways than one.

Back at the station, Justin circled the male students on the list the curator had given him. He concerned himself with only the men who had signed up in the past year. There were five names. Four of those matched up with Alex's list. He crossed off Bodkin. He called the remaining three and made appointments for the next two hours.

Gary Epson was gay—and proud of it. He lived with his mother and two sisters in a dilapidated old house on Second Street. He told Justin he had signed up for Alex Carlson's class hoping to meet someone who shared his artistic interests. Maybe, with any luck at all, he'd felt a meaningful relationship would ensue. "But," Epson said with a delicate snort, "the place was full of jabbering biddies and this one ol' fart." He had dropped out.

The next student was a Vietnam veteran named Lester Calvado. In a shabby hotel room overlooking

169

the railroad station, Calvado, left leg gone above the knee, had sat tall and straight in his wheelchair despite the irreparable damage to his spinal cord. Calvado had told Justin he'd signed up for the art class as a form of therapy. Mrs. Carlson had been a talented and extremely patient instructor, but his deteriorating health and frequent stays in the hospital had forced him to drop out.

The third and last student, Scott Withers, was a cocky, golden-haired Adonis in his late twenties. He lay sprawled on the couch of his sparsely furnished apartment. He reminded Justin of the cloned, bronze surfers who flocked to the beaches of Southern California.

Withers, displaying a mouthful of perfect white teeth, offered Justin a beer. When Justin declined, Withers shrugged, sauntered to the refrigerator, and got out a Coors Light. He returned to the couch and flopped down.

"So," Withers said, pulling off the tab with an exaggerated motion, "you wanted to talk about Alex?"

"What can you tell me about her?"

"Hey, man, do I look like the kind of guy who kisses and tells?"

You look like a blue-ribbon asshole, Justin wanted to say. "I'm not interested in the notches on your bedpost. I'm investigating a crime committed against Mrs. Carlson."

The bright blue eyes narrowed. "She give you my name?"

"I got it from the Art Center."

"Oh." He looked both relieved and disappointed. "So why you investigating her art students? Someone paint her a dirty picture?"

Justin ignored the smirk. "Someone broke into her house and stole some valuable property."

"Hey, man, it wasn't me. Look, I took a class from her. That's it."

"You didn't try to see her outside of the Art Center?"

"Whadda I look like, a fucking retard? Sure I did. You've seen her, right?" Justin nodded. "She's a sexy chick. Mature. You know what I mean? I go for older women. They can always teach a sly dog a new trick or two."

"Are you an artist?"

"Naw. I work in the pizza joint across the street. She'd come in a couple times a week after class. We got to talking. You know how it is? I wanted to see more of her—literally."

"So you turned on the charm. Tried to score," Justin said evenly. "Was that how it was?"

"Yeah, only I wasted my hard-earned bread trying to make it with that chick. Besides the ten bucks for that one lousy class, she has me buy paint, canvas, brushes. Then she treats me like the rest of those dumb bohemians. Turns me down flat like I'm some snot-nosed kid. Wouldn't even have a drink with me after class."

"That must have pissed you off, huh? I bet a guy like you doesn't get turned down often."

"Not so's you'd notice." Withers brought the can to his mouth, halted without sipping, then lowered the can. He eyed Justin shrewdly. "I wasn't *that* pissed, man. Not enough to break into her house and steal. I called her a couple times, then said to hell with it. I got better things to do than chase after some cold-ass broad."

"These calls, did you talk to Suzanne?"

"You mean Alex?"

"Yes, Alex."

"No, man. I whistled 'The Star-Spangled Banner.' What the hell do you think? 'Course I talked to her.

171

That's what phones are for."

"When was the last time you spoke to her?"

"I don't know. Shit, until you called this afternoon, I'd forgotten she existed."

"When did you see her last?" Justin pressed, leaning forward.

"Aw, fuck it," he spat out. "Last week. Okay? Ya happy?"

"Forgot she existed, huh? You've got a short memory, Mr. Withers. Now tell me about it."

"After her class one night I stopped to say hi. No big deal."

Justin waited.

"She wouldn't talk to me. That's it, man. End of story."

"You going to be around town for a while?"

Withers sighed. "I'll be around. Don't you cops have anything better to do than hassle people?"

"Scotty ol' dog, we live for that shit."

On his way back to the station, Justin told himself that Scott Withers was one to watch. It might be wise to keep an eye on David Sloane as well.

Chapter 11

He worked the glove off his right hand with his teeth, then pulled the butane lighter from his pants pocket. He flicked it. The flame shot up with a loud hiss. He lowered the flame. Holding the photo in his gloved hand, he positioned the lighter under the backside, and, carefully moving the flame in small circles, watched as the glossy skin of the picture blistered and darkened. Several minutes later he returned the lighter to his pocket and laid the photograph on the work table. After replacing the glove, he reached for the pen at his elbow. He wrote rapidly, the felt tip squeaking across the photograph.

The phone rang for the second time since he had been in the house. He moved toward it. Between the first and second ring, he heard her key in the lock.

Pausing, he looked from the phone to the front door. Then he stepped back into the dim recesses of Alex Carlson's painting alcove.

Alex shifted the grocery bag to her left hip and opened the door. The telephone rang again as she entered. She hurried downstairs to the study and snatched up the receiver in the middle of a ring.

"Hello?"

"You okay, babe?" Greg Ott asked, concern in his voice. "What took you so long?"

"I just stepped in the door." She put the bag on the desk and, shrugging off her coat, lifted a bottle from the bag. "I bought champagne. Domestic, but good."

"What's the occasion?"

"I sold a painting. A very expensive painting. The check came this morning. I owe it to myself to get ripsnorting drunk. Wanna join me?"

"Oh, God," he moaned. "How you torture me. I called to tell you I'm leaving for the airport in two minutes to catch the six-fifteen to Denver. Come with me. I'll buy you dozens of bottles of champagne. Dom Pérignon. We'll frolic in a bathtub filled with it. I'll drink it from your bedroom slipper — from your navel."

Alex smiled. "No, Greg, I don't think so."

"Well then, promise me you won't get drunk till I can be there to take advantage of you."

"No promises. How long will you be gone?"

"Two nights."

"Want me to feed the fish?"

"Would you?"

"Sure."

"I'll leave a key in the barbeque."

She heard a soft click on the line. "Greg, are you there?"

"Always — for you."

"Did you hear someone come on the line?"

"No."

Goosebumps rose along her arms.

"Damn," he said, "gotta go, babe. Dinner out when I get back. Get glitzed up."

Alex said goodbye and hung up. Standing at the desk, the bottle of champagne clasped tightly to her chest, she shivered. The click on the line, she told

174

herself, had been Greg's secretary—nothing more.

She carried the groceries up to the kitchen.

Opening the freezer door, she took out a Swanson Salisbury steak and, looking at it with indifference, decided that even cardboard tasted palatable with a glass of champagne.

She put away the groceries and slid the aluminum tray into the oven. After setting the timer, she went downstairs to sketch until it was time to leave for class.

The bedroom was dark. Alex crossed it quickly before the dark could cover her in its claustrophobic veil. She switched on the swing-arm lamp over the center of the work table and adjusted the light.

Her eyes, she decided, must be playing tricks on her. Forcing herself to stay calm, she stared disconcertedly at the photograph that had disappeared from the desk in the study.

She leaned in closer, hands crossed over her mouth, unable to bring herself to touch it.

The color photograph, which showed her standing on the deck of Joe's sailboat, hands on hips and legs parted, had been grossly altered. Her entire body was now a gray-brown. From her face to her feet the glossy paper was raised, rippled. Its texture reminded her of a roasted hot dog left too long over a blazing campfire. Her face had been totally obliterated.

At the bottom of the picture, printed with a felt-tip pen, were the words, "The monsters want you, Allie."

He'd been here again. Alex's heart banged in her chest. Was he still in the house?

She ran across the room, dropped to her knees on the raised platform, and groped under the bed for the shotgun. She cried out when a burning, fierce pain spread over her palm. Jerked her hand away and fell back. Her palm, though burning, showed no sign of a wound.

Panting, Alex threw back the bedspread and, from a distance, looked into the dark space.

The shotgun was gone. But in its place was the thing that had made her hand feel as though it had been plunged in acid. Alex knew then what had stung her. A nettle. Each stinging hair on the plant was like a hypodermic needle filled with an acid irritant. Years ago she had stepped barefoot on one. The pain had lasted for days.

She scrambled to her feet, a strangled cry erupting from her lips. Panic made her clumsy, her hands useless. She groped and fumbled with the heavy drapes in an effort to get at the door latch of the slider. The drape slid across her back, enveloping her in a black void. She hit at the glass with a fist while she worked the latch.

Suddenly the door flew aside on its track. Alex stumbled, off balance, across the concrete slab. Her foot caught the edge of a brick planter, throwing her down on all fours. She cried out again as her hand slammed down hard on something cold and steely. Instinctively grabbing at the object beneath her hand, she lifted it, holding it up, staring at it in confusion and terror. The moon's rays glinted off the metallic blades of a pair of large hedge clippers gaping open like the jaws of an alligator.

The night air smelled of jasmine, sweet and clean. A cricket chirped twice, then became silent. A siren wailed in the distance.

At that moment, on her knees, hugging the clippers to her breast, she could have sworn she heard laughter.

She looked to the top of the bluff. The ragged outline of the ridge stood out sharply against the evening sky. Her eyes moved slowly along it until they came to something upright along the flat plateau. It stood unmoving. Then it was gone. Had it been a figment of her imagination? Or had it been him? A bone-chilling tremor convulsed her.

Where would she be safe? In the garden where unseen eyes laughed at her—mocked her? Or in the house where a madman could still be hiding, waiting to . . . ?

In there? Out here? Where *was* he? Wherever he was, she knew, beyond a doubt, he was watching her.

She rose to her feet, using one hand to push away from the concrete, the other, the hand that felt like it was on fire, held the clippers in a death grip. Swaying slightly she walked across the hard slab toward the house.

Without entering, she used the tip of the shears to move the drapes aside. She peered into the bedroom. The room was dim except for the glare of the swing-arm lamp that spotlighted the photograph.

Her gaze followed the long shadows that crossed the floor of the studio to her bed. The quilt was twisted and rumpled. The pillow had been pulled out from beneath the bedspread and lay propped up against the headboard. In the downy contours of the pillow—in the deep indentation made by someone's head—was the telephone receiver. She bit down on her lower lip. He had blatantly lain on her bed using her telephone—not to talk, but to listen.

Alex felt the anger starting to burn. Why was he doing this to her? What had she done to deserve this? He was trying to drive her crazy. It wouldn't take much, she thought, just a couple more shoves and she'd be over the edge.

She stepped inside, lifted the receiver off the pillow, picked up the base of the phone from the night stand and backed up to the door again. By putting her back against the metal door frame and straddling the opening, she had a clear view inside and out.

Alex tucked the clippers under her arm and dialed the police. She asked for Detective Holmes. A moment later he answered.

"Holmes here."

"It's me . . . Alex. Can you come over?" Her voice, surprisingly, sounded normal.

"Has something happened?"

"Will you come?"

"I'm in the middle of an interroga—"

"He was here again—inside the house."

"Did you see him?" He was whispering, but the urgency was unmistakably there.

"I don't know." She stared at a crusty patch of dirt on the white spread. "I don't know anything anymore. Can . . . *you come?*" Her voice broke.

"I'll be right there. I'll send a squad car, too. Stay calm."

As if in a trance she walked to the work table and opened the drawer beneath the picture. With the eraser end of a pencil, she slid the picture inside then closed the drawer. She returned to her post astride the door. The orange handles of the clippers pressed sharply into her stomach. The open blades pointed menacingly toward the bluff.

The police arrived with sirens screaming eight minutes later. In those eight minutes, which seemed like eight hours, she stood in the doorway, eyes darting right, left, and straight ahead to the hands on the clock.

A sharp pain shot across her shoulders as she left the brace of the doorframe to let the police in. It occurred to her as she was halfway across the room that she still held the bulky clippers. Suddenly feeling foolish, Alex paused, bent down, and slid the clippers under the bed.

At the front door were two uniformed officers.

"I'm Officer Capucci and this is Officer Olinski." The one speaking was female, approximately five feet four inches tall and very buxom. She was pretty in a pixieish sort of way.

"I thought Jus—uh, Detective Holmes would be with you."

"He'll be along," Capucci said in a husky voice. Large expressive eyes, the long lashes thickly coated with mascara, stared coolly into Alex's.

"Ma'am, what's that buzzing?" Officer Olinski, a man of medium build and height with thinning blond hair and a reddish mustache, asked.

"What? Oh, it's the stove timer. Excuse me, I'll shut it off."

"I'll go with you," Capucci said.

Upstairs in the kitchen, Alex removed the TV dinner from the oven with trembling hands. Capucci eyed the foil-wrapped tray with a look of disdain.

Then she and Olinski checked through the house. The three of them met in the bedroom five minutes later.

"No sign of anyone, Mrs. Carlson. Was this door locked?" Olinski asked, opening the slider.

"Yes . . . no . . . I'm not sure," she said weakly. "It was locked when I left today. I don't know if he managed to open it."

"You unlocked it?"

"I went out . . . I can't remember if it was locked or . . ." Her words trailed off.

"Do you know what he was doing in your house?"

Alex sighed deeply, looking from one officer to the other. "Using my phone."

"Using your phone?" Capucci asked.

"Actually he just listened . . . listened in on a conversation between a friend and myself."

Capucci gave Olinski a dubious glance as if to ask, Is this chick for real?

"There's dirt on the spread. I'll have a look out back for footprints," Olinski said quickly, heading for the slider.

Capucci wandered around the bedroom, one hand resting lightly on her gun, the other hand behind her back. She circled the room slowly, bending or stretching, looking at everything. Alex felt her scrutiny was more personal than official.

"Is this the way you found the bedding when you came home?"

Alex was about to answer when Olinski reentered, flashlight in hand. "Can't see much now. There is dirt on the back step, and with the dirt on the bedspread, I'd say he came in through this door."

Alex, standing in the middle of the bedroom, tried to control her trembling, her chattering teeth. She was in a giant blender, being pureed. Where is Justin? she wondered.

The phone rang.

Alex made no move to answer it.

"Shall I get that?" Capucci asked.

Alex nodded.

Capucci answered. She turned to Alex. "It's your husband."

Alex took the receiver.

"Joe? Where are you?"

"I just got in, Alex," Joe said. "Is something wrong?"

"No everything's fine," she lied.

"Did Todd tell you I'd be coming for the tax papers?"

"I have them out, Joe. But it's really not a good

time—"

"Don't worry, I won't barge in on you tonight. I'm bushed. How about in the morning?"

"Yes, that's fine." Alex felt a blessed relief. On a normal day Joe could be a drain on her nerves. His presence tonight would surely deplete her.

"Are you certain you're all right? You sound . . . strange."

"I'm just tired."

Joe paused before saying, "Alex, I've been debating whether or not to tell you about this. I've decided you should know. A Sergeant Holmes called on me—"

"Yes, I know. He's investigating a crime. I gave him your name several days ago. He needed to know about the gun. I'll tell you about it tomorrow."

"He came to see me yesterday. The only thing he wanted from me was my opinion."

"Your opinion?"

"Of your mental state of mind."

It took her a moment to digest that. "I see. And what did you tell him? Did you tell him about the nightmares? My fear of the dark? My father?" Her voice was flat, unemotional. She heard him sigh. "It doesn't matter. I'll see you in the morning, Joe."

Minutes later, upstairs in the living room, Olinski was about to take Alex's statement when the doorbell rang.

Alex started to rise but Capucci put out her hand and said, "Just relax, ma'am. I'll get it."

Her large breasts bounced as she walked. And with each step a rounded cheek undulated provocatively beneath her dark blue pants.

The sound of the door opening and Capucci's muffled voice carried to the upper level. Alex could hear Justin's voice, but his words were indistinct.

Alex clenched her hands into tight fists, her fingernails cut sharply into the palms. The two of them are certainly taking their time down there, she thought, while I sit here taut as a bear trap, set and ready to spring. But then why should Justin hurry? The crazy lady was at it again. No doubt he'd humor her. Play along. See how far she'd go this time.

Shivering, teeth still chattering, Alex slowly turned her hands over. One palm had been gouged by the clippers; a small flap of skin, encrusted with dirt and blood, lay gaping open. The other palm, now visibly swollen from the nettle rash, had been scraped by the rough patio concrete; it was dotted with pricked skin and tiny specks of dried blood. She felt like crying.

Capucci brushed against Justin as they walked up the steps side by side.

"Mrs. Carlson," Justin said, "I came as soon as I could."

So it was *Mrs. Carlson* again. "Good evening, Sergeant. Thanks for taking the time to come out," she responded coolly, unshed tears stinging the backs of her eyelids.

"What happened?"

Before she could reply, Capucci cleared her throat and said, "It seems someone came in through the slider in the bedroom and listened in on that extension while Mrs. Carlson was on another extension." She'd made it sound trivial—like a snot-nosed kid had eavesdropped on his big sister's phone conversation. "Nothing appears to be missing or otherwise disturbed."

A wave of queasiness spread through Alex's stomach. Her scraped hands shook uncontrollably. Her head ached from the fear and tension. Her back ached from the strain of standing stiffly against the slider, waiting for help to arrive—waiting for Justin.

182

She ached all over. Ached because she felt so alone. And because she was terrified. And because Justin still didn't believe her. And because her life was going to hell and she had no idea how to stop it.

"I can handle it from here," Justin said. "I'm sure Mrs. Carlson will fill me in."

Don't be so sure, Detective Holmes.

"Olinski, take a cruise through those hills above," Justin said. "Look for anything out of the ordinary."

"There're a couple houses up there, you want us to check with the residents — see if they noticed anyone prowling around?" Olinski asked.

"Yeah," Justin said, tossing his jacket on the couch.

After the two officers let themselves out, Justin took a chair opposite hers.

"Alex, did you hear him while he was in the house?"

"Oh, it's Alex again, is it?"

"So that's why you're treating me like a goddamn process server, because I didn't address you by your first name?"

She glared at him.

"Look, I'm sorry. Now will you *please* tell me what went on here?"

"Nothing went on here. I made it all up. I haven't called the police in three or four days and I missed the excitement."

Justin stared at her. Finally he said, "Why are you doing this?"

"*You* know," she said, cocking her head to one side. "I'm crazy. We both know that. Right?"

"If you didn't see him," Justin said, as if she hadn't spoken, "did you hear him while he was in the house?"

She turned her head away again and stared out

the window.

He snapped the notebook shut and rose to his feet.

"Where are you going?" she asked.

"Anywhere but here. It's pretty damned obvious you don't want to talk to me."

Oh God, Alex cried inwardly. How she needed someone. Someone to care about what happened to her. Someone to tell her everything would be all right. From the moment she'd lifted the phone to call for help she'd known that someone was Justin. She wanted him to believe her. To help her. But he wanted to be anywhere but here with her.

She held her breath as he grabbed his jacket and strode to the stairs. He stopped, turned sharply. "Screw this!" he said, throwing down his jacket. "You're going to talk to me because I'm not leaving until you do."

She turned her back on him.

He crossed the room, pulled her to her feet, spun her around to face him, and, giving her a hard shake, said, "What happened here!"

Startled, Alex gasped.

"What happened?" he asked, more calmly.

With her chin held high, she said quietly, "My ex called a few minutes ago. He thought I should know that the detective assigned to my case was slightly concerned about my sanity. If you . . . if you think I'm going to subject myself to your silent ridicule, Detective Holmes, then you're the one who's insane."

"Oh Jesus." Justin dropped his arms and began to pace the room. "I should have told you about that. Alex, that was before . . ."

"Before what? Are you saying that now you believe me?"

"I want to believe you."

"But you don't."
He stood there, looking miserable, helpless.
Alex sighed, crossed the room. "Come with me."

Chapter 12

Justin stared into the drawer of the work table.

Alex hung up the telephone—she had called Velda to cancel her class. She turned, watched Justin reach up, take a manila envelope off the shelf and, lifting the photo by the edges, slide it into the envelope. From a carton in the corner he took out a two-foot wood stretcher bar and dropped it into the track of the sliding door. "Do the same upstairs," he instructed Alex.

She picked up a ruler, crossed to the bed and worked the nettle out.

He turned. "What's that?"

"A present."

He went to her. "It's a nettle. Did you touch it?"

She held out her hand, palm side up.

Justin took her hand, turned it over slowly. "Put it under cold water," he said quietly. "Might take the sting away."

Alex went into the bathroom, ran water on her hand, then, blotting it dry on a towel, walked back into the bedroom to see Justin at the head of her bed. He was removing the pillowcase, carefully turning it inside out as he wriggled it off.

"Why didn't you show the picture to Capucci and Olinski?" he asked.

"I don't know."

"Why did you show it to *me?*"

"I don't know that either. My first instinct was to shred it into tiny pieces and put a match to it." She turned to the dresser. "Do me a favor? When you're through with it, burn it."

"Alex, you should have left everything the way you found it. It's important that you don't tamper with evidence."

"I wasn't thinking." When he stared at her skeptically, she added, "Do you think I'd sabotage my own case? I'm having enough trouble trying to make you believe I'm telling the truth."

"I believe you."

"You do?"

"I don't think you'd knowingly handle a toxic plant. I found hairs on the pillowcase that are not yours."

She ran her hand along the smooth polished oak of the dresser top, then looked up into the mirror. The face showed a hardness that was not flattering. An image of the pretty, curly-haired Capucci sprang into her mind. Capucci's face was young and unlined. Her eyes, when she had looked at Justin, seemed to glow with such bright eagerness.

"What's her first name?"

"Whose?"

"Capucci."

"Beverly." He moved behind her. His eyes met hers in the mirror. "Why?"

"I want another gun."

Justin shook his head dubiously.

"Damn it, Justin, he has a gun—my gun. And now the Meachams' shotgun."

"What? Why the hell didn't you tell me he'd taken another gun?"

"I'm telling you now."

"Why are you making it so damn difficult for me?"

"Do you think it's easy for me? I'm alone, unprotected. I need another gun."

"Oh, Jesus, no. Alex, you couldn't hang onto the guns you've had. What is it now—four? You want to give him an arsenal?"

"He won't get another one from me. It's legal to carry a gun in Nevada without a permit. And by God, if I have to carry one—"

"It's legal if it's not concealed. Oh shit, I can see it now." He barked out a laugh. "You packing a gun on your hip."

"I'm losing my sanity and I'm scared to death, and you laugh." She whipped around suddenly, hair flying across her face as she confronted him. "Well, go on—laugh!"

His hand lightly touched hers. She pulled away. "Don't," he whispered firmly, reaching out again and taking her hand. He lifted her tightly clenched fist and opened it. He studied the palm critically. She winced in pain as his thumb lightly stroked the gouged skin. He put his lips to the cut, then raised his head to look into her face.

She stared at his mouth, her gaze following the soft curves of his lips, and she thought how sensuous they were. Don't let this happen, an inner voice whispered as he slowly lowered his face to hers. She watched his mouth come nearer and nearer—as though her eyes had the force of a magnetic field, pulling him in. Her mind and body suddenly felt at odds with each other. Don't let anything get started. She closed her eyes. His lips touched hers . . . so lightly, so feathery she wondered if they were really there at all.

Suddenly she longed to crush her lips to his. She

wanted desperately to crawl out of this nightmare and lose herself to him. Just for a little while. A little while. What could it hurt?

His arms moved around her waist to her back. Sliding her arms around his neck, she slowly raised up on her toes, inching upward against him.

His mouth, though the pressure was somewhat firmer now, moved with such deliberate self-restraint that she sensed they were caught in slow-motion frames, with each frame better than the last. When her mouth instinctively sought a closer contact, he drew back slightly. His lips played and teased, pressing and withdrawing. Lingering, not parting. When the tip of his tongue moved over her lips, teasing the corners of her mouth, her breathing quickened. Her pulse accelerated.

One moment his kiss was playful and delicate, the next it was deep and passionate; his tongue caressing, his mouth sucking, his teeth nibbling. He was in complete control, initiating all the moves. Each time she tried unconsciously to take control, he drew back, causing her to moan inwardly and pause until his lips again took over.

Her fingers wove almost frantically into his hair. His hands, gently working their way under her sweater, were cool in contrast to her burning skin. She pressed forward to meet him as one of his hands glided down until it rested on the small of her back. Pulling her to him, he moved his body against hers. She felt his erection press maddeningly on her pubis. His other hand caressed a breast under the bra, the thumb stroking back and forth across the nipple.

Hesitantly, he pulled his mouth away. She felt a great void, a lack of warmth in her burning, swollen lips. Her eyelids fluttered open to see vibrant

189

eyes gazing into hers. His bright blue irises now seemed darker, nearly black, the pupils fully dilated.

With an urgency that had not been there before, his mouth came down on hers again. Never in her life had she wanted anything so much. No, I don't want this to happen, she thought, struggling for control. Yes you do. Oh, yes you do. He'll help you forget. For the moment he'll help you forget all the bad things.

Her hand moved across his chest, touching the smooth leather of his gun harness, down his flat stomach to rest on his full erection. Slowly she stroked up and down the length of him, tingling at the thought of him inside her.

He moaned, squeezed her tighter to him. And then the doorbell rang.

Alex stiffened. Pulled her mouth from his.

"Sonofabitch," Justin said, letting his forehead drop to her shoulder.

Her hands fell to her sides. He lifted her sweater and bra, put his mouth over a nipple and sucked lightly. Then he stepped back holding her at arm's length.

"It's no secret you're unlucky," he said, his voice husky, "but I never dreamed it'd rub off on me." He touched her lips.

Alex was moving away, heading for the door when he pulled her back and, stepping behind her, lifted her sweater and hooked her bra. He leaned down to kiss her when the doorbell chimed again.

Pulling back, suddenly ill at ease, she moved around him and left the room.

"Joe?" Alex said when she saw her ex-husband. "You said tomorrow."

"I didn't like the way you sounded on the phone. I know you well enough to know when something's wrong." He stepped inside and embraced her.

"Joe, I'm fine. Really," she said. But he seemed not to have heard. He stared past her, surprise, confusion, and that certain look registering on his face.

Alex turned to look at Justin standing on the bottom step of the stairway. He was leaning against the wall, arms folded across his chest, the pillowcase and envelope in his hand. How handsome he is, she thought. Maybe too handsome. It occurred to her that Joe's interruption may have been more timely than she realized. A few minutes more and she would have given herself to a man—a stranger practically—because she was overwrought and vulnerable. Well Joe was here now. She wouldn't be alone after all.

"You've met Sergeant Holmes," she said, pulling her mind back to the present.

Glancing at Alex, Justin mouthed the word *touché* as he stepped down and extended his hand. "Good to see you again, Mr. Carlson."

"Has there been more trouble?" Joe directed the question to Justin as he gave his hand a brief shake. Justin looked at Alex.

"No," Alex said quickly. "We were just going over some things."

The three of them stood in awkward silence.

"I'll be leaving now, Mrs. Carlson." Justin nodded his head at Joe. "Mr. Carlson."

Before Joe could respond, Justin had crossed the foyer, opened the door, and was gone.

"See you," Joe said to the closed door. "Nice-looking guy. He must be working overtime on your case," he said, his tone heavy with cynicism. "Police

191

work can be exciting. Did you happen to notice he had a hard-on?"

"Don't start, Joe. We're not married anymore."

"How true."

"You intended all along to come over tonight. God, I can't believe you. If you're not going to be civil, then I don't want you here."

They stared at each other.

Joe looked away first. His laugh was dry. "I can be extremely insufferable, can't I?" He reached out and smoothed a stray hair from her face. "I don't know how you put up with me all those years. I'm sorry. Alex, I'm sorry."

She looked at him, checking to see if he was sincere. The muscles in his face had relaxed. He smiled.

She returned his smile. "Come on upstairs. I could use a drink; how about you?"

"Sounds like a winner."

"I have champagne. Would you like to help me drink it?"

"What are you celebrating?"

"Nothing special."

Joe popped the cork. Alex got down the glasses. "Alex, you never age. You're just as beautiful as ever. Single life must agree with you."

His double-edged compliment made her conscious of her appearance. She'd caught a glimpse of herself in the foyer mirror. Her hair mussed from Justin's hand. Her mouth—still tingling—devoid of lipstick. On the front of her sweater, where her breasts peaked, were clusters of fuzzballs.

Ah, there was nothing like lust to put a glow in the cheek. A sparkle in the eye.

"How's Todd taking his breakup with Tracey?" she asked, though she knew the answer.

"I think it was over the first day he walked on campus and got an eyeful of all those gorgeous, independent women."

"Well, I'm glad . . . I think. So is he taking time from his ardent pursuits to keep up with his studies?"

"Oh, he's going to do just fine. It was tough at first. All those awesome chicks sort of clouded his brain for a couple of weeks. But when I reminded him that he had plenty of time to satisfy each and every love-starved coed, he finally got down to business. If he'd taken after me in the looks department instead of his mother, he wouldn't have this problem."

She ignored Joe's self-critical put-down and said, "As long as he remembers his major is government and not girls."

"Don't worry about him; his head may turn a little too readily, but it's on straight."

"Where are you staying?"

"At the Nugget."

"Would you mind spending the night here . . . in Todd's room? I'd rather not be alone tonight."

She expected another of his sarcastic remarks, but all he did was nod with a certain measure of understanding.

Alex held out her hand. "Here, give me your jacket, I'll hang it up downstairs."

With Joe's suit jacket over her arm, she stopped at the couch, picked up the one Justin had left behind, and carried both down to the foyer. As she stood at the closet, about to hang up Justin's down jacket, she was overcome by his scent. She found herself hugging the soft feathery jacket to her chest as she pressed her face to the cool lining. That woodsy soap and Justin's own distinctive scent filled

193

her nose and lungs, making her light-headed. With her eyes closed, she breathed deeply and relived that first contact of their lips and the kisses that followed. *Stop it! You were a fool to let it go that far. What would have come of it? Pain. Anguish. That's what.*

"Alex, where'd you go?" Joe called from the living room.

"I'll be right up," she responded after a guilty start.

Justin sat in the overstuffed rocker across from Thelma Klump. She was courteous and gracious, as before, but this time he sensed an impatience, a nervousness. A spasmodic tic below her left eye had begun moments after she'd let him in the house. Klump rubbed at her eye.

"Why, Sergeant, I would have called you immediately if I'd noticed anything out of the ordinary. We women must stick together. There's so much crime these days. Drugs. It's the drugs. Why, one can't pick up a newspaper without—"

"You saw no one enter or leave Alex Carlson's house just before dusk today?"

"I saw Mrs. Carlson go out around two. I didn't see her return. I don't stay outdoors once the sun goes down." She pressed a twisted, gnarled finger to the tic. "That poor woman. So much trouble in such a short time."

The kettle began to whistle.

"Ah, the water is ready. I'll just get our tea." She stood, smoothing down the skirt of her pink dress.

Justin watched Klump disappear into the kitchen. He shifted in the chair, lifted the lacy doily from behind his head, and, without taking his eyes off the door Klump had gone through, quickly folded the square cloth and stuffed it into the front pocket of his pants. Justin thought he heard a door close softly somewhere in another part of the house, the metallic click of a latch bolt. In the kitchen he heard porcelain clinking together. Then the sound of glass breaking. A string of hushed curses followed.

Several minutes later Klump entered the room carrying the silver tea service. Around the neckline of her dress she had attached some sort of frilly collar with brightly colored glass gems. Her cheeks glowed with a florid rouge.

Justin stood, took the tray from her hands. "You live alone, don't you, Miss Klump?"

"Yes. And it can be scary at times. With that man coming and going so freely into Mrs. Carlson's home I don't mind telling you that every little noise gives me the willies. My word, you're not going to stand there holding the tray, are you, Sergeant? Put it down on the table."

"Maybe the intruder is not a man." Justin put down the tray.

"Not a man? You believe a woman would—? Well, I wouldn't know about these things. So many unstable people nowadays. It's the drugs." She lifted the cup and saucer. The two porcelain pieces tinkled in her shaking hand. "Oh dear, would you look at that. My hands are practically useless now. Arthritis. And the pain. Well, I'm not one to bore people with my aches and pains. One sugar, wasn't it sergeant?"

"None, thank you." He took the cup and saucer from her trembling hand. "You say you saw Mrs. Carlson leave her house around two. Were you in the yard?"

"I was."

195

"Did you go anywhere today?"

"No. I never left my property." She stared past Justin's head at the back of the chair. Her eyes narrowed slightly. "I thought you were going to pay me a visit yesterday. I saw you at the O'Briens' house."

"It was closed up tight, just like you said. It's obvious, with the sheets covering the furniture, that they're on an extended vacation. If someone were looking for a place to hide out, the O'Brien house would be ideal."

"Yes, it would, wouldn't it? I'll keep my eyes open. Call you if I see anything."

"I'd appreciate it." Justin put down his cup and saucer, and stood. "Thank you for talking with me again."

"Oh, it's my pleasure. I welcome the company . . . now and then."

After he left the house, Justin walked to the edge of the bluff and looked down on the house where Alex was entertaining her ex-husband. Would he spend the night? In which bed?

Who gives a rat's ass?

He turned, started to walk toward his car when he saw Klump standing at her living-room window. She smiled and waved. The smile looked strained. The tic danced madly beneath her eye.

Klump was lying.

Thelma Klump waited until Holmes had driven off before leaving the window. Things are getting out of hand now, she thought.

She made her way to the back of the house, then down the steps to the cellar. She crossed the large storage area to a narrow door. She knocked. From within she heard shuffling noises.

"Open up," she said.

A moment later the door partially opened. The man looked at her but said nothing.

"He heard you," she said. "He asked if I lived alone. He knows I live alone." She waited for him to respond. He silently stared at her. "I took you in because you understood my problem. You said you could scare her off, make her sell the house. That's fine. That's what I want. What I don't want is my privacy invaded as well as my rights as a property owner. You said he wouldn't concern himself with a woman living alone. Well, he has. And the bitch is still there."

"Patience."

"He stole the doily from my chair. Pocketed it as slick as you please. What if he finds your hair on it?"

"He won't find a thing."

Klump turned away, then turned back. "I don't want her hurt."

"No."

"You'll just scare her?"

"Yes."

She nodded curtly. As she walked away, she told herself at the first opportunity she would have a look at the diary he kept hidden on the inside of that box radio. She had already been through his meager possessions the first week he'd moved in and had found nothing. But positive that he had something to hide, she had sneaked into his room that afternoon while he was down the hill at the Carlson place. For nearly thirty minutes she had searched, finding nothing. Sitting on the bed, perplexed, her gaze had come to rest on the radio atop the bureau. He had brought the radio with him. It dawned on her then that she had never heard it playing. That scratchy old record could be heard most of the night. But never had she heard the radio. Excited, she had pulled off the radio's cardboard back. Inside the gutless cavity she found a neat bundle of papers and a diary.

Yes indeed, she told herself as she climbed the basement stairs, first chance I get I'll read that diary.

198

Chapter 13

Alex fixed breakfast for Joe and saw him off before ten A.M. At noon she was waiting on the porch when the tan station wagon pulled up to the house. Margie opened the door.

"Don't get out," Alex said. "You know how crowded the Steak House can get after twelve."

"I thought you might want to wait for that old gal coming up your driveway," Margie answered casually, climbing out and slamming the door. "And then again, you might not."

"What old gal?"

"The one who looked like a giant canary on a bike."

Alex suddenly felt uneasy. "Oh, shit."

"Who is she?"

"The infamous Thelma Klump."

"Ahhh, the one with the pellet gun."

"Did you happen to see a black cat lashed to her handlebars?"

Margie shook her head. "I'm sure I'd've noticed."

Klump came into view. Upon seeing Alex on the porch, she leaped from the rolling bike. It continued on for several yards before it fell to the ground with a clank, tires and pedals spinning. The tall woman in the snug yellow sweat togs and orange sneakers marched to the porch and halted within two feet of Alex, cheeks puffing with each panting breath.

Alex looked down into the mottled red face. Her position above Klump gave her a false sense of confidence.

"Hand it over, that . . . that murdering sonofabitch! Hand it over to me now and I won't call the cops."

"Are you referring to my cat?"

"You're damn right. Hand it over!"

"Be serious," Alex said, thinking she might have misjudged Klump. The woman wasn't just a multicolored pain in the butt, she was as dingy as a Bronx taxi. Alex glanced over at Margie, who was staring at Klump wide-eyed, her mouth hanging open.

"An eye for an eye, Mrs. Carlson." Thelma Klump shoved a gnarled hand into the pocket of her sweatshirt and hauled out something small and brown. A dead sparrow. Thrusting it toward Alex, she violently shook it. The tiny head, beak open, eyes opaque and staring, whipped about limply. "This is what your precious cat did. I warned you, Mrs. Carlson." Her eyes under nearly lashless lids, were maniacal.

"Look, I'm sorry—"

"It's too late for your puny '*I'm sorry,*'" Klump mimicked Alex in a whiney tone. "What's done can't be undone. I want that animal!"

"There's no way in hell I'll let you get your hands on my cat. If it's justice you want, then go on, call the cops."

"Call the cops? '*Call the cops,*' she says! I'm not blind, Mrs. Hot Stuff. I've seen the police cars come and go from this house. You do filthy things

200

with those so-called lawmakers—admit it!" Drops of spittle flew onto the back of Alex's hand. She quickly wiped them away on her pants.

"You're crazy."

"Oh? That detective, sergeant Something-or-other, he comes knocking at my door moments after leaving your bed. Don't think I didn't see the lipstick on his shirt collar. The same shade you have on at this moment. Whore!"

"Get off my property," Alex said quietly.

Klump stepped back a half-dozen paces. "You don't belong here. You've no respect for the rights of others. Why don't you just move? Sell the house and get out before you get hurt." Then, drawing back her arm, she flung the dead bird. It hit Alex on the right shoulder with a light feathery thump then dropped to the bottom step, its head hanging grotesquely over the edge of the bricks. "Get off this hill before you get what you deserve!"

"What are you talking about?" Alex stepped forward.

Klump laughed as she picked up her bike, climbed on, and pedaled out of sight.

After several silent moments, Margie said, "Holy shit. I never thought I'd be at a loss for words."

"She knows something."

"Imagine getting so pissed over a dead bird that she'd want to retaliate by snuffing Blackie. And to insinuate that you're shacking up with the Reno PD—incredible."

Alex stared blankly after Klump. "And you said I was persnickety."

At Harrah's, Alex turned her car over to an

attendant at valet parking before she and Margie made their way across the plush skyway above Center Street, then headed down again. The Steak House was located below street level in the hotel/casino. Every twenty feet or so Margie stopped to drop a coin into a slot machine. Pulling Margie's sleeve, Alex steered her down the stairs to the restaurant.

The maître d' stepped forward. "Alex, a pleasure to have you join us today."

"Hello, Bernard. Will there be much of a wait?"

"Never for you. I'll just put you in Mr. Ott's booth. Will he be joining you today?"

"No, he's out of town till Thursday."

Bernard led the way through the dim restaurant, to a booth in the back. They slid in. Then Bernard unfolded the heavy magenta napkins and, with two fingers, draped the linen across the lap of each woman.

"Stefan's working the executive banquet room today, but I'm sure he can take care of you ladies as well."

"Oh, don't go to any trouble for . . ." Alex suddenly realized that Bernard had already disappeared around the partition.

"God, I love to go to lunch with you," Margie said. "I feel like a duchess."

"That's Greg's influence. I'd just be a plain ol' commoner without him."

Stefan warmly greeted Alex and Margie, recommended the swordfish, took their order, and left. He returned minutes later with a basket of Lavasch and a bottle of chilled Riesling. After pouring wine into each glass, he planted the bottle in the standing ice bucket, said "Enjoy," and moved off again.

The food came. Margie talked of trivial things, asked Alex about innocuous matters. They ate, then, just as they were finishing, Margie dropped the bombshell.

"You're sleeping with Sherlock Holmes, and I seem to be the last to know. Now why is that?"

Alex looked around to make sure no one else in the room had heard. In a low voice she said, "I'm not sleeping with him."

" 'Lipstick on his collar.' 'The very same shade adorning your lips at this moment.' Did she make that up?"

"No."

Margie waited.

Alex nervously broke the Lavasch into little pieces. "It was an *almost.* But it didn't happen, and it's not going to happen."

"Why?" Margie said in an imploring tone. "Good lord, he didn't try to — he didn't get rough or anything?"

Alex shook her head. "It would have been easier if he had. I can handle that kind."

"Alex, go for it. Give yourself a treat. Don't make such a big friggin' deal out of it."

"Easy for you to say. You've got Bob and the kids."

"If I didn't have Bob, if I were in your position, that man would have been in my bed by now. So what's your excuse?"

"Ease up, okay? I don't need a man. I can take care of myself."

"Why would you want to? What are you afraid of?"

Alex chewed on her lower lip and looked around the room. "I can't handle it. Being a . . . a . . ."

"A what?"

"Being a one-night stand to some guy. Is that so difficult to understand?"

"So when was the last time that happened?"

"Ed Scoggins."

"Ed? Wait a minute. You dumped him. He called, but you refused to see him or even talk to him."

"I had my reasons. Then there was Mitch, the airline pilot."

"Alex, he was crazy about you."

"He was based in Chicago. With him, it would have been a series of one-night stands." Alex sipped her wine. "And there's Greg. We both know how long he'd stick around if I stopped running and fell into bed with him."

"Maybe. Maybe not." Margie speared a piece of broccoli. She brought it up to her face as though inspecting it. "You're afraid of him. That's it, isn't it?"

"Afraid of who?"

"Holmes. Scoggins. The pilot. Men you think you're falling for."

"Don't be ridiculous."

"Why? Why are you afraid?"

Forensic lab technician, Oliver Bernsway, had to tear his gaze away from the microscope to answer Justin's question. He sipped coffee from a mug labeled Lab Rat.

"You know as well as I do, Sergeant Holmes," he said in a monotone, "that a few stray hairs provide little or no proof of a person's identity. When used with other evidence the examination of hair, at best, may implicate or eliminate an individual."

"Cut the crap, Ollie," Justin said, smiling. "Just do the best you can. Okay?"

Bernsway returned the smile. "You got it. But," he said, holding up a hand, "I can't get to it for a couple days. A week would be more realistic."

"No problem. I'll be back in the morning."

"Good. You'll have it then."

They both laughed.

"Stick around a minute. Have a cup of coffee."

"I wouldn't drink anything that came from this lab." Justin looked around the cramped, cluttered room with its laboratory equipment — stainless steel trays, esoteric bottles holding God only knew what. A *Playboy* calendar was tacked on the wall over Bernsway's work table. Justin read the year, 1977. "You could use a new girly calendar, Ollie."

"That's the only one Sarah will let me have. She's seen the current ones."

Justin leaned in, put his eye to the microscope and looked at the dish of lifeless tadpoles.

"Sperm?"

"Yeah. Wish mine looked like that. Sarah's pregnant again."

"What's that now, five?"

"Six."

"Ever hear of the term *vasectomy?*"

"Had one. Those little suckers of mine are like Asiatic roaches — indestructible."

"Have it done again."

"Nah. The way I look at it, if those ol' boys can go under the knife and survive to swim back upstream, who am I to play God."

Justin squeezed Bernsway's shoulder. "Get rid of the calendar."

Thelma Klump and her remark, "I hope you get what you deserve," had been heavy on Alex's mind the remainder of the afternoon. Did Klump know something? Had she seen someone? Or was she just a fanatic, spouting off?

When Alex wasn't thinking about Klump, Justin kept stealing into her thoughts; his teasing lips, his warm hands. She realized she did not know if he was committed to someone, or for that matter, married. But what did it matter? He was the detective working on her case. That was all he was. All he'd be.

At dusk the phone rang.

"You've been bad, Allie," the voice whispered. "Slutting around like her. Just like her."

Alex slammed down the receiver. She closed her eyes and made an effort to control her breathing. Somehow he had gotten the unlisted number. She wasn't surprised. But what he had said rocked her badly.

How did he know so much about her? Was he guessing? Or was he seeing everything she did firsthand?

The house was locked up tight. There was no way he could get in to spy on her. Unless . . . unless he knew of a secret passage. Saying those words almost made her laugh. Her house wasn't a seventeenth century manor with tunnels and trap doors. It was a modern trilevel without basement or attic. There was a crawlspace under the house, accessible from the attached garage only. The cathedral ceilings and floor-to-ceiling windows that had made her father's designs so popular left no room for an attic or overhead crawlspace.

Her father had designed the house . . . for her. Would he have dared to . . . ?

She took the large flashlight from under the sink and, going downstairs to the garage, lifted the square plywood plank from the floor at the back. Clinging to the plywood, suspended in an erratic web, was a huge, black widow spider hovering protectively over her egg. Alex shuddered, but left it alone. She knelt, waved the beam of the flashlight down into the hole. The dirt-packed space, littered with boards and scrap linoleum, was situated directly under her bedroom, and was exactly the same size. She slowly moved the light around the solid walls. To get a good look she would have to climb down inside and search for a door leading up into her bedroom. That was the only room connected to the crawlspace. The sight of the black widow discouraged her. Without disturbing the spider, she replaced the plank.

She went into her bedroom. Four years ago she had replaced the wall-to-wall carpet, and there had been no trap doors in the floor. Inside the closet, she tapped on walls, looked for anything out of the ordinary. Nothing. The bathroom was all marble and tile; she ignored it. In her painting alcove, she tapped the walls and tile floor. Underneath and to one side of her work table were drawers. On the other side was a large cabinet, nearly empty because it was deep and difficult to reach all the way in. Alex removed the half-dozen rolled canvases and shone the light in the empty space. With the flashlight, she went inside and crawled to the back. The smell of mildew and linseed oil was strong. She tapped the end of the flashlight against the wall.

The light blinked out. It wasn't completely dark in the cabinet, but it was dark enough to make her heart skip several beats. She began to back out, shaking the flashlight.

The unexpected ringing of the phone startled her. She jumped, bumping her head on the low ceiling. Her heart raced. She backed out quickly, instantly thankful for the bright lights.

She grabbed at the receiver.

. . . *sun-shine. My only sun-shine* . . .

"Who are you?" Alex asked wearily.

"You know who I am. You just won't accept it."

"*Who are you!*"

"Allie, why did you forsake me?"

Her body stiffened. A moan escaped from her lips.

"They're out there, Allie. Waiting. You know where they are."

"No."

"Can you hear them scratching . . . looking for a way in? Can you—"

"They're not there!" she shouted. "There's nothing out there! You can't make me believe!"

"They want you, Allie. Monsters eat little children and bad girls. Bad girls . . ." She hung up.

Allie. Her father was the only one to call her Allie. The warnings were his. Had he come back from the dead to haunt her? No! Dead people stay dead. But what if he hadn't died that day nineteen years ago? Then where had he been for almost two decades? And why would he come back now?

Alex went upstairs to the kitchen. She poured a glass of wine, drained it, then refilled the glass with trembling hands. Whoever he was, he was playing with her . . . for now. Teasing and taunting, as

Blackie had done with the field mouse before putting it out of its misery.

Oh God, please make him stop.

The phone began to ring again.

Alex grabbed her purse and hurried down the stairs. Without bothering to take a coat, she flung open the door and ran straight into the arms of a man.

She gasped; then, seeing that it was Justin Holmes, she threw her arms around him and held on tight.

Justin held Alex close. He buried his face in her hair, breathing the fresh, sweet scent of her. His fingers gently worked the muscles at the small of her back. He heard the phone ringing inside the house, but chose to ignore it.

With her face against the hollow of his shoulder, she said, "It's him."

He pulled back to stare at her. "You talked to him?"

Alex nodded. She moved away from him, stepped into the house. Justin followed. The ringing stopped.

As Alex climbed the stairs ahead of him, he found himself staring at the neat curves of her hips and buttocks under the polished cotton slacks. He resisted the urge to reach out and touch her. Now is not the time, he reasoned.

He followed her into the kitchen. She attempted to mix him a drink. The Scotch spilled on the counter. He moved her aside and took over.

"Did you put the number on the phone?"

"With everything else on my mind I was afraid

I'd forget it. I didn't think anyone . . ." Her words faded.

"So what'd he say?" He handed her a glass of wine. The wine sloshed over the rim. "Easy, Alex."

She nodded, sipped her wine.

He guided her to the couch. "Tell me what he said."

He listened to Alex's account of the odd conversation.

"Did anything he say make sense to you?" he asked.

"Yes, but it wouldn't make sense to anyone else."

"Why is that?"

"It was something I was raised with. Warnings by my father."

"Things only you and your father would know?"

"And Lora. My sister."

"Your father is dead, right?"

She nodded.

"What about your sister?"

"I don't know what happened to her. I haven't seen her since we were kids."

"Do you think the pistols have some significance here?"

Alex rested her head on the back of the couch. Justin wanted to stroke the long graceful curve of her throat.

She rolled her head back and forth.

He leaned forward, put his hands together, made a steeple with his fingers. "The voice, does it sound like your father's?"

"Yes," she whispered.

"You're certain?"

"No, not a hundred percent. I haven't heard his voice in so long. But there's something—inflections

210

that are similar."

They sat in silence. Justin sipped his drink and watched Alex absently pick specks of cork from her wine.

He rose, walked to the fireplace. After building a fire, he returned to the couch. "Scott Withers."

Alex looked up. "A student of mine. His name was on the list."

"He called you a few times. Any similarity in the voices?"

"No." Alex laughed lightly. "Scott was looking for a mother. A mother with incest in her heart. He has the patience and attention span of a two-year-old. I can't see him being vindictive. I only bruised his ego a little."

"That may be enough. Revenge, hate, jealousy, that has to be this guy's motive. It's obviously not personal gain. Your ex, would he know about these warnings of your father?"

Alex swallowed. "Yes. It's not Joe. He wouldn't wait three years to take revenge."

"Maybe he waited until your son was out of the picture."

Alex stared off into space for several moments. Then she shook her head sharply. "I can't accept that. Justin, Klump said something today . . . something very odd. She said I should sell my house and move before I got hurt."

Justin rubbed at his chin. "She knows something, that's damn certain."

"Do you suspect *her?*"

"I'd like to get into her house. I just don't have enough to request a search warrant." He put his glass on the table and stood. "Come with me. I have something for you. It's in my pickup."

Alex watched from the open front door as he reached down into the truck's bed and lifted out two metallic poles. He returned to the house.

"Charley-bars. For the sliding glass doors. I'm sure that's how he got in last time. C'mere," he said, leading her down the hallway to her bedroom. "I'll show you."

Crouching in front of the slider, he removed the stretcher bar, inserted the metal bar, and demonstrated how it worked. He handed her the bar. "Now you try it."

"It looks easy enough," she said.

"Go on, do it."

She stared at him and, seeing his sober expression, took the bar and crouched down.

Her long hair fell across the side of her face. Her back arched delicately and through the thin crepey material of her blouse Justin could see the lacy straps of her bra. An intoxicating scent stole over him. His mind went back to the night before, and he thought of her breasts cupped in his hand; the silkiness, the weight, the nipples responding to his touch. He felt his own body responding to the sight of her both then and now, responding to the idea of making love to her completely.

His fingertips moved lightly down her back to the curve of her buttocks. He leaned over, his lips touched the back of her neck. He felt her stiffen.

"Justin," she began slowly, "about last night . . . I didn't mean—I don't know why I let it go that far. I . . . I'm just not good at casual affairs."

His mouth covered hers. Moving slowly against her unresponsive lips, his tongue teased and probed. Through her parted lips, her tongue came forward to lightly meet his. He felt a purring current like an electrical charge. Then he was kissing her hungrily. His hands roved over her warm body. She clung to him, returning his kiss with a wildness that made his insides twist and pull.

With a moan, she broke the kiss and came to her feet, pushing at him. Before he knew what was happening, Alex was out of the room. He watched her run down the hall, grab her purse from the foyer table, and fling open the door and disappear outside. Moments later he heard a car start up and the sound of tires crunching over dried leaves as it pulled away.

"Alex?" he said aloud.

What the hell just happened here? he asked himself.

Alex headed toward downtown Reno with no firm destination in mind. Where would she go now that she had run away like a sniveling virgin? The Meacham household was her last choice. Margie would only lecture, and Bob would look stricken and helpless. Without luggage, she couldn't go to a motel. She found herself turning onto Brookhurst, heading west. Greg Ott. Of course. Greg was out of town. She had promised to feed his tropical fish. She could stay there.

She circled the Lakeridge Golf Course and turned into the driveway of unit 17, parking alongside Greg's white Mercedes. His condominium backed up to the fourth hole. She left the car and walked across the freshly mowed lawn to the front patio. Lifting the lid of the barbeque, Alex found the sardine can with the key inside.

After letting herself in and locking up, Alex

turned and leaned against the door. Eerie light, coming from the built-in wall aquarium, shimmered green and aqueous over the furniture and fixtures. A soft bubbling sound filled the room. She walked through the apartment that had recently been decorated by High-Stepping Designs. A two-color scheme of tan and ultramarine meandered throughout. The furniture was a combination of sleek and puff.

She felt most comfortable in the kitchen. After switching on the overhead lights, Alex went to the refrigerator and took inventory. Greg was not your typical bachelor, she noted. There were rounds of cheese, various pâtés, and chilled champagne. She closed the refrigerator door and opened the pantry. She found more pâtés, escargots, crackers, smoked octopus and frog legs, and a case of caviar. Wine bottles, stored at the proper angles, occupied the top shelf. There were mixes of all kinds. An abundance of liquor. The larder was stocked for a party.

Alex opened a package of crackers, a jar of white asparagus spears; and cut a wedge from a round of brie. She chose a chilled bottle of chardonnay. After making up a tray, she took it into the living room and, on the floor, with the wavering light from the aquarium, poured wine into a glass. As she slowly ate her dinner and sipped at the wine, she thought about what was happening to her.

Justin was foremost in her mind. She thought of his kiss and of how hard it had been to pull away from him. She wondered if it wouldn't be easier to just give in, as Margie had suggested — keep it simple and purely physical.

Purely physical.

Those were the exact words her father had used

that night twenty-one years ago as they'd stood looking down at the swollen, lacerated face—which bore no resemblance to the beautiful woman she remembered as her mother—on a slab in the morgue. Alex and her father had traveled five hundred miles by car to the Clark County morgue in Las Vegas to view the remains of a murder victim. The Jane Doe, a prostitute, had been beaten and stabbed. The body had been discovered, bound and gagged, in the air shaft of a warehouse at the north end of town. For several days the police had run a description of her in the newspapers in the hopes that someone would identify and claim the body. To the sleepy morgue attendant, William Bently had shaken his head and mumbled, "No. That's not my wife." Yet, only minutes later, as they were driving away, he had turned to Alex and said, "It was her, you know. Your mother." Alex had been speechless. "I lied," he went on, "because I will not claim her body, nor will I bury her. Let her lie in a pauper's grave where she belongs. She was dirt. The only thing that was ever important to her was the physical. Purely physical."

No, Alex had told herself over and over on that long drive home, *that woman was not my mother.*

The sputtering sound of a motorcycle passing the condo brought Alex back to the present. She finished the last of the wine in her glass, picked up the tray and carried it into the kitchen. She moved to the window above the sink. As she lowered the pleated shade she stared blankly at the window of the condo next door. A dark shape flashed across the front of the lighted window, making a brief silhouette. Her heart thumped. She pulled the shade back up and looked out. Nothing. It must have been someone inside that condo, she thought. It only looked as if it was on the outside. Stop imagining things. No one knows where you are. No one.

She lowered the shade again.

She straightened the kitchen, then fed the dozens of tropical fish in the aquarium. After getting a quilt and pillow from the guest bedroom, she stopped before the shelves holding Greg's video library. One entire shelf was devoted to titles such as *Rhonda's Fantasy, Goin' Down in Beverly Hills, Nurses in White Lace.*

That's the last thing I need now, Alex thought grimly, thinking of Justin's lips and hands touching her. She reached up and took down a cloth-bound edition of Ovid's *Metamorphoses*. Safe enough, she thought. Curling up on the couch with the quilt, book, and a snifter of anisette, she began to read.

Before finishing the *Raven's Story,* she fell asleep.

She didn't hear the light scratching.

Justin waited an entire hour before locking up Alex's house and leaving. There was the possibility that she wouldn't return as long as his pickup stood in the driveway. And despite his irritation and confusion, he was concerned for her safety.

He drove the pickup to the bluff where he could observe, through the trees, both her house and Thelma Klump's. He parked.

Another hour passed. Give up, he told himself. What are you doing wasting time on her? What would she want with a cop? David Sloane was right; the woman was shopping. And when a woman like Alex went shopping it was in classy boutiques, not bargain outlets. She liked to play games with men. And she was good at it. Very good indeed.

Reaching into his pocket, he pulled out the list Alex had given him. He ran his finger down the names, noted an address, and put the list away. He started the car and drove down the hill.

Five minutes later he was cruising the narrow street of posh condominiums. In the driveway of unit 17, he saw Alex's silver Nissan parked alongside Ott's Mercedes.

The windows of the condo were dark except for a ghostly greenish-white light coming from the living room. In an upstairs window, Justin spotted the red glow of a cigarette. It moved upward and then grew bright, illuminating the outline of a man as he dragged on it.

Justin had seen enough. He pulled away slowly, resisting the urge to peel rubber.

Alex woke up, feeling disoriented. She looked around, saw she was at Greg's place and it was still night. She wondered what had awakened her? All was quiet except for the soft gurgling sound of the aquarium's pump. By the quartz clock on the mantel the time was eleven. She had fallen asleep reading the Ovid. Her philosophy teacher would have been appalled.

She closed the book and put it on the chrome-and-glass coffee table. She was about to lie back down when she paused, breathing deeply. She smelled smoke—cigarette smoke. Pushing the quilt away, she lowered her feet to the floor and leaned forward.

"Greg?" she called out. "Greg, are you here?"

Rising slowly, she went into the kitchen, flipped on the light, and looked around. Everything was as she had left it. Shutting off the light, she crossed the living room to the stairway.

"Greg?"

She turned on the light for the upper hall, then climbed the stairs. The smell of smoke was definitely stronger on the second floor. "Greg, please answer me."

She pushed open the door to the master bedroom. It was softly lit from outside by a sodium street lamp. Alex could see the bed was empty and unmade. Nothing had changed since her tour earlier in the evening. The cigarette smell that had been so strong only moments ago was lost to her. Now that she was up here, it was difficult to tell where it had come from. She crossed the room to the window. Looking down, she saw the two cars in the driveway below. From behind her came a faint swishing sound. Alex turned quickly. There was nothing there. She heard it again, sounding like crisp taffeta. She took a hesitant step toward the closet, but before she could go any further, the sound of a car stopping out front distracted her. Turning back to the window, she saw a taxi at the curb. Greg stepped out.

What was he doing home? He had told her he'd be back Thursday. Had he come in earlier, while she was asleep, stayed long enough to smoke a cigarette, left, then returned again? Doubtful.

In the hallway now, Alex heard the door of the taxi close. As she hurried downstairs, she heard his key being inserted in the lock. She crossed the living room just as the door opened and Greg stepped in with a young, red-haired woman at his

218

side.

"Alex," he said, looking alarmed. "I thought that was your car. Is something wrong?"

Alex glanced from Greg to the woman, then back to Greg. She put on what she hoped was a cheerful face. "Hi," she said to the redhead, "I'm Alex Carlson, a friend of Greg's." She then turned to Greg. "No, there's nothing wrong. I'd forgotten to feed the fish so I thought . . . well, better late than never. Right? I was just leaving."

She placed Greg's spare key on the table, snatched up her purse, and squeezed around Greg. Without turning he reached backward and grabbed her hand.

"Diane, would you excuse me a minute? I have to talk to Alex. Make yourself comfortable." He pulled Alex outside and onto the patio. "You're not here to feed the fish, are you?"

"Honest, Greg," she said. "I'd forgotten. I was on my way home from Margie's and decided I couldn't bear to be responsible for the death of two dozen expensive, exotic fish."

"Really?"

"Really."

"Well now that you're here — stay."

"And what will we do? Play three-handed rummy?"

"I'll get rid of Diane. It's not often I get you over here. We'll have one of those homey sort of evenings. Maybe turn on the TV and watch a video or two."

Alex laughed. *"Rhonda's Fantasy?"*

He stared into her eyes. His smile was slow and sexy. "If you like."

She kissed his cheek. "I gotta go. Don't forget

dinner tomorrow night." Before he could stop her, she had slipped around him and hurried to her car.

She drove straight home. When she pulled up her driveway and saw Justin's truck was no longer parked at her door, she felt both relief and disappointment. Blackie ran up behind her as she was opening the front door. She picked up her cat, nuzzling him as she carried him inside. "Well, fella, how about sleeping with me tonight? I could sure use the company."

Chapter 14

"Is that a new dress?" Greg asked, leaning over to rub the material between two fingers. He and Alex were seated in a booth at Le Moulin, an elegant French restaurant in the Peppermill Hotel/Casino.

"No, Greg. You've seen it before." The dress, white silk, had a tank bodice, wide matching belt, and a soft flared skirt. A large red scarf, shot through with silver and gold metallic threads, was draped off one of Alex's shoulders and tied at the other.

"It's very chic." Greg poured more wine into her glass. "It makes me horny."

"A bomber jacket on the right person would make you horny."

He smiled and winked. "So you saw Todd last weekend?"

"Umm. It was brief, but better than nothing."

"Miss him, huh?"

"A bunch. You know, I even miss the sound of his shower running a full thirty minutes every morning."

"God, I remember those long showers when I was his age. I could get my rocks off twice in half an hour and be ready to take on the whole fucking world." Greg laughed when he saw her shocked expression. "I love to watch your face when I get

221

earthy with you."

"You do, do you?" She lifted an eyebrow. "I don't know what you mean. I was about to say that that explains why Todd preferred my shower to his. Mine has two pulsating heads."

"Enough. You're driving me crazy with that dirty talk."

The busboy refilled their water glasses.

"Okay," Greg said, "out with it. Something happened while I was in Denver, and I would be very interested to know what it was."

"What makes you think that?"

"You came by to feed the fish, right?" Alex nodded. "And did you hang around to burp them? There were dishes in the dishwasher. Quilt and pillow on the couch. Book on the table — a rather boring book it was. I have the most revered collection of erotica in the state and you choose — Well, no matter, you were snuggling down for the night. Why? I know it wasn't to surprise me, because you didn't expect me until this afternoon. So why?"

"You should have been a detective," Alex said. Then she recounted the events of the past week, filling him in on the phone calls and the last break-in.

He took her hand and squeezed it. "Honey, I'll stay the night at your place and move some things over tomorrow."

"I appreciate your concern, really I do, but the answer is no."

"Then be reasonable, babe, and come to my place. He couldn't possibly know where you are."

"I'm not so sure about that."

Greg slid over, putting his arm around her shoulder. "Now I offered you two solutions, so which is it

222

going to be—your place or mine?"

"Greg," she said, reaching up to stroke his jaw lightly, "those are not solutions—only postponements. I can't go the rest of my life wondering if he's lurking somewhere out there, waiting for me. Do you understand what I'm saying? Even if he doesn't mean to hurt me—if he just gets some perverse gratification from threatening me—I'd never know for sure. There's only one way . . . and that's to find out who he is and to stop him."

Greg took her fist and unclenched each finger slowly; then, putting her hand to his lips, he kissed the scraped palm. "Okay, sugar. Your feisty spirit is one of the reasons I adore you. Not only are you bright and witty, you're one of the best-looking women around, and," he added, staring across the room, "it appears I'm not the only guy to think so."

Alex had to turn her head slightly to the right to see where Greg was looking. At that moment the waiter reappeared and stood in front of Greg, but Alex was able to look past him to the table halfway across the room. She looked into those intense blue eyes.

Justin was not alone. The woman with him was in profile to Alex. She was young. Stunning. Her pale blond hair, pulled up loosely into a chignon off-set to one side of her head, shimmered like champagne in the candlelight. Alex suddenly felt old and frumpy.

Justin was in a black mood. His mood got blacker when he glanced across the room to see Alex sitting in a booth with a good-looking, silver-haired man. For someone with a whole lot of problems, Justin told himself, the lady looked relaxed and composed. He had watched as she lightly stroked the man's face. The man had lifted her hand and kissed the palm.

He recognized her date as Gregory Ott, the defense attorney. The man was obviously in love with Alex. It showed in the way he looked at her, touched her. Justin wondered if Alex was in love with him. They had spent the night together. She had run from his arms into Ott's, and that was enough to make Justin's insides twist with a sick wretchedness.

"Jus, is something wrong?" Sherry Lowden asked. Sherry was the rich, spoiled daughter of one of Nevada's more affluent casino owners. Between her extensive stints to Europe and the Far East, she rested up in Reno. She always called Justin when she was in town. "I know how you detest those black-tie affairs, Jus, but my father does expect me to at least make an appearance when I'm in town. And I can't think of anyone who looks sexier in a tux than you, darling. Now that it's over, it wasn't so bad, was it?"

Justin pulled his gaze away from Alex to stare absently at Sherry's sculptured face. It's too perfect, he thought. It lacked character, definition. Her voice was perfect. The low, singsong quality threatened to put him to sleep if she said more than a dozen words. Her body was perfect. And boring.

"You look as if you just spotted public enemy number one," Sherry said. "You didn't hear a word I said. I feel terribly neglected."

"You're never neglected. Every man in the room has a surreptitious eye on you."

"I'm not with every man in the room. I'm with

you. And I want your eyes only." As she said those words, Justin watched her gaze move slowly from table to table.

He looked back at the booth. At that moment Alex turned her head and stared into his eyes. Justin watched her expression change from mild curiosity to surprise to something unreadable.

He slowly lifted his fluted glass, nodded his head slightly, raised the glass higher in a mock toast, brought the glass to his lips, then turned his attention back to Sherry.

Alex had no time to react. No time to smile, frown, or even return Justin's ambiguous toast. The sight of him, sitting not more than twenty feet away, with someone else, so unnerved her that she immediately lost her appetite. Putting her fork down gently, she stared in disgust at the food on her plate.

"Sweety?" Greg touched her arm. He was peering at her strangely, the linen-covered bread basket poised over her plate.

"What? Oh, no thanks. I don't care for anything else."

"Well, eat up," he said, taking another piece of bread. "How's the duck?"

"It's very good."

She lifted her fork and poked at the bird, picking at the glazed skin and bits of wild rice. How long had he been there? She stole a glance at his table. The waiter, after serving their entree, was pouring the last of a bottle of champagne into their glasses. They had been there long enough to get their food and drink a bottle of champagne. Had Justin been watching them the whole time? Don't flatter yourself, Alex thought. With a girl as lovely as the one who was possessively resting a hand on his arm, it was doubtful he'd been overly preoccupied with what was going on at another table. He looked striking in the black dinner jacket. His clear blue eyes seemed to glitter in the candlelight. He had been speaking to the blonde. They both laughed. She leaned over and kissed him on the lips.

Placing her fork across her plate, Alex tried to think of something other than Justin and his beautiful date and the kiss that, though brief, had made her go weak inside.

"How did your business trip go?" she asked Greg.

"Let's get married," he said.

She turned to look at him.

"I mean it. Let's get married."

"Greg, this may sound trite and somewhat old-fashioned, but love, not sex, should play a major role in marriage."

"Believe me, sweetheart, *love* is a major concern here. There's nothing I'd love more than to have sex with you. If I have to marry you to get you into bed, it's the least I can do."

Alex laughed. "Greg, you're impossible."

When Justin looked back at the booth a few minutes later, Alex and Ott were laughing. He attacked his antelope steak like a ravenous lion, only he wasn't hungry anymore.

It was impossible to keep her gaze from going to the table across the room. Alex watched Justin

226

meticulously brush a stray hair from the woman's cheek. His hand seemed to move in slow motion. Exact. Precise. His fingers a sensuous, instrumental part of his body. Her stomach did a slow roll.

"You didn't answer my question, Alex . . . about marrying me," Greg said, his expression and voice no longer teasing.

Alex stuttered, trying desperately to find something to say. "Greg . . . I . . . I . ."

He smiled, squeezed her hand. "Stay my friend then. I know as well as you do that it's better that way."

She nodded, smiled. Her eyes began to mist.

"Hey, hey," he said, taking her face in his hands. "What's this? Can it be that the lewd Greg turned sentimental is too much for you?" He kissed her mouth lightly.

"You're not lewd, only ribald. Otherwise I wouldn't put up with you."

"And you bring out the satyr in me. Shall we have dessert? An after-dinner cordial? An orgy?"

She smiled weakly. "Can we go, Greg? I'm really tired."

"Sure." He signaled for the waiter.

After paying the check, Greg rose and waited for Alex to slide from the booth.

Now comes the really hard part, she thought. To reach the door, they would have to walk by Justin's table. The room appeared to have doubled in size; the door now seemed a million miles away.

She stood, felt Greg's arm move around her waist protectively. As they walked to the restaurant foyer, she looked straight ahead.

Within several feet of his table, Alex's eyes involuntarily shifted to meet Justin's. An electrical jolt, sharp and intense, seemed to cross those few feet and surge into and through the very core of her being.

"When we leave here," Sherry was saying, "we'll go back to my place. The jacuzzi is steamy hot, and the champagne is icy cold."

"I can't tonight, Sherry, sorry. I've got work to do."

"Ohhh." Her perfect face pouted. "It's my first night back, and I'm very horny. I picked up a new trick in the Orient. It'll drive you mad."

Justin had watched Alex rise from the booth and then cross the room. She was wearing a silky dress that seductively played in and out between her legs as she walked toward him. He'd never seen her in a dress. Jeans, slacks, shorts, a kimono, yes, but no skirt or dress. Then he realized that he had seen, in bits and pieces, at one time or another, most of her body. And what he had seen had only served to whet his appetite for more. He wanted to see every part of her. All at one time. He wanted to touch every part of her. He felt a sexual stirring that he knew was not attributed to Sherry's hand caressing his upper thigh, but to his vivid mosaic images of Alex's body.

With her gaze straight ahead, she closed the distance. Then her cool green-gray eyes were staring into his and he felt something like a molten rush of energy erupt inside him.

In the restaurant foyer, as Greg helped Alex with her coat, she stole one last glance at that damned

228

table. From where she stood, Alex could see that the blonde had her hand on Justin's thigh. Her foot, now shoeless, was caressing his ankle. Alex felt heat rising throughout her body. It was both agonizing and wonderful.

On the drive home Greg chatted casually as Alex in her mind's eye saw Justin and his date sitting at their table. The woman was young, poised, and beautiful. Yet, something told her that the volatile emotion she'd felt when their eyes had met had been felt by him as well.

"I know where I've seen that guy before. The one in Le Moulin," Greg said. "Detective Holmes."

Alex felt her body flush warmly at the sound of his name.

"He stopped by my office a couple of days ago. He seemed more interested in you than in the crime."

They rode in silence the rest of the way to Alex's house.

She said good night to Greg at her door, then locked up, switched out the lights, and went into her bedroom.

After dropping a still-pouting Sherry at her door, Justin drove across town. He pulled his red Corvette under the trees at the edge of the bluff, looked down at Alex's house. The house was dark except for a soft glow from her bedroom window. A shadow moved about in the room. Although her car was the only one in the driveway, he wondered if Ott was with her?

He sat there thinking about her. About the feel of her skin. The smell of her. The way her lips and tongue had burned into his. He wanted to touch her. Hold her. Feel her naked body against his. Feel her moist warmth closing around him. To hell with mixing business and pleasure. He wanted her. God, how he wanted her.

The flat of his hand pushed against his erection, making him sigh.

"This is crazy," he whispered hoarsely. He started the car, pulled out, and drove down the hill.

Alex stood before the full-length mirror in her stockinged feet. The room was dim, with only the glow of a small bedside lamp. Staring into the mirror, she removed first her earrings, then the clips from her hair. As she shook her head gently, her hair came down around her shoulders, full and feral. She untied the scarf, held it out at arm's length before draping it over the lamp shade. The light in the room became warm and rosy.

She undressed slowly, looking at herself, imagining it was Justin watching her uncover her body bit by bit. The dress slid down over her hips to the floor. She lowered her bra's straps and took in a deep breath. Over the top of the demibra her breasts swelled. Her finger traced along the lace of the cup before she unhooked the bra and let it fall. Her open palms stroked the side of her breasts. Her fingertips touched the nipples. In the mirror she watched her nipples slowly grow erect. Her hands moved seductively down her body to her panties. And her hands became his hands—Justin's hands. Chewing on her lower lip, sucking on it, she closed her eyes and imagined him pulling the flesh-colored satin bikinis over her buttocks and down her legs.

230

She stepped out of them. She pressed her fingertips lightly to her pubis and moaned as a wave of pleasure spread through her. Her other hand moved to her breast. She whispered his name. When footsteps lightly sounded on the front steps, she knew.

Reaching into her closet, she pulled out a white kimono and put it on over her nakedness. She moved lithely down the hallway, her entire being so warm she failed to notice the cold tiles under her bare feet. As she reached the door, she heard a light tapping. She unlocked the door, pulled it open, and stared into bright brooding eyes.

Justin crossed the threshold. His eyes took in every part of her as she stood there silently. Her lips were moist and swollen. He saw a pulse throbbing at her throat. The long kimono was unbelted, open, the impression of her nipples clearly visible beneath the shiny material. Without taking his eyes from hers, he closed the door and turned the deadbolt. In one fluid motion he stepped up to her, slipped his hands inside the kimono at the waist, circling her back, and pulled her to him. The kimono slid off her shoulders and dropped to the floor. There was something tremendously exciting about standing in the foyer, his cool, formal black attire contrasting with her warm, creamy nakedness. Her skin was hot and as silky as the lapels of his jacket. He crushed her to him, his lips sought hers in a feverish kiss.

Without breaking the kiss, Justin lifted her and carried her to the bedroom. When he reached the carpeted platform on which the bed sat, he lowered her to her feet. They now stood eye to eye. He slipped off the jacket. With one hand he pulled off his tie and unbuttoned his shirt while the other

231

caressed first one of her breasts and then the other.

She watched as his gaze, cool, unabashed, took in her breasts, her waist and hips, the dark pubic hair, and finally the length of her legs before looking back into her eyes.

He removed his shirt, then pulled her to him again, pressing his furry chest to her breasts.

Alex reached for the hook at his waistband. She pulled down the zipper and helped him remove his pants. When his clothing lay at their feet, he drew her back into his arms, rubbed against her and kissed her with unbelievable passion. Alex sighed deeply. Her body felt like one overly sensitive conduit of sexual energy.

He stepped up, lifted her, and laid her on the bed. While looking into her eyes, he entered her slowly. She pulled in her breath, savoring the feel of him gliding deep inside her.

For the briefest moment, Alex stiffened with apprehension. How could I be so damned weak? she asked herself. Then her increasing passion wiped all thought away. As Justin moved within her, only one thing mattered, and that was to make it last as long as she could.

She felt her climax approaching—too fast, too soon. She wanted to prolong the inevitable. Her body let her down. She plummeted over the edge as wave after wave of pleasure, so sudden, so intense, washed over her. Justin's mouth covered hers fiercely, stifling her cries. He stopped deep inside her. His lips eased their pressure and drew away. Slowly Alex opened her eyes and stared into his. He lowered his head and kissed her again, lightly, sweetly. His hands began to roam over her breasts as he slowly pulled out. Shifting her position, she took hold of him. He was still hard, fully erect.

"No," he said, taking her hand away. "Lie back, close your eyes."

"But—"

"Sssh."

This time he made love to her with an unhurried and accomplished precision. He carried her along to heights of desire she'd never dreamed were possible. When her hands automatically reached for him, he gently pushed them away, leaving her mind and body free to experience all sexual sensations as they surfaced with wanton and uninhibited abandonment. She moaned aloud as his tongue and fingers maddeningly stroked her body. He seemed to know just where to touch; what brought the most pleasure, and when and how. His hands and mouth roved over skin so responsive it pulsated. Oh God, she thought, lost to all rationality, don't stop . . . don't ever stop. Her back arched and became rigid as her empty hands sought something to cling to. Entwining her fingers in her tangled hair, she pulled and twisted.

The vibrating ripples within her became a swirling, dizzying whirlpool. She had the perception of being sucked downward into the depths of a vortex until there was nowhere to go, and then the whirlpool reversed its savage course and exploded up and out like a geyser. Justin slid into her at that moment and filled the throbbing void. She clung to him, pressing eagerly up to meet him. He paused, waiting until the violent contractions eased, and then he began to move his hips slowly, rhythmically. She returned his kisses with a smoldering passion and moved with him, trying to concentrate on bringing pleasure to him, but once again she found

233

herself responding to his lovemaking, his sweltering eagerness, his whispered words of encouragement.

Their bodies, slick, feverish, came together again and again, faster now as he began to thrust with more urgency. His breathing hoarse and ragged in her ear. Her nails digging into his back. Her own breath came in rapid pants as she felt herself drawing nearer and nearer to yet another orgasm. A frenzied wildness swept her along. She wanted to hold back, to luxuriate until Justin was ready to share it with her. The last vestiges of pent-up desire burst forth as he thrust deep into her. She felt him shudder, heard the low moan in his throat as his throbbing combined with her own.

Minutes later, crushing his body deliciously to hers, he kissed her temple, her eyelids, her throat. The rippling waves slowly diminished with the beating of her heart. She smiled as the inner muscles surrounding him involuntarily flexed for the umpteenth time.

"Ummm," he said, "do that again."

Her throat was dry as a new sponge. With her eyes closed, she whispered, "I'm too weak to move."

Justin stirred. She tightened her arms and legs around him.

He settled back down. "I don't want to crush you."

She kissed the corner of his mouth and lightly ran the tip of her tongue along the separation of his moist lips.

"Mrs. Carlson, you are one carnivorous *femme fatale*. But you already know that." He turned on his side, raised up on an elbow, then allowed his eyes to travel the length of her. Their skin, from the red light, glowed rosy, warm and flushed. With the back

234

of his fingers he lightly stroked down her body to her stomach. He traced along a thin blue line just above the pubic hair.

"That's a stretch mark," she said quietly.

"Yes. And this and this." He tenderly touched several others.

Alex placed a hand over his.

"Alex, you shouldn't be ashamed of them. It's the mark of a mother. Bearing a child has to be the ultimate achievement."

After staring at her for a long moment, he let his fingers continue to rove over her body.

She closed her eyes. There was something about his touch, something different from the touches of the few other men she had known. He was experienced, no doubt about it. But it was more than that.

She relaxed, feeling light, tingly. In her semidozing state Alex heard a heavy creaking sound, then a scratching. An overwhelming sensation of malevolence thundered through her. Her eyes flew open, looking upward to the black eye of the skylight.

She shivered.

"Alex," he asked softly. "What is it?"

Exhaling, she threw her arms around his neck, clinging tightly. She buried her face in his warm throat, the pulse in his neck throbbing against her lips.

The convex skylight reflected the red glowing lamp. If there was something up there, seeing it would be impossible. With her eyes closed, she began to chant silently: There are no monsters . . . there are no monsters.

He raised his head and stared at her. "Tell me what you were thinking?"

She opened her eyes, looked upward. "No. It's crazy."

"Tell me."

"I . . . I had this overpowering sensation of malevolence — deadliness," she said quietly. "Jesus, did that come out of my mouth?"

Justin lifted his head, looked up at the skylight. His brow creased. When he looked back at her, she averted her eyes. He kissed her mouth lightly and started to get out of bed.

"Where are you going?"

"I thought you might want me to leave now."

Staring silently at the starry sky, she shook her head.

He lay back down.

"Are you married?" Fine time to ask him that, she thought, after inviting him to spend the night.

"I *was* married. For five years. Once was enough. She found monogamy a bore."

"I see." She sensed he was staring at her. Studying her. Turning to look into his eyes, she asked, "What is it?"

"Your husband was jealous, wasn't he?"

"Very. What did he say about me?"

He was silent.

"What did David Sloane say about me?"

He waited a moment before saying, "Sloane said that you weren't always truthful. That you went through men — I think the expression was — like a person with a head cold goes through Kleenex."

Alex laughed lightly. She wanted to cry. He didn't have to tell her what Joe had said, she knew it couldn't be good. Justin had believed Sloane. Was that why he was here with her now? The easy mark. All the guys were getting it, so why not him?

And as long as he was assigned to her case, he might as well have some fun. The nights were beginning to get cold.

She was beginning to get cold.

A good time? Was that all she was to him, Alex wondered with a sinking feeling in her stomach, just *a good time?*

"That friend of yours, Ott, what if he finds me here with you?" Justin asked, not looking at her now.

"What if he does?"

"He's in love with you."

"That's between Greg and me."

"Oh? Then I take it you have no qualms about sleeping with him one night and me the next?"

Alex scooted up to sit with her back against the headboard. She pulled the sheet above her breasts. "You know where I went last night?"

He nodded.

"I was alone."

It was Justin's turn to laugh. "All night?"

"Yes—no, but—"

"Was he there with you last night or not?"

"Yes, but only—"

"Then why did you say you were alone?"

"Damn it, I don't have to explain myself to you."

"No, you don't. If you want to sleep with Ott . . . or Sloane, or your ex or . . . or the seven dwarfs for that matter, it's your business and your business only. Just don't lie to me. That's the one thing I cannot tolerate."

"I went there. I was alone until around eleven. That's when Greg came in. I left immediately."

"I don't think so," he said quietly.

She got colder. She began to shiver. He was

calling her a liar. Was that how he made his exit from a woman's bed? "Maybe you'd better leave after all."

"Fine. Great." He climbed out of bed. As he put on his clothes, he silently stared at her. Alex had pulled the quilt over her naked body, denying him any part of it. She stared at the wall opposite her. With his shirt gaping open to the waist, his jacket and shoes in hand, he crossed the room, then stopped.

"Alex . . . ?"

She continued to stare straight ahead.

He stood there a moment longer. Then he strode quickly out of the room, taking an extra second to punch his fist into the open door.

The front door slammed shut. A minute later Alex heard the engine of his car roar, and tires peeled rubber as he screeched down the driveway.

Well, Alex, how's it feel to be a one-night stand . . . a piece of ass . . . a good time? Not very good. *Don't say you didn't ask for it.* I won't.

From the top of the bluff Justin had a clear view of Alex's house through the trees. He'd much rather protect her from her bed, with her warm body alongside his, than up here in his usual spot, in the dark, the cold.

Justin slammed his fist against the steering wheel. He winced. It was the same hand he'd used to punch her bedroom door.

Women!

Good riddance, he thought angrily, she was a goddamn cop's nightmare. It was impossible to know if, and when, she was lying. Klump, Sloane,

238

and Alex's ex had implied she went through men like locusts through Brigham Young's crops. Why would she lie about being with Ott last night? At ten o'clock he had seen both their cars there. And he had seen Ott having a cigarette—a postorgasmic smoke?—in an upstairs bedroom.

He knew better than to get involved with women on his cases. Business and pleasure don't mix. He could learn from the TV detective shows. As soon as the hero fell hard for that certain woman, then *bam*—it was all over—the kiss of death. Everyone knew that. To top it off, he had committed the cardinal sin. He had asked her about her relationship with another man. No, two men—Ott and her ex. And hadn't he tossed in Sloane for good measure? God, nothing like showing he was jealous and insecure.

Why was it that everything he did where this woman was concerned was wrong? He had enough women to screw around with; he didn't need this one—this *walking calamity*. The woman had hang-up upon hang-up. Sensitive, cynical, possibly neurotic, definitely a liar.

She had told him she was no good at casual affairs. Yet earlier, when he had come to her door she had been ready and eager for him. Ready and eager for *someone*. In bed she had been wonderfully wanton. And then, when they had finished, she had seemed to turn . . . well, sexually shy. The woman was a network of complexity.

Thoughts of them together, their naked bodies pressed against each other, had him stiffening, growing erect inside his jockey shorts. With a grunt he shifted his position on the seat. Christ, he was behaving like some horny teenager. His heavy breathing was fogging up the inside of the Corvette. He rolled down the window.

A movement, about a hundred yards to Justin's right, caught his eye. The rays of the full moon glinted off silver hair. Was that Klump moving up toward her house? What had she been doing out in the dark by the edge of the embankment? Looking down on the house below? Klump's preoccupation with her neighbor, Justin decided, stretched beyond the considerate duties of Neighborhood Watch. It was little wonder that Alex had felt she was being spied upon. Tonight, two people, he and Klump, had been looking down on her.

Had there been a third?

Chapter 15

The temperature hovered at the freezing mark at eight o'clock the following morning. Light flurries swirled through the frigid air, announcing the first snow of the season.

From the living-room windows, Alex watched Hawkins's old truck chug up the driveway. The snow, beginning to stick to the icy pavement, made his progress slow and nerve-racking.

By the time his battered pickup slid to a stop near the garage, she had stepped out on the porch. Briskly rubbing her arms to keep the blood circulating, she walked out to meet him.

"I won't be needing you anymore, Mr. Hawkins," she said as he climbed out of the truck.

He cocked his head to one side. Glared at her. "You firin' me?"

"I don't need you anymore. May I have the keys to the garage and shed, please."

"That cop—he's been telling you things about me, ain't that right?"

She held out her hand. "The keys."

He nodded, his eyes mere slits. Then, reaching into his pocket, he brought out a cluster of keys. Slowly slipping two off the ring he held them up, inches from her fingers. Alex reached for them. He pulled them back. She moved for them again, and he pulled back farther. With lightning speed she closed her hand around the keys, but Hawkins caught her wrist with his other hand before she could pull away. He squeezed.

Fear gripped her. This man is a murderer, she thought. Women are sublife to him. Why was she doing this alone? She should have asked Greg to fire Hawkins.

Hawkins glared at her. She glared back unflinchingly. He suddenly released her wrist. Without another word, he got into his truck and slammed the door. The engine sputtered, caught, and then revved. Yanking the steering wheel sharply and pressing down hard on the gas pedal, he whipped the truck rapidly around in reverse. The pickup backed off the pavement, jounced over the rocks that lined the edge of the driveway, and in one thumping motion shot forward, clearing the rocks and showering a spray of debris in its wake. It fishtailed for approximately fifteen feet before Hawkins got it under control. He descended the slippery driveway, exhaust pipe belching black oily smoke.

Alex returned to the house. Taking her time, shivering, she went upstairs to the living room. She picked up the phone and dialed.

"Margie?"

"Oh, honey, I'm glad you called. Bob wants to leave a day early for the islands. Business first, then ten days of fun and sun. Are you going to be all right? I hate to leave you right now with all that crap going on in your life."

Alex sighed deeply. "When?"

"Two this afternoon. Alex, are you okay?"

"I . . . Oh, Margie."

"Hon? I'll be right there."

Thirty minutes later, after Alex had told Margie about her evening with Justin, Margie reached across the dining-room table and patted Alex's hand. "You love this cop, don't you?"

Alex shook her head. "I'm only human; I have desires and needs like everyone else. Look, he was a diversion—someone who was there when I needed someone. So, please, don't try to make more out of it, okay?"

"Damn it, why don't you admit you love him?"

"Because I don't."

"Bullshit! I've never seen you this torn up over a man."

"And what if I were in love with him? Margie, he's a playboy, a jock, a stud. The kind of guy who screws you and then says 'screw you.' And the really funny part is, he thinks I'm just like him."

"Alex, call him. Swallow your insufferable pride and tell him you're sorry."

"Sorry for what? For being upset because he used me?"

"You don't know that. Honey, you have an uncanny knack of alienating the men in your life. I've seen you do it so many times."

"I can't pretend to like someone when I don't?"

"You don't like Holmes?"

"He's all right." She pinched off a piece of donut and rolled it into a small ball of dough. "I guess I like him as well as he likes me. He's not bad in the sack." She squashed the dough ball between her fingers.

"Alex, look, most of us are insecure in some way. But not everyone takes his insecurities out on others the way you do—with the force of a jackhammer, ramming it down their throats."

Alex was silent.

"Why?"

"Why what?"

"Why do you push men away?"

"You think I have some deep-rooted problem?" Alex tried to keep her voice light. "Something from the past, perhaps, hindering my chances of ever finding happiness with a man?"

"Yes, I do. Alex, you're smart and pretty and personable. You shouldn't be alone. You should be sharing your life with someone you love. For God's sake, don't destroy your own chance for happiness."

"Love makes the world go round," Alex said, and drained her cup of coffee.

"Oh, that sounded so cynical."

"Well, maybe that's how I feel."

"You're afraid to fall in love. That's it, isn't it? Someone broke your heart and—"

"No one broke my heart," Alex cut in. "If you never love, you never hurt."

Margie looked up. "Joe? What about Joe?"

"Joe asked me to marry him. He was the first man I'd ever been alone with."

Margie opened her mouth to say something, then closed it. She shook her head, incredulous.

"It's obvious you want to play Freud, so okay, let's psychoanalyze Alex. Let's see now, when I was in kindergarten—"

"Stop it. That's not fair. I don't want to know anything you don't want to tell me. Let's drop it, okay?"

Alex disliked herself then. Her best friend only wanted to help, and she was acting like a bitch. She hesitated, then said quietly, "My father adored my mother, and when she left him he went to pieces. You wouldn't believe what Lora and I had to go through to prove we weren't like her. Joe was to have been my salvation."

"Your father didn't want you to marry Joe?"

"He didn't want me to marry anyone. He wanted me to stay with him forever. Be his baby always." Alex laughed lightly. "I married Joe to spite my father. And I divorced Joe because he turned out to be just like my father. Possessive. Jealous. Insecure."

The snow was coming down hard. Not the fluffy light flakes of a few hours before, but coarser, icier granules. Alex watched those falling white bits through misty eyes. "Allie," her father had said just before he'd disappeared that fateful day, "You're just like your mother. Your eyes. Your hair. *Everything.*" And she had answered "No. Honest, Daddy, I'm not."

Just like your mother.

At nine-fifteen Justin walked into the forensic lab to find Oliver Bernsway sitting on a stool, eating sardines from the can. When he spotted Justin he held out the can.

"Yummm," Justin said, waving it away.

"Great for the ticker. Lowers the cholesterol."

"I'll take my chances. What did you find, Ollie?"

Bernsway's brow furrowed; he feigned ignorance. "The hairs?"

"Oh. Did I say I'd have something for you this morning?"

Justin walked to a microscope and, with his hands clasped behind his back, bent and peered through the lens. "Did I tell you I'm getting another mare? A real sweet, gentle gal. Loves kids, I'm told. Horses should be ridden often. Keeps them young and healthy."

"You've a nasty mean streak, Sergeant."

"Yeah, I know."

"The two samples—those from the pillowcase, and the ones from that lacy thing—are close enough in color, length, and diameter to suggest they came from the same source."

Justin turned to face Bernsway. "Human hair?"

"Synthetic. A cheap wig. Probably thousands of them like it out there. Sorry, Jus, wish I could give you something conclusive, but no can do."

"You've given me plenty, Ollie. Thanks. Bring the family over next weekend. I'll put on a pot of chili if Sarah will bring her home-baked bread and a couple of her rhubarb pies."

"Deal."

Outside, as he headed for his car, Justin thought about the lab results. A wig. Klump wore a wig. It was doubtful he could prove that the hairs had come from her wig, but there was one positive aspect. The gray hairs on Alex's pillowcase had not come from the head of Gregory Ott.

An hour later Justin was at the art center viewing the paintings of Alex Carlson. On a bench in the middle of the room he sat, elbows on his knees, chin in his hands, and studied the paintings one by one. His eyes were repeatedly drawn to the night-scape titled *Depth*.

With a sigh he rose and walked out to the reception desk. Velda Lancaster looked up and smiled.

"Good afternoon, Sergeant Holmes. Something I can do for you?"

246

"Mrs. Carlson's painting, *Depth*. Is it sold?"

"I'm not certain. That's the one with the Not for Sale sticker, right?"

"Right." Justin cleared his throat. "I'm interested in buying it. Could you call her? Ask her if she'd consider selling it?"

"Of course."

"Uh . . . would you mind not telling her it's me?"

Velda smiled, reached for the telephone.

Justin walked back into the gallery. Five minutes later Velda joined him.

"She's willing to sell it, Sergeant. But not cheaply, I'm afraid. Evidently it means something special to her."

"I'll take it with me."

"I haven't told you the price."

"It doesn't matter. Will you take a check?"

With the painting wrapped in brown paper, he headed for home.

An hour later, back at the station, Justin looked up to see Gunther standing stiffly on the other side of his desk.

"Can I have a word with you, Sergeant?"

Justin leaned back in his chair. Nodded.

"It's about that woman . . . Mrs. Carlson."

"Go on."

"Well, I'm thinking I might've said some things about her that could, well, give you the wrong impression of her."

"Oh? Now what would that be?"

"I think you know, sir." Gunther swallowed, his Adam's apple rose and fell. "I didn't lie. I told you what I saw. But maybe what I saw, and how I related it to you, wasn't really how it was. If you know what I mean."

Justin stared at him. "What reason would you have for wanting me to think ill of Mrs. Carlson?"

"Because of that prick Ott. Her boyfriend. I guess I wanted to get even. She was sort of a scapegoat."

"What you're saying is that you didn't see the Carlson woman and Corvette man embracing?"

"No, sir. I did see them. As clear as a bell. What I'm not certain of is if she was actually a willing participant."

Justin leaned forward, elbows on his desk, hands clasped in front of him. In a calm, even tone he asked, "Are you telling me that you sat there—or stood there, or whatever—and looked on impassively while a woman was being assaulted?"

"I didn't say that, sir. I don't know that for sure."

"What do you know? And where the fuck were you?"

"In the patrol car at the bottom of her drive. I, uh, had the binoculars. I was just about to go back up there and check it out when this guy on a motorcycle pulls up and asks me for directions. I got rid of him real quick, but by then the man had come out of the house and was getting into his car. So I took off."

"I see. So take off now," Justin said, picking up the file in front of him.

Gunther moved away.

Justin slammed down the file. He reached for the phone, his hand pausing on the receiver a moment; then he lifted it and dialed. He put in a call to Dallas and requested a criminal check on David Sloane. Dallas responded promptly. David Leroy Sloane had been arrested twice in the previous year.

248

Assault with intent to commit rape: acquitted. Rape: charges dropped. Justin followed a hunch and checked on Sloane in the Reno files. Five years ago, while employed at the Nevada branch of Norday Investments, a petition had been filed by a female employee accusing Sloane of sexual harassment. Upon Sloane's transfer to Dallas, the petition had been withdrawn.

Alex had been damn lucky. Somehow she had been spared the pain and anguish of being yet another victim of David Sloane.

But Alex had been a victim of prejudice and hate. Of the people Justin had interviewed regarding Alex, all those with an unfavorable opinion of her had had a spiteful motive. An ex-husband, an angry neighbor, an alleged rapist, and a cop with misdirected animosity.

And he had believed them. You're an asshole, Justin told himself. You should have seen through Sloane.

But knowing that Alex had told the truth about Sloane didn't rectify the fact that she'd lied to him about being with Ott at his condo on Wednesday night.

Was there also a reasonable explanation for that incident? *Forget it. Leave it. It's over and done with.*

At dusk, Alex turned on the lights throughout the house. She had been unable to shake that feeling of malevolence from the night before. And now, without Justin, it was twofold. Being alone had never been a strong point for her. Several times she had dialed Greg's number, but had hung up before it rang. The last time she had completed the call, only to get Greg's answering machine. She'd left no message.

Through most of the evening she found her thoughts alternating between Justin and the intruder. Was Justin at home, alone, as she was? Was he out with the blond woman from the restaurant? Was he thinking of her? Then: Who was the intruder? Why was he after her? When would he come again? Where was he now?

He stood in the bathroom looking at his image in the mirror. Light filtered in from the hallway.

She was nothing but a whore, he told himself as he chewed on his lower lip. The same as her mother. Grief and heartache, that's all she was capable of giving. He thought back to the night before, thought of her standing before her bedroom mirror undressing, touching herself, preparing herself for that man she'd known less than two weeks.

Through the skylight, in a state of rage, disgust, and desire he had watched the two of them, naked, writhing, clutching shamelessly, until, sexually sated, she had sent the cop from her bed and out into the night.

He whispered, "I'm the one who should be with you, Allie. I'm the one who has the rightful place in your life." He bit down slowly, watching impassively as his teeth disappeared into the flesh of his lower lip. Blood oozed up around each tooth.

Upstairs in the living room the grandfather clock chimed the hour. He looked upward, counting the bells. Ten o'clock. He twisted the knobs on the bathroom faucet; water gushed out into the sink. He turned off the light in the hall. Then he moved into the study, lifted the receiver, and held it to his chest. With the back of his hand, he wiped at the blood

250

on his mouth and chin.

They could have been happy together all these years, he thought with contempt, if only she hadn't been like her, like the other one.

Curled up on the end of the sectional sofa, Alex thought she heard something. Turning down the volume on the TV, she listened to a hissing sound coming from somewhere downstairs. She lowered her feet to the floor, sat up straight, and listened again. It sounded like running water.

Rising slowly, she moved to the top of the stairs. With caution, she went down to the main level, turned left, and walked down the hall to her bedroom. Whatever was making that noise was not coming from the bedroom or master bath. She listened again. It sounded as though it was coming from the lower level, where the study and other bedrooms were.

She backtracked to the foyer and had begun to descend when suddenly, two steps down, she stopped. The hair rose on the back of her neck. The downstairs hall light that she had switched on earlier was now off.

Poised like a guarded doe, Alex listened. Over the rushing sound of blood pounding in her ears, she heard water running. She backed up carefully to the foyer, then, turning, she ran back to her bedroom. Snatching up the receiver, she punched 911.

"Hello! Hello! Damn it, someone answer me! Please answer!" she whispered frantically.

"It's time, Allie," the hoarse voice on the phone said. "They've waited long enough. The night is theirs."

251

He was in the house with her.

There were four telephones in the house, at least one extension on each level. Which extension was he on?

She put the receiver on the bed and backed up to the glass slider. Quietly, keeping her gaze steady on the hallway, she reached for the lock lever at the handle. A piece of jagged metal scraped her finger. She risked a look. The lever had been twisted and broken off. It was stuck in the lock position.

She stepped into the studio alcove and wrapped a sweaty, trembling hand around the cast-iron statuette.

Keeping hysteria at bay, she switched on the light of the swing-arm lamp. Then she moved to the night-stand lamp and turned it on. The room was ablaze with light. If she found herself trapped in the dark she would go mad — stark raving mad.

She ran.

Justin pulled up to the unmarked car parked under the trees. De Solo leaned over and rolled down the window.

"Anything happen while I was gone?"

"Not much. About an hour ago the old lady left her house — on foot. Unless I missed her when I took a leak, she hasn't returned."

"What's going on below?" Justin nodded his head toward Alex's house.

"She's still got the place lit up like a Christmas tree. Must be scared of the dark, huh?"

"Anybody with her?"

"Not that I know of."

"I'll take over, De Solo. Thanks for the relief."

"You gonna sit here all night?"

"I don't know. Couple hours at least."

"Why don't you see if you can get an invite in? Would sure be a helluva lot warmer."

"I doubt that," Justin said to himself.

It had stopped snowing by mid morning, and the snow had melted away an hour later.

De Solo drove away with only his parking lights on.

Justin took the .38 police special from the glove compartment and set it on the passenger seat.

Straight ahead, through the trees, he could see Klump's house. The lights were on in the living room. He saw a silhouette pass behind the shaded window. So she was back in the house again. De Solo had missed seeing her return.

He looked back down the hill. The house—with a light blazing in every window—suddenly went dark.

"What the hell . . . ?" Justin said. There was no way all the lights could go off at the same time unless someone hit the circuit breaker. There was no reason for Alex to do that. A power failure? He glanced over to Klump's house; her lights continued to glow.

Shoving the gear shift in reverse, Justin backed out, his rear tires spinning on the loose gravel.

Alex froze. She had gotten as far as the hallway when everything went black.

Now she would go mad.

She could hide. She could make a run for the front door. Or she could stand here and wait for him to come for her.

The statuette was heavy in her hand. She

253

switched it to the other one, wiped her palm on her denim skirt, then gripped the statuette again. In the oppressive blackness of the hall she sensed his presence. Her feet refused to move. She could go neither forward nor backward. A moment later, in a state of paralyzing terror, she felt, rather than heard, footsteps advancing toward her. From behind, she felt an arm close around her as a cold hand moved across her mouth.

Chapter 16

It isn't happening. Oh God, Alex prayed, *let it be a bad dream.*

"Pretty, Allie. Sweet, Allie." He ground his body into hers, and she felt with sickening horror his erection hard against her. "Whose baby are you?" Those words. That voice. Her muffled sob bounced back off his hand.

The statuette dropped from her numb fingers. She was pulled roughly from the wall and propelled toward the bedroom. She began to resist.

"Don't fight me, you slut. I'll hurt you if you fight me."

Alex moaned softly.

His hand tightened over her mouth and nose, cutting off her air. He kicked at her feet, partially dragging, partially carrying her a few steps farther down the hall.

Her head felt light. Bright spots danced before her eyes. On the wall, in the dimness, she stared at a family photograph—the one she had kept hidden from her father. A professional photograph of her parents, sitting side by side on a loveseat, four-year-old Lora sitting cross-legged on the floor between them and baby Allie on her father's lap. As she stared, her father's image began to waver—waver slightly to and fro. "Daddy . . . *no,* Daddy," she breathed, expelling the last bit of air from her lungs onto the salty dampness pressed to her mouth.

Her head was forced against the photograph. She heard the crack of glass.

"You fucking bitch. Because of the two of you, my life was a living hell." Alex heard him spit; felt droplets on the side of her face. "You'll pay for the both of you. Hear me? You'll pay!"

Dark. Everything was suddenly so dark. Where was the light switch? She had to find daddy again. Had to tell him something . . . something very important. But what? What? Yes. Of course. She had to tell him to help her . . . help her get out of this hot dark box . . . this smelly refrigerator. Then his face was before her again, like the diaphanous, detached head of the Wizard of Oz in the palace. Strong. Handsome. Powerful. She felt her body relaxing, felt the muscles in her legs go limp as her knees began to bend. She was lifted up by strong arms and carried with ease a few paces before the ghostly features of her father's face became rigid. "Over my dead body, Allie!" the floating head shouted at her. "You promised. You promised you'd never leave me!"

Her father's face was gone, and there was only darkness again.

An instant later she was gasping for air. Air filled her lungs as she sucked greedily with everything she had. She drew it in, afraid to let it out—afraid the supply would be depleted again. Then a steel band wound around her chest and squeezed, forcing the precious air from her lungs.

She cried out in sheer frustration.

"Shut up!" the voice said in her ear as she was dragged through the doorway of her bedroom.

Struggling again with the strength heightened by a blast of adrenaline, Alex managed to free her mouth from his grasp. "No," she croaked, the sound barely above a whisper. Drawing in a deep breath, whipping her head from side to side to keep his hand clear of her mouth, she screamed, "Nooo!" The word resounded in her head.

She fell over the raised platform and was pushed down to the floor on her stomach, the weight of his body crushing her. At the edge of the bed Alex tried to rise, but was knocked back down. Her hand groped along the floor, under the bed, searching for a handhold. Her fingers touched cold metal. She knew instantly what it was—the hedge clippers she'd found on the patio the night he'd been in her house. With a strangled cry, she grabbed up the clippers, pulled them out and, with all her might, arched them up and over her left shoulder. She felt a pointed tip puncture solid matter. She heard him grunt, curse. Alex struggled upward, made it several feet before she was grabbed by her shoulder.

"Bitch!"

She heard pounding and shouting.

Suddenly she was hurled down. The oak night stand seemed to come at her like a runaway Mack truck, slamming against her hip with a solid thud. She cried out sharply as the pain in her side exploded, making her knees buckle. She fell to the floor.

Pressing the side of her face to the smooth wood, Alex watched as the dark form ran out the door, down the hall, and disappeared into the garage.

"Alex, open up!" The voice at the front door was Justin's.

She heaved herself away from the night stand and

rushed to open the front door. Justin pushed his way in. Grabbed her. In a breathless voice he asked, "You all right?"

"Yes."

He flipped the switch for the foyer light. "Where's the breaker box?"

"Garage. Be careful!" she called out as Justin charged through the foyer door into the garage.

Within seconds the lights were on again.

Alex watched as Justin, gun in hand, crossed the garage and disappeared outside through an open side door. Wearily she lowered herself to the bottom step of the stairway. She looked up at the photograph on the wall. A crack in the glass ominously crossed the heads of her mother and father. Spittle blurred the smiling faces.

Within minutes Justin was back. He knelt down, his eyes darted over her, a muscle worked in his jaw. "Did he hurt you?"

"I hurt him, I think."

"How?"

"Yard clippers. I stabbed him."

"Show me," he said, pulling her to her feet.

Seconds later they were in her bedroom. Alex pointed to the clippers. Justin looked for blood, but found none. "Are you sure you stabbed him?"

"One of the blades . . . went into him. He cried out. Cursed."

"Let's go upstairs."

On wobbly legs she climbed the steps ahead of him.

"Sit," he commanded, pointing to a rattan dining-room chair. He strode to the kitchen, picked up the phone, and called the police. Then he took down the bottle of brandy and poured a hefty shot.

"Drink some of this, then tell me what happened." She took the glass from him. He removed his jacket and hung it over the back of a chair. Next he loosened his tie and undid the top two buttons of his shirt. Alex waited for him to roll up his sleeves, but instead, he towered over her, arms crossed, legs planted firmly apart, the butt of a gun protruding menacingly from his waistband.

She handed the glass back. "I don't want any—"

"Drink it."

With both hands gripping the glass, Alex lifted it to her lips. Brandy sloshed over the top and dripped off her fingers into her lap. She took a small sip and allowed herself a few moments to gain some composure. The liquor burned a path to her stomach.

"What happened?"

She swallowed. "I heard noises. He was . . . he was here . . . in the house. Downstairs. He grabbed me . . . from behind—did you see him?"

"Did *you* see him?"

Alex shook her head vigorously.

"Any part of him? A piece of his clothing? His shoes?"

"Nothing. It was dark. The lights went out. He grabbed me from behind."

"Okay, he grabs you, he's got a hold of you—is there anything you can tell me about him?"

"No."

"Nothing?" he asked, glaring at her again.

"He was tall, strong, and he had an erection. All right?" she said in exasperation. "Does that help?"

Justin turned sharply, putting his back to her. "How'd he get in. Did you leave the doors unlocked?"

"I'm not that stupid."

"Well how, then?"

"I don't know *how* he got in. Isn't that your department? Or am I in charge of that detail?"

"Damn you, Alex, this is no time for your sarcastic remarks."

Why was he doing this to her? She began to cry.

"Shit." His hand moved to touch her, but halted in midair before dropping back to his side.

Alex heard sirens. Red and blue lights whirled above the house on the top of the bluff.

"Okay, pull yourself together while I talk to them."

"And with those comforting words . . ." she said under her breath as she tried to control herself.

He lifted the gun from his belt, put it on the table beside her, and headed toward the front door.

She took a sip of brandy and rose to pace the room. The small oval mirror on the wall between the living room and dining room caught her reflection. She moved closer to it and examined her face. Mascara tear tracks ran down to her throat. Her hair, knotted on top of her head, escaped in wispy strands. There were chafe marks across the lower half of her face. A white, bloodless scratch marred her right cheek.

She pulled a Kleenex from the box on the breakfast counter, returned to the mirror, then roughly removed the mascara streaks. Pulling the pins from her hair, she shook her head until her hair fell to her shoulders.

The brandy, on her empty stomach, was already going to her head. In addition to being frightened and shocked, she was angry. That sonofabitch, she cried inwardly, staring at the wreck in the mirror

260

before her. She was going to get another gun if she had to steal one. And she'd carry it with her everywhere. He'd never get that close to her again.

"Why!" she cried, hurling the glass at the mirror. Both glass and mirror shattered with a deafening crash.

Justin was up the stairs in an instant, his eyes wide and questioning as he looked at her and then at the broken glass. Neither of them spoke.

She began to pick up the broken pieces. He took a shard of glass from one hand and shook her other hand at the wrist until she let what she held drop to the small table. Still holding her wrist, he led her back to the chair.

"Now tell me the rest."

"Where are the police?"

"They're looking for him."

"Don't they want to talk to me?"

"I'm talking to you. Talk."

She sighed. "He dragged me to the bedroom. I couldn't breathe. He fell on top of me. That's when I . . . I stabbed him."

"Then what happened?"

"He ran away."

"Did he say anything to you? Christ, Alex," he said harshly, "give me something to work with."

"Stop it." She looked up at him. "Stop it, damn you. Maybe you don't care for me personally, but — and correct me if I'm wrong, Sergeant — aren't we supposed to be on the same team?" They stared at each other. "Well, *aren't we?*"

He ran a hand through his hair and squatted down in front of her, being careful not to touch her. His voice softened as he said, "I'm sorry."

She crossed her arms over her chest, trying to

control her shivering body, tilted back her head, and stared at the ceiling. "I was so scared."

"I know," Justin said quietly, finally reaching out to touch her consolingly. His hand moved slowly up and down her thigh. "I know. But he's gone now."

"He'll be back." Tonight? Tomorrow? Who knows when? That was part of the game: to keep her guessing, to keep her scared; to make her crazy. She thought grimly, He will be back.

"Was his voice the same as the voice on the phone?"

"Yes."

"What did he say?"

"It's all such a jumble." She tilted her head back again, closed her eyes, and tried to think. "He said I would pay—"

"Pay? Pay for what?"

Alex squeezed her eyes together tightly, trying to bring his words back. " 'You'll pay. You'll pay . . .' " She opened her eyes and blurted out, " '. . . Because of the two of you my life was a living hell!' " Justin stared at her silently. "For a few moments, in the hallway, I felt certain it was my father. Now I'm not so sure. If I can just sort everything out—what's the matter with you? Why are you staring at me like that?"

"How did he get in?"

"What difference does it make now? If I can—"

"It makes a helluva lot of difference. He definitely did not force his way in."

She glared at him in astonishment. "You don't believe me. You think I'm lying to you." She shook her head ruefully. "Oh, my God."

"Alex, I believe you. You look like you just wrestled a gorilla." He touched her cheek near the

262

scratch.

"Not a gorilla. Not a ghost. A man. A living, breathing man. I could feel him, smell him, even taste the sweat on his hand."

"Jesus, how did he get in?" Justin asked the blackness beyond the window.

"I don't know." She was losing patience with his one-track line of questioning. "I sure as hell didn't give him a key to the house and invite him over for a rollicking evening of rape and mayhem."

"Key." Justin rose to his feet. "You had the locks changed after the initial break-in, right?"

She nodded.

"Then he comes in again, but this time through the bedroom slider." He paced to the breakfast counter then slammed his fist down hard on the tiles. "What a goddamned idiot I am. How many keys do you have to that door." He jerked his thumb in the direction of the front door.

"I keep a set there." She pointed to a fuzzy key ring on the table below the broken mirror. She rose from the chair and strode to the key holder on the wall in the kitchen. "There was another one on this rack." She fumbled through the keys. "It's not here. That lunatic has a key to my house."

"Okay, okay, let me think. He took the key when he broke in through the slider. He's had it for several days, and he waited until tonight to use it. Why? Probably because Wednesday night you went to Ott's. And Thursday night I was here—for a while anyway."

A shudder went through her. Barely above a whisper, Alex said, "He's had a key since the first break-in. And he's been coming and going at will."

"But you had the locks changed."

263

"Different locks, different keys. But he's been here."

"Explain."

"Things broken and out of place. Thuds in the night. The fire in the kitchen."

"Then I'd say he's had it longer than that. He broke the window to make it look like a forced entry. He could have come through that small pane, but I doubt if he did. Did you notice anything out of the ordinary before that night?"

Alex paused to think. *"Yes.* Hawkins said he put the bedroom window screen back on. A day or two before the first break-in he found it lying on the ground. It'd been hot that week. I must have left the windows open."

Justin nodded slowly.

"What made you come tonight?" Alex asked softly.

He lifted the gun from the table and held it out to her. "For you. Can you shoot it? Do you know anything about firearms?"

"Joe taught me." She took the gun. "Won't you get into trouble, giving me this?"

He shrugged. "I'm leaving the force in January, so I guess it doesn't matter. Now that we've established how he got into the house, tell me again what he said. What was that about your making his life a living hell?"

The more Alex thought about it the more she persuaded herself that what she had heard was nothing more than the rantings of a madman. For her to have committed an act against anyone so horrendous, so unforgivable that person would want to kill her was inconceivable. The man was obviously crazy. "He said a lot of off-the-wall stuff.

264

Probably meant nothing."

"No, he was trying to tell you something. Think about it."

She chewed on her lower lip. "He said I would have to pay for the *both* of us."

"Any idea who he meant?"

"My mother, I think," she said quietly, seeing again the spittle covering the face in the picture.

"Because she ran off and left him?"

Alex looked up at him, surprised. She nodded. "We're back to my father again, aren't we?"

"Do you have any of his personal papers?"

Alex nodded.

Minutes later, from a shelf in the garage, Justin helped her take down a carton labeled Bently—Desk Contents. He carried it upstairs, set it on the floor in front of the couch.

"This stuff was in my father's desk. Joe cleaned it out and put it in the garage. I never looked at any of it."

"Why?"

"I was afraid of what I'd find."

Alex sat on the floor. From the stack of papers at her knee she lifted an official-looking document. She found herself reading it twice before she could comprehend its meaning. Then she read it a third time.

Justin came into the room, carrying two cups. "I put all that crap in your coffee. Sweet'n Low, Cremora. You suffering from a synthetic deficiency?" He looked at Alex's face. "What is it? What did you find?"

"My father adopted my sister."

He stared at her curiously.

"I didn't know that," she said. "I thought she was his natural daughter. According to this, her surname, before my father gave her his name, was Hunter—my mother's maiden name. Lora was illegitimate."

"How old was she when he adopted her?"

"Two. My parents were married in March of that same year."

"Do you think she knew?"

"I don't think so."

"When was the last time you saw her?"

"When she was seventeen she ran away from home. We never heard from her again."

Alex picked up a batch of letters held together by a rubber band. The band, rotten, sticky, fell away.

She felt the blood leave her face. Her hands began to tremble.

There were ten letters in all. Seven of them had been addressed to her father. The other three had been addressed to her. All were from Lora.

Justin sat on the floor watching Alex's face as she read each letter. When she finished she looked up, stared vacantly out the window, then sighed.

Justin leaned forward.

"It seems my sister got pregnant when she was seventeen. My father turned her out. Disowned her. In these letters she begged him to let her come home and bring her baby with her. She also wrote to me. He managed to intercept and read my letters. Listen to this." Alex lifted a letter to the light. " 'Little sister, you're the only chance I have now. We can't come home unless Dad comes for us. Something very scary happens to me when I try to leave this house. It feels like I'm going to die. Alex, I'm sick. I think I'm going crazy. I have no one to talk to except the baby. Please, only you can make Dad bring us home.' "

Alex looked at Justin. Her expression quizzical. "How could he be so cruel? Even if she wasn't his real daughter, he raised her as his own.

"When she disappeared, he said it was no great loss since she was just like our mother. He would say over and over how Lora cared nothing for the people who loved her. That she thought only of herself. And I believed him."

Justin picked up the top envelope. "Lora Bently, Haller, Oregon. May I use your phone?"

She nodded.

He went to the kitchen extension. Alex sorted through the rest of the papers as Justin talked on the phone. When he returned, she was putting the papers back into the box.

"If your sister still lives in Haller, the local police will find her. We should hear something by morning."

Alex rose. "I could use another drink. How about you?"

"I'm fine, thanks," Justin said, following her into the kitchen. He leaned against the wall. "Did he hurt you?"

"I'm not sure." She rubbed her right hip where it had hit the night-stand.

He crossed to her. "What is it?" Without waiting for an answer, he knelt down and pulled up her denim skirt.

"What are you doing?" She tried to push her skirt down, instinctively looking to the windows.

"This is no time to be modest." He struggled to peel her pantyhose down below the bruised area. "I'd like to get my hands on the guy who invented

267

these damned things. Lift your foot so I can take your shoes off."

He slipped off her shoes and the pantyhose followed. His fingers tenderly touched the red puffy area below her hipbone.

"Stay here. I'll get ice for that. It won't help the discoloring, but it might keep the swelling down."

He put a handful of ice cubes in a dish towel. Alex shivered when the cold pack touched her skin.

The doorbell rang.

He handed her the ice pack. "Keep this on for another few minutes."

He went down to the front door.

Moving into the dining room, Alex leaned against the wall with the ice at her hip, and caught bits and pieces of conversation as it drifted up to her. ". . . no sight of him? . . . probably won't come back tonight . . . eyes open anyway . . . be right here if you see anything . . ."

She went limp with relief. He was going to stay with her. She wouldn't be alone. Not even a loaded gun could make her feel safe tonight. When he returned, she was back in the kitchen retrieving her shoes and hose.

"You look tired," he said. "Why don't you go on to bed?"

"What about you?"

"I'll be okay."

Going down the stairs, she could feel his gaze on her. Turning at the bottom, she looked up at him. "Thank you for staying."

He ran a hand through his hair, but said nothing.

She stared at him a moment longer, then continued on to her room.

268

As she undressed by the light from the foyer, she heard him talking upstairs. Holding her robe in front of her, she walked to the open door and called up, "Are you talking to me?"

"I asked if you wanted your cat inside," he called back. "He's on the deck."

"Yes. Thanks."

Silence.

"Good night," she said.

" 'Night."

She leaned against the doorjamb, thinking—not about the nightmare that had taken place earlier in the hall, that was something that had to wait for light of day. She thought about Justin. Upstairs keeping vigil.

Justin suddenly appeared at the bottom of the stairs. A startled look crossed his face when he saw Alex leaning against the doorjamb.

"The light." He pointed to the chandelier.

Pulling the robe up to cover herself, she put a hand to the switch. "I can get it from here."

He stared at her for several moments as though he wanted to say something. Finally he nodded, turned, and headed back up. Waiting until she was sure he was off the stairway, Alex turned off the light.

She took a hot shower, roughly scrubbing her body with the back brush until it stung. Then she wearily climbed into bed.

When she closed her eyes a torrent of memories rushed at her. Everything she remembered about her sister, the way she had looked, talked, laughed—the things they had done together—all came back vividly, as though days, and not decades, had passed. She prayed for her sister and then she

269

cried herself to sleep.

Sometime in the night Alex opened her eyes to see Justin, wearing nothing but his slacks, silhouetted in the doorway to her room. She had been dreaming about him. In the dream he'd told her he loved her. She'd wanted to tell him she loved him as well, but each time she'd opened her mouth to speak, her father's face appeared in place of Justin's.

Fully awake now, she softly called out his name.

He turned and slowly walked away.

As if drawn along by an alluring magnetic force, Alex left her bed, put on her robe, and went upstairs. Although the house was dark, she could clearly see him standing at the windows, hands in his pockets, looking out toward the casino lights.

As she crossed the thick carpet to him, she wondered if what she felt for him was some mad obsession. He had begun to invade not only her every waking moment, but her dreams as well. Her attraction to him could not be anything more than a superficial infatuation. She was thirty-eight years old. Too old to love for the first time. And how, she wondered grimly, could she have fallen for someone who was incapable of returning her love?

All those thoughts racing through her mind dissolved as she stopped behind him. There was no stopping now. She was burning up with anticipation and longing. With a feathery lightness her hands moved over his naked shoulders.

Justin turned slowly, hands still in his pockets, and looked at her questioningly. She rose on tiptoe, leaned in, tilted her head upward, and kissed the corner of his mouth. She pressed her lips to his eyelids, first one, then the other. Her tongue slowly traced the separation of his lips as her hands roved

270

over his chest, thumbs playing over the nipples. One hand tracked lightly down his chest, across his stomach to the front of his pants. Through the cloth she felt him growing against the palm of her hand, heard him suck in his breath. She stroked him, kissed his sedate lips, teased his nipple.

"If you keep this up," he said in a low, husky voice, "I'm going to have to rape you right here and now."

"Uh-huh." She put her lips to his ear. "Lie to me. Tell me I mean something to you. Tell me you're not just out for a good time."

"Is that what you thought?"

"Tell me."

"You mean something to me," he said quietly. "You mean a lot to me."

"Yes. You're a good liar."

"I don't lie."

"I didn't lie to you."

"It doesn't matter."

"Yes. It does."

"Then I believe you."

She dotted his lips with light kisses.

"I won't use you, Alex."

He started to pull his hands from his pockets. She held them in place.

"I know you won't," she said, dropping her robe to the floor. She reached for his belt buckle. "Because tonight, *I'm* going to use *you*."

They kissed long and eagerly. Alex lowered herself to the floor, bringing him down with her. She made love to him, passionately, almost desperately, with no thoughts other than those of the moment.

Chapter 17

A hand caressed her back. Warm breath moved against her ear, a whisper, "Alex, wake up."

She opened her eyes. In the gray light of dawn, Justin, fully dressed, was sitting on the edge of the bed, leaning over her.

"Humm? Something wrong?"

"I have to leave. I want you up and dressed."

"What time is it?"

"Almost six."

"Ohhh," she groaned, rubbing her eyes. "You are definitely an early riser."

He lifted the robe from the foot of the bed and handed it to her.

Sliding her legs out of bed, she gasped when her hips pressed against the mattress.

"Hurts now, huh?" He pulled back the sheet, crouched down and studied the purple bruise. "It looks bad."

"I'll survive. I've had worse skiing."

His hand rested on her hip. His eyes moved slowly up her body to her face. "The locksmith has come and gone. New keys on the kitchen counter."

"A locksmith in the middle of the night?"

He chuckled. "It's a twenty-four-hour town. I made coffee. That should perk you up."

"It'll take more than coffee to get me moving this

morning."

"Oh yeah?" His hand moved up her thigh.

She smiled. "I thought you had to leave?"

He sighed. "I do. Get dressed."

She went into the bathroom, washed her face, brushed her teeth, then returned to the bedroom.

Justin was stretched out on the bed, head propped up on one hand, smiling.

"What are you grinning about?" she asked.

"Y'know, you don't look half-bad in the morning."

"I'm too sleepy to fight with you."

"Some women are downright spooky. And y'know what else? You don't look half-bad naked." He dodged the rolled-up socks she threw at his head.

"Where are you going so early?"

"The station. Paperwork. Looks like I'll need a warrant to search Thelma Klump's house. She refused to allow the investigative team in last night."

"Anything about my sister?"

"Not yet. I'll make a few calls myself. Hurry, I'm taking you to your friend Margie's house."

"Margie and her family are sleeping under an island moon right now. It's three-thirty in Maui." She stepped into her panties.

"Then you'll have to come to the station with me."

"Sounds exciting, but I think I'll pass. I'll be okay for an hour." She reached behind her and hooked her bra.

He opened his mouth to protest.

"Really, Justin, I'll be all right. I have the gun."

He sighed. "Okay, but lock up. Don't answer the door to anyone, understand. Stay inside."

She smiled, nodded.

"C'mere a minute."

She finished pulling her head through the frayed

neckline of an old sweatshirt and moved toward him, lowering the shirt over her breasts as she walked.

He swung his legs over the edge of the bed, pulled her in between his knees, then lifted her sweatshirt. As he kissed her midsection he said, "Get naked again."

"I thought you were in a hurry to get to the station?"

"It's too damn early to go out."

She knelt down in front of him. With his hands holding her face, he kissed her. Kissing, she mused, was definitely one of his strong points.

As he kissed her, he lifted the sweatshirt and pulled it over her head.

Thirty minutes later Alex watched Justin drive away. A patrol car pulled up the driveway and parked near the house. A lone policeman remained in the car. Justin, she realized, had assigned her police protection.

Klump knocked again. After several long moments she slid the duplicate key into the lock, turned it, and opened the door. She looked in and called his name.

The bed was unmade, though she knew he hadn't slept in it the night before. He hadn't returned to the house at all. The cops had come around midnight, tromping through her ice plant and azaleas, wanting to come inside and have a look around. She had exercised her legal right to turn them away.

She was sorry now that she had taken the tall stranger in. From the day she had lied to the sergeant about living alone, she had been guilty of

274

aiding and abetting a criminal. She realized she could be held accountable, as an accomplice possibly, for his actions. He had assaulted her neighbor. That was serious. Very serious.

There was only one thing to do, she reasoned. Get the goods on him. Go to the cops with something substantial before they had a chance to get back to her with a warrant. She'd say he had threatened to harm her—kill her; had kept her a virtual prisoner in her own house. What was a poor helpless woman to do?

She crossed the room to the bureau, reached for the radio and paused when she saw the painting on the floor. It faced the wall. Klump stooped and turned it around.

A nude painting. The figure was of a woman in a three-quarter view, face turned away, hands holding long, dark hair atop her head. It had been painted by the hussy herself—Alexandra Carlson. Klump grunted. Although the face was not visible, she was certain the body had been modeled from the artist's. It was no wonder the man living in the basement was after her. Decadence begot decadence. She positioned the painting the exact way she had found it.

She started to go back to the radio, eager to read the papers tucked inside the cavity, when something under the rumpled bedclothes caught her eye. She stiffened. Someone was in the bed. No. Impossible, she told herself. There was no mound, just crumpled covers. She flung back the blanket. On the dingy sheet, looking like a squashed animal, lay a gray wig. It was similar to the one she was wearing. Similar to the ones she kept in the hatbox on her closet shelf.

With a rigid forefinger, she flipped it over. The Tress House label in the netting told her the wig was hers.

Why that sonofabitch, she thought. Not only had he gone back on his word about hurting the Carlson woman, he had used her wig—no doubt in an effort to implicate her. "Well," she said aloud, "we'll just see who implicates whom."

Feeling anger now, she took down the radio and, no longer concerned with being careful, yanked off the backing, threw it down, and pulled out the thick sheath of papers. Sitting on the bed, she began to read.

He worked quickly. Sitting on the floor of Klump's storage shed, he pulled a length of fishing line from the spool and snapped it off with his teeth. He made a cinch knot, worked it over the sparrow's head, and pulled it tight. He opened the shed door a crack and tossed the bird out. It landed directly beneath the bird feeder.

He crouched on the balls of his feet, waiting. He didn't have long to wait.

The black cat moved in with an inherent stealth, wary of the woman with the pellet gun who had already taken several off-the-mark potshots at him. His body was low, his tail twitching, his eyes luminous.

The man in the shed jerked the line. The bird seemed to leap through the air to land inches from the shed door.

The tomcat stopped dead in his tracks. He opened his mouth and made strange clicking sounds. He advanced. Stopped. Clicked. Advanced again. Just before he pounced on the dead sparrow, the cat's rump wriggled from side to side.

While waiting for Justin to return, Alex kept herself busy by writing in her diary. The month of October had begun with routine daily trivia. It now went beyond that. The events she entered in the log were macabre and far too eventful. She could write a book. With goosebumps rising along her arms, she brought to mind the attack in the hallway and wrote it down.

Alex heard a light thump. It came from the direction of the redwood deck. She paused, listening. A succession of soft snorts followed. Picking up the gun, she rose and walked to the slider.

Blackie was on his side under the patio table. The cat was kicking his hind paws at his throat. "Blackie?" Alex slid open the door.

Frantically now, the cat continued to kick. As Alex stepped out she heard a gagging sound. *My God, he's choking!*

Running to the table, she knelt, dropped the gun, reached for him. The needle-sharp claws raked painfully across her hand. The gagging sound changed to a wheezy cough.

She tried to grab Blackie's back legs to keep his claws from ripping into her arms and hands. On his back now, the cat thrashed wildly, eyes wide and terrified, tongue protruding from the side of his mouth. The horrible wheezing noise became a whistling hiss.

In Alex's panicky state she could have sworn her cat was being attacked by a bird—a small sparrow. The bird was bouncing up and down on his chest. Alex grabbed the bird and tugged as claws tore into her wrist. The sparrow, she realized, was tied, by its neck, to Blackie's neck with clear fishing line.

277

"Oooh, Blackie, stay, kitty, stay," Alex whispered hoarsely as she tore into the house, grabbed the scissors from a drawer, and ran back to the thrashing cat. Sticking her finger along the back of his neck, she found the line and cut it, fur and all.

Blackie leaped to his feet, shook his head, coughed, and shook his head again. Alex gently picked him up. She hugged him to her.

Klump had read the legal documents and was well into the scribblings of what she assumed was a journal. She felt the skin on the back of her scalp tighten. Most of what she had read was bizarre and without reason. And what she understood made her insides crawl.

She sensed a presence in the room. She turned her head toward the door. The scream that tore into her eardrums could have come straight out of the journal—straight out of hell. It froze her. Anchored her to the mattress. It came at her like an avalanche. A powerful blow wracked her shoulder. Another pounded the back of her head, jarring her brain stem. Driven to the floor by one blow upon another, she clutched at the wig, holding it desperately to her head. The man's face frightened her more than the fists that rained down on her.

It was inhuman.

Alex hugged Blackie to her until he squeaked out a weak meow and fidgeted to be let loose. Then she put him down and watched as he ran across the deck and jumped onto the rail before leaping to the roof and disappearing.

Alex spun around, glaring up at the house on the hill. "You bitch," she said between clenched teeth. "You crazy, evil bitch!"

She snatched up the fishing line with the dead bird and ran, tripping and almost falling twice, down the wooden staircase to the yard below. She ran across the lawn to the sagebrush incline and started to climb in the direction of Thelma Klump's house. Halfway up the hill, her breath coming in ragged spurts, she heard shouting from below. She looked down to see the policeman running across her backyard, shouting at her to stop.

What am I doing? she asked herself. Running off half-cocked—without the gun—exactly as Justin had told her not to do.

She looked up at the house, threw the bird as far as she could throw it and screamed, "You stupid bitch!"

In anger and frustration, Alex was about to start back down when she noticed wisps of smoke curling skyward.

Black smoke and flames.

The house was on fire.

Turning to the policeman, she shouted, "Call the fire department!" She pointed at Klump's house. "It's on fire! Her house is on fire!" She watched the policeman turn and run back toward his squad car. Then, her heart in her throat, she scrambled upward, slipping and sliding on the loose soil.

Reaching the top of the ridge, Alex stopped, and gasping, trying to catch her breath, she stared in morbid fascination at the burning house.

Flames and smoke rose from the roof. She heard the sound of breaking glass as a window at the side of the house blew outward. Was Klump still inside?

"Thelma! Thelma! Where are you?!" Alex ran to the back of the house. There, on the other side of the window, wide-eyed from terror and shock, clawing frantically at the glass, was Klump, covered with blood and fighting for her life.

Alex pulled up short, frightened by the manic look on the woman's face. Klump's mouth, gaping open, was pressed against the window, like a wet suction cup, her cheeks puffing in and out as she tried to suck air from the glass.

Alex moved then. She ran the few steps to the window, put her palms to the warm sash and pushed. She cried out in frustration. It was locked.

Klump pulled away from the window, her mouth leaving a foggy disk of condensation on the glass, and slid, still clawing, out of sight.

She's dying, Alex thought, she's dying before my eyes.

Around the corner of the house was a set of French doors. As Alex ran to them, she glanced down the hill to see the policeman, now joined by Justin, running across her lawn to the rocky incline. There was no time to wait for them, she thought, no time at all.

Shaking the doors violently, she looked around for something to break the glass. She reached down, grabbed the garden hose and swinging it with all her might, smashed the glass with the metal spout. The heat hit her like a blast from a blowtorch, sending her back several feet. Putting her forearm across her face, she stumbled forward, reached through the broken pane and unlocked the door. Shoulder to the door, she pushed against it. Taking a deep breath, she rushed inside, heading in the direction of the window where Klump had been. It was impossible to see through the dense smoke, and she hoped she would find the old woman before her air ran out. Something caught her foot and she went over. Alex grabbed hold of the first thing her fingers touched—hair—and pulled. The hair came free and angled limply from her fingers.

Alex threw down the wig and reached for Klump again. This time her fingers gripped real hair, oily and drenched with sweat and blood.

She dragged the unconscious woman across the room, through the door, across the patio—gasping fresh air. Over the lawn, and would have kept going until she collapsed if hands had not disengaged her fingers from Klump's hair and pulled her away.

"Alex, stop. She's safe. You got her out," Justin Holmes said, holding her tight. "Easy, honey, easy."

"Her house . . . her house . . . on fire." Alex doubled over, then sank to the ground.

Justin sat beside her, put an arm around her. "Fire engines are coming now. Ambulance too. Hear them?"

"Thelma?!" Alex looked around to see the policeman hunched over, giving mouth-to-mouth resuscitation to Klump. "Dead?"

"No. Listen."

Alex listened. She heard coughing, moaning.

"She's alive."

Alex winced as she shifted on the couch.

Fifteen hours had passed since she had pulled Thelma Klump from the burning house. Justin had taken her to the hospital as soon as the ambulance had driven away with Klump. In the emergency room a doctor had cleaned the cat scratches, put three stitches in the back of her hand where broken glass had sliced through it, and had then given her a tetanus shot—by far the most painful of the three—in the left hip. They had stayed at the hospital most of the day, hoping to talk to Klump who, drifting in and out of consciousness, was the only one with knowledge of her attacker. At seven o'clock they had given up and left.

Back at Alex's house, Justin had drawn her a steamy bath in which he'd placed some Epsom salts. She had soaked for almost an hour, adding more hot water as it cooled. It was Justin who cooked dinner.

Now, her hair drying in the heat of the firepit, wrapped in the white kimono, Alex sipped brandy-laced coffee and watched Justin as he talked on the phone.

He hung up and motioned her to join him on the couch. When she sat he lifted her hand and squeezed it.

"There's nothing to indicate that your sister ever lived in Haller, Oregon. It's a small rural town. Less than a thousand people. Those letters are twenty years old. She may have come and gone without so much as a stir in the community. Yet, if she looked anything like you, folks would surely remember.

Alex felt a deep sense of disappointment. "We looked alike."

"We're checking the neighboring communities too."

"Did you find anything at Thelma's?"

"He was living in a room in the basement," Justin said. "That's where the fire was set. We found the pistols and the shotgun, what was left of them.

Klump managed to get out and make it as far as the window in the dining room. If there was anything in his room to tell us who he was, the fire got it."

"Thelma knows."

"Yeah, she knows."

Justin picked up the phone again, dialed. He placed Alex's hand on his thigh, his hand over hers. Speaking into the phone, he asked for Dr. Jacobs, waited, then said, "Yes, Doctor, Detective Holmes here. Has Thelma Klump regained consciousness yet? . . . It's imperative I talk with her . . . Yes, I understand . . . Whatever time you say . . . We'll be there, thank you." He replaced the receiver, turned to Alex. "She's conscious and asking to speak to you. But the doctor says he won't permit it until tomorrow morning."

Alex nodded.

"How's the hand feel?" He lifted her hand and kissed the crisscross network of cat scratches along her arm.

"Feels okay."

"How's this feel?" He ran a hand over her hip, where she'd had the shot.

"Hurts like hell."

"I'm sorry." He pulled her around to lie across his lap. One hand stroked her face, the other rested on her hip. In a soft voice he said slowly. "One night, a million years ago, I held you in my arms just like I'm holding you now. You were wearing a kimono like this one. I watched you sleep. Your lips were swollen from crying. Through the opening in your kimono I watched your breasts swell with each breath. I thought you were the most desirable woman I'd ever seen. My need to kiss you, to touch

283

you, was overwhelming. I slid my hand inside your kimono and cupped your breast. I kissed your mouth. You . . ."

Alex put a finger to Justin's lips to silence him. She took his hand and slid it inside the kimono to her breast. Looking into his eyes, she arched her back and raised up, her lips lightly touching his. They kissed, tentatively at first, then with an urgency they both knew would stir and abate many times before the night was over.

Chapter 18

Thelma Klump had suffered multiple contusions, a fractured skull, acute smoke inhalation, and second-degree burns to both hands. Considering her age and the circumstances surrounding the trauma, the doctors gave her less than a thirty percent chance of recovery.

Wearing a plain white cotton hospital gown, her head covered in bandages, Klump looked frail and very old. The once fierce eyes now stared at Justin with a watery placidness. Justin leaned over her. "Who is he? What's his name?"

"Will . . . Will Bently." Her voice, affected by the smoke in her lungs, sounded like crackling cellophane.

Alex stiffened. "William Bently? Are you sure?"

Klump nodded.

Alex squeezed Justin's arm. "My father."

"How did he get around? Did he drive your car?"

"Motorcycle. Kept in shed."

"Miss Klump, can you tell us anything about him? Where he comes from? Why he was after Alex? Anything?"

Her eyes widened, became frightened. She looked at Alex. "Careful. Be careful. Fire. Monsters. Crazy . . ."

"What else?" Justin asked. "Please, help us."

285

"Westgate." She cleared her throat. It sounded like dry leaves being crunched underfoot. "Dr. Penn . . . Pennburg."

"Dr. Pennburg and a place called Westgate? Is that correct?"

She nodded, looking again to Alex.

"Can you describe him?" Justin asked.

Klump lifted a bandaged hand and pointed to a glass of ice water on the night stand.

Justin looked to the nurse standing in the corner. The nurse stepped to the bed, lifted the glass with the flex-straw, and put it to Klump's lips.

Klump sipped, coughed, then whispered, "Scars."

"Scars?"

"Face . . . hands."

"What kind of scars? Burns? Cuts? What?"

She nodded.

"How old is he?"

Klump closed her eyes.

The nurse reached a hand to the bandaged wrist, took a pulse. "She's about done in. Maybe tomorrow . . ."

Klump opened her eyes and rolled her head from side to side. She coughed. Pain distorted her face. Reaching out a hand, she looked beseechingly at Alex.

Alex laid a hand on Klump's shoulder. "I know we've had our differences, Thelma," Alex said quietly. "But I don't believe you really wanted him to hurt me."

"No," Klump whispered. "So shamed . . . I . . . you saved my . . . life . . ."

"You would have done the same for me."

The woman closed her eyes again and turned her head away.

286

Thelma Klump died one hour later.

"Westgate is a private asylum in Portland, Oregon. And Pennburg turns out to be a Dr. Penndulbury, a psychiatrist," Justin told Alex after hanging up the telephone.

Kneeling on the floor in her art alcove, she was fitting a painted canvas into a frame. She looked up at Justin. "Then he *is* crazy."

"Looks that way." He left the bed and came to her. Dropping to his knees, he took the screwdriver from her hand and finished screwing on the clamps. "You heard Klump's description of him. Do you recall ever seeing anyone with scars on his hands and face?"

"I've been racking my brain. But, no, no one." She handed him two screw eyes and a length of picture wire. "The name William Bently. My father. Lora. Oregon. The lapse of years. It's all tied together some way. Justin, what if my father survived the accident on the boat, but from a blow to the head or something got amnesia? That could explain the need for a psychiatrist."

"Anything is possible, Alex."

"Suppose he just got his memory back after all those years. It's possible he thinks I betrayed him by marrying Joe. Now he's come after me."

Justin stopped twisting the picture wire and stared silently at Alex.

Alex laughed. "What is it about me that seems to attract sex fiends, degenerates, and crazies?"

"Are you saying I'm a crazy degenerate?"

"You're the sex fiend."

"And proud of it."

287

She turned serious again. "Justin, did you get any feedback from the town where Lora lived?"

"No, not yet. The county authorities are doing what they can to find her, but I can't wait while they dingdong around. I've got to go to Westgate. This Dr. Penndulbury should be returning my call any time. I doubt if he'll talk to me on the phone. I don't even know if he'll talk to me in person, but I've got to try."

"I'm going with you."

"We'll see."

Alex picked up the jar of screw eyes and the box of clamps. She rose, carried them to the supply shelf on the wall above her work table. "I'm going," she said. "It's not a matter for debate." As she stood on tiptoe to put away the framing supplies, she knocked over a coffee can of nails. Grabbing for the can, trying to keep hold of the jar and box in her other hand, she called out, "Justin, help! I can't let go here."

Justin came up behind her, but instead of helping her, he stood close to her. His hands cupped her hips, moved up and down, caressing.

"Jus, the nails."

His arms went around her waist, his body pressed against hers. He kissed the nape of her neck, her throat, her earlobe. His hands roved over her breasts. The snap on her jeans popped open, the zipper slowly came down. Alex made a few feeble protests. Then, passion rising, her breath quickening, she stopped struggling, closed her eyes and let herself feel—everything, just as Justin had taught her.

Justin's breathing became hoarse in her ear. His fingers hooked into the waistband of her jeans. He worked them down over her hips and legs as he kissed the curve of her lower back. Her panties came down next. Alex stepped out of them. Naked from the waist down, she sighed as the coarse denim of his Levi's rubbed against her soft flesh.

"You're wicked," she whispered, still stretching out to hold onto the supplies on the shelf.

"Ummm." He began to unbutton her shirt.

With a moan, Alex pulled her hands away from the shelf and, amid the clinking din of falling nails and clamps, she spun around in his arms, locking her body to his. As they kissed, he backed up toward the bed.

Dr. Penndulbury saw William Hunter to the door. It was five o'clock. Hunter was his second to last patient of the day. He was tired. It had been one of those days. Everyone had had an emergency. Everyone had been on the verge of hysteria. The only one who had been calm, who had seemed relatively normal, had been Hunter. A success story, Dr. Penndulbury thought. He wished they could all be that way.

Back at his desk, he pressed the intercom for Abigail Leger, his receptionist. "Mrs. Leger, send in Mr. Post."

"Yes, Doctor."

"Is that it? No more squeeze-ins?"

"That's it, thank the Lord. We both deserve a medal for getting through this day."

"I'll settle for a drink and a cigar."

"Oh, Doctor, there was a call from a Sergeant Holmes in Reno, Nevada."

"In regard to what? Did he say?"

"No, Doctor."

"I'll get back to him after I've seen Post." He started to hang up. "Oh, Mrs. Leger, bring in a new box of Kleenex, please."

"Are your parents living?" Alex asked, running her toes up and down along Justin's leg.

He adjusted the pillow, propped himself up, then pulled Alex back into his arms. "No. Both gone."

"I'm sorry."

"It happened a long time ago. They died together. Asphyxiation. We lived on a farm in a small community outside of Boise, Idaho. One night the pilot light on their gas furnace went out. They died in their sleep."

"Where were you?"

"San Francisco. College. The University of California. At the time I had three years of premed behind me."

"You wanted to be a doctor?"

"Not really. My father was a doctor and he wanted his only son to follow in his footsteps. After they died I realized I wasn't cut out for medicine, never had been, so I dropped out of school and moved to Reno."

"What made you decide on police work?"

"I guess I was influenced by the father of my college roommate. Tim's old man, Patrick O'Farrell, was the typical Bronx Irish cop. He was retired when I met him. Living in Sausalito. God, the tales that old man could tell around the kitchen table, never once repeating himself. I had a standing invitation to Sunday dinner at their house. I rarely missed a dinner." Justin smiled, letting his mind drift back in time.

"You said you were leaving the force in January, what will you do then?"

"Ranch."

"Like a cowboy?"

"Got myself a spread just outside o' town. Aim to poke some cows and buck some broncos."

"You're making that up."

"Nope."

"You don't look like a cowboy. Don't dress like a cowboy."

"You ain't seen me on the spread."

"And you sure as shootin' don't sound like a cowboy."

"Reckon I'll get the hang of it, by and by." He dropped the drawl. "Tell me about you."

"Well, I'm thirty-eight, divorced, with a son eighteen who—"

"I don't want vital statistics. I want to know about Alexandra Carlson. What does she like? What does she hate?"

"Well, let's see. She likes escargots, bubble baths, and having her back rubbed. She's afraid of grasshoppers, the dark, and crazy people out to do her in. She doesn't like bigots, anchovies, and football." She turned in his arms. "Justin Holmes . . . tell me about him?"

"He likes football, anchovies, and rubbing the back of a beautiful woman. He's afraid of bubble baths, a beautiful woman, and cop killers. He doesn't like the ballet, escargots, and crazy people out to do in that beautiful woman."

"Children?" she asked.

"A daughter. Her name is Casey. She's ten."

"Do you see her often?"

"Not as often as I'd like. She and her mother live in southern California."

Alex lightly pulled at the hair on his chest, curling it around her fingers. "How'd you get so good?"

"Good at what?"

"You know. . . ."

"For a woman who's absolutely decadent in bed, you have a problem saying what's on your mind."

"I'm a doer, not a talker. So how'd you get so good?"

He caressed a breast. "Have I told you that you have perfect breasts?"

She shook her head. "A little smallish, don't you think?"

He pretended to study each one with care. "You're right. I take it back, they're not perfect, they're incredibly small. Not even worth touching."

"They're not *that* small."

"They're just right. Now, do you want to talk, sleep or—"

The phone rang.

Alex sighed. She answered. Justin watched the muscles in her face tense. She handed the phone to Justin and mouthed the words, "Dr. Penndulbury."

Justin took the receiver. "Dr. Penndulbury, thank you for returning my call. I'll get right to the point. You have a patient by the name of William Bently. We believe Mr. Bently is involved in several criminal activities here in Washoe County. I need to talk to you as soon as possible."

There was a pause on the line, then, "I have no patient named Bently."

Justin felt the air go out of him. Had this one big lead turned out to be nothing? If so, where would he go from here?

"Can you describe the man?" Penndulbury asked.

"Scars."

"Tell me about these crimes, detective Holmes," the doctor said.

"But—"

"I have no patient named Bently. But I believe I know who you're speaking of."

Justin felt the air coming back. "Yes. Well, we'd like to question this man about an attack made early this morning on an elderly woman in Reno."

"Impossible. William was in my office today for his weekly session."

"He's there? In Oregon?"

"That's what I said."

"When? How long ago did you see him?"

"Not more than an hour ago."

"He's back then," Justin said more to himself. "Dr. Penndulbury, I'm flying to Portland. Can you meet with me tonight?"

Justin heard the doctor sigh. "I'm exhausted, Sergeant. Whatever you have to tell me—whatever I choose to divulge to you about my patient—can wait until morning. I'll see you in my office at eight."

"Until eight then." Justin hung up. He dialed O and asked the operator to put him through to the county police in Portland. After talking to a Sheriff Thompson, Justin called the airport and booked a single seat on the six-twenty flight.

"I'm going with you," Alex said when he hung up. "Call the airline back and book another seat."

"No. You're safer here. He's back there now. I don't want you in the same state with him."

"I'm not staying in this house alone, Justin. He's crazy. He just bludgeoned and torched an old

293

woman who took him in."

A chill bowled down Justin's spine. "You'll go somewhere else."

"Where?"

He paused before saying, "I don't believe I'm about to suggest this, but would you feel safe at Ott's place?"

"I don't want to involve Greg in this."

Justin was silent.

"It's not what you think," Alex said. "We're friends. That's all. We've never—Greg and I—well, we just never . . ."

"Are you saying the two of you have never been intimate?"

"Yes. That's what I'm trying to say."

"Then you were telling the truth about not being with him at his condo that night?"

"Yes," she said emphatically.

Justin pulled away from her and turned around to stare into her eyes. Like a jolt from a stun gun, it hit him. Someone had been there that night. He had seen him. Of course Ott had been the obvious choice. But he knew now that the man in the window could only have been Alex's tormentor. Klump's killer.

"I'm telling the truth," she said, drawing back, her voice rising in anger.

He grabbed her shoulders. "Oh, Alex," he said, suddenly crushing her to him. "He could have killed you that night. And I drove on by."

"What are you talking about."

"He was there. Smoking a cigarette at an upstairs window. I thought it was Ott—with you. I was mad, jealous. *Stupid!* I drove away thinking the worst."

Alex went limp against him. "I smelled smoke. I went upstairs. Greg came home. I left."

"Thank God."

"That was the day he listened in on the phone while Greg and I talked." She spoke slowly. "Greg told me where to find the house key. I was to feed his fish."

"He must have followed you there."

She nodded.

Justin felt sick when he realized what could have happened if Ott hadn't come home at that moment. If she had been attacked or killed, he would have been responsible.

"Don't blame yourself," she said, as though reading his mind. "I'm the one who ran off."

"I made you run away."

"I should have stayed. I wanted to."

They held each other without speaking. Justin stroked her back until he felt the taut muscles relax.

"My place," Justin said, out of the blue.

"Hmmm?"

"He doesn't know where I live," Justin said. "You'll be safe there."

"Alone?"

"I'll get someone to stay with you."

"Justin—"

"Please, Alex, do what I say for once, okay?"

She sighed deeply. "Okay."

That night, wrapped in Justin's arms, Alex dreamed of the monsters. They crawled up through the heater vents, oozed out through the electric sockets and surfaced through the drains. She let out an agonizing cry. Justin shook her awake. He held her tightly to him while she trembled.

When he felt she had gotten a grip on herself, Justin asked, "What was it? What did you dream?"

"I can't remember."

Justin waited. Then he said, "You kept saying, 'I don't believe in you . . . you're not real.' What's not real, Alex?"

"Monsters."

"What kind of monsters?"

"Whatever kind my mind can conjure up."

"I don't understand."

"It was a little game my father used to play, called 'Monsters in the night.' In order to keep Lora and me inside after dark, he'd tell us there were monsters hiding in the bushes, waiting for us to come out. Knowing it wasn't true didn't stop me from being afraid. I slept with a night light, yet the night terrors still got to me. It never fazed Lora, though. Late at night, after my father would go to bed, she'd sneak out of the house."

"What kind of a man *was* your father?"

"A man who had been hurt. An overprotective man." Her finger nervously traced a pattern on the sheet. "He lectured us constantly. Don't go in the street. Don't talk to strangers. Don't go near the water. Don't, don't, don't."

"I did the same with Casey. It's only natural to want to guard our kids against harm."

"But, you see, he reinforced his warning with facts—hard undeniable facts."

"Such as?"

"Every day he read to Lora and me from the newspaper. Tragic items. Whatever he came across, he never failed to pass along to us. If a picture happened to accompany the story, hey, all the better. Visual aids are so much more effective, don't you think?"

Justin remained silent.

"I remember, when I was five or six, he made us watch a TV newscast about a girl my age who'd been raped and murdered. Teenagers had found the mutilated body rolled up inside a feather mattress dumped in the woods. The story seemed to go on and on, day after day. For years I had nightmares about that little girl in the mattress."

She fell silent. Justin kissed her temple, held her snug in his arms.

She realized then that the room was completely dark. She had gone to sleep the past two nights without a night light. Justin had been the only security she had needed. Even now, after the nightmare, she felt safe and serene in his arms.

"Do you have a picture of your father?" Justin asked.

"In the hall."

"I'd like to take it with me tomorrow."

Chapter 19

Justin and Alex had driven the twelve miles from her house to his with only minimal conversation. It was five A.M. She was not a morning person.

Although it was still dark, Alex sensed the sky was roiling with storm clouds. Wind rocked the car. As they cleared the city limits and drove along a deserted country road, sand and bits of sagebrush snapped at the windows.

Justin went through the open gate onto his property. As the Corvette bumped along on the gravel driveway, Alex saw a white Volkswagen Rabbit parked at the east side of a one-story ranch house. A dark-haired woman paced behind the car.

"Good, Capucci's already here," Justin said.

"What did she say when you asked her to baby-sit a grown woman."

"She said, 'no problem.' Capucci takes her job seriously. Off duty as well as on."

Justin pulled in behind the Rabbit. Capucci walked back to meet them as they climbed from the car.

"Looks like a Tonapah Low coming in the back door," Capucci said, looking to the north, her hair whipping about her face. "That usually means trouble."

"Hurry, let's go in," Justin said, leaping up the

steps. He opened the front door and ushered the two women inside. "Thanks for coming, Bev. I owe you one."

"You owe me two, but who's counting."

"I'm going to grab a quick shower. Bev, would you mind fixing coffee?" Justin called out as he headed down the hall. "Make yourselves at home, both of you."

Alex followed Capucci into the kitchen. She watched as the other woman, seeming to know where everything was, busied herself making the coffee. And she walked around the kitchen, taking in the rustic decor of used brick, sandstone tile, and hammered copper. Finally she moved toward the dining room. Leaning against the doorway, she looked into the living room and the long hallway Justin had gone down.

It had been apparent to Alex the moment she'd walked into the house that it was a man's domain. Warm and comfortable, with heavy wood furniture and a lived-in look, the rooms were both messy and inviting. Plants flourished everywhere. No dinky knickknacks or frills, only functional accessories. Magazines and newspapers lay neatly stacked on the table in front of the couch and on the floor at the side of a large reclining chair. An apothecary jar, two-thirds full of unshelled sunflower seeds, sat on an oak table alongside the recliner. A pair of reading glasses leaned against the jar.

Over the running water Capucci said, "I remember now. Last week, Rockridge Drive. You're the one whose house was broken into. What was it the intruder did? Listen in on your extension?"

"That's right," Alex said without turning. "He also killed my cat. Attempted to kill my other cat.

Attacked me and then killed the woman whose house he was staying in."

Capucci shut off the water and stared down into the coffee pot. "Jus didn't tell me that."

"Guess he didn't have time. It's all happening very fast."

A few minutes later Justin came up to Alex. He silently pulled her into the dining room and, with his body, pressed her against the wall. He was dressed casually: slacks, sport shirt, and jacket. His hair was damp, and he smelled fresh and woodsy. He whispered in her ear, "If you get scared, don't hesitate to call the station. Ask for De Solo. He'll assist Capucci if you need him."

"We'll be all right," she whispered back as he kissed her temple, stroked her throat.

Capucci stepped into the dining room. "Coffee will be ready in— Oh, sorry," she said when she saw the two against the wall. She retreated into the kitchen.

"Reno PD checked out the shed at Klump's house. No motorcycle. They're out looking at the airport now. If it's there they'll stick close to see if he comes back for it. If he does, they'll have him." Justin kissed Alex long and sweet. "I've got to go." He backed up. "I'll call."

Alex nodded. She stayed where she was as Justin strode into the kitchen and said something to Capucci. A minute later she heard his pickup truck start up and pull away, tires crunching on the gravel drive. "Be careful, Justin," she said quietly to herself.

Dr. Clifton Penndulbury tapped a fingernail to

the tortoiseshell frame of his eyeglasses as he listened to Justin Holmes. Justin wondered if the doctor's distracting habit carried over into his therapy sessions. Penndulbury reminded him of Woody Allen. An aging, meatier Woody Allen without a shred of humor.

"You're certain the man you're after is a patient of mine?"

"Reasonably sure. I got his name, your name, and the name of this place from Thelma Klump before she died. The description she gave of her attacker was of a badly scarred man."

"I see." The doctor leaned forward, made a steeple with his fingers, and cleared his throat. "You realize, of course, Sergeant Holmes, I don't have to tell you anything that went on within these walls between my patient and me. Privileged information."

Justin nodded.

"It's common knowledge William Hunter—that's his name by the way—committed a crime ten years ago and was declared insane. You can get that information at the *Portland Star*. But you say he has allegedly committed a crime since his release?"

"Yes. And that was only to get to Mrs. Carlson. God only knows what he has in mind for *her*." Justin felt a wrenching in his stomach when he thought of Alex. Although she had tried to appear cool and calm, he'd sensed that she had been just short of terrified.

"Can you tell me why he was incarcerated? It might help to shed some light on his motive for wanting to hurt Mrs. Carlson." Justin stared at Penndulbury. "Hate, revenge, jealousy? What?"

"What's his relationship to this Alex Carlson?"

301

"I don't know. There's a possibility he could be her father."

"Impossible. Will is twenty-two—twenty-three at most."

Justin mulled that over. "The names of his parents?"

"Mother . . . Lora Hunter. Father unknown."

"Lora? Alex's sister. Christ. The *baby*," Justin said. "Then William Bently—Alex and Lora's father—is Hunter's grandfather."

"Appears so."

"Bently again. He's the connecting link. But how? Why?"

"How did this woman—Klump was it?—how did she die?"

"She was beaten and her house set on fire."

The doctor sighed. He rose, stepped to a file cabinet and pulled out a fat folder. "William Hunter was committed in 1977, at the age of twelve, for arson and matricide."

"Gin," Beverly Capucci said, laying down her cards. "That's a game. Play another?"

"Whose deal?" Alex said.

"You sure you want to play? Your mind doesn't seem to be on the game."

"I'll try not to make it so easy for you this time." Alex couldn't concentrate. She was bored stiff with the card game, yet there was nothing else to do. The wind, whipping the trees and blowing dirt across the pasture to the house, had knocked out the television reception.

"Stop fretting. Relax. Even if that goofball is in town, he's not going to find you out here. And if he did—a big *if*—I'm ready for him." Capucci patted the service revolver on the table.

"Maybe you ought to take it out of the holster."

"We'll play to a hundred again," Capucci said. "How about a nickel a point? Loser's points deducted from the winner's."

"Fine." Alex smiled inwardly. Capucci was no dummy. She knew a good tap when she saw one. Like money in the bank. But what the hell, Alex thought blithely, with something at stake, she might be able to get her mind on the game.

A soft thud against the house made both women jump. The gun was out of the holster and in Capucci's hand in a flash.

"What was that?" Alex whispered.

"I'll know in a minute." Capucci was on her feet, moving toward the kitchen with Alex close behind. On the wood siding by the back door she heard scratching.

Capucci went to the window and, keeping to the side of it, looked out, then down. "Come have a look," she said, lowering the gun.

Alex glanced down to see two huge tumbleweeds, meshed together, bouncing forward, rebounding, then advancing again. They looked as if they were trying to climb up the side of the house to the window.

"There's your intruder. Look out there." Capucci pointed to an open expanse of land thick with tumbleweed. "There's a heap more where they came from, and they'll be a headin' this a way. Invasion of the giant tumbleweeds. Makes your blood run cold, don't it?"

The telephone on the desk dinged. Penndulbury ignored it. He opened the file in front of him and silently read for several minutes. "Sergeant, let me begin by saying that we, the hospital staff here at Westgate, felt confident that Will was of sound mind. Rehabilitation complete. We wouldn't have released him otherwise."

"I'm not questioning your decision regarding his release, Doctor."

"He reports to me in person twice a month," Penndulbury went on as though Justin hadn't spoken. "He was here, sitting where you are sitting, yesterday between four and five."

"Then he's flying back and forth from Portland to Reno."

"Perhaps. I just know he reports to me every other Saturday. He'd committed one violent act as a child. Ten years later, we were as satisfied as anyone can be that he was able to differentiate between fantasy and fact. That he was cognizant of his act. Four years ago he finally came to terms with the nightmare of his mother's death."

"Nightmare . . ." The doctor leaned back in his chair, rocked lightly, and tapped at his glasses. "The horrors of the unconscious mind. Until three years ago, my patient was haunted by frequent, recurring nightmares. Violent, self-inflicted punishment resulted from his night journeys into hell."

"The scars on his face and hands that Klump mentioned, they were self-inflicted? His mother didn't beat—"

"No. To my knowledge his mother never raised a hand to him. He clawed and bit himself time and again. In the beginning of his incarceration, we found it necessary to restrain him a good part of the time—for his own safety."

"Why did he hate his mother?"

"On the contrary, Sergeant Holmes, he loved her. Will told me he loved her more than life itself. You see, she was all he had . . . and he was all she had.

"They lived on a farm twenty miles from Portland. In the twelve years they lived on Hanson's farm, the mother never left the house."

"Why?"

"My guess would be agoraphobia—fear of open spaces—complicated by the fear of being alone. Who's to say? The what ifs and maybes are not important. What we do know is for the first twelve years of her son's life she managed to imprison him in that house with her."

"How?"

"Simple. She passed her terror on to him. We now know that one can be controlled and made to do—to believe—anything, if one is conditioned long enough and thoroughly enough. Remember the Jonestown mass suicide?" Justin nodded. "She began to condition him as an infant. He lived in constant terror that some horrible thing or things beyond the confines of their house would one day devour him."

"What in God's name did she terrorize him with?"

"They had no radio or television, but she had at her disposal a wealth of reading material. There were enough books on reptiles, mythical monsters, and God's most formidable creatures to educate a little boy and feed his fear for many, many years."

Penndulbury shook his head slowly. "Monsters, dragons, I don't know what all. Only Will knows what horrors lived under his house."

"Incredible. But why kill the mother if he loved

her and she was all he had?"

"Ahhh, but *he* didn't kill her. In his mind the monsters did. His mother had told him that they couldn't get in. And that they would both be safe as long as they didn't go outside."

Justin's expression showed confusion.

"Somehow, after twelve years, the creatures found a way in. His mother was sick. Dying. She'd been abusing her body with alcohol for years. Drinking from guilt, perhaps, or fear that William would one day learn the truth. After all, the boy, though gullible, was very bright. He was also becoming a man."

"Mrs. Carlson seemed to think the man calling her was well educated."

"Will's education was rather well balanced. Each day his mother diligently put him through the three R's. The horror stories came at night."

"I'm having a hard time following you. She was all he had. She was dying. Instead of trying to help her, he finishes her off. Is that what you're saying?"

The doctor reached across his desk and took hold of a tape cassette. He held it up. "What you're about to hear is a seventeen-year-old, under hypnosis, reliving a most frightening experience."

Without another word Penndulbury slid the cartridge into the recorder. Activated it. Justin leaned forward, turned his ear to the hissing coming from the speaker. The doctor's voice issued forth.

"How old are you now, Will?"

"Twelve and a half." The voice was young. Prepubescent.

"Where are you?"

"Inside the house. Always inside the house."

"Yes, but where in the house?"

306

"In her room. In a corner. I'm scared."

"Why are you afraid?"

"Something bad . . . very bad is going to happen."

"Tell me everything you see and hear. Tell me everything as it happens."

"My tummy is growling."

"Are you hungry?"

"My tummy's hungry."

"How long have you been in the corner?"

"Three, maybe four days. I don't know anymore."

"Where is your mother?"

"She's calling to me from her bed. I don't want to go over there."

"Why?"

"Doesn't look like my mother. All puffy. Her skin's the color of . . . of chicken fat."

"Do you go to her?"

Pause. "Her hand feels hot . . . spongy. She's looking at the ceiling. Her mouth is opening and closing, but nothing comes out. I'm scared. I know if I look up at the ceiling I'll see that man."

"Which man is that?"

"The one in the hooded cape. The one with the skeleton fingers."

"What's happening now, Will?"

"Trying to talk to me. Can't hear her. Don't want to get too close. Stinks. She stinks . . . like rotten garbage."

"Will, try to hear what she is saying. Try very hard."

"She's saying Mr. Waincock will know what to do when he gets here. She says she loves me. She says she doesn't want me to hate her."

"Why would you hate her?"

After a long time the hissing from the recorder was replaced by a soft whiny voice. "She says she lied."

"About what?"

"About the house. The things living underneath. *Everything.*" Silence. Then, "She says he won't be coming for us now. She says he's dead. He's *dead.* Ohhhwww."

"Who's dead?"

A scream.

"What is it, Will? What do you see? What do you feel?"

"It's so bright." Another scream.

"Will?"

"Pain . . . in my eye. It hurts so bad. It hurts to see. Oh God, I don't want to see. I can hear them coming . . . coming for us."

"What? What's coming?"

"She said she lied about *them.* But she didn't lie. Can't she hear them? Can't she see them? How'd they get inside? Oh, oh God. No! Oh, Momma, Ooooh, no no no!"

Penndulbury switched off the recorder. "There's nothing more. Will had to be physically restrained then. At that point, in her room, while frantically trying to save his mother's life, he was actually killing her with his bare hands.

"Something finally snapped in the boy's head," the doctor went on. "After he beat and kicked his already dying mother to death, he set her on fire in her bed. The medical examiner reported finding over a hundred bites; savage, animalistic bites deep enough to be detected in what was left of the charred, shriveled flesh. Human bites."

Justin could only stare. He didn't trust himself to

speak. Somewhere in the state of Oregon was a madman. And that madman wanted Alex. His stomach knotted fiercely. If anything were to happen to her . . .

"In his apparent rage at his mother," Penndulbury said, closing the file, "he became one of the very creatures she had used to terrify and control him for all those years."

After a long pause Justin spoke. "Why did he set her on fire?"

"Fire was the only weapon he had. All creatures are afraid of fire. And though he would never confess to deliberately killing his mother, he did openly admit to torching the bed after she was dead. To kill the monsters."

"This is a private institution. Who paid for his care?"

"Lora Hunter's father."

"But he died when his grandson was only three or four."

"The money was drawn from a trust fund set up by Bently for William the day he was born. The trust was turned over to him on his release from Westgate."

"Why would Bently set up a trust fund for his grandson? I was under the impression he had disowned his daughter?"

"I know nothing about his association with his daughter and grandson."

"Did anyone visit the boy?"

"No family came to see Will. No one inquired about him — except Harley Waincock."

"Who is this Waincock?"

"He was the only person to go out to the farm. Owns the general store in Haller. He delivered groceries, mail-order items, liquor once a week to the Hunters. Ironically, Will works for Waincock now. And what's even more ironic is he lives on the farm again."

"Hunter went back to that house after what happened? After all those years of terror?"

"It's not unusual. He felt it imperative to his mental health that he meet the demons head-on. Stand up to them. Vanquish them once and for all."

"And what if he fails? What if they take control of him again? What if it's Alex they want this time?" Justin was thinking aloud. "What did she do to him?"

"That I can't help you with, Sergeant. He never mentioned an Alexandra Carlson. As far as I know, before his release from Westgate the only human contact he'd had was with his mother and Waincock. Of course, Will had town privileges for over two years before his release. His behavior off the grounds was exemplary."

"It's less than a two-hour flight to Reno."

The doctor nodded slowly. "To my knowledge he never left the state of Oregon. At least not until after he was released four months ago."

Chapter 20

William Hunter had gone through the entire condo, room by room. He stood in Greg Ott's upstairs hallway, squeezed his eyes shut, and growled low in his throat. *Where is that fucking bitch?*

From the airport that morning, in a rented car, he had driven straight to the house on the hill, only to find her already gone. His next stop had been the home of her best friend. Although he knew the Meachams were in Hawaii, Hunter figured Alex would be in need of a safe haven. Upon finding no one at their house, he had gone on to the condo of the attorney.

"Where are you, cunt?" he screamed, kicking a large potted ficus tree down the stairs. Black soil and leaves flew in all directions, littering the tan carpet. The tree became wedged on the staircase.

Hunter took the steps in leaps and bounds and hurled himself over the railing at the bottom. In a low crouch, his head cocked, his eyes darting about the living room, he felt himself slipping. Felt himself being sucked down into the black hole. In an effort to control the rage, he breathed deeply, listened to the melodious gurgling of the two hundred-gallon fish tank, and forced his mind to become as blank as a plaster wall. As the minutes ticked away his rage slowly dissipated, drifting up and away like the rising bubbles in the tank.

Calmly now. *Where is she?* There was only one other place he knew to look. At her lover's place — her lover, the cop.

He opened his wallet and pulled out a tiny slip of paper. Scribbled in his angular handwriting was a rural address south of town. Hunter smiled, proud of himself. He had covered all the bases. From Alex's address book he had discovered where her friends lived. From the glove compartment of the cop's own car, when it sat in her driveway, he had copied down this address from the registration.

She was there. He could feel it in his gut. The bitch was going to suffer. She should never have crossed him. The rage began to build again. With an animalistic growl, he lifted a bronze bust of Chopin and hurled it at the center of the aquarium. The thick glass exploded. A tidal wave of water, sand, and tropical fish gushed out into the living room. Hunter cried out as a fiery pain ripped through his shoulder. The wound, where Alex had stabbed him with the hedge clippers, opened again, bleeding profusely.

He tore apart a throw pillow, pulled out the cotton batting, and, stuffing it under his shirt, covered the puncture on his left shoulder. She would suffer for that too, he reasoned., Before he made her his forever, she would suffer for all the wrongs she had done.

Harley Waincock fit the dummy key into the vise and tilted it into the cutter. It ground the metal away. He removed it, buffed the jagged edges, then handed the heavyset woman the new key. "There you go, Mrs. Vicker," he said. "Now don't go putting it in the glove compartment. It don't do you no good if you can't get to it."

"I'll leave this one with Kurt. I always know where that boy is. Right there in that easy chair, eyes glued to the tube." She turned away, turned back. "Oh, Harley, I need some postage stamps. You got the ones with the seashells?"

"I believe I do." Waincock came out from behind the counter with the sign that read Waincock Locksmith—Emergency Service, and walked into a back room. A moment later he appeared at the gilded barred window. "How many, Mrs. Vicker?"

"The seashells?"

"Yes'um."

"A book should do it. I don't care for those ones with the flags. Not that I ain't patriotic and all that, it's just that they're so dang plain."

The word plain made Waincock think of Mrs. Vicker's daughter. "How's Lilly these days?"

"Fine. Fine. She'll be coming into the store to do the shopping this afternoon."

"Why don't she just call in what she needs? We can run it on out to her."

The woman seemed to blanch. She looked around to make certain they were alone. Leaning forward, she whispered, "Well, Harley, truth is she don't much like having that young man delivering the groceries."

"Will?"

"She says he has the devil in his eye. I know, I know"—she held up a hand—"that's silly talk. But he scares her. I'm sure it's all those scars that make him look so mean—'cause without them he'd be a nice-looking boy, but . . . well, you know. I have to

313

confess he gives me a case of the jeebies too. Other folks feel the same."

Waincock was silent for a moment. He looked down and said, "There's plenty for him to do around the store. I'll be doing the deliveries myself from now on."

Mrs. Vicker nodded, paid for her stamps and new car key, and hurried away.

More problems, he thought. Would the good Lord ever grant him, Harley Monroe Waincock, total absolution for his sins?

Welcome to Haller, Drive Friendly, the sign read. In the right-hand corner riddled with BB shot was Pop. 995.

Justin slowed the rented Chevy Citation, pulled sharply into the gravel driveway of what looked like the only gas station on the west side of town, and eased to a stop at the pumps. It appeared to be a full-service station; gas, tires, parts, and repairs.

"Afternoon. How much you need?" the lanky attendant asked. He leaned down, looked at Justin with heavy-lidded eyes.

"Afternoon. Could you tell me if Harley Waincock still owns the store here in town?"

"Yeah. He does."

"About ten years back do you remember a Lora Hunter and her son William? Lived on a farm somewhere around here?"

"You got the wrong place of business, fella. I'm running a gas station here, not an information center. Chamber of commerce is that place that looks like a teepee on the other end of town."

"Why don't you fill it up for me?"

"Happy to."

Justin stepped out of the car, stretched his legs, stared down the road toward town. "Nice town you have here."

"No different from any other town with a population of seven hundred."

"Thought it was closer to a thousand?"

"Gets smaller every year. Old folks die, young folks get the hell out. I remember that woman you were asking about. Never met her, or the boy, but I remember them. Some kind of fire out there back in 'seventy-six, 'seventy-seven. Mother was killed. The kid was taken in by relatives or something. He just moved back on the farm, I'm told."

"Have you seen him around town?"

"Sure. He drives Waincock's delivery wagon. Comes in for gas." The attendant replaced the nozzle in the pump and grunted. "Two-eighty. I'll be damned if I could even squeeze a lousy three bucks into her."

"Sorry, this thing's been passing up stations all day. Hey, thanks for the information."

"No problem."

Justin cruised Main Street slowly. Waincock's Market was situated in the center of town. He drove on by. The teepee building that housed the chamber of commerce was on the east end. Making a U-turn in the parking lot of a defunct restaurant, he headed back to the market.

After inquiring inside the store, Justin walked around to the back. He approached a man who was unloading cases of canned goods from a flatbed truck, tossing one case after another, without breaking stride, onto the loading platform.

"Harley Waincock? Fellow inside said I'd find you

315

out back. Name's Holmes. Justin Holmes."

"What can I do for you, Justin?" Waincock neither stopped nor looked up.

"Like to ask you a few questions about Lora Hunter and her son."

The broad back stiffened. The biceps bulged, flexed involuntarily. The man dropped the box, straightened, and stared at Justin with fierce black eyes set in a flat, brown face. Waincock was built like a gorilla.

"Who are you?"

"The law." Justin showed credentials. "Reno, Nevada."

"Will?"

"Afraid so. Can we talk?"

"Damn." Waincock's face and body went slack. "What'd he do?"

"He's wanted for questioning in the death of a Reno woman. She was bludgeoned, her house was set on fire—with her in it."

Waincock tipped his head. Stared at Justin. "Know much about Will and his mother?"

"Just what Dr. Penndulbury at Westgate told me. A little about the son. Practically nothing about the mother."

"Let's go for a ride." Waincock tossed the last case on the platform. "Hop in."

Two miles north of town, Justin saw the small white farmhouse at the end of the dirt lane. It looked lonely and oppressive. He felt cold. It's just a house. A little house with green shutters smackdab in the midst of this beautiful scenery, he told himself. There are no fire-breathing dragons. No monsters waiting to leap up through the cellar steps. No ghosts.

"I'm curious," Justin said. "The gas-station attendant in town didn't seem to know much about the Hunters and what happened here ten years ago. I thought people in small towns knew everybody's business."

"They do if it concerns townsfolk. The farmers are isolated. Unless they got kids going to school, or they don't mind folks knowing their business, things stay private with them. Aside from myself and the late Sheriff Archer, who was a man of few words, no one else knows exactly what happened out here that day."

As Waincock pulled to the back of the house, Justin's hand moved toward the gun under his arm.

Waincock glanced at him. "Ain't nothing out here can hurt you."

Justin's hand dropped back to his thigh.

They climbed out of the truck and walked to the huge elm tree. Waincock bent down, picked up a rock, then pitched it through the tire swing suspended from a branch of the tree.

Justin took in the house, the old lopsided barn, a wooden shed. A red tractor, its tires long ago rotted down to metal rims, sat under a veneer of black, white, and green bird droppings.

"Who owns this place?"

"I do. Bought it on the auction block shortly after Will was committed. The money went into the trust for him. Never thought he'd ever want to come back here. But when he did, I let him stay. No one else has lived in it for ten years. It's a good farm. There's a creek over there." Waincock pointed toward a copse of trees. "Good fishing. I grew up on a farm like this."

"Me too," Justin said. "Great place for a kid to

grow up."

Waincock looked away. "Yeah. He was a good kid. Minded everything his mother told him. And she was good to him. Baked him cookies, played games with him. Taught him to read and write. Showed him plenty of love and affection.

"He always seemed happy to see me when I dropped the groceries off. Maybe it was just the mail he was eager about. I brought that from town too. Like I said, he was a good kid. But she never left us alone together. It was like she was afraid I might say something I shouldn't say to the boy."

Without looking at Waincock, Justin said, "Like tell him there were no monsters under the house? Or that she kept him a prisoner because she was afraid to go out? That she was robbing him of his childhood? That there was a good chance he would go crazy and become a murderer all because of her? Is that what she was afraid you might say to him?"

"Don't talk about her that way." Waincock hurled another rock through the tire swing. "You didn't know her. *I did*. I saw her at least once a week for twelve years. Her life wasn't easy. She was just a kid when she moved into this house. She delivered that baby herself. Wouldn't even let me take her and the kid in to the hospital afterwards. She didn't know anything about taking care of a baby. I didn't either, but I brought her books. She learned fast. It was a couple years before I realized she never went outside. And by the time I realized what she was doing to him—the books she'd been ordering through the mails were no longer reference books or fairy tales—he was already seven or eight."

"And you just kept quiet? Minded your own

318

business?"

Waincock smashed his fist into the tire swing. It leaped about, jerking. "I loved her, goddamn it. She was so beautiful—a natural beauty, not that phoney made-up kind. Do you think someone as pretty as her could ever love someone like me?" He pounded his chest with both fists. "Well, do you?" When Justin made no comment, Waincock slumped and looked away. His voice softened, "I felt honored to be let into the house. Sometimes she offered me a cup of tea and some of her homemade cookies and we'd talk. Once in a while she'd ask me to repair something. Most of the time I just volunteered. I 'specially looked for things to do inside. She'd sit and talk with me while I worked. I never worked so slow in my life. It was one of those times, when the boy was about eight, that he asked me had I ever seen any of them in the yard? And how come I wasn't afraid of them? I didn't exactly know what he was asking about, but I got the gist of it. His momma just shushed him and sent him outta the room. I tried to talk to her about him—about what she was doing to him. . . ."

"What did she say?" Justin asked after a time. Waincock had stopped talking and was staring absently at a dilapidated shed.

"She said she knew what she was doing. I was to mind my own business or I'd be very sorry. That's when she started to drink. I know because I brought the bourbon to her each week. Four years later I took the garden hose, stuck it through the bedroom window and put out the flames on Lora and her bed. Then I followed a trail of charred grass to that shed where I found Will, covered in blood and kerosene, one hand burned black, completely out of his head.

"I owed it to that boy to help him. What happened was my fault. Because I loved her I turned deaf, dumb, and blind. I killed her and destroyed him."

"He works for you now?"

"Yeah. In the store. Delivers, stocks the shelves, unloads the crates and boxes. Odd jobs. He even helps out with the locksmithing."

"Locksmithing?" Justin's skin seemed to ripple.

"Yeah. He took a real interest in that. Wanted me to teach him everything about it. Said it was probably because he'd been locked up — at home and in the institution — all his life."

Waincock stared at the back of the house, at a window that was boarded over. "I found a fancy paperboard box behind the dresser in her room. Smoke stained, but okay. There was some odds and ends and papers in it. I gave the box to Will. Hope I didn't do the wrong thing."

"Did you read the papers?"

"No. I don't think Lora would've wanted me to."

"Harley?" Justin's voice sounded strained.

"Yeah?"

"Did Lora ever mention an Alexandra Carlson?"

"Not to me. But Will said something about an Alexandra. Except I think the last name was Benson — no, Bently. Was that the woman he tried to burn up?"

"No. Lora and Alex were sisters."

"I remember him saying that this Allie was all that was left of his family. Said he wanted to kindle warm family ties with his last blood kin. Wanted to share his life with her."

"*Kindle?* He used that word?" Justin asked, thinking of Klump and looking again at the charred siding around the boarded window of the farmhouse.

Waincock looked to where Justin was staring. He nodded, his thick brows furrowing.

"Where is he now?" Justin asked.

"Gone. Back to Reno. I thought you knew. I took him to the airport this morning."

"Ahhh, shit."

They both began to run.

"How fast can this sonofabitch go?" Justin called out as he reached the truck and pulled open the door.

The lights flickered. Beverly Capucci glanced up at the overhead dining-room light, then turned her attention back to Alex. For the past twenty minutes she'd been pumping Alex about her personal life. Although they were on a first-name basis, and Beverly's tone was light and chatty, they were nowhere near to being friendly and comfortable with each other.

"How long have you known Justin?" Beverly asked the inevitable question.

"Not long."

"How well do you know him?"

"Well enough."

"He's something, isn't he? 'Course he's not the steady, settle-down-with-one-gal kind of guy, y'know?"

"And I'm not the steady, settle-down-with-one-guy kind of gal, *you know?*"

"Glad to hear it. One less heart to be broken."

"Did he break *your* heart, Beverly?" Alex asked

lightly, wanting to slap the little bitch silly.

Beverly's answer was a smug smile.

The telephone rang. Beverly answered.

"Hey, Sarge, how's it going? No, no problems. Alex and I were just chatting. You know how women are—but of course you do, what a foolish question." A few seconds later she held the receiver out to Alex. "It's Justin, calling from the airport in Portland."

Alex took the receiver. "Hello, Justin."

"Alex, how are you holding up?"

"I'm fine. Did you find out anything?"

"Yes, but I'll wait till I see you to fill you in. I should be at the house by seven-thirty or eight."

"How about taking me out to dinner. Your fridge is barren. I peeked."

"I'll take you anywhere you want to go," he said somberly.

She felt the hair at the nape of her neck stiffen. "Justin, what is it?"

"Nothing," he said softly. "It's just that I can't wait to see you . . . hold you."

"I can't wait either," she said and glanced at Beverly. Beverly sniffed, looked away, her mouth hard.

"Put Capucci back on."

"Okay. 'Bye."

"Goodbye, hon."

"He wants to talk to you again." Alex handed the receiver to Beverly. Then she stared out the window at the flashes of lightning and wondered if he was going to break her heart too.

"Sure I understand," Beverly was saying. "Yes, I promise to call in if we see or hear anything. Locksmith? Jus, there's no way he could know

322

where she is. Everything is fine, really. So long."
She hung up, turned to Alex. "He's concerned
about us being here all alone. Thinks we should
have a few more uniforms come out."

"What do you think?"

"I'd say there's nothing to worry about. Justin will
be here in less than two hours."

"But . . ."

"Hey, if you're uptight," Beverly snatched up the
receiver. "We'll call."

"No," Alex said almost too quickly. She realized
she was twisting her hands together nervously. She
stopped, examined a fingernail casually and added,
"No, you're right."

Beverly nodded, returned the receiver to the cra-
dle. "I've always loved this house. Did you know
Justin practically built it himself?"

Alex shook her head. "This is my first time here."

"Yeah?" Beverly stood up slowly and stretched.
Her full breasts strained the sheer fabric of her
blouse. "C'mon, I'll show you around."

Alex stood. What the hell, there was nothing to
do anyway. She had beaten Capucci at gin. The
policewoman seemed to have lost her enthusiasm for
the game. Now Capucci obviously wanted to establish her territorial rights. But Alex was curious.
Justin hadn't had time to give her a tour before
he'd had to leave for the airport.

Beverly took her through the house. Each room
was clean but charmingly cluttered. Alex loved it.
Large and sprawling, the ranch-type home was open
and spacious. Spread out for miles, through the
picture windows set along the south and east walls
of the living and dining rooms, was a panoramic
view of farms, ranches, pastures, and mountain

ranges.

"This is the master bedroom," Beverly said, strolling in and flopping on the king-size brass water bed. Alex wondered what the odds were of a lightning bolt coming through the window and striking the water bed, frying Beverly Capucci on the spot.

The lights flickered again, went off completely for several seconds, then came back on, dimmer.

"We'd better prepare for a blackout," Alex said, turning and leaving the room. "Think I saw a hurricane lamp on the mantel."

In the living room, she took down the lamp. It was full of kerosene.

"I'll get matches. I saw some by the stove." Beverly walked into the kitchen.

The lights dimmed, brightened, then went out, plunging the house into darkness.

"Whoooeee," Beverly wailed eerily from the kitchen. " 'Friday the Thirteenth' part six. Isn't this when the crazed killer makes his appearance? Can you hear him, Alex, scratching against the house, trying to get in. Whooowee—*haah*."

Through an icy terror, Alex heard a crack. Then a thud.

"Beverly?"

The only sound was the wind howling outside and that awful scratching. The tumbleweeds?

Alex moved to the wall.

"Bev? Beverly!"

Silence.

"Beverly, this isn't funny." She felt her way along the wall to the kitchen. Was Capucci just having a good time with her? Hoping to scare her? Rubbing her sweaty palms on her corduroy pants, she stepped into the kitchen. She opened her eyes

324

wider, trying to see in the dark. Her throat tightened. "Beverly?" It was a frightened whisper. Damn it, she thought in anger, Capucci is probably about to split a gut from holding back her laughter.

Alex crossed cautiously to the stove. She expected that at any moment Capucci would jump out at her, hollering Boo or Got'cha or something equally infantile. She'd get the matches and ignore her.

Alex's foot touched something soft and yielding. She bent down, waving her hand slowly back and forth in front of her. She felt cotton material. Her hand moved along the shirt, touched curly hair. Touched something wet. Wet and warm and sticky.

Panic was no stranger to Alex, but as she rubbed the stuff on her fingers together, she felt a panic so devastating it literally rocked her on her feet. Oh no. Oh God, *no*.

Alex cried out, whirled around, and made it as far as the kitchen door before the blow on her back knocked the wind out of her. The blow to the base of her skull made the darkness a relief.

Chapter 21

Alex opened her eyes. Through a hazy veil punctuated by pain, a black and white photograph on the dresser slowly came into focus. In the picture were two adults and a young boy. The boy sat atop a large spotted horse. Had to be Justin and his parents, Alex reasoned, before the pain wiped out further speculation.

The heat from Justin's water bed had a soothing effect on her tight muscles. Turning her head slightly, she saw a painting on the wall directly across from the bed. With a tugging in her stomach, Alex recognized it as her own. The nightscape, titled *Depth*. So it was Justin who had bought it. Bought it the day after they had made love for the first time. After she had thrown him out of the house. Oh, Justin . . . hurry!

A warm yellow light floated toward her. The light made her head hurt. She closed her eyes. She detected movement. The soft *swish-swish* of shoes dragging on thick carpet.

A floorboard creaked.

She opened her eyes again and watched as he put the kerosene lamp on the night stand. The subdued light, casting shadows on his face, seemed to make the scars more pronounced. Looking at him, Alex thought of a clay sculpture. A bust that the artist had grown to hate and, through frustration, had dug fingers into, pulling soft clay downward, gouging deep furrows. Clay could be remodeled—the face before her would always remain the same.

He turned to her, staring at her curiously. And then he smiled. Alex's insides froze.

She had seen him before. Without the scars. But where? When? Her mind was a blank. Her head and neck hurt. She wondered if he had killed Capucci. She knew for a fact he was going to kill *her*.

"You're scared, aren't you?" he said. "That's good. That's part of the punishment. I'm going to kill your lover tonight. And if you're still conscious, you can watch."

The gun. Had he noticed Capucci's gun on the table? she wondered. If she could get to it . . .

Reacting suddenly, Alex sat upright and tried to scoot off the bed. Her corduroy pants meshed to the acrylic bedspread like sticky Velcro tape, and the water-filled mattress fought her, sucking her down like a spongy adversary.

He slapped her, open-handed, across the face.

She rolled then. Rolled over and over until she dropped off the far side of the bed. Risking a glance at him, she was surprised to see he hadn't moved. He stood there, hands behind his back, a wily smile on his face.

Alex bolted for the door. The gun. She hoped to God he hadn't seen the gun.

Her shoulder glanced off the door frame. She groaned, not wanting to cry out. He'd like that, a voice in the back of her brain said, he'd like to hear you cry and plead.

327

She pushed through the doorway and looked down the hall. The hallway seemed to go on and on, into a dark void. The light behind her vanished. She was back in that dream again, the dream in which she had moved warily down the dark passage to the eerie light at the end. Only this time there was no light to guide her. It was pitch black. She felt that familiar, suffocating fear rise. Her heart banged. Her blood rushed through her veins, roaring in her ears. She couldn't breathe.

Not now, she said to herself. *Don't panic now. Just get outside and hide until Justin comes.*

Alex moved forward slowly, trying to remember the layout of the house. And after what seemed an eternity, she bumped into something. Reaching down, she ran a trembling hand over the coarse wood and touched the apothecary jar. She recalled the table had been to the left of the hallway. She was certain she had veered right—toward the front door. Waving her hand back and forth, she felt for the recliner that had been beside the table. There was nothing there.

Breathing harder now, she cautiously stepped forward. One step. Something soft touched her face. She put a hand up, felt material. Gasped, swung her fists. Her knuckles rapped against wood. She realized then that what had touched her face was a man's felt hat she'd seen hanging on the rack in the entry hall. She knew she was not in the entry hall now. Two steps more, to her right, she met the ottoman. With her arms outstretched, feet shuffling along the carpet, she kept going. Three steps. She found the recliner. Her body came up against the back of it. How could that be, she wondered? She had to be in the middle of the living room. The recliner, she remembered clearly, had sat against the wall by the fireplace. Fireplace? Before she had been struck down, logs had been burning in it. There was no fire now. She strained her eyes, looking for glowing embers. Where was she? She didn't know anymore. She had lost all sense of direction.

"Alex? Ready or not, here I come."

Apparently he had set up the playground. His rules applied. She wanted to scream and run. But that was just what he wanted her to do. He wanted her to stumble about frantically in the maze he had created. If he had gone to this much trouble to prolong her agony, he had surely found the gun.

But it was still her only chance.

She worked her way around the recliner. Three small steps and she was at a wall. *Wall*. Which wall? Which way was she going?

Why was the room so dark? Where were the windows? If she could just find the windows, she'd have some idea where she was.

"Al-lex I can hear you," he said. "If I can hear you, you're not hi-ding."

This time she listened intently to the sound of his voice. It was coming from her right. A way off from her. If he was in the hallway, and she felt he was, then she was in the center of the main part of the house. The dining-room should be along this wall, to her right. The gun had been on the dining-room table.

She worked her way down the wall, hands flat against the textured paint. Suddenly she ran out of wall.

"Alex?"

His voice was closer now. He was in the same

room with her.

She lunged forward in the direction she hoped the dining room lay. Her hands touched a wooden chair. It was chest high to her. Feeling blindly up along the legs of the chair, she felt another set of legs. Christ! He had stacked the four dining-room chairs one on top the other!

One part of her wanted to give up. Surrender. Get it over with. Another part of her felt compelled to fight. To go out clawing and biting. She was going to die anyway. And if he has his way, she thought, it won't be a quick death.

"Do you need some light, Alex?" His voice was coming from across the room. "Is it too dark for you?"

A loud clattering noise filled her head. She jumped. Gray light diluted the darkness. He had yanked up the blinds.

All the furniture had been pushed into the middle of the room. She stood in the dining room, inches from the table.

Incredibly, Capucci's gun was still lying on the table, exactly where she had left it.

Alex grabbed it, swung around, pointed it at him.

He was holding a gun on her.

"What do we do now, Alex? Count to ten? Take positions behind the furniture? What, Alex? What do we do now?"

Alex pulled the trigger.

The hammer struck against an empty chamber. She cocked the gun again. Pulled the trigger. Another empty chamber.

"It doesn't work without ammunition." He held out his hand. Five bullets rolled around in his palm. "Come and get them, Allie."

She squeezed the trigger four more times. Then in anger and frustration, she hurled the gun at him. It broke through the window with a resounding crash.

He laughed. "Your boyfriend isn't going to be happy about that."

Alex looked around. The front door had been barricaded by the long couch. In the kitchen she could see Capucci, on the floor, blocking the back door. At least she's alive, Alex thought, as she listened to Capucci's soft moans.

He stepped up to Alex. The gun pressed against her throat. He took her elbow, as one would take the arm of an elderly person, and pulled her to him. "This game is over. You're 'it.' Don't try anything stupid," he said, leveling the gun at her head. "I wouldn't want everything to end so soon. I don't imagine you would either."

He led her back to the bedroom, pushed her down on the bed. Then he backed up to the wall-length closet, fumbled around inside and drew out a dark leather belt. All the while his eyes and the hole of the muzzle were fixed on her face.

He was going to beat her.

And then he was going to put a bullet into her head.

Without expression, he sauntered back to the bed, swinging the belt as he came toward her. Alex raised her arm to ward off a blow. He caught her hand in a viselike grip and jerked her across the rough bedspread. With her free hand, she made a feeble attempt to push him away. He quickly joined her hands together, wrapped the belt around her wrists, and pulled the length of it through the buckle. Then he tied the end of the belt to the bedpost.

At the exact moment Justin hurried from the plane, brusquely pushing knots of people aside as he moved to the pay telephone, Alex's hands were being tied together by one of his own belts. *Alex was in trouble.* Justin was sure of it. It was as strong as the feeling he'd had nine years ago, working undercover as a narc, when he'd realized he'd been set up on a drug deal and, in all probability, was going to die. Five men, armed to the eyeballs, surrounded his car in a remote area along the Truckee river. Justin's partner and the backup unit, with no time to spare, had saved his hide.

He shoved coins in the slot and dialed his own number. Busy. He hung up, ignored the money dropped in the coin return, fed in more coins, and dialed again. Busy. He called the station, spoke to the dispatcher.

He ran through the terminal, into the parking lot to his pickup. He was sorry now he hadn't driven the Corvette to the airport. A hundred and thirty and she'd still have passing power.

It was a twenty-minute drive from the airport to his house. If he floored it he could make it in fifteen, possibly thirteen.

William Hunter stood over her. "You were jealous of me because I was a boy. You didn't want to share him with anyone . . . especially not a boy. Were you his little baby? Was that it, huh, Alex?" He reached both hands to the metal waist button of his Levi's. "Whose baby are you?"

She stared at his hands.

He was going to rape her.

Then he was going to put a bullet in her head.

"Don't for God sake . . . don't!"

"Shut up!" he shouted, shoving the gun inside the waistband of his Levi's. She jumped, setting the bed in motion again. She rose and fell with each swelling ripple. The belt, holding her hands, rubbed abrasively against her wrists. He dropped his hands to his sides, and Alex nearly cried with relief. Then he took a cheap lighter from his pants pocket and flicked it. A low flame appeared. He adjusted the flame, watching mesmerized as it grew, becoming more white than red.

Alex, mesmerized as well, swallowed over the knot in her throat.

He took a cigarette from his shirt pocket and, tipping his head to the side, lit it. The lighter flicked out, then went back into his Levi's.

"For a long time I watched you. Followed you. Observed your every move. I got into your house by picking the lock. I came in whenever I wanted, day or night. When you were asleep I stood by your bed and watched you. Sometimes I looked down on you from the skylight. Like that night when you undressed in front of the mirror, touching yourself. Then later . . ." He dragged on the cigarette, eyes mere slits. "With your man."

Alex's mouth went dry. Her face burned. Insane as it seemed, she had felt his eyes on her that night.

"I watched you sleep and whore. And what I couldn't see or hear, I read in your journal."

"Why are you doing this to me?" she asked quietly.

He glared at her, his eyes shining and misty with hate. "You denied me—rejected me like a factory second. Like a . . . a black banana, passed over for the perfect, the unspoiled."

"No—"

"Shut your mouth! I don't want to hear your lies. Understand? No more lies! My mother lied to me. For twelve years she lied. She had no choice; I know that now. She had no choice because of him. And because of you."

"Your mother . . . ?" Alex asked, knowing already.

He stared above Alex's head with an eerie, faraway look. Then rose and began to pace the room, flicking ashes on the floor, stopping now and then to touch some article of Justin's. He paused at the open closet and began fingering neckties hanging from a rack. With his back to her now, Alex could see the bloodstain on his left shoulder. She had done that, she realized. She wished to God she had killed him that night.

A dark tie with light colored stripes found its way into his hand. He stared at the tie, then turning it over slowly, traced with his thumb, the pattern along the edge of the label.

Alex's head felt light, her chest constricted. She realized she had been holding her breath through his silence. She exhaled slowly.

He dropped the cigarette to the floor, ground it into the carpet with his boot. He stretched the tie out straight, rotated his wrists until the silky fabric wound tightly around each hand and then, by flexing his arms once—twice, he made sharp snapping sounds with it.

Blood pounded in her ears as he returned to the side of the bed with the tie, taut and ominous, in his hands. A sharp cry burst from her throat when he sat down beside her. His hip touched her knees.

He sat there. Not moving. Not talking. Just staring straight ahead.

The heavy air filled her ears, nose, and mouth. Alex thought she could almost smell the dead silence . . . taste it . . . feel it against her skin.

He whirled around on the bed, stuck the barrel of the gun to her head, and shouted, "God, how I hate you!" He pulled the hammer of the gun back. "All those years . . . all those years of terror, and you could have spared us that suffering. But you . . . you were too selfish, too righteous to share your life with us. Righteous? Hah! You're nothing but a fucking hypocritical *whore!*" The muzzle pressed painfully to Alex's temple. The pain was nothing compared to her fear.

"My mother loved you. She talked about you all the time. Said you were the only chance we had."

"Lora . . ." Alex said quietly.

"She said you would love me." He laughed. "Do you love me, Alex?"

"I didn't know—"

His hand struck her face with such force her teeth bit into her tongue. A metallic taste, like rusty nails, filled her mouth.

"I didn't know where she was," Alex said quickly before he could hit her again. "She left home when I was fifteen. I never heard from her again."

"You're lying. She wrote to you. She wrote to both of you. He wrote to her once. *Once.* Then her letters were returned unopened. That was before he died. He was a bad man. Bad. Evil."

335

"Yes, what he did was wrong, but—"

"*Wrong?*" William whirled on Alex, stuck his face inches from hers and screamed, "Wrong, you say! He raped his own daughter. Made her pregnant. Then threw her out like garbage. That man was my *father*. Not only did he deny me his name—a name that was rightfully mine—he wanted nothing to do with me."

"No. My father wouldn't do anything that sick. Oh God, he wouldn't . . . couldn't have . . ." Dear God, Alex prayed, don't let it be true. But, staring at him, she couldn't deny it. She understood why he had looked familiar. She saw both her father and Lora in his scarred, twisted face. He had her father's gray-green eyes. Her own eyes.

Before her sat the man who was not only the son of her loved and long-lost sister—her nephew—but he was also the result of rape by her father, which made him biologically her brother. The brother she had always wanted. She shuddered. The emotional impact of such knowledge was utterly devastating.

Her own father . . . with her sister . . .

"How many times did he crawl into *your* bed, Allie?"

The blood left Alex's face. She shook her head violently.

"He kept you pure. But he had my mother to use in his dirty, filthy way until he knocked her up. Then he washed his hands of her. He didn't want us around to remind him of what a sick, perverted pig he was."

"Where is Lora now?"

"Dead."

A heaviness moved over Alex. She could only nod. The realization of her sister's death hung back, reluctant to sink into her shocked mind. It wasn't true. None of this was true.

"How?" she asked.

"He killed her."

"My father?"

"He took her to that terrible house and left her there alone, knowing what kind of a place it was. Knowing we couldn't leave unless he came for us. He was the only one who could show us the safe way out. He left her there to die. And you helped him."

She shook her head.

"I have proof, big sister." Reaching behind him, he pulled an envelope from his pocket and shook it in her face. "Right here—proof that you didn't care what happened to us. Proof that you knew."

With a violent motion he grabbed Alex's hands, made slack in the belt, and roughly pulled her hands free. The buckle clinked against the headboard, its empty noose swaying back and forth across the brass with a sad mewling sound.

"Read it. Go on, read it!"

Alex winced as he grabbed a leaden hand and savagely shoved the letter into it. Awkwardly turning the envelope over, she read the name on the face of it. Mrs. L. Hunter.

"My sister's name is Bently."

"He made her use her mother's maiden name," Hunter said bitterly. "He told her had given her his name and he could take it back. Read!"

The envelope was dirty, crumpled. She slid out the single sheet of paper. It was limp, stained, split in places along the folded seams. The letter had been handled over and over.

Miss Hunter,

As you can see, I have taken back my surname. I forbid you to ever again use it. From this day on your letters to Alex and me will be returned to you unopened. Believe me when I say Alex wants nothing to do with you. She reads your letters, then throws them away in disgust.

If you continue in your effort to foist your shame and disgrace on either of us, I will be forced to cut off all financial support.

I can find no pity or forgiveness for one such as you. You taunted me with your eyes, your voice, your body. You flaunted your infidelity, sneaking off at night to bed down with one scum after another, while denying me my rights as your husband. For that, my whoring wife, I renounce you as you renounced me.

The letter was unsigned, but Alex recognized the large sprawling writing as that of her father.

Crazy. He had actually been crazy. Weaving in and out of sanity for years. Lora, poor Lora, had been forced to become surrogate wife to the man she thought was her father. And because of his own shame and guilt and hate, he had, after mentally transforming her into his perfidious spouse, physically put her out of his life.

An invisible ice pick stabbed at Alex's heart. The rage within her erupted. It blossomed, growing and fanning out in all directions until everything inside her seemed coated with a suffocating blackness.

He had lied about her. He had put the blame for his perverted black heart at her feet. And he had lied to Alex about Lora, letting her think her sister had run away without the least concern for those who loved her. Lora's life must have been a living hell. Alone, with a baby, and . . . and some horrible fear that kept her from leaving the house to which he had exiled her.

William Bently had destroyed two lives, coolly, dispassionately; and had been about to alter her life when the waters of Lake Pyramid had reached out to claim him.

Something that Alex had blocked from her mind for years came suddenly into sharp focus. Not long after Lora had disappeared, Alex had begun to notice her father staring at her. His gaze had seemed to wander appraisingly over her body. More than once he had mistakenly called her by her mother's name. At night, after she had gone to bed, she would hear him enter her room. His breathing, as he tucked the blankets in around her and smoothed her hair, had been heavy. She had lain quietly, pretending to be asleep.

The week before he'd died, he had come up to her as she was brushing her hair at the vanity. With a concentrated gesture, his expression an ambiguous mask, he had buried his fingers into her hair and lifted it. Looking into her eyes in the mirror, he had said, "Wear your hair up tonight, my darling. That was how you had it the day we met. Remember?" Alex had known, at that moment, that she would marry Joe as soon as possible, with or without her father's blessing.

Despite the wind and sleet, Justin made the drive in twelve minutes, passing the two squad cars as he pulled up to his gated driveway.

The four uniformed police stepped from the patrol cars and approached Justin as he jumped out of the pickup. Ice crystals bit into the skin of their hands and face.

"Look, guys, this may be a wild-goose chase, and I hope to hell it is, but let's go in on cat feet . . . just in case. Cohane, Olinski, come with me. Baker, Novak, cover the front and back."

The five men ran silently across the lawn toward the dark house. Upon reaching the gravel driveway, they slowed, then walked over the loose stones as if treading on chunks of glass. Five guns appeared simultaneously.

Two of the policeman followed Justin up the back steps. He took his house key, inserted it in the lock, and turned the knob. The door refused to open. With their shoulders to the door, Justin and Baker pushed, shoving aside whatever it was that had barricaded the entrance. Justin stepped in and nearly fell on something at his feet. His heart leapt into his throat. Dropping down, he turned a limp body over. He ran his hand over the head, feeling curly hair, matted with blood. He felt her neck for a pulse. "It's Capucci," he whispered. "She's alive. Baker, stay with her."

Moving fast now, his heart thumping wildly in his chest, Justin headed for the master bedroom with Olinski on his heels. He ran into the first obstacle in the dining-room.

"What the . . . ?" Justin said under his breath. He took the pen light from his pocket, played the pencil-thin beam over the two rooms. "Shit," he whispered when he saw the maze of furniture clumped haphazardly in the middle of the living

340

room, and the hole in the window. Keeping the light low, Justin and Olinski worked their way around the furniture as quietly as possible.

Hunter cocked his head to one side and listened. He grabbed Alex's hands, again forcing them through the dangling noose of the belt. He picked up the kerosene lamp and pried off the chimney and wick.

"He lied about me," Alex said, tensing as panic rose. Her breathing was labored. "I didn't know about any of this. It's not true. He lied."

"Everyone lies."

Hunter held the upper portion of the lamp to one side, the wick continued to burn as he poised the bottom portion, the portion with the clear kerosene, over her body.

"For twelve years my mother lied to me. 'He'll come for us,' she said."

He tipped the fuel bowl. Alex felt the kerosene hitting her feet, running down to the spread.

"My father was supposed to come and take us out of that house. Monsters lived underneath it. He was the only one who knew the way out."

It was on her legs, dry and cold.

"He never came."

Her stomach muscles clenched when he poured it over her hips and chest.

"He never came because you wanted him all to yourself," Hunter said.

Her nipples hardened. She trembled.

"You'll burn, sister Allie. But you won't burn up like my momma did. The heat will burst the water bed and the water will put out the fire. But you *will* burn. I want you to live, Allie. Live like I've had to live — scarred and ugly and in fear. I'll always be there, wherever you are, to keep the fear alive. And you'll be alone. No one will have you. No one will want to look at you. But they'll look. Oh yes, they'll stare and point and then turn away in disgust. Are you ready, Allie? Ready to share my life?"

And then it was in her hair, running down her face.

Alex gasped, choked, closed her eyes to keep it from blinding her. As she thrashed wildly on the bed, she felt the fluid eating into the cuts and scratches on her hands and arms. Hot. Stinging. Burning. In her mind's eye, the skin on her body puckered, blistered, turned dark like the scorched paper on the photograph.

She opened her mouth and screamed and screamed.

Midway down the hallway, Justin heard Alex's first scream. He charged down the passage and into the bedroom.

When he saw the man, a burning wick in one hand, the other pouring kerosene over Alex's body, Justin didn't even slow down.

"Don't shoot! Don't shoot!" Justin yelled at Olinski as he dove at Hunter, knocking the burning wick aside. His service revolver flew out of his hand. The wick went out. Both men tumbled to the floor.

Justin, enraged, punched and kicked. A fist slashed into his ear, his stomach. But he felt no pain, didn't care if he felt anything except muscle and bone under his own fists. He grabbed at the

342

man, got only a handful of material before a hard-soled shoe caught him on the side of the face. He grabbed at the foot, got hold of it as dancing lights exploded in his head. He twisted it, heard a thud as Hunter again crashed to the floor. Justin lunged forward, falling on his adversary. As his fingers grasped a handful of hair, a knee shot up into his groin. He gasped, let go of the hair, doubled over.

The pain was excruciating. He felt as though he'd never catch his breath. But he sucked in air again when he heard a click and saw the flame. Hunter held a lighter in a trembling hand. The butane flame had been turned to max. It rose a good three inches, hissing like a welding torch, illuminating the cocky smile on Hunter's face and the gun in his other hand.

Justin had seen Olinski crossing the room to come to his aid. But halfway to him, the policeman had stopped, gun wavering in his hand, his expression uncertain. Justin was crouched between both guns. Olinski didn't dare fire a round for fear of hitting the wrong man.

The pain in Justin's groin was forgotten as he threw himself at Hunter, trying to block both flame and gun with his body. At that same instant Hunter charged upward in an attempt to go over the top of Justin to the kerosene-drenched bed. Justin heard the hissing of the lighter above and behind his head. It had to be only inches from Alex, he thought as an image of her body engulfed in flames flashed into his head. With lightning speed, he reached up and, feeling the heat, closed his fingers over the flame. The hissing went on, but the flame died.

Hunter screamed. Fired the gun.

A burning pain seared along the side of Justin's neck.

Before Hunter could flick the lighter again, Justin wrenched it out of his hand. Then he grabbed the muzzle of the gun and pulled it away.

Hunter screamed again.

Justin moved blindly, wanting to silence the screeching forever. His fingers, finding the mouth, were bitten savagely. With sheer animal strength, Hunter broke away and lunged for the bed, his hands like claws. Justin brought the gun up, but before he could fire, he heard two shots in rapid succession. Hunter came down on Alex, his hands at her throat. Justin was behind Hunter in a second. With his arm around Hunter's neck, he jerked back savagely. On his knees, Justin squeezed. The man in his arms, limp, head lolling on his shoulder, did not resist. Still Justin squeezed.

Hands worked at his arm, pulling. "C'mon, Sarge, he's had it. Let go. Let go. I hit him with a couple rounds. I think he's dead."

Justin released the man, pushing him away. He rose abruptly.

Alex!

Jerking the belt off her hands, he lifted her from the bed. He half carried, half dragged her to the bathroom, then pulled her into the shower stall with him, turned the tap on full blast, and held her under the spray. She gasped and sputtered, her eyes still closed. Holding her tight from behind, he rubbed at her hair and clothes. "Open your eyes, honey, let the water wash them out." Alex was struggling, sobbing, whipping her head back and forth, trying to get out from beneath the powerful blast of water. "Alex, don't fight me. Let me wash it off. Please, honey, don't fight me."

She stopped struggling and leaned against him. He turned around to face her. The stinging spray plastered their hair to their heads, their clothes to their bodies, and coursed down their faces. Blood from his grazed neck seeped out to mix with the kerosene and water in a pinkish, oily whirlpool at their feet.

"Try to open your eyes." He tilted her head back out of the spray. "C'mon, open your eyes."

She opened them, blinking.

"Look at me. Can you see me?" Her eyes came up and stared blankly at his face.

Alex shook her head.

My God, he thought, she's blind.

"You're bleeding," she said ruefully, reaching a hand to his neck.

He hugged her to him and laughed with relief, thankful that she could see, that she was alive and in his arms where she belonged. Through the relentless spray of the water he kissed her eyes, her face, her mouth.

Alex sat on Justin's couch, wrapped tightly in a down comforter, staring at the blazing logs in the fireplace. Several hours had passed since Beverly Capucci had been taken to the hospital and the body of William Hunter had been carried out.

Justin handed her a snifter of cognac and sat beside her. She touched the torn skin just under his ear. "I'm sorry," she said. "He could have killed you."

"He could've killed *you*. I should have taken you with me."

"It's over now," she said. "Beverly?"

345

"I think she'll be all right. She was spitting mad. That's a good sign."

Justin lifted her hand, studied the palm minutely. "He blamed you for his mother's death and for all the misery your father caused."

Alex nodded. She had already told Justin everything Hunter had said.

"The pistols," she said, "he felt they were rightfully his. And they were. Through two generations they'd been passed down to the firstborn son. He was that."

"Something else had been passed down through the years. The monsters," Justin said. "You thought Lora hadn't been fazed by your father's monsters-in-the-night stories. She had. It just took some bizarre circumstances to bring that out."

"How did she die?"

"Alex . . . I . . ."

"Please. I have to know."

Justin lifted her hand, turned the ring on her little finger around and around. "First though, you should know that she was very sick, most likely dying. If William hadn't killed her, cirrhosis and pneumonia would have." Alex gripped his hand tightly. "He just went berserk. The monsters, Alex, were a part of his life, too."

The tears came at last. She cried hard, not even trying to mask her anguish and pain. The horror of what had happened to her and to her sister, and to the boy who had been her brother, rained down around her like debris from a collapsing building. Could she ever lead a normal life knowing what Lora and her son had had to endure for all those years? She rocked gently in Justin's arms. "Lora. Poor Lora. She wanted so much to live like normal

346

people. To have a family. Her dream was to marry and have lots of kids and live on a big farm where she could enjoy the wide open spaces. She got her farm, all right, a nightmare place where— Oh, if only I'd known."

"Alex . . ."

"She was the strong one, the rebel. All those years I thought . . . thought *she* had escaped and *I* was the prisoner. It was the other way around, wasn't it? Justin," she turned to face him, her eyes beseeching, "do you think she believed I turned my back on her? Oh God, if she thought that . . ."

"I think she knew your father was crazy and that he lied to her."

"Lies. Everything about my father was a lie." Alex sighed. "So much has happened. The awful way they were forced to live. My sister's death. That man—my *brother*. He killed . . . would have killed— no, would have made me into something ugly, horrible. Dying was too good for me. Oh God—Lora, Klump, Winnie—I should've known . . . should've suspected . . ."

Justin's arms tightened around her. "You couldn't know. It's not your fault; none of it is. You have a lot to deal with, to sort out. But it's not the end, Alex. It's a beginning. A new beginning."

"I don't know if I can deal with it."

"Yes, you can. And I hope you'll let me help."

"After all you've been through, I can't believe you still want to have anything to do with me."

"I love you."

She looked up at him. The firelight made his eyes bluer than ever.

"Allie, I love you."

Alex felt a surge of exhilaration that surprised

347

even her. She realized just how much she had wanted to hear him say those words. And they sounded as wonderful as she'd imagined they would. She squeezed his hand.

"My father used to say that to me. 'Allie, I love you.' I thought there was something the matter with the words. They felt . . . wrong, ugly almost. But, you know what?" Justin shook his head slowly. "When *you* say them, they feel right. They feel . . . special."

They sat together in silence for a long while. Out of the blue, Alex said, "I can't go back to that house. It was a part of my father and . . . and I just can't go back to it."

"You don't have to. You belong here . . . with me. Let that be the start of your new beginning."

The wind picked up again, whistling through the taped-up window. The tumbleweeds that had collected along the back of the house scratched at the siding with prickly feelers.

The soft scratching, which only hours before had put terror into her heart, now lulled her soothingly, like light rain pattering on a tin roof, as she snuggled closer into the arms of the man she loved.

ACKNOWLEDGEMENTS

The people listed below, in one way or another, actively contributed to this book. I wish to thank Patti Specchio for starting my engine and riding with me over the initial uphill climb. Michael Specchio, for continually letting me pick his brain; Joyce Farrell, for her enthusiasm and encouragement; Lucy Beckstead, for opening that first door; Sharon Jarvis, for placing this book so promptly; Ann La Farge for giving it a home; the members of my writers' group for their support; Katina Schafer, for her remarkable insight and advice; and Bob Luce, for his faith, patience and love.

**Have You Missed Any of
These Thrilling Novels
of Romantic Suspense
by Elsie Lee?**

THE DRIFTING SANDS   (1917-3, $2.95)

SATAN'S COAST   (2172-0, $2.95)

THE SEASON OF EVIL   (1970-X, $2.95

SILENCE IS GOLDEN   (2045-7, $2.95)

THE DIPLOMATIC LOVER   (2234, $2.95)

THE SPY AT THE VILLA MIRANDA 2096-1,$2.95

MYSTERIES TO KEEP YOU GUESSING
by John Dickson Carr

CASTLE SKULL   (1974, $3.50)

The hand may be quicker than the eye, but ghost stories didn't hoodwink Henri Bencolin. A very real murderer was afoot in Castle Skull—a murderer who must be found before he strikes again.

IT WALKS BY NIGHT   (1931, $3.50)

The police burst in and found the Duc's severed head staring at them from the center of the room. Both the doors had been guarded, yet the murderer had gone in and out *without having been seen*!

THE EIGHT OF SWORDS   (1881, $3.50)

The evidence showed that while waiting to kill Mr. Depping, the murderer had calmly eaten his victim's dinner. But before famed crime-solver Dr. Gideon Fell could serve up the killer to Scotland Yard, there would be another course of murder.

THE MAN WHO COULD NOT SHUDDER (1703, $3.50)

Three guests at Martin Clarke's weekend party swore they saw the pistol lifted from the wall, levelled, and shot. *Yet no hand held it*. It couldn't have happened—but there was a dead body on the floor to prove that it had.

Available wherever paperbacks are sold, or order direct from the Publisher. Send cover price plus 50¢ per copy for mailing and handling to Zebra Books, Dept. 2921, 475 Park Avenue South, New York, N.Y. 10016. Residents of New York, New Jersey and Pennsylvania must include sales tax. DO NOT SEND CASH.

THRILLERS BY WILLIAM W. JOHNSTONE

THE DEVIL'S CAT (2091, $3.95)

The town was alive with all kinds of cats. Black, white, fat, scrawny. They lived in the streets, in backyards, in the swamps of Becancour. Sam, Nydia, and Little Sam had never seen so many cats. The cats' eyes were glowing slits as they watched the newcomers. The town was ripe with evil. It seemed to waft in from the swamps with the hot, fetid breeze and breed in the minds of Becancour's citizens. Soon Sam, Nydia, and Little Sam would battle the forces of darkness. Standing alone against the ultimate predator—The Devil's Cat.

THE DEVIL'S HEART (2110, $3.95)

Now it was summer again in Whitfield. The town was peaceful, quiet, and unprepared for the atrocities to come. Eternal life, everlasting youth, an orgy that would span time—that was what the Lord of Darkness was promising the coven members in return for their pledge of love. The few who had fought against his hideous powers before, believed it could never happen again. Then the hot wind began to blow—as black as evil as The Devil's Heart.

THE DEVIL'S TOUCH (2111, $3.95)

Once the carnage begins, there's no time for anything but terror. Hollow-eyed, hungry corpses rise from unearthly tombs to gorge themselves on living flesh and spawn a new generation of restless Undead. The demons of Hell cavort with Satan's unholy disciples in blood-soaked rituals and fevered orgies. The Balons have faced the red, glowing eyes of the Master before, and they know what must be done. But there can be no salvation for those marked by The Devil's Touch.